A BRUSH WITH SCANDAL

ALLISON GREY

Storm

Ebook ISBN: 978-1-80508-535-5
Paperback ISBN: 978-1-80508-536-2

Cover design: Rose Cooper
Cover images: Shutterstock

Published by Storm Publishing.
For further information, visit:
www.stormpublishing.co

ALSO BY ALLISON GREY

The Lady Thief of Belgravia

This book is dedicated to the beta reader who first suggested that Violet deserved a story of her own. George, thank you for your inspiration.
And to my family, as always, with love.

ONE

PARIS

September 1882

Smoke billowed and engines whistled as the train from Normandy pulled into the station at Gare Saint-Lazare. Violet waited as a mother holding the hand of a young girl with yellow ribbons in her hair cut in front of where she stood with her portable easel. As soon as they had moved on towards the ticket booth, she snatched up a brush, swirled it about in a pan of black watercolour, and set about capturing the cloud of steam rising from the train as it came to a screeching halt some yards down the track from where she had set herself up. Already the sun had begun to descend, and the waning light angled through the massive glass wall at the end of the station. It was perfect.

Violet's brow furrowed in concentration as she took up another brush, touched it to the yellow paint on her palette, and added highlights to the grey mass of the train she had already depicted on the canvas. It was a race, then, to get the lighting just right before the sun disappeared below the horizon, but she was smiling as she added a touch more white, a spot of lavender, and a bit more grey where the train fell into shadow.

And before she knew it, the sun was gone, the lights were coming on inside the station hall, and her painting was complete. Violet set the brush down and took a step back to examine her work. Not bad... she had captured that hazy afternoon light effectively, but the puffs of smoke could use some work. Still, she nodded and began to collect her materials. She could finish up the details back at her studio in Montmartre.

Violet was just gathering her brushes when she became conscious of a pair of eyes upon her. For the last half an hour, she had been aware of the man standing in a doorway not far away, watching her. She did not meet his gaze but steeled herself as he pushed himself away from the wall and came towards her. He stopped a few feet away, but she made no acknowledgement of his presence as he raised a cheroot to his mouth and drew upon it before nodding towards her canvas.

"Monsieur Monet has beat you to it, I'm afraid, mademoiselle. He was here years ago painting this very station."

The back of Violet's neck prickled with anger, but she continued to fill the leather pouch in which she stored her brushes and spoke without looking at the man.

"And many have also painted the gods of ancient Rome, the kings of England, the crucifixion of Christ himself... there are many ways to paint the same subject, as Monsieur Monet has done himself."

There was a pause as she slipped a brush into the pouch.

"There is a park not far from here – many mothers and their children visit it. You'd surely find some good subjects there to paint."

Violet was biting her tongue now as she deliberately gathered up her piece and slipped it into a canvas bag. "Not that it's any of your business," she said sharply in French, "but I prefer to paint the train station."

He seemed not to notice the threat in her voice. "That's curious. Seems an unusual subject for a young lady."

She sighed deeply. "This was the first place I arrived at when I came to Paris."

"You are English?"

She said nothing, just nodded as she began to fold up the easel. He paused as he drew upon the cheroot once more. "Do you model, perhaps?"

Violet clenched her jaw and gave him a pointed look. "No, but I know many artists up on the Butte who are lookin' if you're volunteerin', monsieur."

And without taking a moment to contemplate his blustering offense, she gathered up the last of her belongings and turned on a sharp heel to make her way to the station's exit. It was only after she had crossed the bustling street beyond and began making her way up the hill towards Montmartre that her stride finally slackened, and her heart slowed its angry race. She could still feel the stranger's eyes upon her and turned at one point to see if he had followed her, but there was no sign of him in the crowds. She frowned, sure she had sensed him behind her, but continued on her way.

Violet drew in a deep breath as she came to a stop outside le Chat Noir. It had opened only a year ago but already it was popular with everyone who had come to this hill to escape the conformity of Paris below – the artists and the musicians, the prostitutes and the pimps, and the bourgeoisie who fancied themselves a little bohemian. Violet shrugged and strode towards the doors. Regardless of who was here tonight, whether they be painter or poet, there was guaranteed to be alcohol and after her interaction with the man at the train station, she was in desperate need of a drink to shake off the lingering sensation of being watched.

It was busy now; music drifted out onto the street and smoke filled the air inside. She hefted up her canvas bag with the painting inside and crossed to the bar, scanning the crowd but seeing no one she knew, and so asked the bartender for a beer. He nodded and turned away as she set down her supplies and leaned her chin upon her hand with a heavy sigh. To think, only a few months ago she had been hanging her work alongside the likes of Morisot and Sisley, some of the biggest names in the Impressionist style. To have her paintings in such august company had been the pinnacle of her career, something she could never have hoped for back in England; not with her low beginnings and the stench of the rookery upon her. But here, in this city of light and cabarets and art, she had positioned herself as an enigma; a pretty, vivacious thing with no history that need get in the way of her rise.

And yet, she was a woman, and as that *imbécile* in the train station had reminded her, women in this world were usually expected to paint pretty things – children and flowers and scenes of domestic bliss. That, or be relegated to the role of muse or model, though the women Violet knew always managed to transcend such simple subjects in a way she had never been able to. She had no point of reference for soft things – not where she was from – and so found her own inspiration in the industry of Paris. The steelworks, the bridges, the trains – all that grinding metal and smoke and filth was so far from where she had come, and so comfortably impersonal. And slowly, bit by bit, she was making a name for herself as the archivist of industrial France, alongside those other artists who sought to record the *fin de siècle*. She nodded as the bartender set a glass brimming with foam before her.

"Violet, my pet."

Violet froze with the beer halfway to her mouth as her stomach dropped. That voice. Not the voice of the man from the train station, but another. One she feared above all else. It had been nearly eight years since she had heard it last, but she would know that raspy, sly tone anywhere. For a moment, she considered not turning to face the speaker, relieved to languish in the moment before confirming who she knew stood there, in this small, crowded bar in Paris, a world away from where she had known them. But turn she did, and all her very worst fears were confirmed.

"Archie." The words left her lips in a disbelieving whisper and suddenly, the din of the crowd surrounding them faded into a low murmur as she stared at the man who had spoken her name. He was dressed in brown tweed and wore a bowler hat low over his heavy brow. His smile was leering. He couldn't seem to smile any other way, as she recalled. The smile grew wider as he contemplated her, for she was in no doubt that her face was ashen with shock. He took a step closer, knocking the brim of his hat back a fraction as though to get a better look at her.

"Violet, look at you – lovely as ever."

A roar of laughter from somewhere at the back of the smoke-filled room broke her trance and she slowly shook her head, conscious suddenly of the glass in her hand. She set it down with trembling fingers upon the bar.

"Archie," she said again, the disbelief now mixed with a trace of fear. She swallowed; tried her voice again. "How did you find me?"

"Why, you're famous, Vi! In the papers and everythin'," he replied, now reaching into his coat to withdraw a crumpled copy of *The Times* before unfolding it and snapping open to a page in the middle. His finger came to rest upon a small block of text in the upper right-hand corner. No picture; just a small, unassuming headline: Painter from St. Giles Making a Name for Herself in Paris.

Archie glanced up and gave her another leering grin. "Now how many artists do you know come from the rookery? Tommy found it and was keepin' it for when I got out. Imagine, my Violet makin' a name for herself. With the Frogs, no less." He leaned in close and Violet would have shrunk back except she knew the pleasure he would take from that, so she remained still, trying not to let the fear show on her face. *He knows.* The wild thought raced through her mind, making her stomach clench with terror. He knew what she had done, and he was here to kill her.

"I thought you were doin' bird at Newgate?" she finally said in a shaking voice, starting when he reached for the beer she had set on the bar and took a slow, deliberate sip. He grinned again.

"Got out, didn't I? I have served my time, and I am a changed man," he said, laying a mocking hand upon his chest and raising his eyes heavenward. Violet glanced towards the door. When her gaze returned to him, his expression was hard and she swallowed again, her body fairly vibrating with the need to move away from him. The edge of the bar was hard at her back. "I went to find you, Vi. Was the first thing I did when I got out of that shithole. Thought we was gonna get married – that's what you promised, wasn't it? When you told me you loved me."

Violet said nothing, but her shoulders did sag with relief. He didn't know. He was here, instead, to force her to make good on her promise to him. A prospect no less terrifying, but one for which her life was not in danger.

"I kept my promise; I got you both outta that home. The boys kept you safe – you'd both be dead now if it weren't for me." His eyes narrowed, eyes black as coal, and Violet's throat tightened. She couldn't help it. She leaned back as he closed in on her and the corner of his mouth turned up. "You were gone, Violet. Boys told me what you did. Didn't even wait for the doors to close behind me." His expression darkened; his eyes full of rage and... hurt? "Went and became a whore... sold yourself rather than be with me. And then Tommy tells me you've up and gone to France, and Della married herself some toff."

Violet's frown deepened as he said this. He'd better leave Della out of his dirty business. She was done with that life.

Violet had tried to be done with it, too. But here it was, standing in front of her in a bar in Paris, the man who, as a boy, had got her and her friend out of the orphanage they had been raised in. The boy she had thought she loved, who had taken them into his gang, the Bruisers, and trained them to be thieves. Della had taken to it like a duck to water, had become Rosie Diver, the greatest pickpocket in St. Giles. But Violet had no talent for diving, and when they finally did escape, she had sold all she had – her body – to keep them fed. It had been Cora, the madam of a brothel in Seven Dials, who had taken her in and told her, if you're going to sell yourself, do it where I can keep you safe.

"I'm not gonna marry you, Archie."

His eyes narrowed and Violet, who had grown up in one of the worst slums, with some of the worst criminals in London, felt the terror crawling up inside her at that look. She pressed back further into the bar.

"What's that, now?"

"I said, I'm not gonna marry you." Violet's voice grew stronger as she said this, even though she trembled in fear. The smile he gave her was chilling and he finally looked away from her, glancing towards the crowds surrounding them. She recognized a sculptor from the École des Beaux-Arts, and an art dealer who would frequent the exhibitions of the Impressionists. Most of these faces were those she recognized in passing. Archie returned his gaze to hers and her breath caught in her throat.

"Do they know, my love?"

She swallowed. "Know what?"

"Do they know you're nothin' but a Seven Dials whore?"

Violet winced and resisted the urge to push him away. Of course, they didn't know. France had been a fresh start for her. Most of these people didn't know Seven Dials from Shropshire. And they didn't know her past. She had been scrupulous in keeping that from her fellow artists. She was pretty and young – they barely took her seriously as a painter. If they found out she had been a prostitute... well, that would spell the end of her art career, and the man at the train station would be her future. *Do you model, perhaps?*

"Archie, please..."

"You made a promise, Violet. I got you and Della out of that fuckin' hole, I trained you both, and I did it all with your word that you'd be mine."

Violet kept her voice low, but it was urgent. "I've got a life here now, Archie. A career, friends... I'm not goin' back to London."

His hand suddenly closed around her wrist and his face was in hers, red with fury. Her heart slammed against her ribs. "I take promises very seriously, Violet. I kept mine, and I killed to do it. You and that bitch Della would be dead if it weren't for me. Let's go."

"Archie..." she started to protest but his fingers tightened upon her wrist, and she gasped, trying in vain to pull away.

"Shall I tell them?" His voice was low, threatening, as he looked slyly about them. Curious eyes turned towards them, and her heart lurched into her throat. For a moment she said nothing, swallowing back the rising anger at this man who would dare come here and threaten everything she had worked so hard for. A promise, indeed, had been made, but she had been young and desperate and had thought she was in love, never knowing at the time what a pledge made to a man like Archie Neville would entail.

"No," she finally breathed out, closing her eyes against the wave of despair. "No, I'll come with you."

"Good girl," he replied, his voice low and taunting. Tears pricked at her eyes as he drew away with a triumphant grin and she paused for a moment to compose herself before nodding towards him to lead the way. She spared a brief glance for the bag of art supplies on the floor near the bar but made no move to pick it up before following him to the door. Outside, night had fallen and though there was a chill in the early autumn air, the streets were busy as people made their way along the Boulevard de Rochechouart. Music wafted out from the many cabarets and bars lining the street and laughter erupted nearby as a group of men and women approached le Chat Noir. Violet made to step back as they reached the door and Archie did the same, stopping to pull on his gloves. She took a deep breath as the two gentlemen bringing up the rear of the group approached the door, both speaking in loud, rapid French and as one of them reached for the handle, she made her move. She darted under his outstretched arm, earning a disapproving shout, but never paused; never blinked to look back as she picked up her skirts and raced towards Rue Dancourt. Her heart thundered as Archie swore viciously and there was shouting – what she hoped was him getting into a scuffle with the two Frenchmen – but onwards she ran, pumping her arms and gasping as she careened down an alley between two restaurants.

Her footsteps echoed in the narrow passage and distant shouting reached her ears over the rush of blood at her temples. Down another alley, and another, until she was on Rue d'Orsel and carriages were rushing by as she skidded to a halt, finally daring to look back. A shadow moved far down the alley and her heart jumped, but she was off again, racing up another narrow lane, heedless of the shouted warnings and disapproving glares of those she passed.

She turned down another mews then, hoping to lose Archie in the warren of alleys and courtyards that he would be unfamiliar with as she made her way north to where her small flat was located just below the Butte, the hill that provided a sweeping view of Paris below. Her chest heaved now, and her legs ached, but she never slowed, knowing if he caught up with her, she faced a fate almost certainly worse than death. Sweat beaded down her back and her lungs burned as she burst onto Rue des Martyrs, pausing for only a moment to catch her breath before she darted across the street, cut through the small park there, and finally reached the neat, unassuming little building that had been her home for the last two years. She slowed to a walk as she followed the lane through to the rear of the building and slipped in through a back door.

Only when she was inside with the door closed firmly behind her did she finally stop to draw breath, leaning against the wall and gasping before she mounted the narrow, steep steps to take her up to the second floor where her rooms were located. Her hands shook as she turned her key in the lock and stumbled inside. It was dark and quiet, the noise of the street below muffled, and Violet bit back a sob as she turned up the gas lamp that sat on the small table in the hall. She turned to lock the door behind her but paused as her fingers alighted upon the bolt when she realized, with a dreadful, sinking knowledge, that locking the door was an utterly futile endeavour. He found her in le Chat Noir, and he would find her here. Archie Neville was coming for her, and it was folly to think a locked door would prove any kind of barrier to him. She had to leave.

Tears pricked at her eyes as she staggered into her small bedchamber, its walls hung top to bottom with her sketches, scribbled on scraps of paper, and framed paintings, some of her own, some purchased from small art galleries around Montmartre. She turned up the lamp on the vanity, its surface scattered with powder pots, charcoal stubs, and scraps of ribbon, before glancing up to the gilt-framed canvas on the wall above her. It was a simple little still life – a ceramic bowl of cherries and peaches, sitting atop a scarred wooden tabletop draped with blue-and-white striped linen. It was the first painting she had completed after arriving in Paris two years ago, and it was with a heavy heart she turned from it and tugged an old leather suit-case out from under her bed.

There wasn't any time to waste. Archie might be temporarily lost in the warren of streets which made up Mont-martre, but there was little doubt in her mind that he would track her down soon enough. She might also have worried that he would simply go back to the busy bar and announce her secret to everyone there, but Archie was nothing if not predictable and she knew he would want her humiliation to be public, revenge for her betrayal. He would find her, and he would make sure she would not get away again. And then he would destroy her.

There was only one person Violet could think of who could help her; only one person she would trust in this world who would know what to do, and she had to get to them before Archie found her. She couldn't help the tears now as they streamed down her cheeks, unchecked, as she stuffed gowns and underthings and food and whatever money she had tucked away into the case. She had a few pieces of jewellery, bought with the money she made from the first painting she sold, and she slipped those in, as well. When she had everything she thought she might need for the next week, she hefted the case up and carried it to the door. For a moment, she stood with her hand on the knob, her head bowed, and thought about turning back for one last look.

She shook her head instead, turned the knob, and carefully shut the door behind her.

TWO

Violet stared out at the passing countryside, rocking in her seat as the steam train lumbered along the tracks. She was cold – no, not cold, hollow – and her eyes ached with exhaustion, but she did not sleep. She leaned her chin upon a fist as clear morning sunlight slanted across a field full of sheep and closed her eyes against the immense loss. Everything would be gone by now – all those sketches, the canvases she had worked so diligently upon, her paints, her brushes, her easels – undoubtedly smashed to pieces as punishment for her transgression, and a tear crept down her cheek. She had worked so hard for that little flat, so hard to be recognized as a gifted artist, to make a life for herself in a new country where her past mattered naught, just her future.

But here she was, back home, where she was nothing but a fallen woman, born in the lowest of circumstances. She had managed to crawl out of that hole and Archie had returned to knock her back in. Her throat grew tight with rising anger and despair as she remembered herself, all of seventeen, desperate for her and Della, her dearest and only friend in those dark days, to get out of the orphanage they had been raised in; to avoid the workhouse they would inevitably be sent to once they grew too old for the home.

Archie had been the answer; a tough, swaggering brute, rising quickly through the ranks of the Bruisers, he had promised a new life for them if only she agreed to one thing when the time came – that she would marry him. And why wouldn't she? He was big and handsome, fearless, and confident. She had fallen for him and for the promises he made, and he had loved her back with a passion she had been flattered by at the time, thinking, in her youthful naiveté, that his fierce devotion to her was a result of their hardscrabble upraising, and that she had likely been the first person to ever show him kindness. And she might have been happy with that, had the real Archie not long after begun to reveal himself to her in ways she found far too frightening to dismiss as simple overprotectiveness. She had known she had to escape... and if he ever found out how, she was as good as dead.

Violet sighed as the train let out a piercing whistle and the station came into view, surrounded by a small, picturesque village. She gathered up her single suitcase and waited until they came to a jerking halt before she stood. Desperate, she had been then, to avoid marriage to Archie once she saw who he really was, desperate enough that she had risked her life. What a fool she had been to think he had forgotten her during those long years in Newgate.

As one of the porters held out a hand for her to step down to the platform, she risked a glance backwards, sure she would see his face in the window looking back at her. Nothing. She let out a breath and nodded at the porter before heading into the station, bag in hand. It was a short walk to her destination and the morning was fine, the air scented with grass and hay, recently cut for the harvest, and so she set out on foot.

Though it was quiet on the hard-packed dirt road that cut through stubbled fields and stands of spindly birch trees swaying in the breeze, she paused to look back every so often. Fear would grip her each time she turned, but the road remained quiet and only the occasional farmer or field hand would wave to her as she passed.

Finally, after about an hour's walk, she reached her destination. The manor lay at the end of a winding drive, lined with massive Lebanon cedars. A pond sparkled at the bottom of a hill, surrounded by willows, their delicate tendrils dipping in the clear water. Violet's boots crunched upon the gravel drive, and she sighed with relief as she reached the massive stone portico at the front of the manor and unceremoniously dropped her bag upon the ground before the grand arched doors. A trio of knocks brought the butler to the door, and he peered curiously at her as she stood before him, no doubt red with exhaustion, her hat askew and her brow damp with sweat.

"Miss Latimer?" he asked, uncertain, and she nodded.

"Yes, Harris – it's been some time. Is Del— Lady Bradford at home?"

The butler's expression grew puzzled. "She is in the village today. Was Lady Bradford expecting you? I'm afraid she did not inform me..."

Violet's shoulders sagged. "No... no, she wasn't expectin' me. It's a... bit of a surprise visit, actually." She paused, not knowing how to proceed. Harris must have seen the uncertainty on her face, for he gave a small, sympathetic smile and gestured to her bag.

"If I may, Lady Bradford shall be returning for dinner. I can have a bath drawn for you in the meantime, and a room prepared – have you walked here from the train station?" He said it kindly, but Violet flushed, knowing she was no doubt a tired, dusty mess. Unconsciously, she put a hand to her ribboned straw hat.

"I did. That would be very kind of you, Harris."

He nodded. "It would be my pleasure. May I announce you to his lordship?"

"He's home?"

"Yes. The countess is attending a meeting with the Ladies Village Improvement Society and his lordship is attending to some matters regarding the estate."

Violet's heart leapt into her throat. "Yes, please."

He nodded as she bent to pick up her bag before following him into what had once been the great hall of the Tudor-era manor. It was quiet here; only the ticking of the intricate grandfather clock at the bottom of the stairs broke the silence. Violet had been here only once, just before she left for Paris. Della had just married the Earl of Bradford, who had hired her for her pickpocketing skills when he had been an operative for the Home Office. She had gone on to take the examinations at Oxford, part of her lifelong dream of becoming a scholar, and had given birth to their first child only a few months ago. At least Violet would finally be able to meet little Clara Winthrop.

The butler motioned to her bag, and she handed it to him with a distracted nod. "I shall be but a moment, Miss Latimer."

He disappeared down a corridor behind the massive oak staircase and returned a few, agonizing minutes later to gesture towards her. "If you would be so kind as to follow me."

Violet inclined her head, her heart in her throat as she followed him across the vast black-and-white checkerboard floor, down a narrow hall paneled in rich, dark oak and through the doorway at the end. Her fingers tightened in her skirts as he led her into what appeared to be a study. Della's husband had always been kind to her, and she had not stopped since she had fled Archie at le Chat Noir, barely sleeping, and not pausing to rest until she had reached England's familiar shores and Headingly Hall, the ancestral seat of the Earl of Bradford. She had come here with a singular purpose; to get the only man of the law she knew and trusted to get Archie out of her life. Permanently. She fairly quivered with fatigue as she entered the elegantly appointed chamber just as Della's husband rose from where he sat behind a massive mahogany desk.

His smile was warm as he came around the piece of furniture, and it was all she could do to remain standing before him, exhausted as she was.

"Miss Latimer, this is an unexpected pleasure! Della did not tell me you would be visiting," he said as he took her hand into his own larger one. He frowned when she shook her head.

"She's not expectin' me. And I didn't come to see her... not really." His frown deepened, but he must have seen the anguish in her eyes, for he gestured to one of the two green velvet-upholstered armchairs which flanked the desk. She took one with a grateful nod as he returned to his seat at the desk to face her before drawing in a deep breath to slow her racing heart and meeting his bemused gaze. "It was you I came to see." She swallowed and he wordlessly pushed the glass and pitcher full of water upon his desk towards her. She poured a splash with shaking fingers and took a deep, satisfying sip.

"And what have you come to see me about, Miss Latimer?"

She managed a weary chuckle. "Don't you think we're beyond those formalities, milord?"

He grinned back at her. "I suppose so, Violet. Perhaps you might call me Cole?"

Her nod of agreement was brief, and her smile faded quickly. "I need your help."

His expression remained unreadable, but he gestured for her to continue. It was now that Violet grew uncertain, and her fingers twisted together in her lap as she cast about for how to explain. If only Della was here. She knew just what Archie was, just what sort of danger Violet had fled, and she would have been able to explain everything to her husband, whom Violet had assisted briefly three years ago to save her dear friend's life.

"There's this... man. Me and Della knew him from back

when we were still in the orphanage. He got us out of that place, got us trained up as pickpockets, kept us out of trouble as we made our way out into the world." Cole nodded but said nothing. Violet took another sip of water to wash away the dust of the road from her throat.

"I promised I would marry him..." She closed her eyes and breathed in, hating herself for having ever made such a promise after coming to know exactly who and what Archie Neville was. But she had been so desperate to get out, to take Della with her so they wouldn't end up in the workhouse, that she would have promised her soul to the devil himself. That she had ever loved him at all made her ashamed to her very soul. She met Cole's sympathetic gaze and continued in a whisper, unable to bring herself to reveal what she had done, as though to speak of it aloud would bring Archie here to this room, the dark specter of her past come back to haunt her. "He was a bad man. He's been in Newgate for the last eight years and I thought he had just forgotten about me – I hoped he had, anyway. Cole, he found me." Her throat tightened as she spoke, and her fists were clenched so hard her nails were digging into her palms. The same terror she had felt when she turned around in the bar to find him standing behind her burst in her chest now and she leaned forward to speak, her throat so tight she was sure she would choke. "He found me in Paris, in a bar. He found me, and he wants me to keep my promise. I can't marry him, Cole, I can't. But he won't ever let me go. I need him gone. For good." Her breath shuddered out, but she still couldn't bear to tell him that, even worse than Archie wanting to marry her, her very life was in danger if he found out what she had done. She grasped the edge of his desk with shaking fingers and leaned closer. "I need your help."

There was a long, agonizing moment where Cole said nothing before he closed his eyes and slowly inhaled. Violet's heart sank.

"Miss Latimer... Violet... you are my wife's dearest friend and you helped save her life, and you know I will do everything in my power to keep you safe... but I cannot help you." His tone was full of regret and Violet knew it must be difficult for him to tell her this. It didn't stop the dreadful sinking feeling in the pit of her stomach as she stared at him in horror. "I am retired. I don't work for the Home Office any longer, and everyone knows I worked for them, anyway. I can hardly maintain a low profile. And I promised Della that I would not go back. That I had escaped with my life and that would be the end of it."

She shook her head, disbelieving. "You were the only one I could think of to go to. I came all this way for your help; I thought you'd know how to get him out of my life. What am I to do? If he found me in a bar in Paris, he can find me anywhere."

"You are, of course, free to stay here with us. I can assure you that you will be safe."

She shook her head again, angry now at the futility of her escape from France. But he had promised Della, and she could hardly blame her friend for holding him to it. "I have a life there now, Cole. A career. Friends. I'm not Violet Latimer, Seven Dials whore... I'm an artist."

His expression faltered and he looked back at her with regret. "I'm so sorry, Violet, if there was something I could do..." He paused and furrowed his brow as though in thought before he reached down and pulled open one of the desk drawers. He snatched out a sheet of paper and a fountain pen, nodding now. She looked on in confusion as he scrawled something on the paper. "I cannot help you, but there is someone who might be able to." He looked up and pushed the paper towards her. "You remember my valet, Mr. Barrow?"

She nodded slowly, confused. She had briefly met the valet three years ago during Della's operation with Cole. He had seemed polite if a bit guarded. A former resident of the rookery, just as she and Della had been. But what could a valet do for her? "Well, he is no longer my valet – he left us shortly after your departure to France to pursue a different career." He gave her a small smile of encouragement. "He had ambitions beyond a life of service, and I could hardly hold him back. He's working with the Metropolitan Police – he's Detective Inspector Barrow, now, though I imagine he won't be going by that name given his current position. I'm certain he would be more than happy to assist you."

A spark of hope came to life in her chest, but she dared not feed it, and when she glanced at the address the earl had written, it nearly died. She raised a horrified gaze to him. "He's in Seven Dials?"

The corner of Cole's mouth went up as if he sensed her unease. "Undercover, as I understand it, to aid the Home Office. I do believe he's assisting in infiltrating the gangs working out of that area." His expression softened. "I gather you had planned on never returning?"

She frowned. "Not there, that's for certain."

He smiled. "Then we must find you more suitable accommodations. Bradford House is currently unoccupied, of course."

Violet shook her head. "No, I couldn't. I can find somewhere myself—"

"Violet." His tone was stern, but there was a sparkle in his amber-hued eyes as he sat up straighter in his chair, exuding all the authority of the Earl of Bradford. "I'm afraid I must insist. I rather think if I allow you to seek other accommodation, the lady of the household shall have my neck."

At this, Violet laughed. "I do believe she would. Then I must accept."

Cole put on a look of mock relief as he rose from his chair. "Thank goodness. She is as fierce as ever, you know."

Violet gave him a sly grin as she rose from her seat and followed his gesture for them to leave the room. "I would expect nothin' less."

Cole waved his arm for her to go ahead of him before falling into step beside her as they made their way back down the hall. "She and Clara will be home shortly. I hope I shan't need to convince you to stay for the night?"

"Not at all."

"Very good. And Violet..."

She turned to face him and saw his gaze was full of concern as he put a hand out and touched her arm, halting her. "Barrow is a fine detective. I have no doubt he will be able to help you – and keep you safe."

And though Violet knew Archie would be on the warpath, stopping at nothing to find her, to force her to keep the promise she had made, Cole's earnest words made the tension in her chest release, just a little, and she offered him a small smile.

"Thank you, Cole. I'm glad Della has someone like you, someone to watch out for her."

"Oh, that's where you're quite mistaken," he said, glancing over at her with a smile as they made their way back to the great hall. "It is she who watches out for me."

THREE

The Fox and Friar had once been Violet and Della's favourite place to patronise when the day ended, and they wanted to share a drink and a meal. On this Thursday night, it was as busy as ever, filled with the swell of voices and the yeasty scent of ale, but it was not the libations, nor the hot meat pies Violet was in search of now. Truth be told, she could already feel the goose-bumps prickling her flesh as the sounds and scents of the rookery assaulted her senses, bringing back memories she had spent three long years trying to suppress; trying to forget the life she had led here and the person she had been. Swallowing back the rising bile in her throat, she pulled her hood high up over her head as she ducked through the press of bodies, praying not to be recognized, for it would take but one word of her appearance to the right person and Archie would know exactly where to find her. She made it to the back of the room without anybody calling out her name and slipped down the narrow, dimly lit staircase leading to the cellar below.

As she reached the bottom steps, the shouts and dull thuds of the bare-knuckle boxing match being fought reached her ears. Keeping to the damp stone walls, she edged her way around the room, staying in the shadows where she hoped the crowd gathered around the makeshift boxing ring wouldn't take notice of her. A bell rang, the people gathered to watch cheered, and the two men in the centre of the ring approached each other, fists raised. Violet stood near a stack of crates, careful to keep her golden hair tucked under her hood, and watched as money exchanged hands, men leaned over to shout their bets, and the two fighters in the middle of the room pummeled each other. One man, slightly taller than the other, grinned as he ducked a fierce left hook, his dark blond hair matted with sweat to his forehead. The other boxer, dark-haired and massively muscled, shook out his arms, raised them once more, and made another quick jab.

The taller man parried the strike and before the other fighter could regroup, delivered a swift back fist, catching his opponent in the jaw and sending him flying back onto the floor. A raucous cheer rose up from the crowd, mixed with some groans, and they shouted at the fallen man to get up.

But it was over. The tall blond man had won, and as money exchanged hands once more, the defeated boxer was unceremoniously dragged out of the ring and the crowd began to disperse. Violet waited in the shadows behind the crates, watching the victor as a handful of notes was stuffed into his bandaged fist. He accepted them with a wide grin and nodded to one of the barkeepers as he was offered a pint of ale for his troubles. He drank it quickly before turning away to tug on the shirt draped over a nearby chair. For a moment, Violet stood transfixed by taut muscles moving under sweat-dampened skin, of the steep slope of broad shoulders and the narrowness of a firm waist. Her heart was beating faster. Why was her heart beating faster?

She waited, watching, until the man shoved his winnings into the pocket of his overcoat and headed towards the stairs. She stepped out from behind the crates as he passed. "John

Barrow?" she whispered, aware of the remaining men on the other side of the room.

He glanced up and frowned, as if surprised to find a woman in this dingy cellar. "Who's askin'?"

She gestured to the stairs. "I must speak with you."

The man didn't move but regarded her suspiciously until she sighed and drew her hood back a fraction. "It's me – Violet Latimer." She kept her voice low, despite the din of the pub upstairs.

He stared at her with narrowed eyes as recognition dawned on his expression before it quickly hardened, and he took her by the arm to steer her towards the stairs and back up to the pub.

He pulled her through the crowd, receiving thumps on the back and shouts of appreciation for his win as she struggled to keep her hood up before they stepped out into the street beyond. He said nothing, just tightened his grip and tugged her down a narrow alley across from the Fox and Friar, finally pulling her into the shelter of a dilapidated doorway. He glanced out into the alley before turning to her with blazing eyes.

"How did you find me?" was his sharp whisper. He had dropped the harsh Seven Dials voice of his youth, undoubtedly part of his cover, in favour of the more refined accent he had acquired in the Earl of Bradford's service.

Violet paused for a moment to pull down her hood. "I'm sorry, detective inspector, it was Lord Bradford who told me—"

Mr. Barrow immediately shook his head and put a finger to his lips as he glanced over his shoulder with a worried expression. "Don't say those names here. Titles aren't safe, especially mine. I'm simply Mr. Barrow here."

"Sorry," she whispered, unconsciously drawing farther back into the shadows of the doorway. "You remember me?"

"Yes, of course. You're the countess's friend."

Violet wrinkled her nose at that. She still hadn't got used to

Della's new title, so at odds with how Violet had known her – as a talented pickpocket and lifelong resident of the slums of St. Giles. Still, she had been thrilled for her friend to finally achieve the life she had always dreamed of.

"Yeah, that's me."

The dim light of the nearby streetlamp highlighted the sharp angle of his cheekbones when the furrow between his brows finally disappeared, and he smiled. "I hear you've become quite the artist."

And despite the constant dull ache in her chest and the fear that at any moment, Archie would appear to claim her, she blushed. "You're too kind."

He glanced down the street to confirm there were no eavesdroppers before returning his attention to her. "What are you doing here?"

She drew in a shaking breath, fear beginning to churn in her belly once more. "Mr. Barrow, you know about Della and me, growin' up in the orphanage?"

He inclined his head, and she continued in a low, urgent voice.

"And you know what happens to children there if they're not claimed; if they don't get work?" Another slow nod. "I'd have done anythin' to keep me and Del out of the workhouse. Anythin'. But I was young, and desperate... you know about the Bruisers?"

His eyebrows lowered a fraction and his head tilted to the side. "Yes... of course."

Violet might have noticed the subtle shift in his expression then, the hint of worry that tightened his jaw, the widening of his velvety brown eyes that seemed to suggest he feared what she would say next. But she saw none of this, so consumed by terror she was, and the words tumbled out of her, unchecked.

"It was their leader – Archie Neville – he promised me and Del he'd get us out of there, train us to be divers, take care of us, 'cause we knew what happened if you went into the workhouse – you'd probably not come out again. And I believed him; I believed every bloody lie that came out of his mouth, and I only had to promise him one thing, that I'd marry him when the time came. And I... I wanted to marry him. I thought I loved him." Her breath caught for a moment, the shame at making that promise in the first place causing her cheeks to grow hot. "But then I started to see what he really was – should have seen it from the start. He killed one of the guards who tried to stop us leavin' the orphanage, and I just told myself that it had to be done – he did it to save us. But then things started to change, and I became so scared of him. I knew I couldn't marry him. But... but I also knew he wasn't gonna let us go." To her horror, tears began to well up in her eyes and she shook her head, furious at herself. Mr. Barrow merely watched her, listening, his head tilted to the side. Violet paused now as the tears fell and the next words she said came out in an agonized whisper from behind her fingers as she held her hands to her mouth, finally speaking aloud the terrible truth she had carried with her for so long, she was sure it had poisoned her. "I turned him in." She closed her eyes for a moment as the words spilled out. "I knew the police were lookin' for whoever was runnin' the Bruisers, but they didn't know who it was. There was a constable I knew, and I told him all about Archie – the robberies, the beatin's, the pimpin'. I even told him about the guard he killed, but I don't think they ever got him for that. He's been in Newgate nearly eight years now and the first thing he did when they let him out was to come and find me. He found me in Paris, in a bar – he knew exactly where I was." She gasped out the last word as Mr. Barrow snatched up her hand, his whisper urgent.

"Does he know? Does he know you turned him in?"

Violet raised her tear-filled eyes to his as a sob welled up in her throat. "I'd already be dead if he knew – Mr. Barrow, he can't know it was me!"

"Hush, now, Miss Latimer. I can help you." He glanced up the street again and, following his gaze, she spotted the group of men coming around the corner. She recognized them from the fight and looked up at Mr. Barrow in a panic as they drew closer, their laughter ringing off the damp brick walls of the buildings surrounding them. His grip tightened on her hand and, turning to look in the direction they were headed, he started to pull her out from the cover of the doorway as though to make a run for it, but they were too close. She shook her head, tugged him back and reached up to cup the back of his head. Without thinking, she pulled him down and pressed her lips to his.

Oh no.

It was the first thought that went through Violet's head as he froze for a moment, no doubt shocked, before he seemed to understand her intentions and leaned into her. He pressed her back against the peeling door, raising an arm as he did so to rest a palm upon the wall behind her, shielding her from the view of those passing by. His mouth, which had remained firm against hers to simply give the impression of them being lovers in a secret embrace, softened as he pushed closer, just a fraction, his lips now moving slowly over hers, gently seeking. Violet's hands were still on the back of his head, and as the kiss deepened, she became lost, barely hearing the shouted jeers and catcalls of the men as they passed by, laughing loudly as they disappeared into the night. Yet even after the echoes of their voices had long since died, Violet was still kissing Mr. Barrow. She couldn't help it; she sighed against his mouth as his free hand traveled up her back, pressing her closer, and she was reeling, Archie forgotten, Paris forgotten, when all she had meant to do was create a diversion.

A shout in the distance startled Violet and she broke away with a gasp. Mr. Barrow's body blocked the light behind him and in the shadows, she could not see his expression, but he was breathing heavily, and his hand hadn't moved from the wall behind her. Neither said anything for a moment until he rasped out, "We should be going."

Violet swallowed and nodded as she reached with trembling fingers into her pocket. "Lord Bradford gave me this letter for you – says we're to go to Bradford House."

Mr. Barrow didn't break eye contact as she pressed the sheet of paper into his hand, holding her gaze for a fraction longer before slowly stepping away and raising the letter to the light of the streetlamp and breaking the seal. He scanned the words upon the paper and glanced up at her. "Come on, then," he said in a low voice. She drew the hood back over her head and followed him out of the doorway and, blessedly, away from Seven Dials.

He hailed the first hansom that passed and as she climbed up inside the cab, Violet's hands began to shake, the shock of her action in the alley finally hitting her. Mr. Barrow followed and banged on the roof with his fist as he took the seat beside her. The carriage lurched into motion and Violet sat, stunned and uncomfortably aware of the heat of him, her mind a whirl of confusion. She could do nothing but stare ahead, trying to find reason in what had just happened. It had been three years – three long, peaceful years during which she had not so much as held a man's hand. A deliberate choice on her part, after the heartbreak of discovering that the only man she had ever loved turned out to be a monster, followed by years of selling her body to keep her and Della out of the workhouse. After that, she had turned to the one and only thing she needed in her life – her art. Art would be her new love, her only passion. She would need for nothing else; she wanted nothing else.

But that kiss. It had come from nowhere, unbalanced her, shifted the axis of her world. It had been... good. Very good.

She blinked as Mr. Barrow let out a low hiss and turned to see him flexing his fingers; the bruised, bloodied fingers of a fighter. She gave her head a shake to dismiss the unsettled sensation in the pit of her stomach as she finally spoke.

"So, what's the former valet to an earl doin' bareknuckle boxing in a cellar in Seven Dials?"

He glanced towards her and smiled, then winced as he cracked a knuckle. She offered him a sympathetic look and would have taken his hands to examine them but feared what touching him would do to her already fragile equilibrium.

"I gather Lord Bradford has informed you of my business here?"

"A bit," she said as he massaged the palm of one hand. "You've gone and become a detective yourself, and that you're investigatin' the gangs. I'm still not sure what bareknuckle boxin' has to do with it—"

"I'm in the Bruisers."

Violet froze. The air grew still between them, as if it had been sucked out of the carriage. She was suddenly aware of her heartbeat, the blood rushing at her temples, and, without hesitating for even a second, whirled in her seat to reach for the latch on the door. Just as quickly, Mr. Barrow's hand closed around her wrist, and he growled in pain as she jerked away from him.

"Miss Latimer!" he called out as her fingers grabbed for the latch once more, but the hint of laughter in his voice gave her pause and she slowly turned to face him. He leaned back in the corner of the cab, grinning at her as her breathing returned to normal and she withdrew her hand.

"I am, of course, not properly with them – I'm here as part of an operation to put an end to the gangs who run the rookeries. I'm undercover."

Violet breathed out a long sigh and slowly returned to the seat beside him as his expression grew grim.

"Were you really going to jump out of a moving carriage if I were in the Bruisers?"

She stared at him as though he had taken leave of his senses. "Have you *met* Archie Neville?"

At this, he raised his brows and gave a small shake of his head. "Not yet. I was meant to infiltrate his inner circle – he's the key to the whole operation. I was waiting for him to get out, but then he left. To go looking for you, apparently."

"Then you haven't a clue what he's capable of. I'm tellin' you, if he knew what I'd done, I'd be dead. And it wouldn't have been a kind death. He's gonna come lookin' for me – the Bruisers can't know I'm here. And they certainly can't know who you are and that I came to you tonight or we'll both end up in the Thames with the mudlarks scavengin' our pockets at low tide."

Mr. Barrow's expression softened a little and he reached across the dimly lit space to take her hand in his, a gesture that seemed fiercely intimate rather than comforting as she was sure he meant it.

"I promise you that won't happen, Miss Latimer. Lord Bradford was an excellent mentor, and I am hardly anything but myself – John Barrow of Seven Dials. That's all they know me as. And you'll be safe at Bradford House. We just need to keep you hidden away until this operation is over."

Hidden away. At these words, a crushing ache filled Violet's chest and tears welled in her eyes as she squeezed her hands into fists. "Goddamn him," she choked out, shaking her head as a wave of hopelessness rolled through her. "I can't believe I'm havin' to hide away from that man just when... just when..." The sob burst out of her, and she buried her face in her hands.

"There now, Miss Latimer – this operation has been in the works for some time now. If everything goes according to plan, Archie and the whole lot of the Bruisers will be put out of business and locked away, and you'll be back in Paris, drinking wine and painting portraits, before you know it."

Violet raised her tearful gaze to him and managed a trembling smile. "I don't paint portraits."

The corners of his mouth turned up. "What do you paint?"

"The railyards... the factories. The docks. I'm paintin' the future."

"Then I promise I'll have you back painting railyards before you know it."

She nodded gratefully at this, but worry still gnawed at her, and she was quiet for the remainder of the short journey until they reached the high brick wall which surrounded Bradford Hall. Mr. Barrow followed her out of the carriage and took them through a small iron gate nestled in the wall before leading them to the door at the back of the house.

"No sense waking anyone up at this hour," he said as he let them into the house, stopping to turn up the gas lamp on the wall to illuminate the narrow hallway. He gestured for her to follow him down another corridor and finally into the kitchens, where he moved ahead of her to light the space and lay his coat over the back of a chair before turning to where she stood in the doorway.

"Are you hungry?"

Violet dipped her wearied head. "A little."

Mr. Barrow gave a single nod and disappeared into another room off the main space. He was clearly familiar with the house, having lived here for several years as Lord Bradford's valet, and returned shortly with a loaf of bread tucked under one arm and a small ceramic jar in each hand. He deposited them on the large trestle table in the centre of the room along with a knife before tugging out one of the chairs and gesturing to her.

"Come and have a seat. You must be tired."

Tired was an understatement. Violet hadn't slept more than a couple of hours at a time in the last few days, always waking to nightmares of Archie tracking her down, his broad face looming over her in the dark. She was drained down to her very bones, and her body ached as she lowered herself into the chair before propping her cheek upon her palm, her elbow resting on the tabletop. Mr. Barrow offered her a sympathetic smile as he crossed the room to the larder and returned with a bottle of red wine and two glasses. Setting them down upon the table, he pulled the cork out in one swift motion and filled the two glasses.

"I reckon you could use a drink," he said, taking up one of the glasses to take a swig as Violet managed a grateful nod. He set down his glass and moved to the large cast iron sink on the far side of the room, turned the spigot and cupped his hands under the flow of water. She took up the knife he had left and began slicing up the loaf but paused with her hand in mid-air as he suddenly bent over the sink and brought two handfuls of water up to douse his head, sighing as he scrubbed his fingers through his hair. She could do nothing but sit there, mute with shock as water dripped from his dark blond hair onto the collar of his shirt. Something stirred in her as he pushed his fingers through his hair, slicking it back and offering her a crooked smile.

"Apologies, Miss Latimer – those fights are a sweaty business." He snatched up a nearby linen towel and rubbed it over his head, snatching two plates from the massive china cabinet as he returned to the table and dropped onto the seat beside her. She blinked, shook her head, and set about slicing the bread with far more determination than required.

"Is that how they found you?" she asked as she set a few slices upon his plate. He nodded as he pushed one of the glasses towards her. She gave him a quick, uneasy smile and took a long sip, letting the wine sit for a moment, breathing deep to slow the ever-increasing tempo of her heartbeat.

"I let them find me. We knew they recruited from the underground fights – I've been in the gang now for the last few months. They send me in to test the other boxers when I'm not prizefighting."

Violet sniffed as she spread a generous spoonful of marmalade from one of the jars over her bread. "Only the very best for the Bruisers, eh?"

Mr. Barrow's expression grew solemn now and he leaned forward in his chair. "I need Archie to come back to London, Miss Latimer. Do you think he's still in France?"

The cold grip of fear took hold of Violet once more and she shivered. "He'll be there until he finds me or gets word that I came back home. He won't stop lookin' for me."

He nodded slowly. "Who can get word to him that you're here?"

She let out a shuddering breath and snatched up the wine, taking another sip before she replied, "His brother. You know him?"

"Tommy, yes. He's the one who organizes the fights."

"Tommy's a loyal little lapdog; he'll be lookin' for me same as Archie and he'll have been runnin' things while his brother was away. If he gets word that I'm back, Archie'll be on the next steamer across the Channel before you can snap your fingers. But, Mr. Barrow," she added in a low, pleading tone, reaching out to lay an earnest hand upon the table, "he can't know I'm here. And if he hears even a whisper about what you are, I can promise that your body will end up in the bottom of a gutter somewhere and no one will remember that John Barrow ever existed. You understand?"

Mr. Barrow's expression softened, and he laid his free hand over hers where it rested so imploringly near his arm. She fought the sudden urge to pull away, disconcerted now with his touch. "I understand. Remember, I've been running alongside these gangs since I was a lad, myself. I'll be careful."

Violet managed a quick smile then and slowly withdrew before taking a bite of her bread. They ate in companionable silence for a while until a clock chimed from somewhere deep within the house. It was then, as her glass of wine emptied and the hour grew late, that the long days with little sleep and simmering fear began to catch up with Violet and her eyelids grew heavy. When she tried to smother a yawn, Mr. Barrow took out his watch to check the time before he began to gather the dishes.

"I'm certain that Lord Bradford has sent word ahead of your arrival. Shall I show you to the guest chambers?"

"Oh... yes, of course. Thank you, Mr. Barrow."

He set the dishes in the sink and led her back into the quiet, dark corridors beyond the kitchen, then up the stairs at the back of the house. A gas lamp burned low on the landing, and Violet found herself reaching for the banister as the exhaustion and the effects of the wine began to make her head spin. It was an effort now to lift each of her legs to go up another step and Mr. Barrow turned back as they reached the top of the stairs.

"Just down the hall," he encouraged her, reaching down to offer his hand. She took it, not without some reluctance, but was grateful for the sturdy support as she pulled herself up the rest of the stairs and followed him down a dimly lit hallway lined with dark wood and paintings in gilt frames. He stopped at a door near the end of the hall and quietly swung it open as Violet peered past him into a room shrouded in darkness. Mr. Barrow cleared his throat as he followed her gaze.

"Perhaps I can show you where things are?"

Violet's mind was a tired whirl, and she could only nod in response. He moved past her into the darkness, and a sudden, warm halo of light appeared when he found a lamp and lit it, revealing a room papered in cream damask with gold silk drapes. A large four-poster bed dominated the far wall, and Violet looked with fierce longing upon the crisp white linens which had been turned back in anticipation of her arrival.

"Is there somewhere to wash?" she asked, still feeling the

stench of the rookery upon her and desperate to wash it off before she could even dream of throwing herself onto that plush mattress. Mr. Barrow turned from where he had been drawing the curtains and pointed to the washstand in the corner. Violet heaved a sigh of relief and took up the lamp to bring it over, only to find, disappointingly, that the basin and ewer were empty.

"There's no water," she said, looking over to where he was lighting another lamp beside the bed. He frowned.

"Perhaps the staff weren't expecting you until the morning. If you'd like, I can fetch some for you?"

Heaven help her, she could barely keep her eyes open at this point. She should say no, leave the washing for the morning, and just get some sleep. But she could already feel herself crawling out of her skin, the smell and the dirt of the rookery wrapped around her, bringing back a host of memories she did not care to recall. She sighed.

"Would you? That would be lovely."

He smiled faintly, the light of the lamp flickering across his sharp features.

"Not at all." He crossed to the door and opened it. "Won't be long."

When he had gone, Violet finally began ripping at the hooks of her bodice, hating the cloying sensation, hating the memories of the rookery the dress now brought back. She had already spotted a wrapper of soft cotton flannel hanging from the hook on the wall near the washstand, and happily flung her bodice to the ground, followed by her overskirts and petticoats, in anticipation of pulling on a garment which didn't carry with it the essence of Seven Dials. A shiver of relief raced up her back as she finally stripped down to her chemise and stockings, feeling as though a weight had been lifted from her. She was just reaching for the dressing gown when the door opened and Mr. Barrow stepped back into the room, ewer in hand.

Violet froze with her hand upon the hook as his eyes

widened in surprise and he immediately spun around to face the door, clearing his throat as he did so.

"My apologies, Miss Latimer – I should have knocked. I didn't think you'd—"

"Think nothin' of it," she said quickly as she tugged on the robe. She supposed she ought to have been scandalized, but given her past occupation, she felt only a mild amusement at his embarrassment, and she smiled as she tied the sash and gave a little cough.

"Thank you for the water," she said, and he finally turned, grinning lamely as he crossed the room to where she stood beside the washstand and, meeting her gaze briefly, lifted the ewer to fill the basin. There was a moment of quiet as the water splashed into the ceramic bowl, and Violet found herself holding her breath as the light from the lamp on the table behind her softened the sharp line of his jaw and burnished his dark blond hair into a rich gold. His arm brushed the voluminous, lace-trimmed sleeve of her gown as he emptied the ewer and he stepped back, looking up at her once more. His embarrassed smile was gone now, and Violet slowly released a long breath as he held her gaze, his eyes black and burning in the flickering light.

"Would you like me to stay the night?" he asked suddenly. Something between offense and lust rocketed through her at these words, and she stared at him, unsure if he thought that one kiss was enough for her to contemplate bedding him, or that he was willing to pay for it. But a small part of her did briefly consider what it might be like to feel those muscles, which had only a few hours ago been delivering punishing blows to his opponent, moving beneath her fingers. It had been so, so long since someone had touched her, and even longer since it had brought her pleasure.

He must have seen the confusion in her expression, for he added, "My old chambers will be empty while the household is in the country. I can introduce you to the staff in the morning and show you around. It's very easy to get lost in this place if you don't know your way."

Relief and, strangely, disappointment filled her, and she gave an uncomfortable laugh. "Yes, of course – that would be very helpful. If you haven't somewhere else to be."

One corner of his mouth hitched up at this. "Nowhere else, Miss Latimer."

She opened her mouth to say something, but no words came to her and so she gave him a lame smile, which he returned before slowly inclining his head.

"Then I'll say goodnight. I'll see you in the morning."

His voice, low and rich, sent a frisson of electricity through her and she could only nod, her mind too weary and muddled with wine to form a response. The door closed with a quiet click behind him, and Violet found, once more, that her heart was beating a rapid tattoo in her chest, and it was not out of fear this time.

FOUR

John Barrow stood for nearly a full minute in the hall outside the guest chambers as he tried to make sense of what had just happened. Miss Latimer hadn't been aware of it, but with the lamp sitting behind her in the dark room, he had seen every luscious curve of her body silhouetted through her light linen chemise and it was leading his thoughts down some very inappropriate paths.

The sound of water splashing behind the door made him breathe out a long sigh before he turned away and made his way back down the corridor to the narrow stairs leading up to the attic. Lord Bradford's current valet ordinarily occupied the space, but he would be with them in Oxford, and John didn't want to go to the trouble of waking anyone to prepare another guest room. He trudged up the stairs, his body now feeling every one of the blows which had landed during the fight before reaching the door at the top of the landing.

After a bout he would usually go home to his rented rooms in Covent Garden, get into a cold bath and polish off a glass of whisky, but he supposed tonight had been a better use of his time. Of all the people to have run into, the woman who had turned in Archie Neville was the last person he expected. And he certainly hadn't expected it to be Violet Latimer.

Oh, he remembered Violet Latimer. Their first meeting had been brief – three years ago, outside the brothel in Seven Dials where she had lived, and where the Duke of Salisbury had held her friend, now wife of his former employer, captive after being exposed by the couple as a traitor. She had the same hard stare he remembered from all those years ago, the same firm set of her jaw. But there was something a bit different about her now – a softness she hadn't had before. He recalled her seeming rigid; angular. But that wasn't unusual for what she had been at the time – selling one's body in a place like Seven Dials tended to make one hard. It seemed the past two years in Paris, eating French food, drinking French wine and making her art had done her good, and all that built-up tension had eased.

John dropped with a sigh onto the mattress, absently rubbing his battered ribcage as he stared up at the ceiling, recalling only now that the chaos of the last few hours had ended, that she had kissed him. And... he had kissed her back? He shook his head, worried that perhaps the blow landed by the other boxer – an up-and-coming young pugilist named Jemmy Sullivan, who ostensibly had saved himself the fate of being drafted into the Bruisers by losing tonight – had perhaps landed a bit too directly and he had imagined the whole thing.

No... no, she had most certainly kissed him in her attempt to keep the men who had been at the fight from recognizing her. And, God help him, he had kissed her right back. A wicked heat surged through him at the memory, but it was quickly tempered by the knowledge that Archie Neville, of all people, was looking for her. John could only imagine that after giving him the slip in Paris, if he found her, his revenge would be swift and violent. Archie would not take kindly to being snubbed in so blatant a way – no, Miss Latimer was very much in danger. John's chest tensed as he rolled to stare into the empty hearth. And if he found out she had been the one to turn him in... John grew cold at the thought, but he was nothing if not a pragmatist. It could have taken months – years – to get close enough to Archie on his own to get any real information that would help the police in their quest to shut down the gangs who ran the rookeries. But with Miss Latimer... She would know all their dirty little secrets; she had once been close to Archie. She had already had enough information on him to put him in Newgate for the last eight years. If she could work with him and the police to bring a real case to the Home Office – why, they could put an end to the Bruisers permanently. They could put an end to all the gangs who prowled the streets, those men with nowhere else to go, who turned to violence for lack of anything else. Violence that was, far too often, directed at those with precious few options; the ones he should have been able to save and had failed to do so.

A sudden pain twisted John's insides, and he blew out a sharp breath to banish the memory of a head of chestnut curls and a rosy smile – turning his thoughts, instead, to the operation at hand. Instead of considering the case, however, all he could think of was the soft surrender of Miss Latimer's lips against his, of her hand slipping around his waist, pulling him closer, and he frowned at himself as he tried to dismiss that memory, as well. There were far more pressing matters at hand but, try as he might, his thoughts kept straying back to the pliability of her mouth and the intoxicating scent of her skin; somehow it had captured the warmth of a summer day, even in that cold, dark alley. Eventually, sleep came to him, his dreams suddenly full of Violet Latimer and her golden hair.

Violet was awake before the sun came up the next morning, lying in the sumptuous bed in the guest room at Bradford House, staring at the ceiling for what seemed an eternity before the first rays of the rising sun began to edge the silk drapes. She glared at the thin strip of sunlight seeping between them; it seemed an affront to the dismal thoughts which had woken her at such an ungodly hour. The room she lay in was luxurious beyond anything she could comprehend yet it was not her cozy, colourful little flat in Paris, the one she had worked so hard for. She had finally got to meet her dearest friend's new daughter, but the circumstances leading to that meeting were not what she had planned. Della was meant to come see her in Paris, bringing little Clara along with her, and Violet was going to show them all the sights; her little studio in Montmartre, the gardens at the Tuileries, the art of the Louvre, and the soaring heights of Notre Dame – Della had been particularly excited about that, having read about the cathedral in Victor Hugo's book. But now... Violet sighed and rolled over to bury her face in pillows made of the finest down and covered with the softest linen... it all meant nothing knowing that Archie was out there, looking for her, ready to pull down everything she had spent the last three years building.

A soft knock upon the door sometime later finally roused her from the bed and she paused, feet dangling from the side of the mattress as she swallowed back the heavy lump in her throat, before she slipped to the ground and crossed to the door. She opened it a crack and peered out into the hall to see Mr. Barrow standing before her, already fully dressed, shaved and hair combed, though a blossoming bruise on his left cheek belied his natty appearance. He nodded, his expression some-what guarded as he held out a breakfast tray.

"Good morning, Miss Latimer. I thought you might be hungry – may I come in?"

Something stirred inside Violet, deep in the pit of her stomach as she wordlessly stared at him before she regained her senses and offered a half-hearted nod, moving back to open the door. He paused before stepping into the room, his gaze dropping down to take her in and she realized, belatedly, that she wore only her chemise before also remembering him catching her in it the night before, far too exhausted and tipsy from her single glass of wine to care about propriety. And the look in his eyes when he finally raised his gaze to hers – oh, she saw him struggle to conceal it behind a mask of cool indifference – it made her insides turn to liquid.

A long moment passed during which they stared at one another, waiting for someone to make the first move, before Mr. Barrow finally cleared his throat and stepped past her to set the tray down upon an intricately carved side table, removing the domed lid to reveal a matching set of bone china decorated with tiny blue flowers. He then set about filling a cup with steaming hot tea and unfolding a napkin to reveal two slices of toast beside a small dish of raspberries.

"Milk? Sugar?" he asked, glancing at her over his shoulder as she drew on the wrapper she had left draped over a chair, conscious of the gaze he was clearly fighting to keep from wandering.

"Just a bit of sugar, please," she said, taking a step closer as he nodded and measured a shallow spoonful into the tea. He then took up the cup and saucer and turned to offer them to her with a half smile.

"Old habits... the valet inside me simply refuses to let a cup of tea go un-poured."

She accepted the cup and saucer he handed to her, lifting the cup to take a sip before closing her eyes. "That's wonderful," she murmured before raising her gaze to him once more.

"I'm seeing Tommy today," he said suddenly, just as the tea had settled, warm and comforting, in the pit of her stomach. She drew in a shallow breath and nodded.

"He'll want your winnin's, I suppose."

The corner of his mouth hitched up. "Most of them."

Her throat moved as she swallowed before finally broaching

the topic they had both been avoiding. Her voice shook. "And what are you going to tell him about me?"

He sucked in a lungful of air, clearly uncomfortable, but he didn't look away. "I'll tell him I met a pretty little dollymop in Covent Garden after the fight... a little green-eyed blonde named Violet."

Violet's lip twitched and a tiny crease furrowed her brow. "That would be enough for him to get a hold of Archie. But I don't do that anymore – he knows that."

Mr. Barrow's shoulder lifted in a shrug. "Maybe... but if you fled France with naught but the clothes on your back, you might be desperate enough." He attempted a smile. "Desperate enough to take home some bloke who'd just been pummeled in a bare-knuckle boxing match."

Violet gave a small laugh at that. "At least he won."

Mr. Barrow smiled before heaving a dramatic sigh. "It's a shame I had to turn her down, seeing as I was in a poorly way." His mouth twisted in a wry grin. "Wouldn't do to tup Archie Neville's lost lady-love."

Violet's stomach churned at the words, and she had to look away. "No... he'd have your head for that." She closed her eyes against the sting of tears – damn but she was tired of them. "I don't like this," she whispered, her voice strained. "I don't like knowin' he's out there, knowin' he's managed to trap me in this house from thousands of miles away, knowin' my life isn't my own anymore."

A hand came to rest upon hers and she looked up, blinking back the gathering tears. Mr. Barrow's expression was solemn. "He'll receive a far longer sentence this time, for more than just petty crimes. He won't see the outside of a jail cell for the rest of his life if I have anything to do with it. Your life will be your own again soon enough."

Violet said nothing but looked down to where he touched her so gently. He coughed and withdrew his hand before nodding to the breakfast tray. "I've already spoken with Mrs. Cooper. Lord Bradford has left instructions with her regarding your stay here and I'll try to come back to update you when I can. She said she left some of Lady Bradford's clothes for you in the wardrobe – when you're dressed, I can show you around, introduce you to the staff."

Violet slowly inclined her head. "That would be very kind of you." She took another long sip of her tea, clenching the cup tighter to stop her hands from shaking. From exhaustion – her sleep had been riddled with dreams of Archie's broad, grinning face – or fear, or both, she could not tell, but she was grateful for Mr. Barrow's encouraging smile as he stepped away.

"Then I'll leave you to it," he said before crossing to the door and closing it carefully behind him. Violet stared at the door for a moment before glancing down at the tea in her hands and setting it, very carefully, upon the chest. She heaved a deep, shuddering breath and turned to the wardrobe. The doors opened to reveal a handful of tea gowns, relatively plain and unadorned, but of the finest quality. She observed the selection dispassionately before pulling out a gown of pale pink decorated with intricate inset lace. Della was a hair taller than Violet, and so the short train on the dress dragged as she belted it about her waist, but it felt wonderful to be wearing clothes that hadn't been stuffed into a suitcase to cross the Channel with her or been dragged through the filth of the rookery. She found a brush and combs on the vanity and managed to pin her hair into some semblance of order before a very deliberate knock sounded on her door once more. Mr. Barrow stood in the hall, his smile encouraging.

"Ready?" he asked as he held out an arm. She hesitated. She wasn't ready. She didn't want to be here, and she hated Archie Neville as she had never hated anyone, and that hatred sat like a leaden weight upon her chest, so heavy it felt at times that she couldn't breathe for it. But just for that one moment, when Mr.

Barrow gave her an expectant smile and offered his arm to her, the weight lifted, and she placed her hand into his as he led her downstairs.

He was an excellent tour guide, starting her in one wing of the house, showing her where to find the library, the parlour, the music room, the conservatory, all the way down to the kitchens. They were far different from the night before, when they had shared that simple meal by the light of a single lantern. Now daylight streamed in through the high windows, a scullery maid was on her hands and knees scrubbing the stone floors, and a footman walked by carrying the day's newspapers. A middle-aged woman, of fair hair and plump cheeks, stood at the massive trestle table, rolling out pie dough and Mr. Barrow nodded towards her as they stood in the doorway.

"That's Mrs. Beatty, the cook – you get on her good side, and she'll always make sure there's a little treat hidden away for you," he said, leaning close to speak over the din of a delivery driver down the hall shouting for someone to come get the sacks of flour he had brought. His grin was mischievous as he raised his gaze to the cook, whose cheeks grew red as she laboured over her dough. "Good morning, Mrs. Beatty!" he called out and was rewarded with a scowl.

"You go fetch that flour, now, Detective Inspector Barrow! Just because you don't work here any longer doesn't mean you can stand about in my kitchens being useless!"

He laughed and gestured for Violet to follow him down the hall to the service door where he had a quick chat with the deliveryman before he hefted up two sacks from the back of the cart and carried them through to the larder. Violet watched, bottom lip pulled between her teeth, as the cords in his neck stood out under the weight of the flour before he deposited it safely on a shelf. He winked at her – God help her, something sparked to life inside her just at that one wink – before he sidled up to Mrs. Beatty, grinning widely.

"Flour delivered. Have you anything for me, love?"

She gave him a nudge in the ribs with her rolling pin and Violet saw his wince of pain as the cook reached into the pocket of her apron. The smile returned as she thrust a handful of peppermints at him and resumed her rolling before glancing up at Violet where she stood in the doorway, waiting nervously with her hands twisted in her skirts.

"And you must be Miss Latimer," the cook said as she set down the rolling pin and brushed her hands down the front of her apron. She came around the table with a warm smile and extended her hand. "We've heard so much about you from Lady Bradford. She even has one of your paintings hanging in the parlour."

The tightness in Violet's chest immediately eased as the cook reached back into her pocket to withdraw another handful of peppermints. She accepted them with a pleased smile.

"That one's my favourite. And thank you," she added, nodding to the treats as she stuffed them into her pocket. "I won't be a bother here, I promise."

Mrs. Beatty chuckled and waved her hand. "No bother at all. Any friend of Lady Bradford is welcome in this home. Have you met the wee 'un? Isn't she a darling little thing?"

Violet's gaze met Mr. Barrow's for a moment, and he gave her a crooked grin as he popped a peppermint into his mouth. She smiled as the cook returned to her baking. "Yes... she's named after Della's mum, you know."

"Oh, aye? Such a pretty name. Well, lots to do here today. You just poke your head in here if ever you need anything, miss."

"I will, thanks," Violet said as Mr. Barrow gestured for her to follow him. She gave the cook a quick wave as they left the hive of activity that was the kitchens to make their way to the back door. Mr. Barrow stopped and nodded down the hall.

"Mrs. Cooper is ready for you. I have to get going –

Tommy'll be waiting for me." Violet said nothing but shivered as a flash of fear skated up her back knowing Archie would be coming back to London. He'd tear the city apart looking for her. The corner of Mr. Barrow's mouth turned up as though he could sense her unease. "He won't find you here, Miss Latimer, that I can promise you. Lord Bradford didn't work for the Home Office for ten years without putting some security measures in place."

The words gave Violet small comfort, but she did manage a weak smile and gestured to the door. "Then you'd best be goin'. Tommy doesn't like to be kept waitin', not when there's money involved."

Mr. Barrow's expression hardened at that, but he nodded in agreement before his gaze locked with hers. Her skin suddenly tingled with awareness at his proximity as she remembered the sensation of his mouth upon hers, the heat of his body as he had pressed against her in that doorway, the quickening of his breath. She stared back at him before blinking and stepping away.

"Yes, yes, I should be on my way. I might not be able to come back tonight..." He paused as though he would say more, but she forced a smile and shook her head.

"Not to worry. You've done more than enough for me, Mr. Barrow. I'll be just fine."

"I'll do my best to come check on you – perhaps in a day or two. Tommy'll have me busy if he's getting ready for—" He broke off, a frown furrowing his brow before Violet finished for him.

"Gettin' ready for Archie to come back."

He gave a solemn nod. "Yes. I have to be there – Whitehall will be wanting reports on him and his activities, and he needs to see that I've been helping out in his absence."

Violet responded, a little too quickly. "Of course... I understand. I'll be fine. I'm sure there'll be plenty to keep me busy here."

He paused again as though reluctant to leave before smiling quickly and inclining his head in the direction of Mrs. Cooper's office.

"Just check in with Mrs. Cooper, I'm sure she can keep you busy." Another quick smile, though it lacked conviction. "Must be off. Goodbye, Miss Latimer. I'll be back as soon as I can."

Violet said nothing, her throat growing inexplicably tight as he backed away with a small wave and slipped out through the door at the end of the hall. She watched him through the window as he strolled away through the gate, hands in his pockets. When he had disappeared behind the boxwood hedges, she turned with a sigh to make her way to Mrs. Cooper's office, perplexed that the sensation of his hand touching hers still lingered.

FIVE

John strolled up to the warehouse down the street from Covent Garden Market an hour after leaving Violet in the capable hands of the Bradford House staff. Not unexpectedly, he had spent the whole walk over thinking of her, alternating between working her and her inside knowledge of Archie's gang into his plans, and of her kissing him so suddenly in that doorway. And every time he remembered her lips, full and pliant against his, desire spiked through him, and he had to pause outside the door to Archie's warehouse to take a deep breath and recalibrate his train of thought, lest he walk in with an embarrassing bulge in his trousers and no ability to weave any sort of lie which would convince Tommy of Violet's whereabouts. A one-time occurrence that kiss had been – necessary in the moment. It certainly wouldn't happen again, and he would quickly put it from his memory. This was far too important an operation to let one kiss – delectable though it had been – derail him.

With this assurance, he felt suitably grounded again, and he swung open the door into the massive space.

The familiar thud of bone on flesh greeted John as he strolled inside, the air musty and cool, and scented with sweat and sawdust. Behind a row of empty crates was the boxing ring where all the Bruisers practised their sport, and it was to the side of this ring that John found Tommy Neville. He was a huge man, dark-haired and dark-eyed, and he raised an inscrutable gaze to John as he came around the bend to lean casually against one of the iron pillars which supported the roof high above.

"Mornin', Tommy," he said as he nodded towards the two men, one of whom was a brute named Henry from the rookeries of Bethnal Green, the other an unfamiliar face to John. "New fella?"

Tommy glanced over at the two men as they circled one another, fists raised. "Aye, come all the way from Manchester. What d'you think?"

John turned his attention to the new fighter, who dodged to avoid a quick strike from Henry before tackling him around the waist.

"He could be quicker on his feet. Looks to be in decent condition, though."

Tommy nodded in agreement. "Might put him in with the Devil, see how he gets on. How'd the fight go?"

John withdrew the stack of crumpled notes from his pocket and handed them over without a word. Tommy took them into his meaty fist, counted them out quickly and handed back a few without looking at John.

"Shame," he said as he tucked his portion into a pocket. "We had hopes for Jemmy."

"Ah, give him some time, he's young – he's got talent."

Tommy shrugged noncommittally. "We have our eye on another bruiser – does prize-fightin' in Shoreditch. Billy Cahill – heard of him?"

John shook his head as he pushed himself off the column when Tommy gestured for him to follow, taking them through the warehouse to the small office at the back of the space. "I haven't – is he good?"

Tommy turned a crooked smile on John as he opened the door to the office. "We'll find out in a week, won't we?"

John held back a grimace as his body, bruised and beaten, protested the idea of another fight in only a week's time. He instead plastered a cheeky grin on his face as Tommy crossed to the liquor cabinet on the other side of the room.

"We certainly will," he said, dropping into one of the creaking leather chairs facing the desk in the centre of the room. Tommy filled two glasses with the whisky he always kept in the office and handed one to John who swallowed half the contents before leaning back in his chair and propping his feet upon the desk. Tommy, a man to whom good manners were as foreign as unicorns, barely noticed as he took the other seat, taking a swig of his own whisky as he did so.

"Make sure you give him a good run for his money – Archie'll be wanting to recruit now he's back. Wants to expand the territory down to the docks."

John gave him a sly smile as he set his glass down and flexed his fingers, masking his pained grimace with a short laugh. "I always do. Where's he gone, anyway? Thought he got out of Newgate last week?"

Tommy's expression darkened; a nerve had been hit. Archie's right-hand man clearly didn't think it was worth his older brother chasing after some lightskirt when they had businesses to run and territories to expand now that he was out of prison. But of course, being a loyal little lapdog, as Violet had referred to him, meant Tommy would hardly speak out against Archie's whims. John, of course, was not supposed to know about Violet.

"He has some business in France – he'll be back when he finds what he's lookin' for."

John simply nodded and gave a nonchalant shrug, as though

he didn't care either way. They went over the business for the day before Tommy finally stood, jerking a thumb towards the door.

"Comin' to the club?"

That would be the Devil's Den, a casino and men's club owned by Archie where many of their business dealings took place, as well as some of their boxing matches. Tommy usually made it a point to stop by when he was done at practise to check in on their other business and John often tagged along if he wasn't fighting. He shook his head and made a show of standing and arching his back, putting on a grimace.

"Not today, I don't think. Missed out on a cold bath last night and me bones are achin' – wanna be in top form for next week, don't I?"

Tommy nodded as he gathered up his coat and hat from the hook near the door. "Aye – have a feelin' about this fella but I need him to show his mettle. Thought you'd have gone straight home after the fight?"

"Tried to, didn't I? Some cock chafer followed me all the way from the pub to Covent Garden, beggin' for a go. I wasn't in any bloody shape, was I?"

Tommy gave a bark of laughter as he tugged on his coat. "A hag, was she?"

John managed to look astonished as he followed the other man out of the office and back into the warehouse. "Nah, a real looker, she was. If I hadn't just had me ribs done to dust, I'd have taken her up. Little blonde thing."

Tommy gave a leering grin as they made their way back through the rows of crates. "I like blondes. She got a name? Maybe I'll go find her for meself."

John made a show of putting his finger to his chin as they reached the warehouse door and held it for Tommy to pass through. If there was one thing Lord Bradford hadn't had to teach John in his training to join the detective department at

Scotland Yard, it was lying. Surviving a childhood in Seven Dials meant it came as naturally to him as breathing. "Her name? Can't remember if she gave it to me – no! She did, said her name was Violet. You'd probably find her back at the Fox and Friar."

And, predictably, Tommy now turned to face John, the sly smile wiped from his face. His dark little eyes narrowed beneath his heavy brow. "Violet, didja say?"

John, looking blissfully unaware of the change in Tommy's demeanor, nodded as he turned the key in the lock. "Think so."

There was a moment of quiet; John could practically hear the wheels turning about in Tommy's head as he dropped the key back into his pocket. "I'm off then, Tommy. I'll see you in the mornin', eh?"

Tommy only nodded as John walked off, smiling to himself as he left his boss with just that little nugget of information. Hopefully it would be enough for him to summon his brother back to London.

Violet spent the remainder of her first day in Bradford House wandering about the rooms like some sort of silent specter, aimless and without purpose. Mrs. Cooper had been hospitable – certainly not the Mrs. Cooper Della had described early in her stay here when she had found the housekeeper to be rigid and unwelcoming. They must have become friendly along the way, for the older woman treated her as any welcome guest, something to which Violet was wildly unaccustomed. Seven Dials prostitutes were rarely accepted anywhere beyond the street corners they plied, even the ones who had gone on to become well-respected artists. Della must be well-loved in this household to afford her friend such hospitality.

Since Violet had woken so late that morning, she had only the afternoon to occupy, but she was finding it difficult – the library kept her busy for an hour or so, but Violet wasn't as enamoured of books as Della, and so eventually drifted away and found herself in the conservatory, strolling among lush palms and fragrant blooms. She discovered a small stone fountain at the end of the path surrounded by benches and longed for just a few scraps of paper and a stick of charcoal to capture the water burbling out of the amphora held aloft by a small marble cherub. She sighed, feeling once more the sting at the loss of all her art, and left the conservatory, her delight at the space now faded. Eventually, she made her way to the kitchens, hoping Mrs. Beatty might at least have another sweet secreted away for her.

With the household away in the country, the kitchens were quiet, but Mrs. Beatty was in the larder, counting out the inventory of goods and she turned when Violet drifted into the room, at a loss for what else to do and having no one to speak to. The cook smiled as she pulled down a large ceramic jar to inspect its contents.

"Bored already?" she asked as she set the jar back on the shelf. Violet gave her a lame grin and scuffed her shoe against the stone floor.

"I don't even think I can go outside to walk in the gardens... I'm not used to bein' stuck inside."

"Well," the older woman huffed out as she pulled down another jar. "We're taking inventory while the lord and lady are out in Oxford – do you want to help?"

Violet sighed with relief. Even inventory-taking sounded appealing after an afternoon of aimless wandering. "I'd love to," she said before Mrs. Beatty set down the jar and gestured for Violet to follow her.

"Come on, then – I'm almost done in here, but I have silver that needs polishing," she said, leading Violet out of the larder and back to the kitchen. She gestured for her to take a seat at the massive trestle table in the middle of the room and left to fetch one of the solid mahogany boxes which contained the silver cutlery. She set it down in front of Violet along with a jar of polish and a heap of rags.

"You ever polish silver before?"

Violet glanced up with a raised brow and the cook laughed. "Just make sure you get all the tarnished bits and dry them before you put them back."

And with that, she left Violet to it. For the next two hours, Violet dutifully scrubbed all manner of knives and forks and spoons, stopping only when Mrs. Beatty popped her head in to say the staff were sitting down to dinner and asked whether she cared to join them. Only a skeleton staff remained with the household away, but Mrs. Beatty and half a dozen maids, in addition to the two remaining footmen, sat down in the servants' hall to share a lovely dinner of roast beef with potatoes and peas.

"Do you really live in Paris?" one of the scullery maids, a little wisp of a thing named Penny, asked, her eyes wide with awe as Mrs. Beatty set out bottles of wine. Violet smiled, even though her heart broke a little at the reminder.

"I do... I hope to be goin' back as soon as Mr. Barrow gets everythin' sorted."

Penny's gaze grew wistful. "Oh, it was so nice to see him again – it was such a shame when he left."

One of the footmen, a young man with a mischievous smile, shook his head at Penny as he casually crossed his arms over his chest and leaned back in his chair. "He never looked twice at you, Pen – what do you miss him for?"

Penny scowled at the footman while Mrs. Beatty tutted and waved her knife at him. "You mind yourself, Richard – he was a nice fellow."

Richard rolled his eyes, but smiled as he resumed his meal and Penny raised her chin in triumph. "He *is* a nice fellow – he's helping Lady Bradford's friend, isn't he?"

All eyes turned to Violet, who shrugged. "He's very kind to help me – and Lord Bradford was very kind to let me stay here. Insisted, was more like it."

Mrs. Beatty sent a sidelong glance her way as she helped herself to another dinner roll. "If you don't mind my asking, what's he helping you with, anyway? He was cagey about it this morning. Would only say you'd gotten yourself in a bit of a jam, so he brought you here to keep you safe."

Once again, the fear made Violet's chest grow tight as she remembered turning away from the bar in le Chat Noir to find Archie standing behind her, that leering smile raking over her. She swallowed it back and gave a quick smile. "Not sure I'm allowed to say – just that I once knew someone he's investigatin'." She couldn't even say his name, and when she took a bite of her roast beef, it stuck in her mouth, dry as dust, and she had to work to swallow it. She tried not to think about what Archie's retribution would be like; tried not to think of the thousand ways he would surely delight in torturing her; the thousand methods he would use to hurt her; to remind her that she belonged to him and that he was not going to let her go. But occasionally, just for a moment when her mind was not otherwise occupied, those thoughts would invade her mind, and her stomach would churn and her breath would grow short, and she would have to close her eyes against the sting of tears.

It was with an effort that she swallowed back the remainder of her dinner and a third glass of wine – she welcomed the hazy fog it brought to the edges of her mind and after much discussion of the staff's plans for their upcoming day off, the kitchen soon emptied, leaving Violet alone with Mrs. Beatty. The older woman nodded towards her as she swallowed back the last dregs of wine in her glass and leaned her elbows upon the cleared-off table with a sigh.

"You're going to feel right terrible in the morning after all that wine."

Violet heaved a shuddering breath as she scrubbed her hands over her face and glanced up at the cook as she set the last plate back in the china cabinet.

"Maybe I want to feel awful from the wine... it'll distract me from all the other awful things I feel."

Mrs. Beatty tutted as she returned to the table and plucked up the empty wine glass. "If it's a distraction you need, you can come down and help me tomorrow. We've bread to bake and vegetables to pickle. Keep your mind off things."

Violet slowly inclined her head, for it was already spinning and her eyelids had grown heavy. "Yeah... I could do that. I've never baked bread before. Or pickled anythin', for that matter."

The cook gave a sharp nod of agreement as she shooed Violet out of her chair. "Then off you go, get a good night's sleep. I'll expect you in here bright and early."

Bright and early sounded positively barbaric to Violet, but she nodded nonetheless and pushed herself away from the table before making her way to the library to find a book that wouldn't be too taxing to her wine-addled brain. Back in her rooms she washed and changed into her nightgown before tucking herself into the big, upholstered armchair which sat beside the fireplace, where a small fire had been banked up for the night. She tried to read for a time, but her thoughts kept straying back to Archie and the terrible sensation in her gut that he was just determined enough to find her no matter how well hidden she was here. Eventually, she set the book down with a defeated sigh and leaned her head back against the chair to stare at the ceiling. It was time to set her mind to other matters.

She thought of Paris, and the exhibition she had participated in only months before, and how proud of herself she had been to show off her art along with other great artists she admired. Pissarro himself had even commented that she had great talent and had bought one of her smaller still lifes.

And then she remembered fleeing Paris, and that there was

no more art for her, and no more studio with the big windows and the little balcony in Montmartre, and all because of Archie, so she banished the memory from her head. Violet's fingers clenched around the armrests as she tried to put her mind to something else, and right there, hovering at the edges of her consciousness, was Mr. Barrow. She closed her eyes as she propped her feet up on the small footrest, and she thought of him in that cellar in Seven Dials, dodging and feinting, his muscles bunching under sweat-dampened skin, his dark blond hair matted to his forehead, his grin bloody but confident as he had ducked blows, only to return them in greater force. And then... when she had pulled him back into that cramped, dingy doorway and pressed her mouth to his, she had marveled at the strength of those muscles as she had moved her hand over his waist, over his chest, and felt the raw power of him.

Violet's breath hitched as she recalled, with devastating clarity, the sensuous slide of his fingers over her hips, and the nerves which had sparked to attention at that touch. She hadn't so much as looked twice at a man since she and Della had moved out of Seven Dials three years ago and she had finally been able to start making a living off her art. For so long, it had felt like her body hadn't belonged to her, just to those who paid for it, and she had been more than happy to fill her life with her friends and her career instead. It had taken a long time for her to feel comfortable in her own skin again, and in the space of a few hours, and with just one kiss, John Barrow had managed to waken something in her which had been long dormant; to consider the possibility of... wanting someone again. *He won't want you back,* an insidious voice whispered in her head, the one which had followed her from Seven Dials all the way to Paris and back, the one which always sought to remind her of her history and the men who had passed through it.

But Violet had always been a practical person and she shook her head to dismiss the voice, rolling her eyes at herself.

Men were, in her vast experience, simply a means to an end – to money, to pleasure, to a hot meal, sometimes – not uncommon growing up in Seven Dials. And John Barrow, wickedly handsome as he was, would also be a means to an end. He would keep her safe while the Metropolitan Police did whatever they needed to do to get Archie back to prison and out of her life permanently. She had spent three perfectly happy years eschewing men, after all, trying to find herself once more in her art, and to leave behind Seven Dials and that voice. Her only goal, whatever came of things with Archie, was to get back to Paris, to her art, to her friends, and resume her life. Nothing else mattered.

Since the book no longer held any appeal, she rose from the chair and found herself wandering to the window where she pushed back the drapes to look outside. Night had long since fallen, and the gardens beneath her window lay in shadow. Beyond the wall which surrounded Bradford Hall were the lights of London. Archie wasn't out there – not yet – and that thought gave her a small measure of comfort as she let the drapes fall back into place. When she sat at the small vanity to plait her hair, she glanced at her reflection and sighed. Dark circles still lingered beneath her eyes, for sleep had eluded her since her escape from France and she glanced at the small silver clock on the wall nearby. Nearly eleven o'clock. If she was to be up bright and early to help Mrs. Beatty, she supposed she ought to get some rest. She stood and crossed to the bed, pulling back the linens to settle down on a mattress that was undoubtedly luxurious, but it was not hers. She snuffed out the candle at her bedside and stared up at the shadows as they danced across the ceiling.

Would Mr. Barrow return tomorrow? And had he convinced Tommy that she was back in London? Her stomach churned with worry – what if Tommy grew suspicious of him? What if he hadn't taken the hint? He wasn't exactly the sharpest wit, after all, more of a blunt instrument. What if Archie tracked her down? What if he found her here, dragged her out, took out his knife...

Violet let out a gasp and squeezed her eyes shut. Her fingers clenched in the counterpane, and she counted to ten, counted to ten again, and opened her eyes once more. No. She was safe here, in this upscale little street in Belgravia. Archie wouldn't be comfortable here, wouldn't know all the back alleys and dark little corners; he wouldn't be protected by the fear that kept the police out of Seven Dials and all his dirty business.

Slowly, slowly, she released a long breath and thought, instead, of Mr. Barrow. Thought of the long, lean muscles in his arms as he had jabbed, diligently and precisely, at his opponent, thought of the taste of his mouth, of his charming little wink at her that morning... and her whole body began to thrum with anticipation of seeing him again. It couldn't hurt to imagine... And so it was, in thinking of only Mr. Barrow, and his devilish smile, that Violet finally slept, a deep, restful slumber, until morning came to wake her bright and early, just as she had promised Mrs. Beatty.

SIX

John arrived at the warehouse again the next morning for sparring practice, but no one was in the boxing ring waiting for him. He made his way through to the office, where he found Tommy making notes in a ledger. John was carefully casual as he leaned against the doorframe, pausing to pull out a pocket watch and check the time.

"The Devil here yet? If not, I was plannin' on goin' for a run," he said as he slipped the watch back into his pocket. Tommy didn't look up, but he did give his head a quick shake.

"He's not comin' today. I have somethin' important I need done."

John pushed himself up and strolled into the office, snatching up a newspaper from the desk and taking a quick glance at the front page. "Of course – what d'you need?"

Tommy looked up now, his brow furrowed as he set down the pen he held. He jerked his head towards the door and John reached back to close it as Tommy slowly stood and contemplated him for a moment before speaking.

"That whore – Violet. I need you to find her."

Awareness hummed through John and the muscles in his

body tightened, but the laugh he let out was easy. "That bit o' tail who followed me after the fight? Cor, Tommy, you could walk down the street and find a dozen just like her."

Tommy's expression grew thunderous. "I don't want another fuckin' girl, I want her. Go find her for me."

John held up his hands and gave the other man a placating smile. "All right, all right – I can go back to the Fox and Friar, see if she's been hangin' about." He turned away and opened the door but stopped when Tommy spoke again.

"Archie's comin' back."

John turned around. "Is he now? Found what he's lookin' for?"

"He will when you find that girl."

John's brows drew together briefly, and he tilted his head, as though in consideration of these words. "Then I'd best be off."

Tommy did not reply, and John was careful to shut the door behind him.

He did, indeed, make his way back to Seven Dials and the Fox and Friar, entering a pub devoid of its usual crowds and noise. It was early, and one of the serving girls was at the back of the bar sweeping under the tables. The owner, a middle-aged man, burly and black-haired, looked up from where he was wiping out glasses and nodded towards John as he entered the pub.

"Hey there, Johnny, you fightin' tonight?"

John shook his head as he took a seat at the bar. "Not tonight. I'm here for somethin' else."

He saw the sidelong look the man gave him. He knew John was in the Bruisers, and he knew that you stayed on their good side, or you found yourself in a world of trouble, which was why he let them use his cellar for their boxing matches. A moment passed before he cleared his throat and said, "And what's that?"

"I'm lookin' for someone. Bit o' tail who might have been hangin' about here. Blonde, said her name was Violet."

The man finally turned and set down the glass he held. His brow furrowed for a moment before realization dawned on his face. "There was a pretty girl named Violet who used to come here – worked for Cora. Haven't seen her in years."

John nodded gravely and tented his fingers upon the scarred wooden bar top. "Tommy's lookin' for her."

The other man frowned. "John, she's not been around in years. I heard she'd gone off to France or somethin'. Why's he lookin' for her here?"

John drew in a slow breath. "Met her in Covent Garden, askin' for a toss. She followed me from here. Wanted to know if you'd seen her."

The man shook his head. "She weren't in here, Johnny. I'd have recognized her – someone would have recognized her. You sure it was her?"

"I certainly hope so." John sighed deeply, as though his plight was great. He slapped a hand down on the bar as he rose from his stool, leaving behind a handful of shillings. "Let me know if you hear anythin'. Tommy wants her found." He gave the man a meaningful look at that last sentence, and he gave a quick bob of his head in response. He didn't need to say anything else. As second-in-command of the Bruisers and younger brother of Archie, Tommy was judge, jury, and executioner here – if he was looking for someone, they'd be found. John turned to the owner as he reached the door.

"Archie's comin' back."

The bar owner did a commendable job of hiding the flash of panic in his expression, giving John a shaky nod. "I'll get the word around."

"See that you do."

With that, John left the pub and began to make his way west, to Charing Cross Road. He knew no one would follow him – Tommy had at least reached that level of trust with him – but he was careful to stop along the way, for an orange from one of the girls selling them on the street; for a newspaper from one of the boys on the corner. He then headed south and took The Mall across to Hyde Park, where he found a bench and sat to peruse the paper and eat his orange. When he was certain that no eyes were upon him, he rose from the bench and made his way through the park, enjoying the soft breeze that held the chill of the coming autumn in it. Already the leaves of the plane trees were becoming burnished in gold, but the sunlight streaming through their branches was still warm, and John whistled a tuneless ditty as he reached the edge of Belgravia.

As he drew closer to Bradford House, he found himself walking a bit faster, as though eager to see her again. He couldn't imagine why; he was simply delivering news, relaying to her that Archie was returning to London, as had been his plan all along. His bosses at Whitehall were eager to get this operation wrapped up, keen to begin the task of clearing out the slums, but John was eager for something bigger. There had been whispers from his colleagues – from the superintendent himself, Lloyd Culpepper, the man assisting with the government's mandate to clear the East End slums, that there was an opening for detective chief inspector. And John wanted it. The years he had spent in the gutter, scraping and clawing for survival in a Seven Dials flash house, working his way out, becoming valet to an earl, no less, had all been in service of making sure no one else would have to fight as he had, as Lucy had. Little Lucy, with her shining ringlets and sparkling blue eyes, had been his to protect after their mother died and their father left them at the flash house where they had been raised. Another twist of guilt tightened his stomach as he crossed the road. He had failed to do that duty; failed in the worst possible way. This operation and its success would be his redemption, his chance to prevent what happened to Lucy from ever happening again.

He stopped at the corner, across the street from the red brick wall which concealed the elegant stone manor behind it and frowned. If Miss Latimer agreed to help him – and he was certain she could help – then he felt far more confident in stopping Archie for good. *If* she agreed to help.

Heaving a sigh, he made his way around to the back door and entered the house. It was quiet, but he could hear voices down the hall, and so he followed them and found himself in the doorway to the kitchen, watching as Mrs. Beatty demonstrated to Miss Latimer the proper kneading of bread dough. She looked up as he entered the room, her pert little nose dusted with flour, and she smiled widely. God help him, he wanted to kiss her again.

"Mr. Barrow!" she exclaimed, stepping back to brush the flour from her hands.

"Good morning, Miss Latimer. Mrs. Beatty," he added, nodding towards the cook who took up the lump of dough they had been kneading and dropped it into a ceramic bowl.

"A fine day, is it not, detective inspector?" Mrs. Beatty asked.

"It is indeed. May I borrow Miss Latimer for a moment?"

The cook glanced at the younger woman, whose smile quickly faded as she untied the apron she wore and draped it over the back of a chair. She stepped towards John, hesitant, her expression tight with anticipation, and followed him as he led her back down the hall and out to the parlour. He shut the door carefully behind them and turned to find her looking back at him with worried eyes, her fingers twisted in her skirts.

"Is he back?" was the first thing she said, her voice low. He shook his head.

"Not yet... but he will be soon."

She swallowed, gave a short nod, and turned away to make her way to the window where she leaned over the deep sill to look out into the garden.

"Tommy has me looking for you."

She gave a short, harsh laugh, but didn't look at him. "He knows people will talk to you. Everyone's scared of him."

John said nothing as she stared out into the garden, her knuckles turning white as she gripped the edge of the windowsill. After a moment, he spoke. "You could help me."

She turned slowly to face him, a small furrow between her finely arched brows. "I'm sorry, Mr. Barrow... I worked so bloody hard to get out of that place. Della nearly got herself killed to get out of that place. I know you wanna stop Archie, and so do I, but I don't know if I can help you. I just want to go back to France. I don't want anythin' more to do with Seven Dials."

He took a step closer to her. "You don't have to go back to Seven Dials, but if there was any information you could share... From what I understand, Archie's not the trusting sort."

Miss Latimer said nothing but did shake her head.

"Tommy knows me by now; he likes me winning fights for him, but Archie won't know me. And they're not going to share the information I need until they trust me."

She still said nothing but did slowly dip her head in agreement.

"You knew them, Miss Latimer... what does it take to get Archie Neville on your side?"

He held his breath as her jaw tensed and she looked away for a moment before meeting his gaze. "Doin' whatever it is he asks. He doesn't like to hear no."

"That's hardly surprising."

Her lips turned up in a smirk. "Archie Neville is evil down to his bloody core, but he's also a man of simple tastes. Give him what he wants. Don't question him."

John nodded, glancing around the room to note the delicate cream and gold striped wallpaper, the fire surround of pale marble, the fine mahogany sideboard upon which sat a pair of ormolu candlesticks. It had all become so familiar to him during his time working here; it had become a second home of sorts. He had enjoyed it and been proud to hold such a position as valet to the Earl of Bradford. But his work with the Metropolitan Police had brought him back to his roots in St. Giles and given him the opportunity to make the lives of those who also called it home better. Getting rid of Archie and Tommy Neville and their gang of brutes and thieves would bring him one step closer to that mission – to rid that place of the crime and vice which had taken Lucy from him. Miss Latimer had finally turned away from the window to face him once more and he decided he had extracted enough information from her for now.

"How are you finding it here so far?"

She lifted her shoulders. "I can hardly complain; I'm gettin' to live like a toff. Mrs. Beatty's been showin' me around the kitchen. It's keepin' my mind off... well, it's keepin' me busy."

John nodded but didn't know what to say. She sounded defeated as she strayed towards the mantel and traced her finger over the scrolls carved into the marble. No doubt she was used to being independent, coming and going as she pleased, using her art to express all her innermost thoughts and desires. He glanced up at the painting of hers Lady Bradford had had framed and placed proudly on the wall between the windows. It depicted a narrow street in short, evocative brushstrokes – not Seven Dials, but something similar; the buildings close together, the sky grey, but two women walked side by side, facing away from the viewer, one in pale blue, one in deep green.

"I don't suppose we could take a walk in the gardens?" she asked suddenly, facing him with a hopeful look. He hesitated, just for a moment, then smiled and held out an arm.

"Come on then – before Mrs. Beatty comes looking for you."

Miss Latimer grinned as she came towards him. "I quite like Mrs. Beatty, actually. I made a loaf of bread this mornin' – I've never made bread in my life."

John chuckled as he led her away from the parlour and towards the conservatory. "Was it any good?"

"Terrible, actually. But Mrs. Beatty says there's always room for improvement."

John laughed again as they entered the conservatory, the air thick and perfumed with exotic blooms. She strayed away from him to approach a large potted palm, tracing her finger over the curve of one of the fronds, then pulling away with a small sigh. He observed the tightening of her lips as they came upon the fountain at the back of the glass enclosure, and she seemed to look with longing upon the little cherub and the water burbling out of the vase it held. He stopped where she stood beside one of the benches flanking the fountain and glanced sideways at her.

"Penny for your thoughts?"

She didn't look at him, but the corner of her mouth did turn up. "Archie never thought I'd go anywhere with my art. Thought it was only for schoolgirls doin' watercolours till they could find a husband." She sniffed and turned to face John with a smirk. "More fool him. I make more doin' paintin's in Paris than I ever did divin' for him or workin' for Cora." She sighed again and looked away. "I did, anyway... everyone there's gonna wonder what happened to me. I don't suppose..."

"Yes?"

She turned to face him again, her expression hopeful. Damn, he'd forgotten how beautiful she was.

"Could you send a letter for me? Anaïs Duchenois – she lives on Rue Cortot – she's one of my friends in Paris and she'll be worried for me. Tell her I had to come home to my sick grandmother or somethin'."

"Of course. I can get that to her." He paused. "Were you unable to tell anyone before you left?"

Her eyes narrowed, anger sparking in the emerald depths. "Course not. I ran. I ran the second I got a chance, all the way from the bar where he found me to my flat, took whatever I would need to get home, and got on the first train to Calais." She shook her head and reached out to let the bubbling water wash over her fingers, staring at her hand as she spoke. "He must have been followin' me the whole time. I'm sure everythin' in my flat is gone."

"What do you mean?"

Her short laugh was full of disdain. "What do you think Archie would have done after I ran off? Wait around for me to come to my senses and go back to him? No, if he was able to find me in a bar in Montmartre, I know for sure he would have found my flat." Her breath came out in a ragged sigh and her voice cracked when she spoke again. "I can almost guarantee you that he made sure to ruin my life there. To make sure if I ever went back, there would be nothin' left." Grief pinched her face, and she pulled her hand back, shaking the water from her fingers. "All my paint, my brushes, all my art... it's all gone. I have nothin' now, nothin' but what I packed in that suitcase."

The despair in her voice was unmistakeable, and he couldn't help reaching out and laying a hand upon her arm to comfort her. She did something then he had not expected, turning into him with bowed head to press her face into his shoulder, laying one hand upon his chest as she did so. Slowly, her fingers curled into the material of his waistcoat, her knuckles growing white and her whole body tensing as though she were holding back some great tidal wave of emotion. A little startled – she had a knack for doing that to him – he raised a hesitant arm and loosely folded her in his embrace, gently stroking her back as she let out a great, shuddering sob. Her fist grew tighter on his waistcoat as she seemed to cling to him, her gasps muffled against his shoulder. He rested his chin upon the top of her head, letting the anguish empty from her as that warm, summery smell of hers filled his nostrils. After a few moments – one did not wallow in grief coming from the rookery

– her tears subsided, and she raised a saddened face to his. Her long, dark eyelashes clung together where her tears had wet them and her cheeks were mottled with red, but her emerald eyes shone no less bright.

"You kissed me back."

"What?"

"In Seven Dials, I pretended to kiss you and you kissed me back."

"Yes... well, I suppose I did."

She blinked up at him as her brows drew together.

"I haven't kissed anyone since I left Seven Dials three years ago." Her voice was the barest whisper and his breath caught as she gazed up at him with wide, fathomless eyes.

"Why not?" he couldn't help asking, hearing what sounded like disbelief in her tone, as though she had been shocked by their kiss. She slowly shook her head.

"I didn't want to. I just wanted to be me. I'd had enough of..." She trailed off and glanced away, as though searching for the right words. A small furrow marred her brow as she spoke again. "Enough of my body bein' used, whether I wanted it or not. Enough of... feelin' like I didn't belong to myself. I just wanted to be Violet again, not a whore – I could be respectable. People look at you different when they respect you and I didn't want anythin' to get in the way of my art."

John glanced down to where she still stood in the loose circle of his arms before offering her an apologetic smile as he took a step back.

"My apologies, then, Miss Latimer... I wouldn't want to be the one to stand in your way."

The air in the conservatory, dense and humid, seemed to close around them as she leaned into him, so close he could feel the soft curves of her breasts flattening against him.

"No, don't apologize. I... I liked it. I'd forgotten what it was like, to enjoy—" She broke off her words, seeming startled again by her reaction before lifting her chin, meeting his gaze with fierce determination, and whispering, "Do it again."

Jesus Christ. The words had barely left her lips when he bent to capture them with his own, turning her fully against him so that he could enfold her in his embrace as his mouth muffled her surprised gasp. Her fingers, which had been loose around the edge of his waistcoat, now dug into him, her long nails scraping his flesh. The sensation sent pleasure spiking through his body and a low growl reverberated in his chest as she seemed to melt into him. Some rational part of his brain told him it was unwise to be kissing the woman he was supposed to be hiding from Archie Neville, and one who seemed to have sworn off all men for the last three years, but goddamn did she taste good. She smelled even better – of grass warmed by the sun; of honeysuckle and sweet pea – and he pulled his mouth from hers to bury his face in her neck to inhale that intoxicating scent before pressing his lips to the smooth column of her throat. Her breath rasped out and her hands were suddenly upon the back of his head, fingers threading through his hair, pulling him back to her mouth. Her soft, deft hands trailed down his back, his hips, until she finally broke away with a small gasp and stepped back. Her chest rose and fell with the quickened rhythm of her breathing and for a moment she said nothing as he looked back at her, not daring to make a move.

"No," she finally said, softly, touching an experimental finger to her lips. "I suppose I'm not ready yet." She met his gaze and offered a small smile. "Though I reckon you could make a girl change her mind."

John couldn't help laughing at that. "High praise, indeed." His smile faded quickly when her gaze dropped to the floor and her lips tightened. He reached out then and touched her chin, drawing her attention back up. "Fear not, Miss Latimer," he said softly. "I won't let Archie get away with his crimes... I will find a way into his circle, this I promise you."

"It won't be easy," she remarked, almost to herself.

"No, it won't." He smiled as she turned to him. "But you forget that I am *incredibly* charming." He put a mocking hand to his chest and saw the corner of her mouth turn up, just a little, so reached out a hand to her. "The garden awaits."

She glanced down at his outstretched arm, hesitated for only a moment, and placed her hand in his. "Lead the way."

Violet had strolled through some of the finest gardens in France during her two years living there – the Tuileries, Versailles, the Jardin du Luxembourg, and though the gardens surrounding Bradford House were not nearly so vast as those, they were no less lovely. She and Della had often sat out under the shade of the ancient oak after Della had married the earl, and it had become one of her favourite parts of the estate. The early autumn chill still hung in the air, but the sun was bright in a cloudless sky as they followed the flagstone path which led around the circumference of the house.

Yet, despite the loveliness of the day and the beauty of the gardens, Violet could not shake the uneasiness in her belly. The kiss had been a test to see if her dreams of his actually meant anything. Was she ready to let herself experience pleasure again; to let someone close? She sighed... no. A very good kiss it had been – that she could not deny. But she had felt herself recoiling during it; had felt overwhelmed by his embrace. He had kissed her with such... passion. With such willingness. And men rarely, in her experience, kissed her in that way unless they wanted more. She would give it, wouldn't she? Slip a few coins her way, and she'll lift her skirts 'cause it's all she's good for. Certainly, they would sometimes try to woo her, to take a bit of time to get to know her, in the shallowest of senses, but when it came time... all they had ever wanted was her body. *He's not like them*, she tried to tell herself, and shook off the feeling before Mr. Barrow spoke.

"Are you finding your rooms suitable?" he asked, somewhat stilted, as they skirted a bed overflowing with nodding mallows and azaleas, their blooms still vivid despite the lateness of the season. Violet glanced at him with a half-smile.

"Mr. Barrow, any room that isn't crawlin' with fleas or damp from a leaky roof is suitable by my standards. It's positively luxurious."

His short, deep laugh made something spark to life deep inside her belly and her stomach clenched. "When the earl first brought me on as a footman, I thought I'd died and gone to heaven. And I only had a little chamber in the servants' quarters."

"Do you miss livin' here, workin' for him?"

He shrugged. "Sometimes. I was so proud to hold that post – valet to the Earl of Bradford. Never thought some grubby little nobody like me would end up working for a peer, of all things. But I'm doing alright. I'm back where I started, trying to make the rookery better for the folks living there now." He glanced over at her, his expression serious. "I am being considered for a promotion at Whitehall. Detective Chief Inspector for the Central Investigation Department. I think, if I were to get it, I could do some real good, make real changes. No one else will care about those people if they don't know what it's like to live in the rookery." He paused and turned his attention back to the path. "And if this operation goes well, I would be that much closer to getting it."

Violet glanced over at him as they strolled by the little pond in which water lilies floated and goldfish swam, unable to imagine any world in which she would willingly return to the slums she had escaped the first second she had a chance. Still, she supposed it was admirable... the residents of the rookery were certainly the most in need, but the most often ignored.

"Oh... I hope you get it." And though his commitment to the place that had brought her only misery and hunger and longing for more perplexed her, she was sincere in her words. He gave a little smile as mottled sunlight danced over his features – sharp, they were, as though carved from stone. He reminded her of those statues she had seen while strolling through the Louvre with her little sketchbook and pencils. She had drawn many of them; the slash of brows, the sharp indents of cupid's bows, the straight lines of noses. And here, before her, was one of those statues come to life. Every line on him was an angle, as though he had been created entirely with the straight edge of a ruler, and he was hard; hard as one of those marble gods. He was not big with muscle, as Della's husband was, but she had touched him, had seen his naked chest that night in the cellar at the Fox and Friar. Every muscle on him was dense and sinewy – he would be deadly to those who dismissed his lack of bulk as weakness.

And for someone who had no doubt fought every day for survival growing up in St. Giles, as she had, it seemed he had not lost his humanity. It was easy to do that growing up in a place like Seven Dials.

He stepped ahead as they approached the weeping willow which bowed gracefully over the path to sweep the long tendrils out of their way. She nodded and ducked beneath the boughs to continue, but soon they had reached the far end of the wall that surrounded the property and Violet turned to look back the way they'd come. Mr. Barrow reached into his waistcoat pocket to withdraw his watch, glancing at it with a frown.

"I'll have to be going soon. Tommy'll want me at the club when it opens for lunch to take shipment of the produce. And I'll have sparring practice after that." He paused and looked up at her. "I could try to come back tomorrow? If I'm not needed?"

A sudden ache coiled through Violet's chest at the idea of him going away again, back to Tommy and the rest of the Bruisers, and all the danger that entailed, but she plastered a bright smile on her face. "Only if you're able – I'm sure Mrs. Beatty will keep me busy. I think I might have another go at the bread, see if I can't make somethin' halfway edible."

When he gave her a skeptical look, she forced out a laugh and took his hand to lead him back to the house. "Come on – you know Tommy won't stand for people bein' late."

Mr. Barrow didn't argue but he didn't look convinced as she walked with him to the gatehouse and laid a hand upon his arm as he stopped.

"If you start disappearin' too often, Tommy's gonna get suspicious, especially if Archie's comin' back. He's gonna have to report to him when he gets home, and it would be helpful if he lets Archie know that you've been around, makin' yourself useful."

The very idea of helping in any way with Mr. Barrow's investigation, of being forced to relive all those terrible years in Seven Dials with Archie, made her skin crawl but she could at least keep him safe. He gave a short nod and finally smiled. "You're right. Now wouldn't be the time to be disappearing. I have another fight later this week – Archie should be back by then."

Violet's chest grew cold, and she tightened her grip on Mr. Barrow's arm. "Then you had better go out there and win that fight. If Archie's there and your first meetin' with him is after you lose a bout, he's gonna think you're not game and it's gonna be that much harder to get in his good graces."

He grinned and laid his hand over hers. It was warm and heavy, and she resisted the strange urge to trace her thumb over his.

"Never lost yet, Miss Latimer. I'll come back when I'm able and let you know what's happening."

Violet almost told him to be careful, but bit back the words and watched as he slipped through the gate and out into the street. She waved as he turned to cross the street, heading towards Belgrave Square. Even after he had disappeared around the corner, she stayed at the gate, her fingers resting lightly upon the metal bars, feeling as though she had lost her anchor in this world and was now adrift in an unfamiliar sea. Della had once been that anchor for her; they had kept each other moored to reality when the harshness of the orphanage had threatened to break them. In France, it had been her art; her means of expressing the parts of herself women were ordinarily meant to keep quiet about. It was her passion, her voice, her freedom. But here, trapped in a house that was not hers, though Della's mark was all over it, she had nothing holding her down any longer. Mr. Barrow was a relative stranger to her, but he knew the hardships of her past and he knew the danger she now faced. And with her departure from Bradford House as yet undetermined, he was her only link to the outside world.

Violet sighed and turned away from the gate to make her way back to the kitchen and that stubborn loaf of bread. If she was going to be trapped in this strange limbo, she might as well make the best of it.

SEVEN

"Have you found her yet?"

Tommy's voice reached John as he jabbed at the punching bag being held steady by one of the other boxers among the Bruisers crew, the enormous Irishman known only as the Devil. His flaming red hair and violent temper lent him the moniker, and he glanced over at Tommy as John shook out his arms and stepped back. Sweat beaded on his skin and he wiped a bandaged fist across his forehead before shaking his head.

"I've not heard a single whisper about her, Tommy – she's disappeared, or it was never her to begin with."

The other man contemplated him from outside the makeshift ring with dark, unreadable eyes as John took up a nearby towel and dragged it over the back of his neck. An uncomfortable silence descended as he looked back at Tommy. The Devil's eyes were on him as well, curious. No doubt he, too, had been tasked with tracking down a pretty blonde whore named Violet. Finally, Tommy sighed and stepped forward.

"You sure she was called Violet?"

"I'm sure... had a cousin named Violet; it reminded me of her."

Tommy narrowed his eyes and John looked back at him, unwavering.

"What did she look like?"

"Like I said... blonde, green eyes. Bit on the short side. Pretty thing. She seemed desperate."

Tommy's eyebrows lowered a fraction. "Desperate for you?"

"Desperate for money." John's voice was flat. "She kept offerin' me lower – gave her a whole shillin' to leave me 'cause I felt bad."

Tommy was quiet again and a knot of tension began to grow in John's chest. It didn't show – he kept his expression carefully impassive as the Devil slowly stepped away from the punching bag. Eventually, Tommy shrugged and nodded towards the other man who immediately stepped out of the ring and disappeared through a door at the back of the room into the warehouse.

John glanced back as the door closed behind the Irishman, then slowly began to unravel the bandages from his hands as Tommy strolled forward into the square of light spilling in through the small, grimy window set high up in the wall. He said nothing as he withdrew a watch from his pocket and glanced at the time before raising his hard, implacable gaze to John, who stared back with equal indifference.

"Ready for the fight?" he asked, his voice deceptively nonchalant. John Barrow was no fool, however, and he heard the underlying threat in the other man's voice. He took a moment before answering.

"Ready as ever."

Tommy stepped closer. He set his large hand upon the length of rope which marked the boundary of the ring, and scrutinized John for an uncomfortable amount of time, but he wasn't about to let any uneasiness show and continued to unwrap his hands.

"Archie's comin' back here under the impression that she's

in London. If he gets back and we don't have her, he's gonna be right pissed. Even more if she's back to liftin' her skirts – he wants her for himself and if he finds her with someone else, he'll fuckin' butcher them. Where the hell is she?"

John let out a disbelieving laugh and raised his hands. "I don't even know the girl, Tommy. I'm just tellin' you what I saw. She could have been anyone – there's probably a dozen blonde whores named Violet in St. Giles alone."

Tommy's expression didn't change – not really – but every muscle in his face seemed to tighten as he stared at John, his dark eyes unreadable. John was very careful not to look away as the other man's lips flattened, and he could almost hear Tommy cursing his brother for this fool's errand. Eventually, he turned away with an obscenity hissed out under his breath and kicked at a nearby bucket. It skittered across the floor, the noise echoing off the rafters, but John didn't flinch as the other man turned back to him.

"Keep lookin' – bring her to me if you find her."

"I will, Tommy. I heard she used to work at Cora's – I can stop by and see if she's gone back."

The other man wasn't listening, though, and he muttered something about bloody lightskirts as he turned and left the room, slamming the door behind him. John didn't move but did continue to slowly unwrap the sparring bandages from his hands. It was going to take some world-class rubbish to convince Tommy that he was truly looking for Violet, but he was prepared for that. A few well-timed conversations with a few specific individuals – the owner at the Fox and Friar had been the first – would ensure that word would reach the Bruisers' second-in-command that he was making a concerted effort to find the missing fiancée of Archie Neville, all before he ever set foot back on England's shore.

Finally, John gathered up his coat and tugged it on as he stepped out into a chill drizzle that had started earlier that morning. He tugged up his collar and pulled the brim of his bowler low over his forehead before heading home, stopping just once on the way to make a very special purchase.

John was only four rounds into his fight with Billy Cahill and his skin was slick with perspiration, his muscles quivered with fatigue, and his head reeled. The other fighter was good. Very good. Tommy would be sure to want to speak to him afterwards about joining the gang. But something else drove John today, beyond his usual desire to keep whoever he could out of the ranks of the Bruisers.

Archie Neville stood at the edge of the boisterous crowd, watching the fight with almost frightening intent. Tommy stood beside him, and every so often, Archie would lean towards him and say something, with Tommy responding in kind. At one point, he nodded towards John, distracting him for a moment and allowing Billy to land a vicious blow right in the gut. John staggered back, winded, as a wild cheer went up from the crowd. Archie shook his head and John forced himself up, stepped back for a moment to collect himself and then, before Billy could even see it coming, struck out with a swift lead hook that caught his opponent in the chest and sent him sprawling upon the hard-packed dirt floor.

Another raucous cheer went up from the crowd and John coughed as he staggered back, still reeling from the blow to his stomach. He raised shaking fists, though, anticipating Billy's retaliation, but none came, and the crowd jeered as the countdown reached ten without him standing. The cornerman stepped under the ropes surrounding the ring and hauled the other fighter off the ground before pushing him out to vicious taunts and shouts. John finally dropped his arms, resting his hands upon his knees as he bent over, trying to catch his breath. The air sawed in and out of his lungs and his knuckles were raw and bloodied, but he had prevailed – by the skin of his teeth.

A huge hand suddenly clapped down on his shoulder, and he glanced up to find the leader of the Bruisers staring down at him. There was no doubt he was Tommy's brother; both men were equally large, equally dark-haired, and equally menacing.

"You must be John Barrow."

Shouts sounded close by and there was a flurry of activity over Archie's shoulder as money was paid out to those who had won their bets on the fight, but John didn't look away from the other man as he slowly rose.

"I am. You must be Archie."

Archie's grin was quick, calculated. His hand remained heavy on John's shoulder.

"That I am, that I am." He glanced over at John's opponent, who had been pushed onto a stool and was having a wide gash on his jaw examined, then looked back. "That was one hell of a hit. Thought he had you for a minute there."

John nodded slowly, never looking away from the dark eyes watching him back.

"He's good. Tommy should speak with him."

Archie nodded as though this were a fine idea and his hand finally fell from John's shoulder. "I'm sure he will." He now made a show of adjusting his cuffs and checking his pocket watch, before smiling again – a cold smile, one which never touched his eyes. "My brother tells me you may have run across someone we know."

John said nothing for a moment as he began to unravel the bandages around his fists. He didn't look to see if Tommy was in the vicinity.

"I only told him a girl followed me to Covent Garden, offerin' a tup. She was blonde, said her name was Violet. That's all I know."

Archie's gaze was sharp, suspicious, and it never wavered as

John balled up the used bandages and held them in his fist, not looking away. Another uncomfortable moment passed before the other man spoke.

"Hear you've never lost a fight."

John paused to dissect this new direction in the conversation before he answered carefully. "No, I haven't."

Archie Neville's grin was cunning, and his big hand came up to clamp down on John's shoulder again. He leaned in close as his fingers tightened their grip. Still, John did not look away as he kept his expression carefully impassive.

"But you haven't fought me yet." His grin widened and he let out a sharp bark of laughter. John knew all about Archie's past as a bareknuckle champion – indeed, he was known to have killed men in the ring. It was one of the reasons he had become the Bruisers' leader, and why they continued to recruit from boxing matches. John was sure that nearly eight years in Newgate hadn't dulled his skills, but he didn't comment on Archie's words, just held his gaze until the other man leaned in even closer, his fingers now biting into John's shoulder. He didn't flinch.

"Listen here, I came all the way back from bloody France thinkin' Violet was found. You know why we're lookin' for her, eh?"

John only shook his head.

"Me and Violet was engaged before I went in the jug. She made a promise. You keep your promises, don't you, John?"

A pause. "I do."

"Good lad. I'm just makin' sure that Violet keeps her promise, that's all. I don't know if it's her you saw, but I do need her found."

Archie's words couldn't be clearer, and his tone suggested what the results of failure would bring. John nodded. "I'll find her."

Archie's smile returned and his grip finally loosened. John's expression didn't change. "That's what I like to hear. She's a mouthy little bitch, is my Violet, but she's the prettiest thing in this shithole and she's mine. Anyone lays a hand on her, and they'll answer to me. And she'll wish she'd never been born." He paused now, and his eyes narrowed. When he spoke, his voice was low. "There's somethin' else I need you to do for me, John."

John's head cocked to one side. "What's that?'

Archie's expression grew dark now – the anger that had been lingering just below the surface now revealed itself and his mouth compressed into a hard line.

"I spent eight years in fuckin' Newgate and I wanna know who put me there. Tommy's been tryin' to find out what bastard turned me in since the day they locked me up. Eight years, and he's not heard a single bloody whisper. He let me down, John, but I've heard you're a clever lad." He now raised a finger and jabbed it into John's chest, his dark eyes simmering with rage. "I'm Archie Neville and I didn't get to where I'm at lettin' some bastard snitch on me and get away with it. You understand?"

John held that gaze which radiated with fury and slowly nodded.

"I understand, Archie."

The cunning grin returned just as quickly as it had disappeared. "You go on home now, rest up – my Violet won't be easy to find."

John's mouth curved into a flat imitation of a smile. "I'll do my best. A pleasure to finally meet you, Archie."

The other man laughed, a rough, callous sound, as he stepped away and set his hat back upon his head. "The pleasure is all mine, John, all mine." He was grinning as he turned away, but the final look he flashed was knowing as he strolled out of the ring.

John stared after him as he gestured to Tommy on his way out of the warehouse. He drew in a slow breath as they left together before tugging on his shirt and waistcoat, gathering up the overcoat he had left at the side of the ring and slipping out through the back, unseen. It was dark outside the warehouse, but not too late – she might still be awake.

John made his way up to Tower Hill and hailed a hansom cab. Once seated, he leaned back on the faded leather squab with a long, agonized groan. Everything ached. Jesus, but that other boxer had been good. Very good. He had been reckless to let Archie's presence distract him – he was lucky to have landed that final blow. Grimacing, he reached into his pocket for a handkerchief and pressed it gingerly to his split lip as he closed his eyes. It was Miss Latimer he saw in his mind; it was all he seemed to see lately, and his pulse began to race as the carriage trundled past Whitehall, his place of employment, and on towards Trafalgar Square. He was not far now.

Lights still flickered in the windows of Bradford House when he arrived, but the servants' quarters were deserted when he made his way in through the back door. He poked his head into the kitchen, but all the lights had been turned down, and so he made his way to the main hall. The parlour was dark and so he followed the corridor which led to the conservatory. A light glowed near the back of the space, and he followed it, down the narrow winding walkway, brushing the trailing tendrils of ivy from his path until he came to the little stone fountain. And there, sitting upon one of the benches, surrounded by strategi-cally placed lanterns, sat Violet Latimer. She wore a simple wrapper of floral chintz, and her flaxen hair had been plaited and tied back with a ribbon. Most notable, however, was the easel which sat in front of her, and she observed the canvas set upon it with a frown, tapping her chin with the end of a paint-brush as she seemed to contemplate the painting before her.

So absorbed was she in her art that she had not yet noticed him standing at the end of the path and observing her. He could happily have noted the fine arch of her brow, the sensual curve of her lips, or the deft flick of her wrist as she brought brush to palette for hours. For days. But then Archie's words came to him. *She's mine.* And any and all inappropriate thoughts quickly abandoned him. He shook his head and cleared his throat and finally, she turned with a startled gasp.

Almost immediately, her whole countenance lit up in the brightest, most joyful smile he was sure he had ever witnessed. *Goddammit.* It was a cruel twist of fate that the woman he suddenly found he wanted to please more than any other was the one who was completely off limits. She had to be. Archie's words, said with a threatening growl, still echoed in his head. *Anyone lays a hand on her, they'll answer to me. And she'll wish she'd never been born.* It would be in their best interest, then, to maintain a professional relationship.

She jumped up from the bench with a gasp, dropped the brush she held and raced towards him to throw her arms about his neck, pressing a quick, eager kiss to his cheek before pulling back to gaze up at him with a wide smile. And every single thought he had just had regarding her and his need to keep his distance immediately fled his mind.

"Oh, Mr. Barrow, thank you! I haven't stopped paintin' since Penny found me this mornin' and told me you had sent me a package! I couldn't believe it – you can't know how grateful I am, truly!"

She gave his arms an enthusiastic squeeze before stepping away and gesturing to the easel at which she had been sitting. "And look! I've wanted to paint this fountain since I first saw it – what d'you think?"

John followed as she returned to the bench, clasping her hands in front of her with an excited grin as he stopped and took in her painting. It was not yet finished, but he could see the little cherub taking shape, its feathered wings captured with short brushstrokes, its round face expressed with a few simple lines. The amphora it held was but an outline at this stage, but he could see it all coming together and nodded his head.

"I'm no art critic, but that's a fine painting, Miss Latimer. I'm glad I could help you."

Her expression grew serious now and she reached out to lay her hand over his arm. He should shake her off, step back; she was entirely too familiar, even after knowing him for only a short while, and he worried this closeness would only create problems down the road. But he didn't – that smile of hers had done something to him, deep inside. He would do anything to be the cause of that smile.

"More than help, Mr. Barrow – I don't know what I'd do if I couldn't paint. I was worried I might go mad here." She started to smile again but must have caught the anxious tightening of his face and frowned, stepping back. It only took her a moment to realize what he was doing here and why he must look so concerned. She swallowed. "He's back, isn't he?"

John closed his eyes and gave a solemn nod before meeting her gaze again. "He is."

All that joy drained out of her face, and she pulled her bottom lip in between her teeth to worry at it, looking away as she seemed to contemplate this news.

"That's good... isn't it? You can finally get your investigation started?" She sounded unconvinced of the benefits of Archie being back in England and he offered a small smile.

"I can. I'm only involved in the boxing matches at the moment. We know they're running brothels and some illegal bookmaking, but I haven't been made privy to any of it yet. And if you want Archie gone for good, that won't be enough. If he allows me access to their inner workings, I'll be able to finally gather real evidence – enough to bring down the whole gang, not just him."

Violet's brows drew together, and her lips flattened into a hard line, as though she had something to say and was reluctant to say it. He raised a brow in expectation and her mouth twisted into a little grimace before she spoke.

"The docks," she said.

"The docks?"

She gave an unwilling nod. "Archie always resented being from Seven Dials – bein' seen as rookery scum. He's happy to run the place, happy to make everyone there as miserable as he is, but he's always wanted more. He's never gonna get rich puttin' on fights for people who've nothin' to give, or runnin' his little club. Prostitution and gamblin' in St. Giles will never get him where he really wants to be, and I know he doesn't want to be a gangster forever. He wants businesses that can afford to pay him big money so he can sit around in his club and have everyone fawnin' all over him. He wants a protection racket, for all them warehouses full of expensive swag, just like Edward Brill had."

"The leader of the Limehouse Gang," John added, turning this new information over in his head. Whitehall knew Archie was planning to expand his territory, but it was good to have someone close to him confirm it. A protection racket – something involving multiple members of the Bruisers – especially for valuable businesses like the warehouses at the docklands, would net some very serious charges. The Limehouse Gang, which ruled most of the East End down to the docks, had made a fortune off such a scheme before their leader, Edward Brill, had turned to reform and started a multitude of businesses to serve his people.

"They almost certainly would have gone to war if Archie hadn't been locked up. He's been plannin' ever since – he wants access to the docks, but Edward and his gang have always kept him out. He'd already started to move closer before he went away, settin' up shop in Covent Garden. He wants protection money – real money. I haven't spoken with Archie in eight years, and I've tried to avoid the Bruisers, but if I were a bettin' man, I'd wager that's his goal. Take out the Limehousers and take the docks and the whole of the East End for himself."

John nodded slowly. This was welcome information, though she had clearly been reluctant to share it. He would press no further today.

"There is something else he wants."

Her throat moved as she swallowed, but she said nothing and looked back up at him, her eyes wide and expectant.

"He wants you found, Miss Latimer. In no uncertain terms. Says you made a promise."

Her mouth – that lovely mouth with the sharp little cupid's bow – flattened into a tight smile. "I did, indeed. What a fool I was."

He couldn't help it. He reached out and took her arms in his hands, holding her gaze.

"Don't ever regret getting you and Lady Bradford out of going to the workhouse. You know it was the right thing to do."

Violet looked away. "I know that... I'm more ashamed that I ever fell for him to begin with. I thought I loved—" She cut herself off with a shake of her head. "And when I saw what he really was... how could I ever trust my own mind again?" She paused and slowly lifted her face to his once more before frowning suddenly and reaching up, startling him when she touched a finger to his lip. He winced in pain, but it was nothing compared to the shock of awareness that bolted through him at that one, simple gesture.

"How'd the fight go?"

John forced out an easy laugh, stepping away from her gentle touch as he made a show of reaching into his pocket for his handkerchief.

"Still undefeated."

The furrow between her brows deepened as she watched him press the square of linen to his mouth. "Looks like the other fella got a few knocks in himself."

He favoured her with a devilish smile. "I've had much worse."

She rolled her eyes at this and crossed her arms over her chest. "That's not somethin' I'd brag about."

John shrugged and shook his head. "I don't know... there's something about a black eye and a split lip that some ladies simply cannot resist."

One fine brow arched up at this. "Is that so?"

He grinned and shoved the handkerchief back in his pocket. "Not really."

Miss Latimer did laugh at that, but her smile quickly faded when she caught his sober expression. "What's wrong?'

"There's... there's something else he wants."

She didn't even have to wait for him to explain. She took one look up at him and nodded.

"He wants whoever turned him in."

"I won't let him find out, Miss Latimer," John was quick to add. "He'll die in a prison cell before he ever finds out it was you, I promise."

A ghost of a smile appeared on her lips before disappearing. "Let us hope."

The sudden, distant tolling of a clock interrupted the quiet of the conservatory and John reached into his pocket to glance at his watch. When he met her gaze, those fathomless emerald eyes were wary.

"Please be careful, Mr. Barrow," she whispered. "He's dangerous... and he'll get what he wants, one way or another."

John didn't offer her an easy smile this time – he saw the fear in her eyes, and instead, reached out to take her hand in his.

"I'll be careful." He paused. "I won't be able to come back here... not for a while. Archie'll be keeping a close eye on me, no doubt. And if what you say is true, I'll have a great deal of work ahead of me."

She nodded, reluctantly, and gave him a forced imitation of a smile.

"Not to worry. I have my art, now... I say it'll keep me busy for long enough. And that bread – I haven't given up on that just yet, either."

John let out a soft laugh at that. He should have pulled away then – he realized he was still holding her hand – but found he could not, and he held her a trifle longer than he ought to have before she withdrew herself with a quick smile.

"Then I shall leave you to it. Good night, Miss Latimer."

"Good night, Mr. Barrow. And thank you, again... this means the world to me," she added, gesturing to the easel. He nodded quickly and stepped away.

"You are most welcome."

It was with an effort he turned away from those wide, grass-green eyes and left the conservatory to make his way home, ready to face his first day with Archie Neville.

EIGHT

A week passed. Two weeks. Mr. Barrow had not yet returned – had sent no word of what was happening – and all Violet could do was bake bread and paint. Her baking had improved significantly – Mrs. Beatty had even served her last loaf for the staff dinner the night before and everyone had proclaimed it to be perfection, causing the cook to beam proudly at her protégée. Her painting, however, had taken a different turn. The little winged cherub in the conservatory had become her muse. She spent hours there now, dressed in an old, paint-splattered wrapper, and had already produced three different paintings of the statue. They had grown darker, somehow, the burst of colour in the background from the riot of tropical flowers fading from the first painting to become a muddle of greys and browns in the latest.

A letter came from Della, and she read it over and over, as though it were a lifeline in a stormy sea.

Dearest Violet,

I have been assured that you are safe at Bradford House, and I hope you are finding it comfortable. I know Detective Inspector Barrow will be working hard to conclude this operation so that you may have your freedom once more. He was taught by the very best, you know. All the same, I worry. I've been kept awake at night with dreams of Archie and the time we spent with him. Our training. Our escape. I've told Cole about what happened. Not everything. There are some things I cannot bring myself to speak of even after all these years, and I'm sure you would agree. I wish with all my heart I could be there with you, but Cole says it would not be wise for me to return to London and draw attention to Bradford House. Archie will surely know who I am now, and he will be waiting for me to contact you. It is quite difficult to remain incognito as the Countess of Bradford, I'm afraid.

Instead, little Clara and I shall wait until we can finally make good on our plans to visit you in Paris. Notre Dame awaits! And if you should ever need anything – anything at all – Mrs. Cooper will be happy to oblige. She has become a trusted friend and I know she will care for you as she cared for me. I'll write often, and I look forward to your response. Please be safe... we have plans, you and I.

Love always,
Your friend,
Della

After reading the missive, Violet carefully refolded the paper and tucked it into the small drawer in her bedside table before taking up a fountain pen and fresh sheet of paper to respond.

Dearest Della,

I am safe and well. I cannot thank your husband enough for letting me stay here. I don't know where I would have gone without him. Detective Inspector Barrow has been most helpful. He even sent me some art supplies and I haven't stopped painting since. I shall send you one of my pieces when it's finished.

He's back now. He's looking for me, and he's looking for whoever turned him in. Della, I hardly sleep at night, thinking about what he would do if he found me. Worse, if he knew it was me that got him put away. I know Detective Inspector Barrow will do his best, but you and I both know how single-minded Archie can be. He trusts no one, and he'll be even less trusting now, knowing whoever turned him in is still out there. I'm afraid I'll be here in this house forever, and we'll never get to meet in Paris. I'm afraid I'll never see my little studio again, I'll lose my patrons, I'll lose everything I built there.

I think often of those talks we had at night, of what we would do if we had the money and the power to change the rookery. I hadn't thought of those talks in years, but I have so much time now, I can't stop thinking. I don't believe we ever thought we'd actually get out of there, but I never dreamed I'd have to go back. I hated it there, Della, it felt like I couldn't get clean of it, and I was there for hardly more than a few hours.

Did you ever consider going back, like we talked about all those years ago? Or is it all a bad memory?

I look forward to your next letter and seeing you and Clara again.

Love always,

Your dearest friend,
Violet

Violet set down the pen and stared down at the letter as she waited for the ink to dry on the last paragraph she had added on a whim. She and Della had, indeed, discussed what they would do to change the rookery, given enough money and power, whispering to each other at night in the orphanage before being scolded by the matron. When they had left and had to worry about food and shelter, and how they might escape Archie and his gang, they had forgotten their talks and their dreams of making St. Giles a better place for those who called it home. But Mr. Barrow's words hadn't stopped playing in her head since that day in the garden: *I'm back where I started, trying to make the rookery better for the folks living there now*, and they had reminded her of the dreams she and Della had shared.

But she had gone back – been forced to, but had gone back, nonetheless – and she had hated it. She couldn't wait to scrub it from her skin, as though the very essence of the rookery had clung to her, reminding her of her past self. And Violet never wanted to be her past self again: the woman who had fallen utterly and completely for a man who had revealed himself to be a monster, who had risked her life to escape him, who had sold herself rather than be married to him. It was nearly a decade of her life that she would be happy to wipe from her memory and never revisit. She could hardly believe that Mr. Barrow, finally freed of the grasping poverty to rise to such heights, had gone back of his own volition.

Violet shuddered as she stood from the writing desk and drifted to the window, envelope still in hand. She peered down at the gardens below, as though he would appear there, and sighed. The garden was quiet, not even a gardener to be seen, and a small knot of worry tightened in her chest. It had been two weeks now, two weeks without so much as a note to let her know how the operation was progressing, or if he was safe. She swallowed back the rising lump in her throat. Had Archie found him out? Was it as she had warned him, and he was now drifting along the banks of the Thames, another unidentified body, another victim of the gangs who controlled the rookeries?

She exhaled a short, sharp breath and turned away from the window to leave her room, making her way down to the kitchens in the hopes of finding a footman to post her letter. She poked her head around the door, but the room was empty. A stack of newspapers had been left on the table and, curious, she drifted idly towards it to pluck up one of the papers. There was little of interest on the front page – something about the war in Egypt, about the founding of a new football club, and she slowly turned to the next page, and the next, until a small headline caught her eye.

Dismembered Body Found in Covent Garden, Police Report

A cold shiver ran up Violet's back as the knot in her chest tightened once more. She read on. *The unidentified body of a man, approximately 25-30 years of age, was discovered outside a brothel in Covent Garden on Thursday evening, police report. The body had been dismembered, but so far police have been unable to find witnesses to this ghastly crime. Neighbours attribute the murder to the work of local gangs, who have become increasingly violent over the last several weeks. An anonymous source blames the leader of the Bruisers, one Archie 'Iron Fist' Neville, who was recently released from Newgate Prison after serving a sentence of eight years in relation to charges of assault, prostitution, and robbery. With no witnesses, however, police say the investigation may be unable to continue. If anyone was witness to this crime or has any additional information, they are asked to contact the Metropolitan Police.*

Violet's hands shook as she slowly closed the paper and stepped back, the envelope left, forgotten, on the table. A terrible dread filled her, suffocating her, until she was gasping, bent over the table, her fingers clutching the scarred wooden top. Mrs. Beatty found her thusly and rushed over to lay a comforting hand upon Violet's back.

"What's wrong, dear?"

Violet could barely say the words. "I think... I think Mr. Barrow might be dead. Oh, no." Her hand came up to her lips as the last sentence gasped out of her. Mrs. Beatty stilled and put a hand to her chest.

"Dead? How?"

Violet almost didn't hear the woman as she stared down at the text on the paper, the words blurring together as tears filled her vision. But slowly, rising through her like water boiling in a kettle, anger replaced the fear as she thought of all Archie had done – to her, to the people of St. Giles and Covent Garden, and the rage filled her like a terrible storm, battering at her until she turned, her jaw set, and made for the back door. Mrs. Beatty rushed after her.

"Where are you going? What's happened to him?"

"I don't know, but I'm gonna find out."

She had just about reached the door when Mrs. Cooper stepped out of her office and set her hands upon her hips, staring Violet down with an admittedly fierce expression.

"Where are you going, Miss Latimer?"

Violet stopped short. "I'm gonna find out if Mr. Barrow is alright."

There was a flash of emotion in the older woman's grey eyes before she slowly shook her head, softening her features just as she reached out and laid her hand over Violet's.

"Now you know I cannot let you leave without word from the police. You are an important witness. If you are referring to the story about the man found in Covent Garden" – her voice wavered briefly as she said this – "we do not yet know if that was Detective Inspector Barrow. Let us not go rushing headlong into dangerous situations without first understanding the facts."

"But I must know—"

"Calm, Miss Latimer, let us remain calm. I am certain if anything had happened to him, someone from Scotland Yard would have sent word. Let us wait. And pray." She paused and gave Violet a meaningful look, squeezing her hand before withdrawing. The rage continued to burn, but Violet pushed it down for the moment, took a deep breath, and managed a small nod of agreement.

"Yes, Mrs. Cooper. You're right. We mustn't be rash."

"Very good. Now, why don't you go on up to your rooms and I'll send Penny up to help you dress for dinner."

Mrs. Beatty's hand touched hers, taking it to guide her back to the kitchens, and Violet followed mutely, numb with shock, burning with rage.

Dinner with the staff was decidedly restrained, no one daring to breathe the name Barrow. Penny's eyes were noticeably red, and she was subdued as she poked at her beef stew. Mrs. Beatty was unnaturally cheerful, her attempts to get the staff talking valiant indeed. Violet said little and ate her meal with cold determination as the anger continued to simmer low in the pit of her stomach. By God, if she ever saw Archie again, she would not run this time – she would claw his cursed eyes out of his head if he had laid a single hand on Mr. Barrow. Dinner ended quickly, for no one seemed eager for conversation with the unspoken understanding that their former co-worker may be dead; dismembered in a back alley in Covent Garden.

After helping to clear the dishes, Violet returned to the conservatory, making her way through scented blossoms and waving palm fronds to where her easel had been left at the back of the room. For a long moment, she stared at the canvas and the half-finished painting upon it but could not find the will to put brush to paint and so sat with a heavy sigh and picked up the leather-bound sketchbook she had left on the bench. Her thumb caressed the soft cover as she unspooled the twine which held the book closed, opening it to where she had tucked a scrap of ribbon between the pages. There, beside smaller drawings of the cherub she had used to map out her canvas, were several sketches of a man's face, drawn from different angles. They were little more than line drawings, done during moments of idle musing, but they were all of the same man. John Barrow, brought to life on the page with a series of slashing lines and subtle shading. Unusual for her, and she frowned at the page. Faces, and people in general, were something she had always struggled to draw – it had always seemed too personal, too inti-mate, as though she would be seeing into someone by capturing their likeness. She had always preferred her subjects to be closed to her – railyards and bridges rarely asked anything of her and demanded little introspection. But with John Barrow... she had been compelled to depict him in some manner. Certainly, he was handsome, with all those sharp lines and defined muscles, but there was something more, something in his eyes, that she couldn't help but want to recreate.

Anger rose in her suddenly, at the same time tears stung her eyes, and she quickly closed the book and set it aside. For a long time, she sat in the quiet of the conservatory as night closed around her until someone cleared their throat and she looked up.

And there he was, standing at the end of the path which led to the fountain as he had the last time they had been here together, very much alive. Something broke inside Violet at that moment. The last month spent hanging on by a thread, the constant fear and worry and sleepless nights, collided with the sudden, gut-wrenching relief to see Mr. Barrow still alive. Her face burned and she couldn't help it; the sob burst from her as she pushed herself up from the bench and raced to him. Last time it had been in gratitude for the art supplies; now it was only immense relief and she gasped as she flung herself into his arms, clinging to him as though she would never let go. He said nothing, just folded his arms around her, holding her as she sobbed against his chest.

"I thought... I thought you were dead," she choked out against the soft wool of his overcoat. His hand came up to caress the back of her head as he tutted softly.

"I'm safe, Miss Latimer, perfectly safe. You must have seen the paper."

She drew away from him now, wiping hastily at her eyes before she spoke, her voice low. "Who was it?"

He sighed and stepped back, pushing a hand through his hair. "A member of the Limehouse Gang. Archie's getting very serious about finding whoever turned him in, and he suspects Edward Brill."

Violet froze as she was struck by the sudden, terrible realization. A man was dead. For something she had done. Someone had been murdered while she sat amid ferns and palms, painting her little cherubs, foolishly thinking that Archie would just go on looking for the person who had sent him to Newgate and there would be no consequences. Worse than foolish. Stupid. Ignorant. Her hands balled into fists, and she lowered her tearful gaze to the ground, unable to bear Mr. Barrow's scrutiny.

"Miss Latimer," he said softly. She shook her head, refusing to look up. "This is not your fault."

"A man is dead. A man is dead for what I did."

"Miss Latimer."

She raised a reluctant gaze and met warm, brown eyes.

"You know as well as I do that Archie belonged in Newgate. Still belongs. He wasn't convicted of anything serious enough to be put away for good last time, but I promise you that he will not get off so lightly again. This was not your fault." He said the words again, stronger this time and touched a finger to her chin so that she was compelled to meet his earnest gaze. Violet's heart sank.

"He's gonna start a war."

"It's likely his intention."

"Likely?"

He sighed again. "I can't be sure... Archie hasn't been forthcoming with his plans."

Violet shook her head, confused. "You've been gone two weeks now and you still don't know his plans?" Despair edged her voice and suddenly, Paris and her art and her friends seemed to grow even further beyond her reach.

Mr. Barrow's brow quirked up. "He's not a trusting man. Less so since leaving Newgate. All I do for him now is fight and search for you."

Violet looked down, saw his arms were still around her and felt a warm flush. She cleared her throat as she stepped out of his embrace, turning away to draw in a deep breath.

"What do I do to get him to trust me?" he asked as she rubbed a hand over her face. She shook her head.

"I told you – give him what he wants and don't question him."

There was a long pause.

"You know there's only one thing he really wants."

Violet's breath came out in a shuddering sigh as she turned back to him.

"I know."

The corner of Mr. Barrow's mouth turned up. "Not to worry – got another fight next week, some fella from Holborn. If I keep winning, I'm sure he'll come around."

Violet was beginning to doubt that any amount of winning would get Archie to trust John Barrow, but she had to hold on to that paper-thin shred of hope. How else was she to get out of this place and back home? She forced a smile and gestured to his mouth, noting the split lip he had been nursing when she saw him last was now almost healed.

"If you've a sweetheart you're goin' home to, she's done a decent job patchin' that up for you."

He gave a short laugh and absently touched a finger to his mouth, while Violet immediately chided herself for making such a personal remark. Why on earth would she want to know who he was going home to or not?

"All my doing, I'm afraid – I've become rather good at fixing myself up. A necessary evil in my current line of work. Though it would be nice to have someone else do it for me."

His words hung in the air between them, seeming to last an eternity before Violet spoke, concerned. "You don't have a cornerman during fights?"

He shrugged. "Tommy'll act as cornerman if he's at the fight, or one of the other lads, but we're not exactly following the Queensberry Rules."

Violet managed a lame grin as she rubbed an awkward hand over the back of her neck, chiding herself for uttering something so daft, and at the same time feeling a mild thrill at the confirmation that there was no woman waiting for him. *Why do you care, you silly twit? You'll never be his woman. You'll never be anyone's woman.* She swallowed back the rising flush creeping up her cheeks, hating that voice that seemed to follow her; it was a constant and unwelcome reminder of her past and how she could not escape it, no matter how much she wanted to. In a feeble attempt to change the subject, she asked, "I don't suppose you want to stay and have a drink? I'm sure Lord Bradford won't mind if we help ourselves to the good stuff."

Mr. Barrow laughed at that, a deep, rumbling sound that she felt all the way down to her bones. He shook his head.

"I'm afraid I can't stay. I'm expected back at the club to

work the door. I'm security now, as well, it would seem. I just... I didn't want you to worry."

"Oh... of course. Then I suppose you ought to get goin'." Disappointment filled Violet, but she fought to keep it from her voice. He clearly heard it anyway, for his expression softened and he reached out then and, much to her shock, brushed away the stray tendril of hair she didn't realize had slipped from her chignon. His hand lingered there by her ear as he tucked it away and all the muscles in her belly grew taut, desire coiling down from her sternum to between her thighs. He held her gaze, his velvet-brown eyes growing darker with something Violet would recognize from a mile away – lust. Dozens and dozens of men had looked at her like that when she had dealt in engendering lust, but few had ever caused her to reciprocate the feeling.

And oh, wouldn't it be so easy to let him fold her back up in those arms, hard with sinew and muscle, and kiss him again. Perhaps let him lift her onto one of the potting tables and open her legs around his hips, forgetting Archie and all he no doubt had in store for her.

But it had been so long, and there was still that small part of her, deep inside, the part of her body she had sold, that was suspicious of intimacy; that whoever was offering it only sought a warm body, never anything more. Worse, that the instincts which had let her fall for Archie would be wrong again. And so, she slowly took a step back and said again, in a strained whisper, "You should get goin'."

Mr. Barrow blinked at her and shook his head. "Yes, yes, of course. I'll return when I'm able to update you... and please don't worry about me, Miss Latimer. Archie doesn't trust me just yet, but he's not suspicious. This will take time, and we anticipated that it would." The corners of his mouth turned up, just a little. "I will be very careful."

She nodded but didn't smile as he paused, seeming to want to say something to her before he dipped his head.

"Goodnight, Miss Latimer."

"Goodnight, Mr. Barrow."

He pulled away and disappeared into the darkness and Violet tried not to think of where he was headed and the danger that awaited him.

NINE

A brisk autumn morning dawned seven days after John had found Miss Latimer in the conservatory at Bradford House to tell her that he was not, in fact, dead. Her immense relief at seeing him had been palpable, but he couldn't help worrying about the agonized guilt in her expression when she realized that a man had died for her actions. She had probably already come to realize in the days since that another murder had been committed in the name of finding whoever had put Archie Neville in Newgate.

She would be devastated. No. He shook his head as he pushed open the door to the warehouse for sparring practice. She would be angry. She would blame herself. And John couldn't let that happen. But dammit, how was he to stop Archie from his streak of vengeance if he barely saw the man? He was certainly not involved in the rash of killings and violence Archie was meting out upon the residents of the East End as he sought out those who had got him jailed – John hadn't come close enough to insinuating himself in Archie's inner circle enough to be tasked with performing shake-downs and threats, let alone murders. The failure to get close to the Bruisers' leader had his bosses at Whitehall worried, especially now with the explosion of violence, and John's stomach was in knots as he nodded towards the Devil, who was already in the ring with another one of the ranks, a burly dark-skinned man who ducked and weaved to avoid the Irishman's swift strikes.

John threw his coat over the back of a chair and took a moment to surreptitiously watch the two fighters as he warmed up, noting carefully that the Devil, while quick for a man so large, nevertheless favoured his right knee. The other man, named Alexander Turner, lacked reach in his arms but had a powerful hook. When they finally drew apart, the Devil turned and nodded at John, who had finished warming up and ducked under the ropes.

Alexander stepped out of the ring as John shook out his shoulders and tilted his head side to side to loosen the muscles in his neck. The Devil, a man of few words, simply nodded at him, and John raised his fists in response, ducking back immediately when he attacked with a straight strike. They danced about the ring for a while, John taking advantage of the Devil's weak knee by keeping him moving to the right. The Devil had noticed and frowned as he parried a hook and struck out, landing a blow on John's shoulder. John shook it off; the Devil wasn't going to waste his energy on a sparring match and had pulled the punch, but John had been on the other end of one of the Irishman's real hits and his nickname was well-earned.

It was only in the ring, with sweat beading on his skin and his breath growing short, that John was able to momentarily forget Miss Latimer and the haunted look in her eyes as she realized the grave consequences that had come with sending Archie to the one place he surely belonged. And as he jabbed and grappled and parried, the sweat slicking down his back and his muscles burning, his focus narrowed on the man opposite him. That was until someone cleared their throat behind him and broke the trance. The Devil, facing the person behind him, immediately dropped his arms and stepped back, his expression blank. John, shaking his head and blinking to refocus his attention, turned.

Archie Neville stood in the shadows beyond the ring, hands in his pockets, bowler hat pulled low over his brow. He jerked his head towards the door and the Devil dutifully stepped out of the ring and gathered his shirt before disappearing. John now met Archie's shadowed gaze as he stood in the empty ring, chest heaving as he fought to catch his breath. The Bruisers' leader slowly withdrew his hands from his pockets and shrugged out of his tweed overcoat. He set it carefully over a nearby chair and, never speaking a word, removed his jacket and waistcoat and began to loosen his tie. As he raised his arm to unbutton his cuff, he finally spoke.

"You still good to go?"

John drew in a deep breath to slow his racing heart and released it before shrugging.

"I reckon."

Archie nodded as he tugged off his undershirt, revealing a massively muscled chest adorned with a dozen tattoos of varying quality. The most prominent, indelible over his heart, was a crudely drawn square in black ink to symbolize the fighting rings most of them had come from, the one given to all members of the Bruisers once they reached their one-year anniversary. John had several months to go until it would be his turn, though he hoped the operation would be concluded before it came to that. There was a slew of others; women in various states of undress, the five dots given to those convicted clustered between his thumb and forefinger, a heart curling around his right bicep, but on his left arm, a small set of initials, VL. It didn't take much work to conclude that this particular tattoo was for one Violet Latimer. Every muscle in John's stomach tightened at the thought of her, of her name marked upon that man's skin; the man who had threatened her, taken her life from her and would kill to get her back.

John's skin prickled with rage as Archie slipped under the ropes marking the boundary of the ring, but his expression remained blank as the other man took up a roll of linen and began to wind it about his huge hands, all the while his gaze fixed on John. His eyes were unreadable, but John could sense the fury in the Bruisers' leader. A muscle in his jaw twitched as Archie strolled across the ring as though he hadn't a care in the world, tucking in the ends of the bandages on his hands and flexing them as he raised his dark gaze. The corner of his mouth kicked up as he drew a line in the dirt floor between them with the toe of his boot.

"Will you come up to scratch?"

John did not miss the goading tone in Archie's voice, but he smiled easily and raised his fists.

"Let's go."

Without hesitating, the other man immediately drew his right arm back and slammed it forward again in what would have been a devastating hook had John not ducked out of the way just in time to feel the whistle of air as Archie's fist swung past him. There was no pulling back on that punch, and there was no pause before the next as Archie swung again, and again, crossing easily over the line he had drawn as he pressed forward. John feinted and parried, giving ground to the other man as he took a moment to collect his thoughts and turn his analysis to Archie's form, to find a weakness. He leaned back to avoid another sharp strike, then straightened, and struck out with a swift right hook, finally landing a blow on Archie's shoulder. The other man shook it off, but his brows drew together in a menacing scowl as he took a moment to collect himself before he gave a quick, shrewd smile, stepping back and lowering his arms a fraction. John straightened, cautious, but kept his fists raised.

"Any word on my Violet?" Archie asked suddenly as he bounced from side to side, rolling his immense shoulders, and shaking out his hands. John shrugged and raised his fists once more as Archie did the same.

"Heard a girl fittin' her description was seen workin' Narrow Street by the docks. I'm headed there after practice."

Archie shook his head, jabbed, missed. "You go there, you're not comin' back. Limehousers are out for our blood."

John didn't respond that this was because Archie had already had two members of the Limehouse Gang murdered and dismembered, though the Bruisers denied any involvement. He instead struck out with a quick left hook, then a back fist that caught Archie on the shoulder. Once again, he shook it off and feinted left.

"She's not here, Archie. You want her found or not?"

The other man laughed. "If you're willin' to die to find her, you go right ahead. I've a dozen other fighters who'll take your place."

John grinned. "But none who can best Archie Neville," he said as he found the gap in Archie's stance, slipping behind his strike to hook his arm across Archie's chest and throw him backwards over his hip, unbalancing him and sending the Bruisers' leader to the ground with a deafening thud.

It was a calculated move, and John stepped back to wait. A moment passed, the dust settled, and he finally lowered his arms, his chest heaving as Archie recovered himself and glanced up. For a passing instant, John thought the gamble had paid off; the corner of Archie's mouth turned up in a grudging smile as he pushed himself up off the ground and brushed the dust from his trousers. He gave a short laugh.

"Tommy said you were good."

John remained silent as the other man shook his head, as though in disbelief, and began to unwrap his hands. He laughed again.

"Didn't think you'd have the guts to do it." When he finally looked up, he was no longer smiling, but John didn't look away as his lips turned up in a sneer. "But if you can't find one fuckin' whore in this city, then you're no bloody use to me. You've a week."

John again said nothing, though he did clench his jaw together as the other man turned and stepped out of the ring, his silence a rebuke, to gather his things and leave through the warehouse door, slamming it behind him.

The knot in John's stomach tightened and he cursed into the silence. *Now what?*

Days passed, locked away in Bradford House, and Violet began to grow angrier and angrier. Her rooms, lovely and well-appointed though they were, began to feel suffocating. The gardens, once her favorite part of the estate, began to bore her. Even her art suffered. She would set up her easel with a fresh canvas, ready to be inspired, but nothing would come. She made a few half-hearted attempts to paint the massive oak tree she and Della had picnicked under, but always ended up abandoning the work.

In the mornings, as she breakfasted with the staff, she would draw one of the newspapers scattered upon the tabletop towards her and find article after article about the increasing violence happening in Covent Garden and the surrounding areas. Another mugging, a business ransacked, a fire set. No one was ever caught, and there were never any suspects, but Violet knew who was responsible. Archie would burn the rookery to the ground to find her. And no member of the Limehouse Gang was safe from the cloud of suspicion that one of them had turned him in.

The guilt made her sick. And Archie's cruelty made her angry. Worse than angry. Vengeful. She hated that she had run away from him that night in Paris, knowing now that if she had gone with him, she might have stopped all this from happening.

Mr. Barrow hadn't returned since his last visit, and every news story about another act of violence made her stomach clench in terror. This time it had been him. This time Archie had found him out. But no word came from the police, and so she convinced herself that he was safe, and she pushed down the fear.

But the anger remained. And the guilt was not far behind.

On a chill autumn afternoon, the sky leaden with low clouds, she stood in the kitchen near the hearth, vigorously kneading a lump of dough. Mrs. Beatty was nearby peeling potatoes for the staff dinner when Mrs. Cooper suddenly spoke up from where she sat at the big trestle table, quietly stitching a linen napkin.

"It's a good bit of luck you're staying here with us, Miss Latimer. It looks as though Covent Garden has gone completely to pot. Why, look here – just last night another body was found inside one of the tenements. It must be terrifying to be a resident – not even safe inside your own home!"

Mrs. Beatty tutted in agreement, but Violet remained silent as she shoved the dough with the heel of her hand, the rage mounting inside her as she tried to hold back the string of curses she longed to shout at Archie Neville. After she slammed the dough into a bowl to let it rise, Mrs. Beatty paused her peeling to give her a worried look as Violet marched over to the table to Mrs. Cooper, who had now moved onto a small hole in one of the tablecloths.

"May I have that newspaper, Mrs. Cooper?"

The housekeeper looked slightly taken aback but nodded. "Of course."

Violet snatched up the paper to view the article Mrs. Cooper had been reading from. Indeed, another dismembered body had been found inside a bedroom in one of the tenements, not far from where she had worked at Cora's brothel in nearby Seven Dials, a life that seemed to have been lived an eternity ago. She read quickly, her face growing hotter as the gruesome details were listed, her stomach churning with revulsion until she reached the last few lines of the article. *The victim has been identified as Mr. Joseph Pomeroy, a former member of the Limehouse Gang and owner of the Queen's Head public house in Wapping. Witnesses are asked to contact the Metropolitan Police with information.*

Mrs. Cooper looked on with a concerned expression as Violet lowered herself, shaking, into the chair beside her, never taking her eyes from the paper, reading the name over and over again. She had known Joseph – he had been a regular client of Cora's, a quiet, reserved man who had been widowed and would visit the brothel where she worked once a week. He had been kind to Violet and the other girls. She remembered him speaking fondly of his wife; that they had wanted children but never been blessed. He had an old lurcher named Boots, on account of his white feet. Violet's heart raced as she read more stories from the rookeries – there had been a violent assault at a bakery, and a man pushed in front of an oncoming horse and cart just a few days past, and she swallowed back a wave of nausea. Joseph – a man who surely had never laid an angry hand upon anyone in his life – was dead, and Violet would bet her life that Archie was the one responsible. No... not Archie. Joseph was dead because of Violet. She was just about to lay the paper down, sickened by the guilt curdling her stomach, when another headline caught her eye.

Edward Brill, leader of the Limehouse Gang, suspected of building a fortune through extortion and protection rackets throughout the East End over the last twenty years, makes surprise donation to the Spitalfields Ragged School. A sum of £1,000 was given in order that the school may stay open in the face of closure due to much-needed repairs to the facility. This follows the opening of a gentleman's club in Soho by Mr. Brill by the name of the Brooklyn Club, said to have one of the finest menus in London and already attracting a clientele of the city's most prestigious residents.

Edward Brill. Violet frowned down at the paper in her hands. A thought, an idea so outlandish she dared not say it out loud, began to form in her head. For a long time, she told herself it was madness; it would only bring her closer to the one place she sought to avoid, and to the one person she dared not confront. But she couldn't stay in this house one minute longer while people died. Innocent people. There was no time left to wait for Archie to warm to Mr. Barrow – who knew how many people would be hurt or worse before then? She was going to stop Archie. She glanced up at Mrs. Cooper, who had taken up a small pair of scissors to snip at some loose threads.

"How do I get word to Mr. Barrow?"

TEN

Edward Brill had been born in low circumstances, that was certain. His father had been an itinerant dock worker, though his employment had been spotty as he often preferred to spend his time and money at the pubs rather than looking for work. His mother worked occasionally as a seamstress, stitching by the light of a single, sputtering candle until her eyesight failed her. The alcohol had killed his father in Edward's thirteenth year, which was when he had taken up the dock work himself to keep him and his mother fed.

And it was working at the docks, moving between Limehouse, Wapping and St. Katherine's, that Edward began to develop an affinity for the work. He was strong, tall for his age, and built like a barrel. He was always the first to be picked from the groups of men who would gather every morning to move the cargo from the ships to the warehouses, and it was during this time he grew to see the value, not in the moving of the cargo, but in the value of the cargo itself. Wine from France and Italy, coffee from Africa, sugar and cotton from the Americas – none of it for him, of course, or the people of the East End. No, all this luxury was bound for Mayfair, for Belgravia, for the country estates of the wealthy and aristocratic. And they paid handsomely for it. Most importantly, they paid handsomely to store it. Dozens of massive warehouses, filled to bursting with thousands of pounds' worth of goods. Edward had been all of sixteen when he and some friends had been caught breaking into one of those warehouses and, rather than allow the threat of the police being called to spoil their fun, had threatened the owner of the warehouse that he had better keep quiet or they would return and do far worse than steal.

Their little enterprise grew from there. Soon, they were extracting money not just from the many warehouses around the dockyards; they were protecting shops, factories, pubs... And not just from the other gangs who fought for control of their territory but from them, as well. For a price, of course.

The profit allowed his aging, nearly blind mother to retire from her sewing work. And he liked that. He brought in more people, other men he worked with side by side each day, and soon there was hardly a business in all of the East End who did not make a monthly payment to the growing group of men and women he had dubbed the Limehouse Gang, named for the dock where they had their humble beginnings. It had taken many years, many threats, and countless bribes to the few policemen who dared to try to investigate, but they were soon one of the most successful gangs in the whole of the country.

And then he had met Lizzie. And she turned his world upside down.

She was the daughter of a publican, one of many who paid the Limehousers to protect his business. It was a job that, despite the questionable morality of their methods, they took very seriously. No other gangs dared encroach upon the businesses they protected, and there reigned a long, if somewhat fraught, peace for many years. And then Lizzie came along, and he wanted to be with her more than anything. She was the most beautiful woman he had ever met, and her smile rivalled that of the sun for its brightness. But she wanted nothing to do with him. Of course, she didn't. He and his gang had spent years siphoning money from her father's business, a business that was not exceptionally lucrative to begin with. He could have forced her – he possessed enough power to do so – but he didn't want her that way.

He ended the protection payments for her father. But she would still have nothing to do with him. She asked him, what of all the other businesses locked in this arrangement, struggling every month to pay the bills, to feed their children, to keep a roof over their heads? Could he not see what damage his gang was doing to the people? Did he not want better for the men and women who had come from the same low circumstances into which he had been born?

And Edward learned, if he was to earn the love of this miraculous woman, he would need to change. And he did. It took time and many of his men were unhappy with his newfound benevolence, until he showed them that there was a better way to make a living. He opened his own businesses and employed those same men to run them, and then opened schools for their children. Edward, with Lizzie now by his side as his wife, wanted more for the people under him. He did not rule through violence or threat; he was beloved by his people. And if anyone stepped out of line and threatened them, well... he wasn't afraid to administer suitable punishment.

And thus, he spent two wonderful years with Lizzie, working with her and all of the Limehouse Gang to improve their lot in life. But it was not enough. After a particularly cold winter, a virulent strain of typhoid swept through the dock-lands, and it took his Lizzie. For a long time, he was angry, as he had been in his youth, and it seemed pointless to continue all he had built with her. However, he could not disregard all those who now counted on him for their livelihoods, and he knew Lizzie would have wanted him to keep going. And keep going he did. But as much as he could improve, there was always a cold winter, or a sickness, or a lack of funding, or crumbling housing, that always remained to keep down the residents of the East End. And he knew there must be more he could do.

But when Archie Neville, leader of the Bruisers, the gang who had been a constant thorn in Edward's side, finally got out of Newgate, he knew there would be chaos to follow. Archie wanted what Edward had built all those years ago – not the businesses and schools and charities – no, he wanted the protection rackets, and the extortion schemes that Edward had long left behind. And there was not a chance in hell that Edward was going to allow that again. Especially not now that Archie had made the very grave and very dangerous mistake of targeting his people.

It was a chill October afternoon when Edward sat in his office, overlooking the warehouse he had bought with his very own money. He was supposed to be reviewing the ledgers for the Brooklyn Club, the gentleman's club he had also bought with his own money – it was his pride and joy, his ticket into high society and the influence that came with it, among the many other businesses he and the rest of the Limehouse Gang ran. Instead, he sat in his fine leather chair, staring at the wall of windows opposite his desk, the ones looking out over Limehouse Basin, the dockyard where he had made his start. Anger roiled inside him; an anger he had not felt in a long time, not since he was a boy and his father had come home from the pubs, drunk and screaming, to beat his wife and lash out at his son. Two of his men were dead, cut to pieces and discarded, like so much refuse, in nearby Covent Garden. There were no witnesses, his contacts within the Metropolitan Police had no leads, but Edward knew, as sure as the sun would rise, that Archie Neville was responsible.

Edward's network of informants had already given him the reason – Archie was convinced it was he who had turned him in and got him sent to Newgate. Truthfully, Edward would have gladly done it himself, but now the Bruisers' leader had gone too far. No one attacked his gang – no one.

Edward was stewing, plotting the many ways he would get revenge for the men who were dead as he toyed aimlessly with the pen he held, when the door to his office opened and his right-hand man, a former docker like himself named Matthew Gibbons, entered the room. Edward blinked, banishing the dark thoughts chasing through his mind, and turned to face the other man, who looked back at him with a forbidding expression.

"What is it, Matthew?"

"Boys caught someone wanderin' around our patch, brought them back here for you. It's her."

"Who?"

"Violet Latimer."

Edward sat back in his chair, disbelieving.

"What? Here?"

Matthew nodded slowly.

"Yeah... and you won't believe who she has with her."

Edward's brow rose in expectation and Matthew smirked as he folded his arms over his chest.

"She's with John bloody Barrow."

Edward's head tilted to the side at this information and a long, drawn-out silence passed between the two men before he finally rose from his chair.

"Bring them up, Matthew."

Matthew nodded and turned, closing the door behind him. In the silence which followed, Edward glanced down and slowly reached out to open the top drawer of the plain wooden desk he stood behind. Nestled inside, gleaming upon a stack of blank paper, was a small knife. Small, but deadly. He left the drawer ajar as the door opened once more and a woman stepped into the office. She had a crown of golden hair, fashionably styled, and tucked up under an equally fashionable hat of crimson velvet and feathers. Her gown was constructed of impeccably tailored crimson wool to match her hat, and over it she wore a voluminous cloak of black velvet. But it was not the gown nor the hat which drew his attention, it was the determined look in her emerald-green eyes, and she held his gaze the instant she crossed the threshold.

It took Edward a moment to register, then, when someone followed her into the room, someone he was also familiar with. John Barrow towered over the lady, and he looked every bit the bareknuckle boxer he was – a fading yellow bruise marred one eye, and a recently split lip had begun to heal. He didn't enter the room, however, waiting in the doorway instead as the lady strode towards him and stretched forth a gloved hand across his desk.

"Good afternoon, Mr. Brill. My name is Violet Latimer."

Edward glanced down at the outstretched hand, covered in fine white kidskin, then back up at those blazing green eyes.

"I know who you are, Miss Latimer." He took her hand in his and grinned. "Everyone knows who you are."

She blinked, as though confused, and withdrew her hand. He chuckled as he gestured for her to sit in one of the chairs facing his desk.

"Archie's got the whole city out lookin' for you." He glanced over her shoulder. John Barrow remained hovering in the doorway, silent and impassive. Edward met her gaze once more, but he was smiling no longer. "Is that why you're here?"

It was now she cleared her throat and perched upon the edge of the proffered seat, folding her hands primly in her lap.

"It is, Mr. Brill, yes." She paused now and her gaze became earnest. Her lips pursed before she spoke again. "I know what Archie's done. To your men."

A heavy silence descended upon the room. No one spoke for a minute, but Edward never looked away from the woman sitting opposite him. The figure in the doorway didn't move.

The knife in his drawer was within inches of his hand. Finally, he spoke.

"What d'you know about Archie?"

Miss Latimer let out a long, beleaguered sigh.

"All too much." She drew in a breath and shook her head. "Perhaps I should explain." She gestured now to John Barrow, who still stood in the doorway, and he came forward at her signal. Edward's hand inched towards the drawer. No Bruiser was going to catch him unawares.

"This is John Barrow—"

"I know who he fuckin' is," Edward said with a growl as he snatched up the knife and pushed himself up, toppling the chair behind him. The lady gasped as he came around the desk just as her companion stepped forward and raised his fists, ready to defend himself when Miss Latimer inserted herself quite firmly between the two men.

"Stop!"

Her small, gloved hand was upon his arm, the one which held the knife, and he looked down into those emerald eyes, eyes that spat fire, and lowered his arm. Her fingers tightened around him.

"He's not here to hurt you," she explained in a low voice. Edward stared down at her, breathing heavily, as a gentle but firm hand moved down his arm to touch the handle of the knife he held. He scowled at her and tugged away, tossing the knife back in the drawer as he made his way back around the desk and laid his palms upon the top, fixing the lady with a glare. He jerked his head in the direction of her companion, who was cautiously lowering his fists.

"What's he here for, then?"

She sighed and gestured for Barrow to come forward again.

"As I was sayin', this is John Barrow. He's a detective inspector for Scotland Yard, and he's been undercover with the Bruisers for the last three months. He's tryin' to *stop* Archie."

Edward raised a skeptical brow as his gaze slid from the boxer, who stared at him with an unnervingly unreadable expression, back to Miss Latimer.

"And what are *you* here for?"

That determined expression of hers faltered a fraction and she drew in another deep breath, closing her eyes for a moment before meeting his gaze once more. Edward noted with interest when Barrow's hand came up and gently touched hers, as though to encourage her. There was a moment of heavy, expectant silence before she finally spoke in a rush.

"I turned in Archie."

In the silence, he could hear the blood rushing in his ears. The anger returned, coiling down through Edward's chest as he scowled across his desk at the lady. Barrow stood behind her, still as a statue, but Edward could see the veins flexing in his hands, the tremble of muscles held in check as though he were anticipating another attack.

"So," he began, slowly, as Miss Latimer raised her chin a notch in a gesture of defiance. "You're why two of my men got cut up in Covent Garden."

Her chin went up again, but he saw the quiver of her lip.

"Yes. And that's why I'm here. I'll not have any more blood on my hands. I knew Joseph. He was a good—" Her voice cracked then, and she shook her head as she looked away towards the windows, her eyes shining. Edward frowned at her as he pushed himself away from the desk and crossed his arms over his chest.

"He *was* a good man. So, if you're the one what turned in Archie, why's he goin' after my men?"

She swallowed and Barrow touched another encouraging hand to the small of her back before she turned a reluctant gaze back to him.

"He doesn't know it was me. I was... I was gonna marry him. Until I saw what he was doin' in Seven Dials, and what kind of person he really was, and I knew I wasn't gonna get away from him so... I turned him in. I was in Paris when he found me and I... I ran off and came home."

Edward's frown deepened. "Then go tell him what you done so he don't kill any more of my men."

Those emerald eyes widened. "You know what happens to me if I do that."

He shrugged. "Better you than my people... it ain't fair they should die for you."

Her lips flattened into a hard line, and she closed her eyes, as though to compose herself, before she glanced up at him once more.

"No, it's not fair. Look, I didn't want this... I did what I had to do to get out of marryin' him, and everyone was better off when he was in Newgate. And I could have hid away till Mr. Barrow here got whatever he needed for the police to put him away for good, but I wasn't gonna let any more people get hurt because of me. I'm here to make a proposal."

Edward stared at the woman across the desk, sparing only a glance for Barrow before he returned his attention to her.

"What sort of proposal? You don't have anythin' I want, not unless you can bring back those men."

Once again, her eyes welled with tears, and her voice was raw and strained when she spoke. "Look, I'm tryin' to stop any more blood bein' shed. I know you're a decent man, Mr. Brill. I know what you do here to help your people. And I can help you with that. But first we need to stop Archie."

"Mr. Brill." John Barrow finally spoke, stepping forward to stand abreast of Miss Latimer. Edward's gaze went to him. "The Metropolitan Police, with assistance from the Home Office, have been building a case against Archie Neville and the Bruisers for some time now. I was brought in to gather evidence of the illegitimate businesses they run. The police can continue to arrest individual members for petty crimes but to put a stop to them for good, they need more. I must become a trusted member of Archie's inner circle."

Edward narrowed his eyes at the other man.

"And what's in this for you, eh? Why should I help the bleedin' coppers?"

That copper – detective inspector, Edward corrected himself with a sneer – now drew himself up to his full height.

"I shouldn't like to lie to you, Mr. Brill. There is a promotion available at Whitehall – detective chief inspector. And should this operation go well, I might be considered for it."

Edward let out a huff of laughter at this.

"A promotion? I'm to risk my life so you can rise up the ranks?"

Barrow let out a long breath. "If I were to become detective chief inspector, I would have the power to do a great deal more to help the people living in the rookeries."

Edward sniffed at this. "When have the police ever done any good for people like us?"

The other man's expression changed at this remark – not growing angrier, only sadder. "I want to help in any way I can. I grew up in Seven Dials, Mr. Brill, and I know what it is to struggle. I know what it is to lose someone to that place. And if this goes well, I can try to stop that from happening again."

Edward did not miss the little frown Violet Latimer directed to Barrow at these words, and finally shrugged.

"So, what's your plan to gain Archie's trust? He ain't exactly the trustin' sort, is he?"

"Detective Inspector Barrow is gonna return me to Archie." Miss Latimer spoke solemnly, and Edward caught her companion's flinch, as though her words pained him. "If Archie is to trust him enough to allow him access to these businesses, then he needs to give him what he wants. And that's me."

Edward took a moment to observe the pair, his arms still

crossed over his chest. "And what have I to do with any of this? Apart from losing my men to that lunatic?"

"We need your help." Barrow spoke again in a low voice, glancing down at the lady. "What does Archie want even more than Miss Latimer?"

Edward said nothing but raised an expectant brow.

"He wants what you had – a protection racket that will guarantee him the wealth and power he's always been after. He's going to come for you and your territory whatever the case, and we are simply going to... remove the impediment. Thus, the police get what they want – insider knowledge of his crimes and everyone involved, and you will not have a war on your hands, which I assure you, Mr. Neville is very prepared to wage." He looked down at Miss Latimer once more, and she tilted her head up to meet his gaze before turning back to Edward. "Scotland Yard would like to arrange a meeting between you and Mr. Neville. At your behest."

"No." The words came out before Barrow had even finished speaking. "Get out." He thrust a finger towards the door. Meet with Archie Neville? If he was meeting for any reason with that bastard, it would be to kill him.

"Mr. Brill, please," Miss Latimer spoke urgently, holding up a hand as he came around the desk to push them towards the door. "Please, listen..."

"You're outta your bloody minds if you think I'm meetin' with Archie Neville." He had almost got them through the doorway, ignoring Barrow's urgent pleas to listen when the lady planted herself firmly in place and glared up at him, pointing a finger at his chest.

"Do you wanna help the folks livin' in Limehouse or not?"

Edward just laughed. "I'm already helpin' the folks livin' in Limehouse, Miss Latimer."

"But you can't get the people who can really help on your side, can you?"

He paused in the middle of trying to close the door on them and met her determined gaze. "What are you on about?"

She lowered her voice now and leaned into him as though to impart a great secret.

"I know you want more, Mr. Brill. You want the attention of the people who can really get things done. That's why you opened your club. You want all them toffs to know about Limehouse and the rest of the East End, because they have the real influence. Money. House of Lords. They can make the real changes. But they ignore you, 'cause you're just rookery scum. Like me. Like Detective Inspector Barrow. You were an extortionist. And they won't associate with you, no matter how much money you have now or how fancy your club is."

Edward sneered. "And what are you gonna do to help? They're not gonna listen to a Seven Dials whore any more than they'll listen to a gangster."

Her eyes were fairly snapping with anger as she took the edge of the door he had been about to close on her and pushed it back open.

"No, but they will listen to the Earl and Countess of Bradford. You know about Della, don't you? The thief who became a lady – she has influence now. And she has friends. Marquesses. Viscounts. Dukes. And that's who you want at your club, isn't it?"

Edward's hand was on the doorknob, but he paused, and her eyes narrowed on him, assessing.

"You meet with Archie Neville. You tell him if he leaves your people alone, you'll give him the docks, and all the businesses who once gave you money. Let him think he's won. You'll be in Society, hobnobbin' with all the toffs, gettin' their money and their laws to *really* make changes. A protection racket will get the Bruisers' put away for good. As long as we have someone on the inside." She glanced up now at Barrow, who nodded in agreement. Edward stared at them both for a minute, half ready to shove them both out of his office and half ready to grudgingly pull the door open. He shook his head.

"Archie thinks I snitched on him – he's as likely to shoot me dead the moment he sees me as he is to sit down and have a meetin'."

For the first time since she had entered the office, a hint of a smile began to play about Miss Latimer's mouth. "We've taken all that into account. There was a lad who used to dive for the Bruisers – he got stabbed in a brothel in Whitechapel a few years back. Had no family, and he was a shifty little bugger. We're gonna tell Archie that it was him who ratted. That should stop the violence against your gang for long enough to get this racket business sorted."

Edward's jaw clenched and he looked down, once again torn between telling them to get the hell out and actually entertaining this bloody nonsense. As though he had any desire to entangle himself with Archie Neville or any of his gang. Still... He glanced out those big windows overlooking the dockyard, grey and damp under a sunless sky, and saw the tiny figures moving below: crates swinging beneath cranes, smokestacks, and sails as far as the eye could see under the drizzle. It was home and he loved it... but it could be better. He wanted better. Safer. Easier. The world passed through these docks but went right by its people. He sighed.

"You ran off from Archie, eh?"

Her eyebrows drew together briefly at his words, and he let out a short huff of laughter. "How are you gonna help me if you're dead?"

Her lips pursed and her eyes narrowed on him. Barrow was the first to speak.

"He's not tearing apart the rookery to find her just so he can kill her."

Edward chuckled and leaned against the door. "Is that what you think?"

Miss Latimer glowered at him beneath her dainty crimson hat.

"You leave Archie to me, Mr. Brill. If he kills me, you can do whatever you want to him, but it won't stop the violence and it won't help your people. Detective Inspector Barrow will be in touch once we're ready to arrange a meetin'. You just be ready to give Archie whatever he wants."

Edward finally straightened with a muttered curse and met Barrow's gaze. "And what about the coppers? They gonna be pokin' around in my business? What's to stop them puttin' me away for extortion as well?"

Barrow drew his broad shoulders back and fixed Edward with an unwavering stare.

"At the moment, Scotland Yard is far more concerned with the increase in violence since Archie's return to St. Giles than a man who now runs legitimate businesses and has become a public face for reform. The government's giving money to local authorities to clear out the rookeries, buying up the land so they can rebuild, but they're not going to go in while Archie's running things, threatening any work they do. They don't want reformers and journalists getting the word out about him, about how the gangs run the rookeries and that the police haven't been able to stop them."

Edward smirked. "And you're gonna be the one to stop him, are you?"

Barrow's gaze never wavered. "If you'll help us."

Edward cursed again and looked down at Miss Latimer, who gazed back at him with pleading in her eyes. Again, the urge to push them out the door warred with the very real opportunity to accomplish everything he had ever hoped for the people of the East End, and he sighed, stepping away to let them back into the office.

"Come on, then. Tell me what needs to be done."

ELEVEN

Violet's heart raced as she stepped out into the fading light of the afternoon and drew the hood of her cloak over her head to shield herself from the chill drizzle. The door closed softly behind them, and she felt the warm, radiating presence of Mr. Barrow standing beside her. She sensed his hesitation and took a step away, breaking the tension herself, taking away the urge for him to touch her, or for her to reach out to him. With enough distance between them, she turned to face him. His expression was hard, but there was concern in his soft brown eyes. They said nothing for a moment before she forced out a laugh.

"Well... that went better than expected."

He didn't smile. "Miss Latimer... I must ask you again to reconsider. I cannot in good conscience bring you to Archie—"

"Mr. Barrow, please." She held up a hand, closing her eyes because she couldn't bear the look upon his face any longer. "I don't want to do this, but Archie's not comin' around to you. He's not. And I want my life back." She opened her eyes to find him looking back at her, his brow furrowed, his jaw tense. "You know this is the only way. He's just gonna keep killin' people and I can't... I can't let that happen. I can't live with that on my conscience."

He started to shake his head.

"It's the only way," she repeated. She drew herself up straighter and put on a brave face that was not matched by how she felt. "He's not gonna hurt me. He wants to marry me. And I'm gonna let him think I might. And besides," she added with a false smile, "you'll be there to watch over me."

His brows drew together. "I can't help you if he tries to hurt you." His voice was low, raw. "I'm undercover. And there I must stay if this is to succeed."

Violet swallowed, doubt creeping back into her mind after the success of their meeting with Edward Brill. She drew in a sharp breath and squared her shoulders. Let Archie try to hurt her. She wasn't running away anymore.

"I'll be fine. We should get goin', before the club gets busy."

His jaw worked, as though he were going to say something, before he gave a sharp nod and jerked his head, indicating for her to follow him. They walked in silence until they reached Cable Street. Dozens of hansom cabs passed, but he never paused to hail one and Violet expected he meant to walk all the way to Archie's club in Covent Garden. It would take over an hour on foot, but she didn't dare protest. Every minute she could delay meeting with Archie was a relief, and she followed along beside him as the sun drew closer to the horizon and the breeze grew chill. After several blocks, he finally spoke.

"How do you find living in Paris?"

Startled by his abrupt question, she looked over at him with a raised brow, suspecting that he was trying to divert her attention away from their eventual destination, a scheme in which she was more than happy to participate.

"I... it's everythin' I ever wanted. I love livin' there." She returned her attention to the street before them, sidestepping a pile of horse dung as they crossed a side road before she spoke again in a low voice. "I have no past there."

"I see." He was quiet again for another block or so before glancing down at her. "It must have been liberating, starting fresh in a new city."

She shrugged, pausing with him as a dray trundled past, loaded down with kegs. "It was. I've been looked down on from the moment we left that orphanage. I was the lowest of the low. But in Paris... in Paris I'm an artist. I've exhibited with Monet and Pissarro and Cassat. I even had a paintin' up at the Salon. Do you know what it takes to get your work up there?"

He didn't answer, just shook his head and she continued, feeling the rising anger in her chest. "And then Archie showed up. And he threatened to tell everyone what I was." She sent Mr. Barrow a sidelong glance. "Listen, I'm not ashamed of what I was. Della and me never went hungry, and we always had a roof over our heads. We did better than a lot of folks livin' in the rookery, and Cora always kept me safe." She swallowed and looked away. "But I ain't exactly proud, either. And I know what would happen if people found out I was a whore. Whores aren't artists. They're muses. Or models. Or worse. Every man in Montmartre would think he could just pay for it, and I'd be willin' to give it. I'd likely never sell another paintin'." She scowled, heat prickling at the nape of her neck. Mr. Barrow said nothing. "That's why I've been on my own since me and Del got out of the rookery. I didn't want to be anythin' to anyone. It was so nice, just bein' Violet Latimer. Not the orphan. Or the prostitute. Or the girl from Seven Dials." She sighed and Mr. Barrow offered her a faint smile.

"You know, for all the places I got to travel to as Lord Bradford's valet, I've never actually been to Paris."

Violet glanced over at him as they strolled past a pair of women sitting together on a stoop, one dandling a baby upon her knee. She couldn't help notice the admiring looks they gave

Mr. Barrow as he passed and suppressed a smile before returning her attention to him.

"Never?" she asked, and he lifted his shoulders.

"No... is it nice?"

At this, she did smile. "It's the most beautiful city on earth." A chuckle. "Though I've never actually been anywhere else, so I can't really say for sure," she amended, and he grinned. "I live in Montmartre. It's where all the artists live, and it's up on a hill. You can see all of Paris from the top. I go to the Louvre during the week to practice drawin' the sculptures. They used to train artists that way, you know – the best students at the *École* would be sent to Italy to copy the old masters and send the paintin's back to Paris to hang in a museum of copies. That's how they decided who was a proper artist." She chuckled again. "Thank God they don't do that anymore. I'd never have made a single paintin' otherwise. Imagine, copyin' a load of old men who've been dead for hundreds of years."

Mr. Barrow gave her a small smile as they left behind the crowded tenements of Whitechapel and drew closer to the Tower.

"I've been writin' to Della," she said suddenly as they passed beneath the shadow of the building. Leaves, turned rust with the coming winter, swirled about her ankles as a chill breeze blew off the Thames. He looked down at her.

"I'm sure she would have preferred to be here in London with you."

"You mustn't tell the earl of our plan... Della would worry." She gave him a pained smile. "She'd probably storm her way into Archie's club to stop me. She'd kill him herself given the opportunity."

Mr. Barrow frowned at the thread of anger in her voice, and she swallowed before adding, "And you must bring me any letters she writes so I can write back."

A muscle in his jaw twitched and his brows drew together

as though in disagreement, but he finally nodded. "I'll do my best."

They passed the Tower without a word to one another, Violet chafing with the one question which had been on her mind since Cole had told her where to find John Barrow. She finally couldn't bear the silence any longer and the words burst from her.

"Why are you back in Seven Dials? You got out... how can you stand bein' back in that place?"

He glanced over at her, as though startled, and she was shocked by the grief in his eyes – it looked raw, recent. She almost felt compelled to apologize and tell him it was no matter, but he blinked, looking away before he spoke.

"I suppose it was partly to prove myself. My mother was a fence, and I grew up pickpocketing for her, area diving, card sharping – whatever I could do to make a bit of money. I was a petty criminal, as were so many of us. I wanted to show the police that not every criminal is a bad person."

Violet hesitated, thinking back on his remark to Edward Brill about having lost someone to the rookery, before she ventured to ask, "And the other part?"

There was a long moment of silence before he sighed. "A long story... and not one I've ever shared."

Violet looked sidelong at him, noting the tension in his voice, the hint of an unhappy ending. What else was to be expected coming from the rookery?

"You told Mr. Brill you lost someone... but you don't have to tell me. I know what it is to have stories too terrible to speak out loud."

He was silent for a long time as they crossed another thoroughfare, dodging horses and carts along the way. She was sure that would be the answer to her question and that no more information about his return to the streets of his childhood would be forthcoming, but as they passed beneath the overarching boughs of a linden tree, he spoke suddenly.

"When I left to work in service for Lord Bradford, I think I was of the same mind as you – I had done it. I had escaped and no power on earth would make me return. Except... I couldn't leave. Not really. There was too much keeping me there." A muscle in his jaw twitched and he gave Violet a quick glance. Her throat tightened as she braced for the inevitable tragedy. Rarely were there any other endings when it came to the rookery.

"I had a sister. Lucy. She was four years younger than me, so I was responsible for her. Our mother had died, and our father had left, and for years it was just us, livin' in that flash house on Queen Street. When I got that job with the earl, I thought it was our chance for a better life. I left 'cause I knew I was never gonna make a decent living in Seven Dials. I sent money to her every month, and the girls in the flash house looked after her for me." Seven Dials was seeping back into his voice as he spoke, but he seemed not to notice, and he swallowed before continuing. "I didn't go back nearly as often as I should have. I was always too busy, so I told myself, and I traveled often with the earl." He rubbed a rueful hand over his jaw. "I last saw her when I escorted Lady Bradford to see you before she and the earl married. She was well." The ghost of a smile crossed his lips as they paused at an intersection to let a carriage roll past. "She even had herself a beau – nice fella who worked in a factory."

The smile faded as they walked along side by side; the evening grew cooler and a biting breeze sprang up, whipping her skirts around her ankles.

"I didn't go back again until after you left for France." His jaw grew tight now, and his eyes narrowed, but he wasn't looking at anything as he stared ahead. "Could have been anyone, really. I'm told the men who did it had been goin' around, robbin' anyone walkin' alone. She fought back, I suppose. They weren't ever caught. What copper was gonna go after a gang of thugs, robbin' and beatin' the people livin' in the rookery? Even if they cared enough about stoppin' them, they were too afraid to end up on the wrong patch. So…" His voice caught now, and he cleared his throat, but he never looked over at Violet, who watched as his mouth twisted up, as though to hold back some great emotion. "So, I went straight to Lord Bradford, and I asked him to give me a letter of reference so I could join the Metropolitan Police. I would care about those people when no one else would. And I wouldn't be afraid. Lucy won't have died for nothin'.'"

Violet said nothing – what could she say? – but she did reach out and give his fingers a quick, meaningful squeeze. He said nothing in reply, but did return the gesture, though his jaw was taut, and his throat moved as she withdrew. They were entering Covent Garden now, and as they came to a large puddle at the end of the walkway, he swiftly angled himself and held out a hand for her as leverage so she could step over it. Upon reaching the other side, he finally met her gaze, and though she had somehow expected grim determination or hopeless grief, she saw only misgiving. He was still unwilling to hand her over to Archie Neville, though this plan would almost certainly bring him the redemption he no doubt sought. And though Violet had some very serious misgivings of her own, she saw that in sacrificing her freedom for now to bring Archie to justice, she would not only be helping herself, but helping Mr. Barrow as well.

Ever the worthy protector, though, his fingers tightened on hers, and his jaw worked as though he would say something, but she knew what his words would be – that he couldn't turn her in to Archie, that she was risking her life, that he would find another way – but she was more determined now that they must go through with this. She, too, would not let Lucy, or any of those poor souls who fought and scraped to climb their way out of the rookery only to be taken by it before their time, die in vain. She held a finger to his lips and shook her head.

"Come on, it'll be dark soon."

The Devil's Den lay at the end of a row of once-stately Georgian terraces, occupying the largest of the homes which had long since been converted into pubs and pie shops and brothels. John's chest ached with the confession he had just made to Miss Latimer. What had compelled him to tell her about Lucy, he couldn't say – perhaps that she, too, would have seen friends and family lost to the violence and decay of the rookery, or that he had held in his guilt over Lucy's death for so long that it had taken just one person willing to listen and the words had burst from him like water from a broken dam. And still, he could not bear that they now stood across the street from Archie's rundown little club, ready to give him Miss Latimer in exchange for the opportunity to become part of his inner circle. If something happened to her... He shook his head and steeled his jaw. She had already insisted this was the only way, that she could not bear if one more life was to be lost to violence on her account, and he could hardly oppose her on that.

He turned to look across the street instead. Two men stood sentry at the door, and the windows had been blacked out, but John was more than familiar with the revelry that would be taking place inside shortly. Archie Neville held court here, a king returned from exile to rule with an iron fist once more. The main floor held the gaming tables and the bar. Upstairs the men of Covent Garden might find female companionship for a price. Below stairs was John's domain. Boxing matches were held once a week in one of the cellars, and he was a popular attraction.

The women from upstairs would come to watch his fights – 'Bonny Barrow' they called him, giggling and tittering at the edge of the crowd and shouting out lewd comments before his fights. He would always favour them with a wink and a nod, knowing that while everyone else dismissed these women and treated them at best as invisible and at worst as objects, they were the eyes and ears of the club. One of the girls, a buxom redhead named Bess who possessed the voice of an angel, had already whispered to him about the illegal bookmakers which operated out of the back of the casino. John had not yet been made privy to it as Tommy always made sure he was working the front door if he wasn't fighting, but now he had information he could take back to his superiors at Scotland Yard. It might not be enough, though. That was why this operation must proceed. Archie would look fondly upon the man who returned his errant fiancée and would certainly be more willing to include such a person in his much longed-for protection scheme.

He glanced down at Miss Latimer and saw the firm set of her jaw and the furrow between her brows where they stood in the shadows of a portico, watching the front door of the club from across the street.

Every muscle in John's chest tightened as his breath grew short, terrified that the moment he brought her into Archie's office, she would be met with swift and violent revenge for her fleeing him in Paris. He wanted desperately to pull her back into the doorway and tell her there had to be another way, that he would find another way, that she was going to end up dead. But he knew what her response would be. That no one else would die on account of her actions, and that she wanted to go back to Paris and her life there. How else would they get Archie on his side? And so, he stretched a hand towards hers, paused for a moment, and touched her gloved fingers. She glanced up at him, her eyes giving nothing away of what she felt, and he nodded.

"Are you ready?"

She paused – just barely – and said, "Yes", before pulling her hand away and drawing in a deep breath. John did the same, though it did nothing to slow the dreadful thud of his heartbeat.

"You're not gonna like me after this."

She shrugged and returned her gaze to the club. "Has to be done."

John said nothing as he clamped his hand down on her shoulder and pushed her out into the street. Her face settled into an expression of sullen resentment as they drew up to the front door. The two guards observed them with suspicion as John nodded towards them.

"Evenin', Danny, George. Is Archie in?"

The two men looked at one another, then towards his captive, who glared back at them and said nothing.

"'E's in his office," Danny said, returning his attention to John.

"Is Tommy with him?"

"Tommy's out tonight," George answered before jerking his head towards Miss Latimer. "Who's she?"

John tightened his grip on her, but she didn't react as he pushed her past the men and up the steps.

"She's for Archie," he called over his shoulder as he thrust open the door. The guards made no objection as he entered the main floor of the club. It was already bustling and noisy, and Bess herself stood on the small stage at the front of the room, singing a ditty about sailors arriving at the London docks after months at sea, the subject matter much at odds with her sweet soprano. She caught his eye from across the space and her expression brightened, a smile creasing her face as she lifted a hand to wave to him. She paused, though, as she caught sight of the woman he held before him, and her smile faded as she dropped her arm. She knew who he was pushing down the hall to Archie's office at the back of the club floor, and she knew what was in store for her.

John tensed his grip on Miss Latimer's shoulder as they turned down a deserted corridor at the back of the gaming floor. She swallowed as they neared the door at the end of the hall and he tried to think of something to say that would comfort her, but he couldn't promise she'd be alright in the end, and he couldn't promise that he'd keep her safe. Though, truthfully, if Archie did try to hurt her, he wasn't sure he'd be able to stop himself from interfering.

They both stopped at the door, John with his hand upon her shoulder. She was silent, still, as though waiting for him to make the move neither of them wanted to make – to open the door. He drew in a breath, instead, and reached down to take her hand in his and squeeze her fingers.

There was nothing he could say, of course, but he wanted her to know that he cared, and he peered over at her when she let out a short, wavering breath. She was looking up at him, her eyes shining with tears, and gave him a smile full of sadness before she sniffed and wiped away the tears with the sleeve of her gown. She shook her head and, just as quickly as the smile had appeared, her expression fell back into the look of simmering dislike she had worn on her way in. John drew in another breath, gave a sharp nod, and reached up to knock on the oak portal.

She shivered beneath his touch when a sharp voice called out, "Who is it?"

"It's Barrow."

A pause. "What d'you want?" Archie's tone was acidic.

"I have somethin' for you."

Another pause. "Come in."

Miss Latimer closed her eyes as John turned the knob and shoved the door open. It rebounded against the wall with a crash as he took her by the shoulders and thrust her inside. There was a long, terrible moment of silence as she stumbled to a stop before the massive oak desk which dominated the centre of the room. John kept his hand clamped down on her shoulder as Archie looked first to him, as though in disbelief, and then to Miss Latimer, who glared at him with a very real, virulent hatred.

John's stomach clenched in anticipation, but he kept his expression carefully blank as a slow smile spread across Archie's face and he rose from where he sat at his desk. He watched, wary, as the Bruisers' leader came around the piece of furniture, his grin wide, hands in his pockets, as though he hadn't a care in the world.

"Well, well, look what we have here." He stopped in front of Miss Latimer, inches from her, but she never looked up at him, just kept her glare trained on his chest. John tightened his grip once more as Archie lifted a hand to grasp a loose tendril of her hair. She had carefully plucked out most of her hairpins on the way over, hoping to convey the effect that she had struggled against John and tried to make an escape, and she winced as Archie held up the strand of golden hair. "Johnny finally tracked you down, eh?" He glanced over at John now, his eyes narrowed. "She give you a hard time?"

John glanced down at the top of the golden head with an impassive shrug. "She weren't exactly willin'."

Archie chuckled and looked back to Miss Latimer, who said nothing, but whose jaw clenched as he took her chin into his fingers and forced her gaze up to his. Her lips flattened into a hard line as she tried to move her head away, but he held her fast. John's muscles quivered and he fought to maintain his blank expression as Archie leaned into her, until his face was mere inches away from hers, a cruel smile curling his mouth.

"Thought you could run from me, didn't you, Violet, my pet?"

Her lips twisted in a snarl, but she still said nothing as Archie nodded towards John. "Where'd you find her?"

John was careful to keep his voice flat, to give nothing away.

"She were with a fella down an alley off Drury Lane."

Archie's expression darkened and he turned a sneer to the woman he still had by the chin.

"Silly little Violet – runnin' away from me only to have to give it up in an alley for a few pennies."

Her glare was scornful. "Better a three penny upright than a single moment spent with you."

Awareness sparked along John's nerve endings as Archie scowled, his fingertips growing white where he still held her by the chin before he finally pushed her away, causing her to stumble back into John. And though he wanted nothing more than to gather her close and keep her safe from the monster standing before them, he scoffed instead and pushed her back, forcing her to right herself against Archie's massive chest before finally stepping back to stand between them, her head bowed, her fists clenched at her sides.

A terrible silence fell upon the room, the tension palpable as Archie glowered down at her, his breath coming quick now, a muscle twitching in his jaw. He spoke without taking his eyes off her, though she refused to meet his gaze.

"Told you she was a mouthy little bitch, didn't I?"

John let out a small exhalation of laughter but said nothing in reply as Archie grinned at Miss Latimer, slipping his hands into his pockets once more, and rocking back on his heels to contemplate her with a wicked gleam in his eyes.

"What should we do with her, Johnny?"

The corner of John's mouth turned up and he made a calculated suggestion. "I reckon there's a room upstairs that's not bein' used."

Archie slowly shook his head, his grin turning cruel. "Nah, she don't need to be around all them doxies. Take her down to the box. I need somewhere more secure – keep her safe till the weddin'."

"I'm not marryin' y—" she started to protest before Archie

cut her off by grabbing a fistful of her hair, knocking off that stylish little cap, and wrenching her head towards him. An agonized gasp burst from her and every muscle in John's body seized, rage crackling through him, burning, and it took every fibre of him not to smash in Archie's broad face, and beat him until he was a bloody mess on the floor. No, instead, with a herculean effort, he stood there in emotionless silence as Archie pushed his snarling face into Miss Latimer's.

"You're fuckin' lucky I don't have you taken apart like those bastards from Limehouse and left in a ditch for what you done. You made a promise, Violet Latimer, and you're gonna keep it." There was a moment of silence, thick with tension, before he spoke again, bending to whisper in her ear. "You said you loved me."

Anyone else would have missed it if they didn't know Archie. But John heard it – the hurt in his tone. Below the rage and the resentment, he was wounded, and he hated it, and hated her for being the one to make him feel that way. Violet's lips flattened into a hard line, and she shook her head, refusing to meet his gaze.

"I did... until I saw who Archie Neville really is."

She winced as his grip tightened, drawing another gasp from her, before he pushed her down with a disgusted snort, sending her sprawling on the faded Turkish rug. John could only watch, furious in his helplessness, as Archie jerked his head towards him.

"Take her down to the box, Johnny. Few days down there should persuade her – keep her from liftin' her skirts for whoever'll pay for it, too. You just remember you're mine, Violet."

John met that spiteful, cruel gaze and gave a short, benign nod, as though he were simply agreeing to share a pint, and reached for Violet, pausing when Archie spoke again.

"And that fella she were with off Drury Lane?"

Archie's eyes were narrow, assessing, as John looked up, forcing his expression into one of cool calculation.

"He was dealt with."

Archie grinned at that as John bent down and took Violet by the back of her crimson gown to haul her up off the floor. She twisted, snarling, as though to get him to release her, but he merely locked an arm around her and held her tight as she spat and thrashed, cursing impressively at them. He dragged her out of the room, slamming the door shut behind them, before pulling her, still fighting against the cage of his arms, and shouting at him to release her, down the hall, away from the gaming floor. There was another door at the end of the corridor, and he pushed it open and pulled her through, not releasing her until he had closed it behind them.

She staggered out of his arms, gasping, before turning to face him. They were in a narrow hall, lit by a few sputtering lamps on the wall, with a staircase leading down into a cavernous darkness. She glanced down into the shadows.

"Is the box down there?"

John leaned against the portal and nodded. "It's where Archie keeps anyone he wants to... question. This is the only way in or out."

"So, I don't come out until he decides?"

He slowly shook his head. "No."

Her throat worked as she swallowed before she glanced down the stairs again.

"Will you be able to come down?"

John's brows drew together. "If he trusts me enough now, he'll probably have me bring you food. He's still suspicious of most people except Tommy. I'll do my very best to come as often as I can."

She squared her shoulders and gave him a nod. "Then lead the way."

TWELVE

Violet's heart was near to bursting as Mr. Barrow took one of the lanterns off the wall and swung it around, filling the void at the bottom of the stone stairs with a sickly, wavering light. This was what they had planned, this was what she had reluctantly suggested, but every part of her screamed to get out, to beg Mr. Barrow to take her back to Bradford Hall. Why in God's name had she ever agreed to help with this operation? Following him down those steps into the darkness seemed so final – and if their plan with Edward Brill failed, then she feared she would never leave and be left to Archie's mercy. And just the idea of that made her heart stutter inside her chest and her throat grow tight.

But when Mr. Barrow, standing at the top of the stairs, turned back to her and offered a hand, she swallowed back the rising, clawing fear and took it, comforted for the moment by the warmth of his fingers laced with hers.

The shadows bent and lurched with the swinging of the lantern, and the air grew cold and musty as they descended into the earth until they reached the bottom of the stairs and were met with another door. Mr. Barrow reached up to a rusting bolt and pulled it back with a deafening squeal to swing the door open. Once again, they were met with shadows and silence and Violet paused, terrified of what the light would reveal beyond the threshold.

Mr. Barrow turned to her now, his eyes velvet black in the dim light.

"Wait here," he whispered before entering the room, followed by rustling and the hiss of another lamp being lit before he returned to where she remained outside, her heart hammering away inside her chest, her hands clammy inside her gloves. He leaned against the doorjamb to contemplate her, his dark eyes unreadable, before he reached out and touched a finger to her chin.

Awareness bolted though her at this one, soft touch and a shiver raced down from her chest to between her thighs as she thought of their kiss in the conservatory and how conflicted she had been afterwards. She had almost wanted more at the time; she had wanted to remember what it was like to have someone bring her pleasure. If it hadn't been so long... if she didn't still harbour so many doubts about opening herself back up in that way, she might have let him keep going. But now, in this moment of doubt and fear, she would give anything for him to kiss her again, to distract her from the dread roiling in her stomach. Her lips parted in anticipation of another kiss as he gazed down at her, and she trembled with the primal urge to turn and run, that she must not enter that room; if she did, she wouldn't come out.

"Did he hurt you?' came his soft whisper, instead, and Violet had to close her eyes against the unexpected sting of disappointment.

"I'm fine."

His hand touched hers once more and she opened her eyes to find him watching her with a faint smile.

"I've half a mind to go upstairs and lay him out again."

Violet tried to return the expression, but she was in danger of coming apart before him and so could only lift the corner of her mouth. "I'd pay good money to see that."

His smile faded and he sighed, tilting his head in the direction of the room beyond. "Come on, then."

Shaking now, she followed him into the mysteriously named box, certain that she would be met with little more than bare stone walls; a dungeon for Archie's enemies and the room where he would break her.

It was, indeed, a dungeon, but not so medieval as she had feared. The bare stone walls had been plastered and lime-washed, and rough wooden boards covered the floor. There was even a small window up near the low ceiling; the promise of daylight come morning. John turned to her as she observed the small brass bed in the corner, covered in threadbare linen and a coverlet of dubious warmth, and the small, worn table beside it upon which sat the additional lamp.

And that was it. There was no rug to warm the floor, no frame nor mirror upon the walls to break up the bare expanse, no chair to sit in. It was a room designed for a single purpose – to hold those who had crossed Archie until he could mete out whatever punishment he deemed worthy. Her punishment would be to stay here, alone, until she would marry him just to get out. She looked up at John, who watched her with brows drawn together in consternation and felt something crack inside her. Not break – she would not let Archie break her – but the very idea of spending the foreseeable future in this spartan room, alone, made the fear surge inside her once more and she had to hold back a strangled sob.

"It's... not as bad as I expected," she said, her voice strained, but the furrow between Mr. Barrow's brows only deepened.

"He's going to be down here first thing in the morning."

Her breath stuttered as she glanced up at the small window. "I know."

Mr. Barrow paused. "It won't be for long."

She nodded slowly. Her hands were shaking, and she tightened them into fists to stop them.

"I'll come as often as I can." He paused again before reaching for something tucked inside his overcoat. The corner of his mouth turned up, just slightly. "I managed to sneak in a little something for you... to pass the time."

Violet's heart, unused to kindly gestures, soared as he handed her the little leather-bound sketchbook she had been using at Bradford House before he reached into another pocket for a narrow, rectangular tin in which she found several lead pencils. Clutching them to her chest, she glanced up at him, her chest swelling with some emotion she could not quite name.

"You really are too kind, Mr. Barrow." On an impulse, she stood on her tiptoes to press a quick kiss to his cheek, but he turned his head at the last moment and her mouth touched the corner of his, instead. And she should have pulled away then, smiled awkwardly, and sent him on his way, but she stopped there, her mouth hovering above his. For a moment, nothing happened as his breath rasped against her cheek, before she turned her head, slowly, so slowly, until her mouth was aligned with his and she was gazing up into eyes of velvet brown.

Violet had hated kissing most men for as long as she could remember; hated their wet, demanding mouths, their beer-soaked breath, their darting tongues. But when John Barrow leaned down to close that gap between them and press his lips to hers, the fear knotted in her chest dissolved and pleasure spiked through her, prickling along the back of her neck, down her spine, and settling between her thighs. This time, however, the sensation of being overwhelmed, of realizing that she was not yet ready for the intimacy of his kiss, did not come flooding through her as it had when they had been in the conservatory. Perhaps, this time, she was ready for... more.

The sketchbook and tin fell to the ground, forgotten, when

his hands moved to her back, fingers digging into her, moving down, down, until he was bending, squeezing her buttocks, lifting her against him with a low, dangerous growl. The sound reverberated through her, setting all her nerve endings alight, and she dug her fingers into his chest, tempted – oh so tempted – to pull him back against the wall, let him lift her skirts... but then it was back, bubbling up inside her. The fear. Fear of this prison. Fear of letting him close. And it won out in the end, rising up her throat, choking her, until she pulled away with a gasp.

He was breathing heavily as his eyes searched hers before he reached for her, taking her hand in his.

"Are you alright?" he whispered, but she couldn't be sure if he was talking about the kiss or her being locked in this room. Neither scenario brought her much comfort, but she dared not speak on her fears, and so gave a quick, determined nod. He hesitated before speaking.

"I won't be far, and I'll come back as soon as I can. Have courage, Miss Latimer... this is all part of the plan."

And his hand gently squeezing hers did give Violet a small measure of courage, enough to offer him a little smile before he spoke, his voice hesitant.

"I should be going, before someone comes looking for me."

Violet's stomach clenched at these words, and she was only able to reply in the barest of whispers.

"Yes, of course." Her throat was tightening, and she nodded again, fighting the desperate urge to grab him and cling to him. She had been at peace with being locked away, to be Archie's prisoner until their plan came to fruition, but now that he was leaving, she was terrified. Terrified of this small room, of the uncertainty, of what Archie might do to her. Her eyes were stinging now, and she forced another smile onto her face. "I'll be fine. You just make sure that no one else gets hurt."

"I will." He paused and the silence fell, heavy between

them before he drew back, his jaw set. "Goodnight, Miss Latimer. And... thank you," was his hoarse whisper. She didn't reach for him but did quickly bob her head in acknowledgement.

"You're welcome."

He hesitated for a moment before turning and leaving, closing the door slowly behind him. There was a moment of silence before she heard the squeal of the bolt being slid back into place. And that was it. She was a prisoner, and a heavy weight settled upon her chest as she slowly lowered herself onto the narrow bed and pulled her knees to her chest to stare at the blank wall opposite her. After a moment, her gaze wandered down to the sketchbook and tin she had dropped when he had held her and kissed her with such passion that she had actually contemplated letting him take her there against the bare plaster walls.

Slowly, she bent and plucked up the book and tin from the floor before kneeling beside the narrow bed. She lifted a corner of the mattress and slipped the items beneath it before stripping down to her chemise and stockings. Violet couldn't face any more of this day. She was tired and heartsick, and she didn't want to think. And so, she turned back the edge of the threadbare blankets, settled herself onto the hard mattress, turned down the lantern and closed her eyes. Sleep was a welcome relief when it came.

There was no knock on the door the next morning, just the squeal of the bolt being pulled back and the creak of the hinges. Violet was already awake and had been for some time. Dawn had only recently begun to show through the dingy film covering the one tiny window up high on the ceiling, but she was ready; waiting for Archie and whatever terrible torture he had planned for her. She pushed herself up from the tiny bed, already dressed for the day. The bold crimson gown was her armour, and she drew her shoulders back, raising her chin in what she hoped was a gesture of defiance as the door opened to reveal, not Archie as she had expected, or even Mr. Barrow, but one of the Bruisers' thugs... Henry, as far as she could remember. She had always done her best to avoid him back when she had been living with Archie, finding his intensity not a little off-putting and his temper a little too quick. It was no wonder to her that he was often employed as an enforcer for the gang.

Her shoulders fell a little as he stepped inside, his huge frame filling the doorway, balancing a covered tray on one hand. A wisp of fear flickered through her chest as he very deliberately put his shoulder to the edge of the door and pushed it closed behind him before facing her with a dark, impenetrable gaze. Violet drew in a small breath as he watched her, not daring to look away as his eyes narrowed.

"It's really you," he finally said, his gaze now traveling down the length of her. The corner of his mouth turned up and he nodded, as though in approval.

"You should have never got found, Violet. He's turned this city upside down lookin' for you."

Violet said nothing, though a lump had begun to form in her throat. Henry let out a small huff of laughter at her lack of response and pushed past her to set the tray down on the bed before stepping back and nodding towards her.

"Glad to see all that whorin' you was doin' after you left us didn't spoil you. You were always a pretty thing."

Violet's heart seized as he reached out and brushed a finger across her cheek, and she squeezed her eyes shut as he leaned down to whisper in her ear, "You know I always did like you, Violet."

His hand was suddenly upon her breast, and she immediately recoiled, reaching to slap him away with a snarl, but he caught her arm in his huge hand, pulling her towards him as she jerked away.

"Get your fuckin' hands off me!" she shouted, clawing at his fingers where they held her in an iron grip. He only laughed, the sound harsh against her cheek as his free hand closed over her breast once more.

"What's the matter, Vi? Need a few bob to give it up?"

Violet's heart was slamming against her ribs now as she pried at his fingers, her whole body shaking with rage as she grunted with the effort to wrench herself away from him, but he held firm, laughing the whole time until the sound of the door opening behind them made Henry push her away with a growl and whip around to find Archie standing in the doorway. Violet gasped as she fell back on the narrow bed and time seemed to slow as Archie came into the room, his face contorted with rage, and laid into Henry with a roar that seemed to echo off the stone walls. She could only watch, frozen in horror, as her captor took Henry by the head and slammed him into the wall. His body began to crumple to the floor, but Archie was already raining down punches and Violet was so aghast that it took a moment for her to register that Mr. Barrow had followed and was standing in the doorway, unable to conceal his shock as he watched Archie beat Henry until he was lying, insensate, in the corner of the room. Archie then slowly straightened, absently wiping his bloodied fists on his coat.

He turned after a moment to face Mr. Barrow, whose expression had shifted, as though by magic, into one of complete indifference. Archie was calmly adjusting his cuffs as he nodded towards Henry.

"Have some of the fellas take him east, leave him for the Bethnal Boys. He ever shows his face in my territory again, I'll fuckin' finish the job."

Mr. Barrow gave a short nod and stepped forward to take Henry by the wrists, dragging him from the room as Violet looked on, her hands pressed to her mouth as she tried to slow her racing heart, swallowing back the rising bile. A long, tense silence followed during which Archie stared out into the corridor, his eyes narrowed until Mr. Barrow returned. He stopped in the doorway, his feet braced a shoulder-width apart, his arms crossed over his chest, undoubtedly returning to ensure she didn't try to escape. Violet didn't dare look at him, but kept her gaze trained on Archie as he slowly turned and came to stand where she still sat at the edge of the bed. She wanted to stand, but he was too close, and she felt small, terrified of his sudden violence, as she tilted her chin to look up at him. His hands were in his pockets – she had always hated that about him: his casual disdain, his glib menace. How quickly he had brushed off his rage. It threw her off balance, and she hated that, too.

"Good mornin', Violet, my love. Apologies for that... some of the fellas don't know how to keep their hands to themselves," he said, nodding down at her, speaking as though he hadn't just beaten a man nearly to death. She glared up at him and said nothing, though her heart was still pounding inside her chest. Mr. Barrow's presence was very much at the front of her consciousness, and she could feel his eyes, not upon her, but upon Archie, watching, wary.

"Sleep well?" were Archie's next words, spoken in a slickly threatening tone. Again, she said nothing. She knew it needled him when he couldn't get a response from her. It was a small gesture of defiance, but all she was willing to display when trapped in this small space with him, especially after seeing him mete out such brutal punishment. His hands flexed inside his pockets and the corner of her mouth curved up, just the smallest amount, at this tiny victory over his self control.

Archie's nostrils flared but he didn't move – he knew his size alone was intimidating. He certainly didn't need to raise his voice or even lift a hand to strike fear into those who crossed him. He knew she feared him. He simply edged closer, his legs now brushing her skirts, forcing her chin up even further to meet his gaze.

"We're at a bit of an impasse, aren't we?"

She finally looked away, not towards Mr. Barrow where he stood silently in the doorway, but to the opposite wall. The sun was up now; a beam of light shone through the small window and the noise of the street filtered through the stone walls – cartwheels rattling, costermongers shouting. She slowly shook her head.

"What are you gonna do, Archie? Beat me as well? Keep me locked down here till I finally go mad and marry you just to get out?" She raised a defiant gaze to him once more. "Why d'you even wanna marry me? You haven't seen me in eight years." She narrowed her eyes at him. "I'd poison you the first chance I got, and you know it." Her voice was low, edged with frost, but inside, she was quaking as she glanced at his bloody knuckles. To her shock, he simply gave a small huff of laughter.

"You hear that, Johnny?" he asked the figure in the doorway without looking away from her. "She's gonna poison me. You heard it from her own lips – if I keel over, you'll know who to blame." The sly smile faded, and he now glared at her, bending down, and speaking in a low tone, forcing her to lean back. "You just fuckin' try it, Violet. You thought you were safe in France? You try anythin' and there's no corner of this earth where my men won't find you."

It took everything in Violet to bite back her scathing retort – how could he be so sure that his men would care to track her down if she killed him? – and instead, look suitably humbled, even a little frightened as he finally stepped away, allowing her to drop her chin and draw in a shallow breath.

Violet wanted desperately to look over at Mr. Barrow; to get some indication from him of where Archie was going with this but dared not. The smile returned to Archie's mouth as he slipped his hands back into his pockets.

"Now, you're a business-minded woman, Violet. Sellin' all them paintin's and little drawin's of yours." His gaze slid down her body, leering in a way only he could manage. "You'll sell anythin' for a few bob, won't you?"

Violet was biting the inside of her cheek now to keep the roar of rage from erupting from her.

"And I like to think that anyone can be persuaded to do almost anythin' for the right price."

A cold chill sparked to life in her chest as she awaited his next words. "I hear our Della's had herself a wee babe. Little girl named after her mum."

Violet froze as the implicit threat hung in the air between them. She was only partly aware of the scream echoing in the room – no, she hadn't made the noise out loud, it was in her head, filling it until she thought she might explode. Her fingers were clenched so hard on the edge of the mattress her knuckles were turning white. If she had a weapon, she wouldn't hesitate at this moment to use it. If he so much as breathed in Della's direction...

She recoiled as he squatted suddenly before her, so his eyeline was level with hers, and held her gaze. He wasn't smiling anymore, and a muscle twitched in his jaw. His voice was the lowest of whispers when he spoke again, and it moved over her skin like a winter's chill.

"You are gonna marry me, Violet, 'cause you're a smart girl." He reached out and put a hand on her knee. She immediately jerked away, but his fingers bit into her, holding her there as his gaze bored into her. "You're a smart girl," he repeated, his voice low and dangerous. "But you were stupid to let anyone find you." The corner of his mouth hitched up and he jerked his head in Mr. Barrow's direction, never looking away from her. "Johnny here knows what it is to keep a promise. And he's gonna make sure you keep yours. Ain't that right, Johnny?" Archie finally looked away from her to direct an unsettling half-smile to the man who still stood in the doorway. Violet finally allowed herself to look over at him, but his expression remained stony, and he only spared a glance for Archie. He gave a short nod.

"That's right, Archie."

And if Violet didn't know Mr. Barrow as she did, she would have wholeheartedly believed in that moment, from the low tone of his voice and the chilling calm of his expression, that he fully intended to do whatever it took to make her marry Archie. She almost – almost – smiled at the thought. If the police didn't give him that promotion after this, then they were fools.

When Archie returned his attention to her, Violet was careful to keep her gaze fixed on him, letting nothing show on her face that would give away any of what she was feeling.

"I have plans for us, Violet – big plans," Archie continued, a hint of a devious smile playing about his lips. "I'm gettin' us out of St. Giles. That's what you always wanted, isn't it?"

She wanted to push his hand off her knee but settled for a pointed look and a low hiss. "I was out of St. Giles, Archie – you're the one that brought me back."

Undeterred, his grin widened. "Ah, Violet, you don't wanna be hangin' about with bloody Frogs. I'm gettin' us the docks. The whole world is there." His eyes narrowed. "And Edward bloody Brill is there, thinkin' he's safe from me." His tone grew dangerous, and his fingers tightened their grip on her knee, making her wince. "And I'm gonna put his head on a fuckin' spike for gettin' me locked up in Newgate for eight years." The corners of his mouth turned up, just a little, and Violet felt a chill. "Just think – all the docks'll be ours, the whole of the East End. The warehouses, the shops – even his fancy little club, the one he thinks will make him a toff. It'll be all ours. I'll dress you in silks and velvets and you'll be drippin' in jewels. You just have to say yes."

Violet's composure finally snapped as she shoved his hand

away from her, sneering. "Edward Brill didn't turn you in, you fool. It was that sneaky little beggar Arthur Potts and he's dead. And I don't want silks or jewels, especially not from you."

Archie's expression froze as he stared at her and a terrible, uneasy tension filled the tiny room. Violet was aware of Mr. Barrow's gaze upon her but dared not look away from Archie as cold rage filled his face.

"What did you say?"

"I said," she spat out the word, "it was Arthur Potts that turned you in 'cause they were gonna arrest him for beatin' his woman nearly half to death. He gave you up to save his filthy little hide before he got himself stabbed to death in a Whitechapel brothel. And there is *nothin'* you could give me that would make me wanna marry you. Go get your docks and your club and whatever else you think will make you important, but it won't be with me."

Violet flinched when Archie rose suddenly, his face red with fury, and turned without another word to storm from the room. Mr. Barrow jumped to the side just in time to avoid being pushed out of the way as Archie made his way back upstairs, slamming the door on the landing behind him.

Mr. Barrow now turned to Violet with wide eyes.

"Are you alright?" was his first question, and she nodded slowly as she became aware of the drumming of her heart. She eased up from the bed as Mr. Barrow watched her from the doorway before making her way over to him and peering up into the shadows of the landing at the top of the stairs where Archie had disappeared.

"I think he bought it," she remarked as he reached out and touched her cheek. She turned to face him, almost absently, and was met with concerned eyes.

"Are you alright?" he repeated, and she narrowed her eyes at him, fury now rising through her after the shock of Archie's abrupt departure.

"Don't you dare let him get near Della and her baby," she whispered, the anger straining her voice, and the concern immediately fell away from Mr. Barrow's expression to be replaced with something darker – something dangerous.

"He won't set foot within a mile of the countess, that I can promise you. I've already sent word to Lord Bradford."

Violet closed her eyes and released a small breath of relief. Della's husband would let no harm come to his wife or their daughter, that she was certain of, and it gave her a small measure of comfort.

"Good," she replied, almost to herself, before starting when his other hand came up to cup her face, forcing her eyes open and her gaze onto his.

"But are you alright? Did Henry...?" The raw anger in his voice made Violet close her eyes, and she shook her head, fighting the urge to lean her cheek into the warm caress of his hand.

"He only hurt my wrist. I'm fine. I'm fine as long as Della and Clara are safe, Mr. Barrow, truly."

And though her words sounded sure, inside she was anything but. Archie's transparent threat against Della and her daughter still rang in Violet's ears and Archie's sudden assault on Henry still had her nerves on edge, so much so that it took her a moment to reflect on what Mr. Barrow had said to her. She looked up at him as he dropped his hands and pulled away, seeming unconvinced by her assurance.

"Does this mean Archie actually told you what his plans are?"

His smile was grim as he leaned back against the door frame, glancing quickly towards the door at the top of the stairs to confirm that no one was coming back before looking at her.

"You were right, of course. Give him what he wants. Don't question him. He told me everything this morning and I managed to get a message to Whitehall to be passed on to the earl."

Violet scoffed. "I suppose you'll be his favourite now – the man who caught Violet Latimer, his errant fiancée."

His smile faded. "I know you wanted no part of this, Miss Latimer, and I'm sorry—" He paused, clenching his jaw. "I'm sorry for what just happened. After all that" – he glanced towards the smear of blood Henry's face had left on the wall – "Archie'll be on edge for a while. Give me some time to show him I can be trusted."

She drew in a deep breath and slowly released it, peering back into that tiny, bare space in which she had spent the night, thinking of another day, another week... or longer, spent within its four walls, and a quiver of anger shook her. If this was what it would take to get her back to Paris, back to her painting and her studio and her life, she would endure this little room and Archie's threats with as much courage as she could muster.

She returned her attention to the man opposite her, but did not look up into his eyes, certain she would only see concern, making it that much harder to tell herself she could endure this imprisonment. Instead, she observed the hands at his sides, saw the slightly off-kilter angle of the pinky finger on his right hand, no doubt the result of a previously broken bone, saw the reddened, raw skin over his knuckles – had he fought again last night? – and tried to bring to mind, instead, the sensation of his mouth on hers, how he had pulled her into his hard body, how he had smelled of clean linen and soap, and how, just for a moment, she had found herself wanting him; something she hadn't felt in a very long time.

When he finally cleared his throat and she raised her gaze to his, he said, without looking away, "I doubt he'll be back. He'll go to Tommy to see if they can find out if it's true."

And she wanted to say, with every fibre of her being, Come in. Shut the door. Please don't leave me here in this room alone.

I'm so scared. *But what if he says no?* the voice in her head whispered. So instead, she swallowed back those words and inclined her head towards the stairs.

"You should go with him. It'll look good."

His expression never changed, but he did give a small nod. "Yes... He'll need someone to keep him in check."

She reached out then and took one of his hands in hers, giving it an imploring squeeze. "Don't let him hurt anyone else."

A pause. "I won't."

He hesitated; she still held his hand and when he began to draw away, she reluctantly let go.

"I'll try to come back tonight – see if Archie will put me on guard duty."

At those words, an unbidden flash of memory came to her; their last time alone in this room together, and her inner muscles clenched, sending a spark of heat up her belly. The sensation only served to frustrate her – did she want him or not? Was she ready for more or was she too afraid of him judging her? If she could not even bring herself to kiss him – even though he was, without a doubt, a very talented kisser – then perhaps she might never be ready for intimacy again. And the thought of that saddened her a little.

But there was work to be done now, and she blinked, the confused thoughts dissolving as she narrowed her eyes on him.

"Do not let him near Della, Mr. Barrow. I mean that... you keep her and that baby safe."

He held her gaze, something dark gathering in his expression and he gave the briefest of nods. "You have my word."

And on that assurance, she finally took a step back, into the room. "Go on, then. Don't let him leave without you."

His hesitation lasted only a moment before he stepped into the corridor beyond and closed the door without another word.

THIRTEEN

Unfortunately, Archie was gone by the time John made it upstairs, but his office was not empty. Tommy sat at the desk, leaning back in the big leather chair, with his booted feet propped up on the desktop. He nodded towards John as he paused in the doorway.

"The Devil's taken Henry – let the Bethnal Boys deal with him. What was that fool thinkin' of, layin' a hand on that girl?"

John shrugged. "Too many blows to the head, I reckon. Where's Archie gone?"

"Took off, was mutterin' somethin' about Arthur Potts."

John took a moment to lean against the doorjamb, crossing his arms over his chest and raising his brows.

"Apparently he's the one what turned in Archie. Least that's what his girl said."

Tommy's eyes widened in surprise before his expression darkened. "He always was a shifty little bastard. Archie'll tear him apart with his bare hands."

"He would," John agreed, uncrossing his arms, and standing upright. "'Cept he got himself stabbed to death in Whitechapel a few years back."

"Bloody hell," Tommy muttered as he swung his legs off the desk and rose from the chair. "Where's he gone then?"

John lifted his shoulders in an insouciant shrug. "Probably gone to find whatever the next best thing is."

Tommy shook his head as he came around the desk. "Arthur didn't have nobody – no family, and no one who liked him enough to call him a friend. Archie's gonna end up back here itchin' for a fight."

John's blood ran cold at this. It was true – he would rage about Covent Garden hoping to find someone, anyone who could take the blame for Arthur, before finding himself a stranger who would bear the brunt of his anger instead. John's expression remained resigned, however, and he jerked his head in the direction of the club floor.

"Should I go find him?"

Tommy sighed as he perched himself on the edge of the desk and it creaked under his weight.

"'Spose so. How'd she know it were Arthur, anyway?"

John shrugged again. "Happened in a brothel... she must've known one of the girls there."

The corner of Tommy's mouth turned up. "She would, gettin' around the way she did. Could have avoided all that if she had just married him to begin with."

John's chest grew hot with anger, and it took an effort to give Tommy a snide grin. "Bloody women never learn, eh?"

Tommy chuckled and nodded towards the door. "You'd better go find him, then. I'll head back to the warehouse, see if he's gone there."

"I'll have a walk round Whitechapel."

Tommy inclined his head in agreement as he tugged on his coat before following John out of the club and into the bright morning sun where they parted ways.

Another quick detour was required before John could set

about finding Archie and trying to talk him out of another violent rampage, and it took him south to Whitehall.

He entered the building and passed through a lobby bustling with police and secretaries, all shouting at each other over the din of rustling papers and echoing footsteps and made his way upstairs to the office of the superintendent, Lloyd Culpepper, his superior and the man in charge of the eradication of London gangs. He was also the man who would be deciding who would be promoted to detective chief inspector, the position John was determined to win to ensure no one would die, pointlessly, as Lucy had; that no one would have to rob innocent people like her in the first place for lack of food, of a home, of a job.

His office door was ajar, and so John raised a fist and tapped lightly upon the door frame, earning a gruff, "Make it quick."

John pushed the door open, and Culpepper raised his head, nodding when he recognized his officer and setting down the pipe he held.

"Ah, detective inspector, come in, come in. Apologies for the mess," he added as he rose to gather the papers scattered across his desktop, gesturing for John to take a seat in one of the faded oxblood leather chairs which sat by the window. "You'll have to be quick; I've another meeting with the MWB in an hour. Any progress?"

John nodded as he settled himself into one of the chairs. Culpepper had been referring to the Metropolitan Works Board, the body in charge of housing and sewage for the city. They were also leading the efforts to clear the slums, a task made difficult in areas like Seven Dials and Covent Garden as Archie ruled with an iron fist once more, making police and engineers reluctant to make any plans for rebuilding the rotting tenements.

"Neville has accepted our cover story – the girl is at his club now. She's told him Arthur Potts was responsible for his imprisonment and he seems convinced, though I can tell you, he was none too pleased."

Culpepper gave a grim shake of his head as he nudged the papers into a neat stack and set them down before taking up his pipe once more. "I'm not going to have more murders on my hands after this, am I?" he asked, breathing out a puff of smoke.

John drew in a deep breath. "I'll talk some sense into him."

"See that you do. Bloody under-secretary is badgering me about it; he's got journalists sniffing around, claiming the police are failing the East End."

"He's not wrong."

Culpepper cut him a sharp look but said nothing as he settled back into his chair, running a hand over his greying chestnut beard and drawing upon his pipe once more.

"I've been at this nearly ten years now, trying to drive the gangs out of the rookeries – they're like bloody weeds, they are. Take out one leader, a new one grows in his place."

John leaned forward and braced his forearms on his thighs. "That's why this will work. No more chasing after the Bruisers for petty crimes – we put them away for good this time. All of them. Make sure they can't come back. Ever."

The superintendent looked thoughtful as he gazed out the window to a bright, cloudless sky, though the chill of the coming winter could be felt in the office, even with a small fire burning below the cluttered mantel.

"And this Edward Brill? Is he to be trusted?"

John nodded. "Let us say we share the same goals. And I don't think he's keen to have us go poking about into his past. Much easier to cooperate."

"And the girl?" Culpepper now turned his gaze back to John.

There was a brief pause before John answered, keeping his tone neutral.

"Reluctant – but willing to help."

Culpepper frowned as he absently tapped the surface of the desk with the pipe.

"And is she... reliable?"

John's brow rose a fraction. "I most assuredly would not have suggested this plan had I not thought her reliable."

The other man shrugged. "Her past was a concern for some of us, detective inspector. She was Neville's fiancée, and a Seven Dials prostitute... it doesn't precisely inspire confidence, does it?"

A muscle twitched in John's jaw, but he said nothing for a moment as he stared across the desk at his superior, with all manner of different scenarios playing out in his head in response to the other man's words regarding Miss Latimer. He liked Culpepper – most of the time – but the man often seemed to forget that they came from two very different worlds. Culpepper was the youngest son of a minor baronet. Not aristocratic, precisely, but gentry, and had lived a comfortable life, rising easily through the ranks of the Metropolitan Police to his current position. John, like Miss Latimer, had grown up in Seven Dials, living on top of a flash house. Women just like her had surrounded him his entire youth, raised him and his sister after their mother died and their father abandoned them. It irked him greatly that a Seven Dials prostitute inspired no confidence in Culpepper. How, then, would he ever compete against all the others clamouring for the position of detective chief inspector when they were all from respectable families – sons of lawyers and clergy and the military, men who had gone to good schools and been raised in good homes and had no criminal past? He had thought that being valet to an earl would shield him from the scrutiny of that past, but even that had not been enough to erase the stench of the rookery which clung to him.

He cleared his throat, erasing the flood of thoughts, and shifted in his seat to lean an elbow on the armrest.

"She was, that much is true," he said slowly, adding careful emphasis to the word *was*. "But I can assure you, I have every confidence in Miss Latimer. She is a respected artist – she's had her paintings shown at the Salon," he added, recalling Violet's pride in that particular part of her career. He paused to find the right tone that wouldn't ruffle Culpepper's feathers. "If the Countess of Bradford, common pickpocket, can become the darling of Society with her skills, then surely we can rely upon Miss Latimer. She did volunteer, after all."

Culpepper's mouth quirked up for a moment before he nodded. "I trust you, Barrow – we'll see how this plays out. And just between you and me – I've already recommended you for the promotion. You've been doing excellent work here. Lord Bradford was quite right that you would be an asset for this department. I know the others were worried that you were nothing more than a pair of fists, but I know you'll prove them wrong – we'll show them that even someone with a past as dubious as yours can be reformed." Culpepper's tone was innocuous, but John had to swallow back a biting retort at this casual prejudice towards the disadvantaged as his superior leaned back and nodded. "But we must be patient, of course – must go through the whole rigamarole of bureaucracy and hand holding. If you can bring in Neville and his top men, it would be all but guaranteed. Don't let me down."

John did not allow that little spark of hope in his chest to grow at that moment – he had learned from a very early age never to hope for too much – but he did allow a flat smile, ignoring the remarks about his dubious past.

"I will do my very best, sir," he said, taking the hand Culpepper offered.

"Good lad. I'll expect another report from you by the end of next week."

John nodded as the other man opened the door. "Of course."

When Culpepper had left, John stood for a moment in the

empty room with the low din of the office beyond fading into the background. He wanted to smile – after all, Culpepper had just confirmed that the role of detective chief inspector was all but his. And while that promotion was now almost within his grasp, it could not help but seem even farther away than before, contingent on whether he was successful or not, on whether he could prove that a former fence and petty criminal could become a trusted member of the police force. His and Miss Latimer's plan *had* to work now.

John shook his head as he gathered up his hat and coat to leave the office. It was time to contact Edward Brill.

Violet furrowed her brow as she dragged her pencil over the page, composing an entire story with a few simple lines. The world fell away when she was creating; she no longer felt the crushing weight of the four walls around her, nor the interminable boredom, nor the constant, simmering fear, just saw the picture taking shape before her eyes. It was, perhaps, all that was keeping her from going mad in this little room. A small smile tugged at the corner of her mouth as she gently smudged one of the lines to create a shadow, the hollow of a cheek. Another stroke of the lead rendered a nose, straight and sharp. She was just touching the tip of her index finger to the page to create the dip of a cupid's bow when the deafening squeal of the bolt on the door being drawn back startled her out of her reverie.

She gasped as her heart seemed to leap out of her chest before she frantically shoved the pencil between the pages and tossed the sketchbook under the bed. In the moment it took her to compose herself and settle her expression into one of stony resentment, the door swung open and her heart, beating painfully against her ribs, suddenly slowed, and gave a warm pulse of... relief? Excitement? She wasn't sure, but when John

Barrow stepped through the doorway, accompanied by neither Archie nor Tommy, all the tension in her chest eased and a little frisson of pleasure spread through her. And again, she was confronted with the conflict between her heart – wanting desperately to let Mr. Barrow in, to explore more than just the kisses which haunted her very dreams – and her mind, which seemed to refuse to let go of the fear that she could never really escape her past, no matter how far away from Seven Dials she got.

But despite that warring of heart and mind, she was standing, smiling, eager as any lovesick schoolgirl. Violet, who had long ago learned love was for fools, who had used men for pleasure when it suited her but had never allowed herself to feel anything for them, now found herself stepping forward, with that silly grin on her face, to greet him. Despite all that had happened since she had fled Paris, despite this room that she was not allowed to leave, despite the man somewhere upstairs who held the power to destroy her life, she smiled for John Barrow.

And when he turned those warm brown eyes upon her, carrying with him, much to her relief, a water basin and fresh linens along with her breakfast, it made something deep inside her spark to life.

"Good morning, Miss Latimer," he began, stepping forward to set down his burden. "How are you?"

She cleared her throat, tempering her smile as she heard the note of concern in his voice. "I'm... well. As well as I can be." She swallowed. "He didn't... he didn't hurt anyone else, did he?"

He straightened and met her gaze, seeming to hesitate before he spoke. "No. Tommy found him at the warehouse sparring with the Devil. Poor fella didn't know what hit him." A ghost of a smile played about his lips. "I've sent a message to Mr. Brill. It's time."

Violet drew in a slow breath and nodded. "Good... that's good. I'm not sure how much longer I can be in this room," she said with a shaky laugh as John stepped back, resuming his position in the doorway. He didn't smile, though, as he reached into his pocket and withdrew an apple. He held it out and she took it with an inquisitive glance.

"It's dry bread and tea," he explained, inclining his head towards the tray he had set down. "Thought that might get a bit boring."

Violet scoffed. "Does Archie think to bore me into marryin' him?" she said as she bit into the fruit. It was perfectly sweet, perfectly crisp.

John finally smiled, though it was faint. "He won't be worried about marrying you once he hears from Edward Brill."

She shook her head, took another bite and swallowed before answering. "Oh, he'll still want to marry me. He's like a dog with a bone, is Archie. But at least he won't be so angry."

The corner of John's mouth turned up. "I'll get you out of here before that, I promise. Go on, wash up – I'll wait," he added as he turned his back to her and shielded the door. She took the opportunity to strip from her gown before filling the basin and squeezing out the sponge. It was a hugely welcome relief to lift her chemise over her head and run clean, warm water over her skin.

"The second that prison door closes, I'm goin' straight back to Paris. I can't wait to be out of this bloody place. At least I can wash it off me now," she added as she splashed a handful of water over her face and neck.

Mr. Barrow shifted his weight from one leg to the other as his head turned, just a little to the side, and his tone was guarded when he spoke.

"It may yet be a few more days – perhaps another week or so, until Edward can sit down with Archie to go over the plan."

"He'd better be bloody convincin'," Violet said with a sniff before she finished washing and pulled on the clean chemise and drawers Mr. Barrow had brought, then tugged on her bright crimson skirts and bodice once more. "I'm decent," she said, and Mr. Barrow finally turned to face her. Her joking tone had produced no smile from him, not even a gleam in those fathomless eyes, and she frowned.

"Are you alright?"

He tilted his head to the side. "Perfectly. Just hoping all goes well with Mr. Brill."

"Oh. Of course." She didn't look away from him, narrowing her eyes at him as though to read his mind, sensing that something was wrong. When a moment had passed and his expression still hadn't changed, she reluctantly turned to lift the lid from the tray of food. As he had said – bread and weak tea. She sighed and set about pouring herself a cup when he spoke, his words not registering until she swivelled back to face him and saw he was holding the sketchbook he had plucked up from where she had slipped it under the bed.

"Is this... me?"

She could only stare, wordlessly, as he slowly turned the page, and she knew precisely what he was seeing – his face, lovingly etched onto the paper in smooth lines and little smudges, drawn over and over again, from all angles. For a moment she couldn't think, but when he looked up at her with a raised brow and an alarmingly inscrutable expression, her heart began to race, and she blurted out the first thing which came to her mind.

"I was just practisin', is all – I'm not much good at drawin' people and I wasn't about to start sketchin' Archie." There. That almost sounded convincing, and disdainful enough of Archie at the end. She could feel the warmth of a flush rising up her chest but couldn't fathom why she would be uncomfortable for him to see her art. She hadn't even thought about what she had been drawing at the time, just put pencil to paper and let whatever was in her mind come to life.

"These are remarkable, Violet." He was perusing her drawings as he spoke, turning the pages once more. His brows furrowed as he reached one particularly intimate portrait, wherein she had drawn him from the back, but he was looking over his shoulder, staring out at the viewer, daring them to look away. She swallowed, and forced an expectant smile onto her face as he looked up. Those dark eyes, so curious in her sketch, were now unreadable, and his smile seemed forced.

"You have quite a talent. And it certainly doesn't look like you need practise." He glanced over at the tray of food he had left. "You should eat. Archie and Tommy are rather preoccupied now with Arthur Potts and finding someone else to blame, but Archie'll be back tonight when the club opens." He handed the sketchbook back to her and she took it, her fingers brushing over his briefly. His gaze flew up to hers and she saw it... he had been concealing it from her the moment he had stepped into this room with that flat voice and shuttered expression, but when her hand lingered over his, that cool façade dropped, and she saw the John Barrow she had come to know in the last month. The one with the easy smile and the devastating wink; the one whose eyes had burned as he had pulled her into him and kissed her, stirring something inside her she had been trying so hard to repress. The one who had entrusted her with his deepest of secrets.

And as soon as he withdrew his hand, his expression became blank once more and she frowned at him as he took a step back.

"Is somethin' wrong?" she asked, and he seemed to hesitate before shaking his head.

"It's nothing. I spoke with my superior at Scotland Yard this morning." He paused and drew in a small breath. "He informed me that he shall be recommending me for the promotion to detective chief inspector."

Violet frowned at him. "You don't sound particularly pleased... isn't that what you wanted?"

He took a slow, wary step back into the room after hovering in the doorway.

"It is, indeed. It's not guaranteed, of course – I came rather late to the game, after all. And I know my past is a concern... some of the men think I was only chosen for this assignment because I can fight, and who better to infiltrate a gang of bareknuckle boxers?" He stopped but an arm's length before her and that spark of awareness lit up between them. Did he feel it, too? His voice dropped when he spoke as though he were worried someone upstairs might overhear. "But if I can gather enough evidence to ensure that Archie and the rest of the Bruisers never see the outside of a jail cell again – then those chances are significantly higher."

She tried for an encouraging smile. "Are you worried our plan won't work? I told you – if you dangle the possibility of all that protection money in front of Archie, he won't be able to resist. It's all he's ever wanted."

His lips tightened. "I don't doubt our plan."

She stared at him, a furrow between her brows, still sensing something not being said. Violet possessed that innate ability, after so many years and so many men, to be able to know when something was amiss, and when she finally spoke, her words came out sharper than she intended.

"What *do* you doubt?"

His eyes widened a little at the intensity in her voice before he shook his head.

"I'm sure I don't know what you mean."

She took a step closer to him, drawing herself up to her full height but only reaching his chin.

"I think you do. What's Archie done?"

He shook his head again and seemed to be trying to avoid her gaze. This man who had smiled at her, and winked at her, and held her when she needed it most, would not look her in the eye, and she took him by the chin and forced his gaze down to hers.

"What's he done?"

He frowned as she released him.

"Nothing. He hasn't done anything. He knocked around the Devil and then Tommy took him out and got him good and scammered. He's probably still recovering."

Her frown deepened and she resisted the urge to shake him.

"Then what's got you so bothered? Why won't you look at me?"

He did, indeed, finally meet her gaze, and her breath caught in her throat as he looked down at her, struggling with his composure even though she could see the desire in his eyes, plain as day.

"It's the other night... I shouldn't have done that." His voice was low, but she held his gaze, refusing to let him look away.

"Done what?"

His cheeks warmed and she almost laughed at him as she leaned into him, challenging him.

"Done *what*, Mr. Barrow?"

"I..." he started, but trailed off, unable to say the words. Bloody hell, had he grown up in a Seven Dials flash house or not? Had all those years in the Earl of Bradford's service turned him into some priggish old moralist? She inched even closer and tilted her face up to look him in the eyes, dropping her voice to speak next in a bare whisper.

"It was a kiss, Mr. Barrow. Just a kiss."

Violet saw the muscle twitching in his jaw, the movement of his throat as he swallowed. She felt the heat of his body, only inches from her, and her insides turned to liquid, even as a small thread of anger coursed through her veins. She didn't wait for him to answer.

"What if I wanted it? Needed it?" The ache in her chest became too much to bear, until she said the words she thought she might never say again: "What if I want more?"

He froze on an indrawn breath as he stared down at her, his chest now rising and falling. He shook his head, causing her breath to catch in her throat. *He doesn't want you.*

"We can't, Violet, not here—"

"Why not?"

"Jesus, we're in his bloody club—"

"He's not here – no one's here."

"Violet..." was his low murmur, followed by a sharply whispered oath as he suddenly bent and pressed his mouth to hers. And though the kiss began fiercely, with John opening his mouth over hers, pulling her tight to him, it soon softened. He pulled back after a moment, and his touch grew gentle, his hands coming up and cupping her face, and he was feathering soft kisses over her lips, dipping his tongue back into her mouth to taste her. The anger dissolved, and her heart was slamming against her ribs in torturous expectation as his fingers slowly traveled up, threading into her hair, undoing the loose chignon she wore. Her face was aflame, and she wanted to grab him, pull him to her and crush her lips to his, but he held her so tenderly, and his kisses were so gentle and caressing, that she could only sigh and lean into him. She felt no fear, this time, no doubt, and his touch made her feel alive, not overwhelmed.

When he finally began to draw away, slowly, she laid her hands upon his chest, as if in supplication, and closed her eyes against the sudden, inexplicable sting of tears. She begged that voice in her head to stay quiet, to not remind her of her spotted past, and what he might really think of it; to let her have this moment. She would break if he said no, and she raised a beseeching gaze to him to offer the one thing she had thought she no longer had to give. "You could have more... if you wanted. John, you can have all of me."

Just saying the words, saying his name, sent a thrill of desire through her. And though she was partly trying to test him, to bring down whatever wall he had built between now and their last time together, she also had to know herself. Was she ready to be close to someone again, or would she forever be uncomfortable with intimacy? She certainly didn't want to be, and if she was going to test herself, she could not imagine a better candidate for that test than John Barrow, with his kind eyes and wicked tongue. But when his expression fell and he stepped back, her heart sank. She had no notions of anything more between them than the physical; she was not a fool. But somehow, she had hoped, deep down in her hard, cynical little heart, that John Barrow liked her.

"We can't..." He squeezed his eyes shut and growled in frustration before meeting her pleading gaze, shaking his head. "What happened with Henry... if he suspects anything... if we are caught..." His throat moved as he swallowed, but he never looked away, though his brow furrowed in consternation. "He's already told me that I must do whatever it takes to get you to agree. He wants me to beat it into you. I can't risk your safety no matter how much..." He didn't finish, but at those words, Violet slowly pulled her hand from his, and he didn't try to stop her as he gave her a remorseful look. "I'm sorry."

She swallowed back the growing ache in her throat as he moved away and nodded towards the sketchbook held loosely in her hand.

"Best make sure Archie doesn't find that."

"Yes, of course," was her whispered reply.

He paused again as he looked down at her, seeming uncertain before he spoke again.

"I'll be back tonight with him. He's not going to wait much longer for you."

She lifted one shoulder. "I can hold out a little longer, until Mr. Brill is ready."

John nodded slowly. "Then I'd best be going. The boys will be at the warehouse soon for sparring practice."

Violet forced the corners of her lips up but found she couldn't speak, so tight was her throat. He stared back at her for a moment.

"Goodbye, Miss Latimer."

He had to go. He had to go now, or she would burst into tears. She attempted another smile – perhaps more of a grimace – and he left, sliding the bolt home before there was silence once more.

FOURTEEN

John all but ran up those steps, down the corridor past Archie's empty office, and out into the brisk morning air. He stopped outside the club's door to draw a deep, shaking breath into his lungs before he hurried down the steps and across the street, narrowly avoiding a cart and horse heading his way. His heart was drumming painfully against his ribs as he made his way down a narrow alley and through to the building where he rented rooms. The halls were mercifully empty, and he locked his door behind him before crossing to the washbasin on the far side of the bedchamber and plunging his hands into the water before bringing them up to douse his head. The water had been sitting since the night before and was frigid, forcing a sharp gasp from him, but he welcomed the shock to his senses and thrust his hands into the water again. Again, and again, until the raging erection in his trousers finally eased and his heart slowed its painful rhythm before he slowly stepped away to reach for a nearby towel.

He was panting as he dried his hair before he growled in frustration and pushed his palms into his eyes, so hard he saw white, trying to erase the image of her from his mind. Of the pleading in her eyes, of those words whispered to him: *You could have more... if you wanted. John, you can have all of me –* but, worst of all, the disappointment. No, not disappointment. It was a wounding, a hurt in her expression when he told her he could not take what she offered. Not that he didn't want to. Indeed, it had taken everything in him not to unbutton his trousers and pull her onto his cock to plunder her sweet, slick core, but he had gone into that room with the image of Henry, crumpled and bloody, replaying in his mind, and the words Archie had spoken to him afterwards ringing in his ears. *Fuckin' bastard, darin' to lay a single finger on my woman – shoulda just killed him.*

John had fully intended to maintain a polite distance between himself and Violet – as he should have done from the moment she whispered his name in the cellar of the Fox and Friar – but then he had spotted her little sketchbook under the bed and plucked it up to return to her with the admonishment that she must not let Archie find it. It had fallen open as he had snagged the leather cover and revealed pages of... him. Not just drawings, but something more. John hardly knew one end of a paintbrush from the other, but he knew when he saw affection. Intimacy. Perhaps... no. He dared not even think the word. She had become far too close.

And she had seen right through that wall he had tried to erect, repeating to himself that they never should have gone as far as they did, that his only duty lay in getting her safely out of this place, away from the rookery she hated, and back to France. That if Archie had so much as an inkling that there was anything between them, he would not hesitate to end them both. But the moment she had looked up at him with tears in her eyes and asked him to give her something – anything – that would ease the terror of being locked in that tiny room by a man she hated, in a city she loathed, that bloody wall had crumbled like dust.

John cursed into the quiet of his tidy little bedchamber as he reached for the bottle of whisky he kept in the cabinet by the bed and, not bothering with a glass, took a quick gulp to wash the taste of her, torturous in its delectability, from his mouth. He hated that he had to tell her no, that he couldn't take what she offered, but he had the means to defend himself if Archie turned on him. Violet had none, and he could not risk her safety just for a taste of what he imagined to be pure heaven. No matter how much he wanted to.

With the cold water and the burn of the whisky in his belly, he felt suitably focused, and John took a deep breath before leaving to make his way to the warehouse where the Devil and Alexander were just starting their sparring match. The two Neville brothers stood in the shadows, observing them silently. John paused near the door to watch the boxers for a moment before making his way over to Tommy and Archie, nodding towards the ring as he stopped beside them.

"The Devil's lookin' good."

Archie spoke without looking at him. "I told him he needed to work on his hook – he's too slow on his feet goin' into one."

John inclined his head in silent agreement as they watched the match for a few minutes before Archie turned to them.

"Come on, then – I need a bloody drink."

They followed him through to the office at the back of the warehouse, where Archie snatched up the bottle of whisky and poured three glasses before taking a seat behind the desk. Tommy sat opposite him, but John remained in the doorway. The older Neville brother gestured to him with his glass before taking a quick swig.

"She still bein' a stubborn little bitch?" Archie's voice was low, irritated, and Tommy let out a huff of laughter. The corner of John's mouth lifted in reply, and he paused to raise his own glass to his mouth before he spoke.

"I think she'll come round. I can be very persuasive." This

was said with a cunning grin as he flexed his free hand and Archie nodded absently, as though he hadn't heard the words.

"No doubt, no doubt. I've waited this long for her; suppose I can wait a little longer." His expression darkened suddenly as he stared down into his glass of whisky, swirling it contemplatively. "Just wish that bastard Potts hadn't got away with snitchin' on me."

Tommy shrugged and downed his drink. "Don't matter no more since he's dead, does it?"

And this was when the air grew chill in the room and Archie turned a slow glare upon his younger brother.

"Are you bleedin' dense?" he hissed. "Eight years I was away, and I'll never get the chance to kill him myself like I shoulda done." His glare turned into a sneer as he inched forward in his seat to fix a scowl upon Tommy as John took a careful and quiet step back. "Eight years you had to find him yourself. And I had to hear it from bloody Violet – if Barrow here hadn't tracked her down like you were meant to, I'd have never fuckin' known."

A tense silence settled upon the room as Tommy slid a dark look over to John before rising slowly from his seat to stare down at his brother.

"No, I didn't find her – I was too busy runnin' this gang 'cause you were stupid enough to get caught."

John took another small step back as Archie planted his palms on the desktop and stood, so his gaze was level with Tommy's.

"Then allow me to relieve you of your burden, Tommy. You go on back to the ring with Barrow and I'll handle runnin' things." His voice was edged with mocking concern and Tommy's jaw tightened in response as John's gaze slid from one brother to the other. The air crackled with tension between the two, but finally, Tommy relented – loyal little lapdog to the last – and turned with a sniff to push past John and out to the warehouse. There was a moment of silence before the warehouse door slammed shut and John turned back to Archie, who picked up his glass and drained the last of his whisky.

"I think my brother got a little too big for his britches while I was away, thinkin' he was in charge of my gang." He raised his gaze to John, who was careful to keep his expression blank. "I got us Covent Garden, didn't I? We was just petty criminals in Seven Dials before I started the boxin' matches. Got us to the top with my fightin' and he thinks he can run this gang without me. I'm expandin' our territory – what's he bloody done?"

John shrugged but made no reply as he took a slow sip from his whisky. Archie scoffed as he poured himself another glass, speaking as though to himself.

"It's time for us to move south. Move beyond bareknuckle boxin'. Limehousers have held their territory long enough and we're gonna take it." He finally looked up at John and tipped his glass towards him. "And I want Violet with me when we do. She was the first one what ever showed me a bit o' kindness, you know? Me and Tommy was too busy survivin' and she showed up one day after I was scrappin' with another lad, patched me right up. Asked if I could help her and her friend get outta that shithole orphanage." He scowled down at his drink. "Promised her the world before I went away, and the bitch threatens to poison me." He let out a sharp laugh and swallowed the rest of his drink. "Give her a good wallop, she'll come round. I'd do it meself but I don't want her hatin' me even more." He laughed as John considered that it was not humanly possible for Violet to hate him anymore than she already did. Archie gestured towards the warehouse. "Come on, the boys'll be waitin' for you."

The sound of the bolt on the door sliding open was beginning to sear through Violet, right down to her bones, and this time was no exception. She sprang to her feet the moment the door squealed open, refusing to be caught sitting again, forced to look up at her captor, and drew in a deep breath as Archie sauntered into the room, thumbs hooked in his pockets. And, behind him once more... Violet only allowed the very briefest of glances towards John who, for his part, kept his own impassive gaze firmly fixed on Archie's back. Her heart was drumming against her ribs as he came to stand before her, the corner of his mouth turned up in a sly smile.

"Evenin', Violet, my love."

She said nothing. The open door was behind him, but John Barrow stood in it, arms crossed over his chest, observing the scene before him with an indifferent, almost bored expression. Archie grinned down at her, though she would not give him the satisfaction of showing her fear.

"So... you ready to get out of here?"

Her gaze slid up, though she moved not another muscle. Archie smiled again.

"Just say the words, Violet, and you'll be free to go."

Her teeth clamped together as she glared up at him. Liar. She would never be free if she said the words he wanted to hear. But he would need to hear something soon, even if it wasn't quite that she would agree to be his wife, or he would lose his patience. And Archie possessed very little of that particular quality.

"Take me back to Paris."

There. That wiped the smug smile from his face.

"Paris?" he finally said, then let out a short, derisive laugh. "You ain't leavin' this room lest it's as my woman."

She drew in a long breath, feeling the weight of John's stare on her from where he stood behind Archie. She could still feel his mouth on hers; she had dreamed about it, along with the ache of him drawing away when she had offered more. *Why would he want more from you?* the small voice hissed at her.

Who would ever want more from you, a common trollop? Violet swallowed and dismissed the thoughts as she turned her attention back to Archie.

"I had a whole life there, Archie. I can't just leave it behind. I must make arrangements, let my patrons know I'm leavin', collect my things."

And at these words, Archie let out a low, mocking chuckle.

"What things?" He leaned in closer. "Your things are gone. You know that."

She did. She did know that; she'd told John as much. She could almost imagine the glee with which Archie had smashed up all her paints and easels and canvases. Maybe he had taken them outside and burned them all. It didn't stop the sharp ache twisting her insides, nor the tears which pricked at her eyes. She furiously blinked them away, refusing to let him see how devastating his words were to her, swallowed back the sob rising in her throat, and met his eyes, summoning a look of disdain as she did so.

"Then you can go. I've nothin' else to say to you."

His gaze darkened as he stared down at her, his fists clenching at his sides, and it took every ounce of control she possessed not to flinch when he stepped closer and bent so his mouth was next to her ear.

"I said you were a smart girl, Violet, and you are... but don't do somethin' stupid 'cause you're stubborn, as well."

When he pulled back, she was glaring at him, once more with the implied threat towards Della and her new baby hanging in the air. She couldn't help it; she was spitting out the words before she could even think.

"If you lay so much as one finger on Della, I swear—"

Archie's hand came up, so fast Violet did flinch this time and instinctively recoiled, squeezing her eyes shut – and then opening them once more when the blow never came, only to see that Mr. Barrow had Archie's arm, raised up over his head as he had prepared to strike, in his firm grasp. He smirked and let out a soft tut of disapproval.

"Easy there, Archie," he drawled, glancing towards Violet. "You'll damage the goods."

Archie cut a swift glare at Violet before Mr. Barrow released him and he let out a sudden, sharp laugh.

"Suppose her looks are the best thing she's got goin' for her." He glanced back at her with a sneer. "But do not mistake me, Violet. I'll have you, one way or another."

She was about to deliver a scathing retort, but the sudden squeal of the door at the top of the stairs drew Archie's attention and he turned as the Devil – Violet didn't remember what his real name was, she only knew he had been a cracksman in his youth and fought his way to the top of the Bruisers – came jogging down the steps. He said not a word as he stepped into the tiny room, and she kept her gaze on the floor as the Irishman wordlessly handed over a crumpled envelope.

"What's this?" Archie asked, but clearly expected no answer as he tore open the envelope and withdrew a single sheet of paper. She could feel John's gaze upon her but dared not look up at him as he spoke to Archie.

"What is it?"

Archie also had no reply as he handed John the paper. When Violet finally dared a glance up, she saw the triumphant sneer upon Archie's face. John was the first to speak, with not a single hint in his tone that he knew exactly what this letter was and who it was from.

"Edward Brill wants to meet with you?" he said, astonished, as he held up the letter in question. Archie was already grinning and rubbing his hands together in anticipation before he gestured to his two men.

"Come on, lads – got to prepare for our guest." The thread of menace was unmistakable in his voice, and Violet watched with no small amount of relief as Archie, seeming to forget she even existed, turned and left the room, with the Devil trailing in his wake. John, facing away from her, did not turn to look back before he, too, followed, but not before reaching back and pressing something into her hand before he left. The door closed behind him, and the lock squealed into place as Violet looked down and opened her clenched fingers to reveal a small square of paper. She glanced up at the door to be certain she was alone before quickly unfolding the note and immediately recognizing Della's neat, slanted writing. Her heart soared and her chest tightened with some unnamed emotion as she scanned the words.

Dearest Violet,

I hope this letter finds you well. I know you must be getting anxious now with nowhere to go, and forced to stay at Bradford House, but I do hope that you're at least able to pass the time with your art. How I wish I could be there with you, but I know you are made of stern stuff, and you will make it through this just as we made it through the orphanage.

Violet paused in her reading as hot tears began to scald at the corners of her eyes, sadness and fear welling up in her chest until it ached. Never had she been more aware of the four walls surrounding her than now, with Della's words to remind her of what she had given up to be here. A shuddering sob escaped her as she read on.

I have been reading the papers – the news from the rookery has been so frightening. I had forgotten what it was like with Archie running things, how he had managed to make that terrible place even worse. And I had to write to you, Violet, because I was so worried you would blame yourself for all this violence. Please believe me when I say that I owe you my life; that if you had not been brave enough to make that promise to Archie, that we would surely have perished in the workhouse. And please also believe me that you were right to turn him in, though I know how you felt for him.

Violet was weeping now, tears dripping down onto the page, blurring Della's words, the same words John had told her in his attempt to assuage her guilt over the fact that people had died for her actions so many years ago.

I only wish they could have put him in prison for good eight years ago. I remain confident, however, that Detective Inspector Barrow will succeed where others failed last time, and Archie and the Bruisers will soon be but a bad memory.

I have also thought on the question in your last letter – had I ever considered going back to Seven Dials? Truthfully, I had also forgotten about those talks we had, back when we had promise and dreams. We became so hard, living on our own, I don't think I let anything like kindness or empathy in for fear that any sign of weakness would make it impossible to survive. I, too, was happy to leave that place and never look back. However, it has come to my attention that Detective Inspector Barrow has been using his position within Scotland Yard to improve matters there. For a long time – far too long, I'm ashamed to admit – I thought him quite mad. Why would anyone ever want to return to that terrible place?

Of course, it was my dearest Cole who made me aware of his good deeds. Cole has been trying for several months to introduce legislation in the House of Lords that might lift the people of the rookeries out of poverty. Of course, this is easier said than done, as so many would rather pretend we don't exist and never did. Do you remember when we dared to venture to Bond Street that one Christmas, after saving up for a bit of silk? One would have sworn we were invisible.

So, in answer to your question, yes, I have thought of going back. We did always say if we had the power to make changes one day we would, and now I do. Even so, it is a challenge to bring about reform, even for the Earl and Countess of Bradford. When you are able to leave Bradford House, I should like to show you what we've been doing. Maybe it's time we both went back – together, this time.

Please be well, for I have not yet forgotten our plans for Paris! I look forward to seeing you again when this is all over.

Your friend,
Della

Violet could not stop the tears which streamed down her cheeks now, thinking of Della and all they had fought for, and how all it had done was get her tangled again with Archie Neville, and taken her back to the one place to which she had sworn never to return. A great, shuddering sob ripped out of her as she folded the letter back up with trembling fingers and slid it deep into her pocket. She neither gasped nor started, numb to everything now, when she heard the scrape of that damned bolt. She didn't look up when the door squealed open, staring down at the floor instead, hugging herself with tears blurring her vision. Footsteps came closer, but she felt nothing. That was, until John Barrow's arms came around her and pulled her into him, and she clung to him, certain now that she would never be able to let go.

FIFTEEN

John held her, as he had that night in the conservatory, wishing with everything in him that he could gather her up right now and take her from this place, wishing he had told her, in no uncertain terms, that he would not allow her to place herself in this position. He had learned, though, that trying to tell Miss Violet Latimer what to do was as futile as trying to tell the sun not to rise in the morning, or the tides to cease their ebb and flow. She was clutching on to him, her long nails digging into his back, her face buried in his chest, her tears wetting his shirt, and he raised a hand to cup the back of her head, gently stroking her golden hair. He didn't know what had been in Lady Bradford's letter, but it had clearly affected her, and he held her as all that pent-up sadness and grief and anger poured out, wishing that he could take it from her and set her free from this place. But, since that was not yet possible, he was content to hold her, knowing they were safe, just for this brief moment, from Archie and his threat to any who dared to even look at her.

As before, she was quiet until all the emotion had finally drained from her, leaving her once more the Violet Latimer who did not care to wallow in grief, and she raised her tear-stained face to his, her eyes wide.

"I thought you were goin' with Archie?"

He shook his head, knowing he should set her back from him, but unable to find the will to do so.

"He and Tommy have gone to gather the lads. Wants to put on a display of force, so to speak, for when Brill arrives."

"And what about you?"

The corner of his mouth lifted in a grim smile.

"I'm to get you suitably attired. He wants you by his side, his pretty little moll, as he so eloquently put it, and so I'm to take you upstairs to borrow something to wear."

Violet made a face as she wiped at her eyes. "And what then?"

John shrugged as he finally stepped away from her, feeling poignantly the loss of her warm, soft curves pressed into his body. "We follow the plan with Mr. Brill. Come on – at least you can get out of this room for a bit," he said with a smile. She didn't return the expression but did let out a sigh of relief as he pulled the door open and gestured for her to go ahead.

The club was not yet open, and so it would be quiet upstairs until Tommy and Archie returned with the men for what they assumed would be a showdown, perhaps with a brawl to follow. They would be whipping up the boys in anticipation. Wouldn't they be surprised when Edward Brill came to them with an offer to give them everything they had ever wanted instead?

When they entered the gambling floor, she pulled away suddenly and marched over to the bar, stepping behind the long, scarred countertop. Bottles clinked as she rummaged about beneath it before emerging with a triumphant smile. She held a bottle of brandy – Archie's best, by the looks of it – and made quick work of popping out the stopper, setting a glass down on the bar and filling it with the clear amber liquid. John watched, a grin playing about his lips, as she raised the glass and took a deep, grateful gulp. She was smiling softly as she closed her eyes, perhaps to better appreciate the flavour, before nodding slowly.

"Ahh... I needed that," she said as she finally looked over to where he stood by a billiard table covered in faded green baize. He didn't respond to her lighthearted tone, however, as he took a few steps closer to the bar. Her smile faded and just as he opened his mouth to speak, to ask if she was well, still concerned about whatever had been in that letter to cause her such sadness, she quickly asked, "What'll it be, sir?" Her teasing grin had returned as she gestured to the wide array of bottles before her, cocking her hip and thrusting out her bosom, playing the saucy bar wench, and he couldn't help but chuckle as he leaned an elbow upon the well-worn oak top.

"A whisky, if you please, miss."

She winked boldly before reaching for a glass and the best bottle of whisky the Devil's Den carried. As she filled the glass, he studied her, noting the delicate curve of her cheek, still stained from her tears, and the stray curls of golden hair which had slipped free from her simple chignon when he had held her. Even thinking of how tightly she had clung to him, how every curve of her had fit so easily against him, made an uncomfortable heat grow in his chest. The unbidden memory of her lips upon his made all the muscles in his stomach grow taut and his pulse quicken, and he snatched up the glass as soon as she slid it across the bar to him, draining it in a single gulp.

The whisky burned its way down his throat, and he coughed before setting the glass back down. When he glanced up, she was watching him with a raised brow, her eyes dark in the shadowed interior of the club, where only a few sputtering lamps were lit against the grey afternoon. He took a deep breath before he pushed the glass towards her.

"I'll have another, please."

She frowned at him now as she refilled his glass, no longer

the lusty barmaid, and passed it to him once more. He again swallowed back the drink before meeting her enigmatic gaze.

"Did Lady Bradford have bad news?" he asked, and her expression fell at his words before she looked away.

"No... no, she's well. I just... I miss her. And I feel like I'm goin' a bit mad down there." She glanced around the empty room and a tiny smile lifted the corner of her mouth. "It's nice to be out – even if it is just in his dreadful little club."

He returned the expression as he swirled around the last dregs in his glass before she propped her elbows upon the scarred and stained bar to capture his gaze.

"Would you tell me about Lucy?"

John, startled by her question, couldn't answer for a moment as that familiar mix of grief and guilt twisted his insides, but Violet's wide, entreating gaze compelled him, and he frowned as he swallowed back the last of his drink and set down the glass.

"Lucy... she would have told me that everything I'm doing is nonsense. That I can't possibly save everyone in the rookery on my own." A faint smile curved his lips as he trailed his finger around the rim of his glass. "She would have made a fine police officer if women were allowed – she had no fear."

Violet smiled at this.

"I should have got her out of that place when I left. I could have got her a job in service somewhere." John pursed his lips as he stared down at his glass. "She wanted to stay. The girls in the flash house were like family; she wouldn't leave them. She was doing alright for herself, fencing just like our mum." He let out a small exhalation. "I hardly slept after she died, blaming myself, knowing I could have stopped it."

Violet started to shake her head in disagreement, and he held up a hand. "I know that's not true, not really, but deep down... I'll always feel responsible." A chill, like a shard of ice, buried itself in John's chest as he looked down at the bar, unable to meet her kindly gaze. "It shames me now to admit... I spent weeks trying to find those men that murdered her. I was going to kill them. I wanted them dead; it was all I could think about. I would wander the streets for hours, waiting for them to try and rob me."

The chill began to spread, and John had to cough to bring himself back to the present, even as the memory of stumbling his way through Seven Dials, with that same chill inuring him to all other feelings, threatened to overwhelm him. He shook his head and lifted his gaze to Violet once more. "No one ever came near me. I suppose I looked like I was ready to do violence. And that was when I finally realized that there was another way to stop men like them, without having to hurt people. And so, I joined the police force."

Violet's expression was sympathetic as she reached across the bar to touch her fingers to his, a gesture which made his throat grow tight with emotion. He gave her a strained smile.

"I've never told anyone about her, you know. Lord Bradford doesn't even know about her."

Violet's expression was soft as she looked back at him over the bar. "After all this, Mr. Barrow... I think you can tell me anythin'."

He chuckled softly at that and gestured towards the stairs at the back of the room. "Come on, Bess'll be waiting."

She hesitated for just a moment, pulling her bottom lip in between her teeth before she slipped out from behind the bar to follow him. He put his hand out, stopping her as they reached the bottom of the stairs, and when she turned to him with a questioning look, he said nothing, directing his gaze up to the next floor instead, to indicate that they had their pretence to maintain. She nodded, understanding, and put on the expression of hostile resentment which had been effective for her thus far, allowing John to push her up the stairs to where Bess and the other girls plied their trade. As it was downstairs, it was quiet up here, too, for the girls had been sent away for the day. Only Bess had been asked to stay to find a few spare dresses to lend out.

John led her down a dimly lit hall, its walls covered in faded wallpaper dotted with tiny pink flowers. The dark oak door at the end of the hall was slightly ajar, and he pushed it open without knocking to find the shapely, flame-haired Bess standing in a small bedroom. A rainbow of skirts and bodices were strewn over the striped coverlet on the brass bed, and she gave a hesitant smile as John entered the room, followed by a sullen Violet.

"Afternoon, Mr. Barrow. Tommy says I'm to find some clean clothes for the... um..." She paused and glanced over at the other woman, who was glaring at the wall, her lips pursed, before clearing her throat. "For the lady, here."

John laughed harshly at this as he wandered to the bed to cast a disdainful look upon the brightly coloured silks and wools. "She ain't no lady, Bess, I can assure you of that."

Bess ignored this quip as she took Violet's hand with a smile and guided her over to the selection, rifling through the gowns before plucking up a simple sprigged cotton day dress in pale green.

"Lettie's about your size – though we've not got anythin' near so grand as what you're wearin'," she said, eyeing the stylish crimson wool gown before handing over the dress. She selected two more outfits, one in peach silk and one in gold and black stripes and smiled as she laid them over Violet's outstretched arms.

"Thank you, Bess," she murmured, and the other woman nodded before casting a wary look over at John, who stared back at her with his most forbidding expression.

"That'll be all, Bess. You can go now."

His gaze never wavered as uncertainty crossed her face before she finally inclined her head towards Violet and left, closing the door slowly behind her. John waited as her footsteps retreated down the hall before he finally spoke.

"The meeting's not until later this evening..." He glanced at the pile of dresses she held, then met her gaze. "I could fetch you something to eat? You'll want to try those on before—"

"No... don't go," she said quickly, stepping towards him and setting the gowns back upon the bed. "I couldn't eat a bite, anyhow. Please... just stay with me?"

Her wide green eyes were full of pleading, and he finally nodded, safe in the knowledge that Archie and Tommy would be occupied for the remainder of the afternoon gathering their men, preparing for a battle that would never come.

"Of course." He waved towards the gilt-framed room divider in the corner. "I'll wait here."

Her grateful smile made his chest tighten as he took a seat in the small, bent-wood chair tucked under the window. She plucked up the peach-coloured dress and slipped behind the screen. Fabric swished and after a few moments, John heard a sigh of relief before she draped her bright crimson bodice on top of the frame, followed shortly thereafter by the matching skirt. After another few moments of faint rustling followed by a muttered curse, John finally ventured to speak.

"I suppose... I never thanked you properly, for volunteering to help with this operation. I know this was the very last thing you wanted." He paused, searching for the right words. "And... thank you for letting me go on the way I did. It felt good to speak of her again."

There was a moment of silence from behind the screen before Violet spoke.

"I was happy to listen."

John allowed the smallest of smiles as he gazed at the screen with its faded cream and blue toile panels, and that shard of ice which had lodged itself so firmly in his chest felt as though it were beginning to thaw. He could get used to Violet listening –

and he could be quite happy doing the same in return. Another moment passed before she stepped out from behind the screen, swathed in peach silk and cream lace. *Goddammit.* Forget listening to her, he was going to end up dead just looking at her the wrong way, and he sat up a little straighter in his chair as she ran hesitant hands down her stomach. The gown had clearly been cut to attract a certain type of clientele, and the boned bodice pushed her small breasts up until they were all but spilling over the top of her lace-edged chemise. The hem had also been shortened to show off shapely ankles and calves, and she frowned at herself.

"Archie'll lose his bloody mind if I come down in this."

John cleared his throat, doing his very damnedest to dispel the memory of warm curves beneath his fingers, of the summery scent of her, and of the touch of her lips, as he rose from his seat.

"Very likely... perhaps this would be more appropriate?" he said as he lifted the pale green cotton dress from where she had left it on the bed and held it out. She reached out, her hand lingering over his for just a moment before she slid the gown from his grasp and stepped back. He could have sworn he saw the skin over her luscious breasts pinken as she warmed with a flush, but she turned before he could see her expression and slid behind the screen once more. Heart racing, he resumed his seat as the peach gown was carefully laid over the top of the screen before she began fiddling with the new frock. After a moment, he ventured to speak again.

"Perhaps... when you're back in Paris, I'll come and visit. You could take me around to all the sites." John immediately grimaced and dropped his face into his hands to stifle his groan. *Idiot!* Had Archie not told her that he had done just as she had said he would and destroyed everything she had built up there? He mouthed a curse and quickly added, "That is... once you're settled, of course."

There was a long moment of silence from behind the screen

and John squeezed his eyes shut, rubbing his fingers over his temple. He really had put his foot in it this time, hadn't he? After what seemed an eternity, she finally spoke.

"Cor, Mr. Barrow... you really have taken one too many knocks to the head, haven't you?"

John stared at the screen, mouth agape as he heard the laughter in her voice before she stepped out, prim and proper in sprigged cotton. He couldn't help but chuckle as she sketched a little curtsy. This gown was leagues away from the peach frock: buttoned up to just below her chin, the sleeves long and fitted, the skirts leaving everything to the imagination. She sniggered a bit as she looked down at herself.

"I'd make a convincin' schoolmarm, but perhaps not the intended to a Seven Dials' gangster."

John smiled as he shook his head.

"Archie'll want something a bit showier, make no mistake."

She sighed and plucked up the gown of black and gold stripes and disappeared once more. As she changed, he thought on the words he had spoken, said in the moment without much consideration, but he found himself warming to the idea. *Visit her in Paris.* Yes, that would actually be... wonderful. There was undeniably something between them... wouldn't it behove him to explore more between them than the frantic kisses they had shared up until now? She had asked for more, after all... John frowned at himself. He wanted to give it – he wanted to give her more, though he wasn't entirely convinced that she was ready to receive it, despite her offer. And, more frighteningly, he knew what danger there was if he took it.

Outside, the grey of the day deepened, and rain began to patter upon the windowpane. John stood and reached for the box of matches which had been left upon a dresser scattered with hairpins and powder pots, striking one to light another lamp. The shadows in the room wobbled as the flame righted itself, and John glanced out the small window to watch as the people in the streets below scattered for cover when the patter became a downpour. Rain streaked down the window and the little room, papered in pink and burgundy stripes, grew dark save for the few spots of warm, quivering light provided by the lamps.

"I hope Bess hasn't been caught in that," John remarked, off-hand, as he edged back the gauze curtains to watch water begin to pool in the cobbled roads. There was a pause.

"Isn't she comin' back?"

John absently shook his head as he turned to face the divider.

"The club's closed tonight for the meeting with Brill. Archie's planning for battle." He let out a dark chuckle as he ran a finger along the edge of the brass bed frame. "Won't he be disappointed?"

Violet said nothing, and John cleared his throat as he glanced back up. That look on her face after he had told her he could not take what she offered still nagged at his conscience. Afterwards, surely – when Archie and the rest were safely put away. Perhaps then, they could explore this attraction, and he forced the words out.

"About yesterday..."

A harsh burst of laughter sounded from behind the screen.

"Yeah, I know... you shouldn't have done that."

John's brows drew together, and he took a step towards the divider.

"No... I never thought that at all." He drew in a deep breath. "I very much wanted more, Miss Latimer..." He paused and swallowed. "Violet. And I'm so sorry if I gave you cause to doubt that."

There was another long silence before he elaborated, drop-ping his voice as he took another step closer to the screen. "It just... with everything happening, I'm afraid the timing wasn't quite right."

Quiet fell, interrupted only by the hiss of the rain and the thrum of his heartbeat. When he was sure he couldn't bear the anticipation any longer, she stepped out from behind the screen. There was no gown this time, not peach or green or striped, just Violet, as he had come to think of her of late, in chemise and stockings, her eyes wide. Everything in him came alive in that moment as she whispered, "Is now the right time?"

And he should have said no. Archie was still very much a threat – to her life, and to his. He could have told her, let's wait. We'll have all the time in the world once this is over – but they wouldn't. She was leaving, going back to Paris to pick up the pieces of her life there. There would be no time. And so, instead of saying no, he found himself whispering her name, reaching for her, and she was in his arms, right where she belonged.

SIXTEEN

It was like a sip of cool, clear water after a drought, a soft bed at the end of a long day, as Violet pulled John's mouth down to hers. It had been so long, she couldn't even find the will to slow down, to take her time to explore him – instead, she was pushing at his coat, fumbling at buttons, seeking the heat of his body. His hands held her to him as his mouth moved over hers, tongue exploring, just as she reached the bare skin of his abdomen, and she sighed against his lips. His shirt, the impediment to her wandering hands, was promptly discarded, and a hot shiver raced through her as she pressed herself to him.

His hands were at her hips now, bunching up the soft linen of her chemise, until he was lifting it up, over her head. That inner voice, the one which told her that no one could possibly want her, was quiet, because he did want her. Violet knew desire; it had been her livelihood, but this man desired her in a way no one else had. It was in his touch, his kiss, the way his fingers dug into her flesh. It could not be doubted, not when he pushed her back against the wall and dropped to his knees before her. Desire shone in his eyes as he gazed upon her nakedness, before he slid a hand – bruised and damaged, but no less skillful – up her stockinged calf to lift her leg over his shoulder before he raised his gaze to hers.

"You said I could have all of you, Violet. Do you still wish to give it?"

Rapturous relief filled Violet at the knowledge that the little voice had been wrong, that someone could want all parts of her, dark or light. And so, she took his face in her hands and murmured, "I'll give you all of me if you'll do the same."

John nodded his agreement, and kissed that place between her legs where she ached for him. His fingers stroked softly over her thighs as he licked and sucked, and his hold grew tighter as she began to spiral, squeezing her eyes closed. Her hips rocked against him, and her fingers tightened their grip in his hair as the pressure mounted, sending her to the edge of a precipice from which she had no fear of falling. Not with him. And so, she let herself go, let the pleasure wash over her, crying out as the crescendo peaked, all as he knelt before her, worshipping her.

In the trembling aftermath, as Violet drifted back down to earth, he was still there on his knees before her, pressing his face into her stomach, breathing in her scent, his hands gliding over her thighs. As she fought to catch her breath, he gently took her leg from his shoulder and rose, his mouth seeking hers once he was standing. And then he spoke, his whisper soft in her ear.

"Of course you can have me, Violet. Whatever comes of this, I will be happy to say that, for this time, you were mine."

And Violet Latimer smiled, because she was happy to be his, even if it only lasted while they were alone in this room together. She slid her arms around him and pulled him down to her mouth. He was kicking off his boots as they stumbled towards the narrow brass bed where he swept all the gowns Bess had laid out onto the floor. Violet fell then, pulling him down with her, opening her legs around him. He was pushing his trousers off as his lips began to drift away from her mouth, trailing across her neck before he was moving down again, dropping soft, hot kisses upon the curve of her breast before he took her nipple into his mouth with a low growl.

Violet surged against him as pleasure rippled through her, and she flung her arms over her head, writhing beneath John as his hands slid around her hips so he could push her further onto the bed. She gasped as he released her nipple before his lips were on her again, pressing to her stomach, lower, lower, until he parted her thighs, whispering her name like it was a prayer, like he couldn't quite believe she was lying beneath him, naked and willing and reaching out for him. And as he stared down at her, his chest rising and falling, she was finally able to see the toll of all that fighting he had done to maintain his cover. What had seemed rock solid and invincible was scarred; bruises in varying shades of purple and yellow bloomed across his skin, which had been opened and healed again, bearing the marks of many fists. And he was doing it all for something beyond himself. Violet did not yet understand it – certainly not him wanting to bring himself back to the rookery – but she saw the punishment his body had taken and could at least understand his dedication. She pulled him down to her, reaching for his cock, unable to wait any longer.

"John," she whispered, swallowing the end of the word as he buried himself inside her, and she dug her fingers into the hard bands of muscle on his back. He thrust again, and she bit back a cry. "John, it's been so long." A moan. "So long."

"Then I will be gentle... Violet, I don't ever want to hurt you."

She smiled and brushed her fingers over his lips. "You don't need to be gentle with me, not here. If I am yours and you are mine while we're in this room, then we mustn't be afraid. I want whatever we could have if we had..." She trailed off, feeling suddenly a sharp pulse of emotion. He must have seen the hesitation in her eyes, for he immediately leaned down to kiss her and all thoughts of what might happen beyond this room fled her mind.

The rain continued to pound against the small windowpane. Inside the room, it was warm and cozy, and Violet was determined that they would have everything they had ever wanted this afternoon, because once they left, she would belong to Archie until an ocean came to separate them.

She clung to John, remembering what it was to revel in the weight of a man upon her, in the languid thrust of his hips, in the mounting pressure, and not feel separate from her body. She was here, experiencing every touch and sound and smell, and loving it. She had never felt worthier, and if she went home to Paris after this and never saw John again, she would remember this always. It was perfect. He was perfect. She clung to him as he thrust into her, wrapping her legs about him, never wanting to let go. When the ache became more than she could bear and she was hovering on the edge of another crashing release, he pulled his mouth from hers to whisper in her ear.

"Let me feel you, Violet – let me feel you take your pleasure." He rocked into her, sighing against her neck. "Violet, I—"

Whatever he had been about to say, Violet never heard as she shattered, coming apart in his arms and crying out as the sensation crested. He moved with her as his breath grew ragged against her neck before he withdrew with a sharp gasp to spend himself upon her belly.

For a long time they were quiet as the rain drummed upon the roof. When their breathing had slowed, John leaned off the edge of the bed, rummaging about in the pile of his discarded clothing and emerging with a handkerchief with which he gently wiped his seed from her belly, placing a soft kiss upon the curve of her breast as he did so.

Violet smiled as she wiggled down in the bedding, stretching her limbs like a contented cat as John passed a questing hand over the fullness of her hip. His lips played at her temple as she finally spoke into the quiet.

"I could stay here like this forever."

He kissed her earlobe, breathing softly against her neck.

"Don't tempt me, Violet." There was a pause and he sighed. "But I'm afraid our time is at an end. We must get you dressed and ready for tonight."

Violet had known they would have to part, but it didn't stop her letting out a small, disappointed sigh as he slipped off the bed before offering his hand. She took a fleeting moment to observe him, magnificent in his nakedness, before stepping to the floor. He gestured to the washbasin in the corner of the room, and she quickly bathed herself as he set the bed to rights and picked up the scattered dresses.

As she dried herself, he approached her with the gown of black and gold stripes and held it out with a small smile.

"Let's hope this one works."

Violet inclined her head, taking the gown from him and stepping behind the screen to draw her chemise back over her head before fastening her corset. When she stepped out from behind the divider, John had finished washing and dressing himself, with not a hint in his appearance that he had just spent the last hour ravaging her, and she warmed at the thought as he nodded in approval.

"Perfect," he said with a little smile and stepped towards her to press a quick kiss to her mouth. It took everything in Violet not to cling to him, suddenly fearful that if she let him go, she would never hold him again. *Silly,* she told herself as he turned away to gather up the discarded dresses. *Whatever happened in this room stays here. You're so close to getting back home. Do not get distracted now.*

With this admonishment to herself, Violet sat at the small, mirrored vanity to put her hair back in order, tucking in the few loose strands with a hairpin and carefully powdering her cheeks to diffuse the flush as she caught his gaze in the reflection.

"I'm afraid it's time to go back down to the box."

His expression was apologetic as she rose, drawing in a long breath, and following him back downstairs to the gaming floor. He stopped at one of the billiard tables to deposit her gown before waving towards one of the chairs at the bar.

"Have a seat; I'll fetch you something to eat before we go down."

Violet nodded. She was, indeed, famished and she waited as he disappeared into the next room before returning with a plate of bread and cheese, a cold meat pie and a bright red apple. As she sat to eat, he stepped behind the bar and poured her another glass of brandy, which he set down with a grin.

"I reckon another one of these is in order."

Violet chuckled as she chewed on a crust of the bread.

"I'd say a good deal more than one is in order, but I suppose I'll need my head about me."

John offered an encouraging smile as he reached out to touch her hand. Their eyes met, and Violet couldn't breathe for the weight of the unspoken words between them, wanting to talk about how the last hour they had just spent had been... earth-shattering... but knowing it would make no difference to what else had to happen tonight. John cleared his throat and withdrew his hand as Violet reached for the brandy and swallowed it back, letting it settle in the pit of her stomach as the corner of his mouth hitched up.

"All you need to do is stand by Archie's side and look pretty – Mr. Brill will handle the rest. As long as Archie agrees to the plan, we'll be set. I'll be able to collect all the evidence we need to charge him with extortion." He gave her a grim smile. "Twenty or so years of penal servitude should put an end to the Bruisers for good."

Violet could only nod as she took a bite of the meat pie,

barely tasting it as she swallowed. Scarcely two months ago, when she had turned to find Archie in le Chat Noir, that dark specter of her past, she had been sure that was the end for her. Archie would bring her back to Seven Dials and make her keep her promise, and Paris would be gone in the blink of an eye. But now... that didn't seem so certain anymore and she smiled across the bar.

"I'll be the perfect little moll. He might even think he has a chance with me," she added with a sly look, popping a piece of bread into her mouth. John grinned at her as she finished the last of her meat pie before letting out a sigh and nodding towards the back of the room.

"Archie'll be back soon. Time to go."

Violet swallowed back the last of her brandy before slipping off her stool and following John through the corridor that would take her back down to the box. This time, there was an end in sight, and Violet felt no trepidation as they made their way down the stairs into the void of darkness. This time, she would be ready for Archie and whatever he had in store for her. And when the loneliness and fear threatened to overwhelm her, she would carry the memory of the rainy afternoon spent making love with John Barrow, and none of that would matter.

SEVENTEEN

Edward Brill arrived at the Devil's Den at precisely the appointed meeting time of eight o'clock. John, in his role as security for the evening, greeted the other man when he stepped up to the door, neither giving any sign they recognized one another. When John guided him into the club where Archie held court with Tommy by his side, the Bruisers' leader let out a short laugh.

"I see you've come prepared, Brill," he remarked sarcastically as he nodded to the two huge men who had accompanied him into the club. By contrast, every fighter in the Bruisers' ranks had been gathered, and stood throughout the gaming floor, all watching Edward Brill and his two men. Every one of them had been itching for a brawl and there was a murmur of discontent as they saw that the leader of the Limehouse Gang clearly did not have the same intention. Archie held up a hand and the club fell silent. John took a step away from Edward to wait in the shadows, careful to keep his impassive gaze trained on a spot on the wall over Archie's head and away from Violet, who stood at his side, resplendent in the striped gown, her golden hair caught up in a loose chignon studded with a bejewelled comb. She was the loveliest thing he had ever seen; a spot of light in this smoky, dimly lit room, and he ached for her.

Edward Brill gave a crooked grin as he cast his gaze over the assembly before returning his attention to Archie.

"Cor, they are an eager-lookin' bunch, aren't they?" He gave a huff of laughter, and Archie frowned. "My apologies then. If they came for a row, they're gonna be disappointed. I'm here with an offer."

Archie stood a little straighter at this, crossing his arms over his massive chest as he regarded Edward.

"What offer?"

Edward let out a low chuckle and once again regarded the dozens of men assembled behind Archie before meeting his gaze once more.

"Perhaps there's somewhere we can speak that's a little more... private?"

Archie's eyes narrowed, as though contemplating whether this was a trap of some kind. He glanced over at his brother, who gave an almost imperceptible shrug of his shoulders before looking back at Brill and tilting his head.

"Alright then. You lot," he said, glancing back at the men gathered behind him. "Stay here." He gestured to John, who reached out to close his hand around Edward's arm. The two hulking men who accompanied him stepped forward, but their boss waved them away.

"This way," John said, before giving him a little shove towards the corridor at the back of the room. Edward dutifully followed along with his two companions. Archie led the way, his hand clamped down on Violet's shoulder as he pushed her into his office. Edward's two men waited in the corridor as the door closed shut behind them, and it was just Archie, taking the seat behind his desk, with Tommy and Violet standing beside him, and Edward taking the seat opposite as John stood sentry by the door.

"So," Archie began, leaning back in his chair and spreading his hands over his stomach, "what's Edward Brill got to offer me?"

Edward allowed a small, amused smile as he deftly matched Archie's posture.

"The docks."

Archie's brow rose at this, and John took the momentary distraction to let his carefully disinterested gaze fall upon Violet, standing on the far side of the room with Tommy's big hand resting upon her shoulder, and noting the firm set of her jaw, the way her hands were fisted at her sides, her lingering fragrance – as always, like a summer's day, even though the rain continued to pour outside. Her eyes met his, but her expression never changed, and she soon looked away. It took every ounce of his concentration to focus on the conversation being held now, and not think about how just hours ago they had been upstairs in Bess's room, and he had been buried inside her, hearing her sharp cries of pleasure, drinking in her scent and the softness of her skin. And now... he couldn't imagine not having that in his life after she left. A dull ache sprang up in his chest and he had to force his attention back to the two men who sat facing one another. Archie was chuckling at Edward's suggestion.

"The docks?" Archie's tone was disbelieving. "Are you serious?"

Edward cleared his throat now and sat up in his chair to fix the Bruisers' leader with a pointed look.

"I know you think I'm the one what turned you in. It weren't me." He gave a dark little smile. "Wish it had been."

Archie's mouth twisted in a sneer before Edward continued, seeming oblivious to the other man's reaction. "Two of my men are dead now. We both know that was you."

To this, Archie said nothing, and John caught Violet's flinch at these words. Edward continued.

"I don't want no more violence. I know you've been after

my patch since before you went away. And I know what you'll do to get it." His expression darkened as he looked over the desk at Archie, who responded with a smug grin. Edward let out a heavy sigh and leaned back once more, as though resigned. "I'll give it to you. The protection racket. No one will challenge you, I can promise you that. But," he added in a sharp tone, pointing a finger across the desk, "this is under the condition that there's no fightin'. You'll get your money, and we won't stand in your way. My businesses are off the table, but the rest of it is yours. Mark my words, though, Archie Neville." A short, fraught silence fell before Edward spoke again, his voice low and simmering with warning. "If so much as one person in any part of our territory gets hurt, I will fuckin' kill you."

Archie's smug grin never faded, but Tommy's broad shoulders tensed, and he stepped forward in defense of his brother, who waved him off.

"And what's in this for you?" Archie asked. Edward tilted his head as he contemplated the question.

"I know I won't talk you out of keepin' to your territory. I know you want what I had. And my people don't want a war. If this is what it takes to keep them safe, then that's what we'll do." He glanced over at Violet now, as if he were just noticing her presence, and the corner of his mouth turned up in a leer.

"Is this the one you was lookin' for?" He let out a small laugh as his gaze raked down her figure before he nodded appreciatively. "I can see why you wanted her found. Fine bit o' tail, that is." He turned his attention back to Archie now, whose expression had grown ominously dark. "Tell you what, you throw in a swive with her, I'll even let you use my warehouse for your little fights."

Violet's face turned a convincing shade of red as she glared across the desk at Edward who smirked as Archie's hands curled into massive fists upon the desktop. His voice snapped with rage when he spoke.

"You look at her again and they'll be findin' a third body in Covent Garden. Not even your fuckin' mother will be able to identify it after I get through with you."

The air grew still inside the room and Edward's smirk quickly faded, replaced by a threatening scowl, and John felt compelled to step forward and place a warning hand upon his shoulder. The tension mounted as the silence drew out until Edward blinked, and the scowl disappeared. He leaned back in his chair once more and John stepped away.

"Do you want the deal or not?"

Archie observed him for a moment, the corner of his mouth turned up before he looked over at John.

"Whaddaya think, Johnny?"

John glanced over at him, startled, but he did not fail to notice Tommy's reaction. His head snapped up and his eyes widened in shock that his older brother, his leader, had failed to turn to his long-time right-hand man for advice. John, for his part, did not react beyond a small shrug.

"All that money just to keep them other gangs out of the East End? Cor, we could do that standin' on our heads," was John's reply as Tommy's seething glare bored into him.

"Do you not think he's up to—" Tommy began to object, but Archie cut him a sharp look of warning and his brother's mouth clamped shut as he took a reluctant step back. Archie returned his attention to Edward with a cunning grin.

"How do I know I can trust you? We ain't exactly on good terms, are we?"

Edward sighed. "You can believe me or not, but I don't want a bloody turf war. Better my people should give you money than lose their lives. Just understand, I don't want this and I ain't doin' it for you. I'm doin' it 'cause I know you're a selfish bastard who'll burn down the East End to get what you want. And since I can't fight you and your crew of animals without a lot of pointless bloody deaths, this is the next best solution."

Archie seemed to mull this over before he responded.

"And what's to stop you goin' back on your word?" His lips curled in a nasty sneer as he leaned forward in his seat. "Because if any part of what you're offerin' ain't true, I'll fuckin' annihilate the whole lot of you."

Edward's expression didn't change; he simply stared back at Archie across the desk before shrugging.

"No goin' back. Everyone's already been informed, it's all yours. I told you; you just make sure no one gets hurt, and no one will stand in your way."

A long silence fell over the room and John found himself holding his breath, praying for Archie to take the bait. He risked a glance over at Violet and saw that she, too, was watching Archie as though waiting for his reply. John vowed to himself then that he would get her out of this place, and so help him, if this didn't work, he would find another way. She would not spend one minute longer in this place than necessary, and he breathed out a long sigh when Archie finally rose from his chair and extended his hand.

"Boys'll be disappointed they didn't get their fight."

Edward stood and took the proffered hand with a little smirk.

"Offer's still on the table for the warehouse," he said, winking over at Violet before he laughed and waved a hand at Archie. "I know, I know, she's yours. Bit skinny for my tastes, anyway." He turned before Archie could reply and opened the office door.

"We're done here, boys," he said to the two men who waited in the hall for him. "Let's go." And without another word to the people inside the room, he disappeared down the hall.

Archie let out a disgusted snort before shaking his head and turning to Violet, his face now wreathed in a smile.

"You see, Violet? I told you I'd get you the docks."

And this time, Violet did not sneer or scoff. Instead, she

looked at Archie now in mild surprise before murmuring, "Yes, you did," and dropping her gaze to the floor, a small furrow between her brows. Archie was practically triumphant, but Tommy was scowling as he pushed Violet to the side to interject.

"Archie, we killed two of his men – do you really think he's just gonna hand over control of the East End to us?"

John watched, wary, as Archie turned to his brother, his broad face growing red with anger. "Yes, because he's smart enough to know that there'll be a lot more if he doesn't. This is what I've always wanted, Tommy. If you've a problem with it, feel free to see yourself back to the boxin' ring. Johnny and me'll take care of it. Won't we?" he added, now turning to face John, who was ready for this question, who had been planning for it, and answered with the simplest of ease, "Of course, Archie."

Tommy glared at John before he swore viciously and stormed from the room, slamming the door behind him. John looked back for a moment at the door as it rattled shut, frowning, before he slowly turned to the Bruisers' leader who was shaking his head.

"Don't know what's got into him," he scoffed as he resumed his seat and took up a bottle of whisky to fill the glass on his desk. "No bloody vision, that's what." He swallowed back the drink and jerked his head towards Violet. "Take her back down to the box, wouldya, Johnny? Lots to plan for, now."

His grin was victorious, and he filled his glass again as John dutifully stepped forward and took Violet by the arm. She put on another admirable display of resistance as he dragged her from the room and back down the hall. They did not speak until they reached the bottom of the stairs and John turned to her with an encouraging smile.

"We did it, Violet," he whispered, bending to press a quick, fierce kiss to her lips. Just as he started to pull away, though, her fingers clamped down on the back of his head and she held him there, opening her mouth to his, her tongue sweeping over his, her moan swallowed by him folding her up in his arms, reveling in the heat of her, the scent of her – he would remember it until his dying day. A summer afternoon would pale by comparison.

When the kiss softened, and she drew back, he found he could not let her go, and he held her a moment longer, touching his lips to her forehead before finally releasing her. John forced another smile onto his face as he reached up to slide the bolt aside to open the door, and she said nothing as he stepped inside to light the lamp before following him. When he turned to face her, she took a deep breath and gave a little smile.

"I think... I think when this is over, I'd like you to come visit me in Paris. That would be... nice."

John grinned as a knot formed in his stomach, something between anticipation and appreciation, that this woman – this wonderful, beautiful, resilient woman – was welcoming him to stay in her life; even knowing that they would soon be separated, that they remained on two different paths. But perhaps this would have to be enough; the occasional letter or visit before she inevitably met some charming Frenchman who would sweep her off her feet. He swallowed at the thought before answering.

"I'd like that." He cleared his throat and glanced over her shoulder towards the door. "I should be going. Archie will want to begin planning." He took a step towards her to lay an encouraging hand upon her arm. "We're getting closer. You'll be out of here soon."

She nodded, her cheeks flushed, her eyes shining. It took everything in him at that moment not to kiss her again and, instead, step past her to the door.

"I'll be back as soon as I can. Goodnight, Violet."

"Goodnight, John."

EIGHTEEN

Knowing now that the plan was in motion – that Archie would begin his unimpeded expansion into the East End – made the next two weeks just bearable for Violet. She still had her sketchbook, which blessedly passed the hours trapped in her little room, and John had even convinced Archie to let her have a book or two. But at night, alone in the darkness, she felt herself crawling out of her skin, trying desperately not to think of the four walls surrounding her. Instead, she would draw upon the memory of her afternoon with John in Bess's room, how the rain had streaked down the windowpane as he had bent over her in the flickering candlelight to press his mouth to hers, to skim his hands over her flesh, taking her in one, hard thrust and dashing any doubts she might have harboured. Those memories, and his brief visits in the morning to bring her breakfast, were all that were getting her through each long, interminable day.

On the fifteenth day, as she lay upon the hard, narrow bed, staring up at the low ceiling and wondering if she and John would ever have the chance to be together again, the door opened. She rose with a long sigh, her breath catching as Archie stepped into the room, followed by John, who once again braced himself in the doorway and stared at some invisible spot on the opposite wall. Violet was very careful not to glance his way, keeping her sullen gaze fixed on Archie, instead. He was not smirking today, or thunderous with anger, as he usually was when he deigned to visit her down here in the cellars, happy to let her rot away until she agreed to keep her promise. He knew she was breaking; she could hardly hide the desperation which threatened to burst from her with each passing day. No, today he looked resigned, if a little resentful as he turned to face her, his thumbs hooked in his pockets.

"Been nearly a month now, Violet," he began, giving his head a slow shake. "How long are you gonna keep this up?"

Violet said nothing as she glared up at him, and he let out a heavy sigh before lifting his shoulders.

"I've been in a generous mood lately and thinkin' that you just need a little push. So, I've decided to put you to work – let you out of here for a bit."

Violet couldn't stop the widening of her eyes, and his expression immediately darkened as he pointed a stern finger at her chest, dropping his voice to speak in a low, threatening tone.

"Now don't go gettin' any notions, Violet – this ain't me lettin' you off the hook. You still made a promise, and you're still gonna keep it." He cleared his throat and stepped back. "That said, since you once did me a kindness, I'm gonna return the favour" – he paused and arched an expectant brow – "with the understandin' that you have until the end of the year to keep that promise. If not..." Archie met her gaze, then, as he let the reminder of his threat to Della hang in the air between them. Violet's chest grew cold, and she fought back a scowl, nodding instead as she looked down to her feet.

"Thank you, Archie."

He sniffed in reply, as though not entirely pleased with the bargain he had offered before he waved a careless hand at John, who remained silent and stoic in the doorway.

"Johnny here says we need help up in the bar, cleanin' it and so on. He's gonna be keepin' an eye on you for me whilst I'm expandin' into the East End. And Violet..."

She looked up and there was a menacing gleam in his eyes.

"Don't you even think about runnin' off."

Archie's tone was sharp, and she shivered beneath his baleful glare, nodding quickly to appease him. He held her gaze for a few, tense moments before turning without another word and motioning for John, who caught her eye before turning to leave to give her a quick, knowing look. She let out a shuddering breath as the door closed behind the two men and lowered herself to the bed. A giddy laugh threatened to burst from her at the thought of finally being released from this room, but she swallowed it back as the weight of Archie's new deadline grew heavy upon her. She closed her eyes, practically hearing the tick of the clock he had set, but quickly reminded herself that it wouldn't matter in the end. John was prepared; he would be gathering all his evidence now, and she would finally get out of here. That night, she slept better than she had in weeks.

Archie was true to his word. Each morning, either Tommy or John would arrive to take Violet from the box and put her to work in the club, wiping down the bar and the tables from the night before, scrubbing dishes in the scullery or peeling potatoes in the back of the kitchens. She grinned as she worked, thrilled to simply be looking at more than four white walls, and if she was alone with John, he would smile back at her, and her heart would flutter as though she were some lovesick schoolgirl.

And then, one chill October morning, John came down to escort her up to the club, as he so often did, but this time, they did not stay to complete the usual chores.

"We have an errand to run," John said to her with a smile as he opened the front doors and gestured for her to go ahead of him. She frowned, confused.

"Surely Archie's not lettin' me leave?"

John shrugged as she slowly walked by him and out into the brisk morning air.

"I'm to pick up some supplies for the kitchen and I said I would need someone to help. He suggested you go with me." He gave her a wry smile as he set his hat upon his head. "I think he's trying to butter you up. Been asking me if you're finally warming up to him."

Violet fell into step beside him as she pulled her dolman coat tighter about her throat to ward off the cold. "And what did you tell him?"

"I said you seemed happy enough, that I even caught you humming to yourself one day. That seemed to please him."

Violet gave a disdainful sniff as they headed towards the market. "Well on my way to fallin' head over heels, I am," she said in a scathing voice as John let out a low chuckle.

Even away from the club and Covent Garden, John and Violet never once allowed the mask to slip; she remained his surly captive and he her put-upon minder. Archie still ruled over this territory and had eyes everywhere. But as they made their way through the narrow alleys and rows of tenement housing which would take them to the market, they found themselves alone in a small courtyard surrounded by brick walls. John did not pause as they made their way through to the gate embedded in the wall on the far side, but he did take the opportunity to reach out and touch Violet, gently, upon the small of her back. She did not break stride as they reached the gate and he pulled it open with a deafening squeal, but she did smile as he gestured for her to go ahead of him.

"I ran into Cora after the fight last night," he said as they passed through the gate. Violet instinctively glanced down at his hands and saw the bruised, scraped knuckles – she would be very much relieved when he no longer had to engage in such brutal fighting to maintain his cover in the gang. She spoke as she looked back up at him.

"How is she? I'm afraid I got rather bad at writin' to her."

He waited until they crossed through a jumbled intersection busy with horses and carts and streetsweepers before he replied.

"She's well. I've been helping her with a few of the girls who wanted to go to school. One of them has even left to do the books at a brewery in Rotherhithe."

Violet glanced over at him, impressed.

"Really? How'd you convince them to do that?"

One side of John's mouth turned up as they stopped in front of a little shop, its grubby window filled with pots and pans and other cooking supplies.

"Oh, they didn't need convincing. They wanted to go. I just made sure they had clothes and books... there's a charity in Whitechapel that helps women *'in need of saving'*" – he emphasized the last words with a knowing smile as he looked over at her – "and I'll send anyone their way who's looking to get out."

"Why, aren't you just a knight in shinin' armour?" Violet said with a wink as John reached for the doorlatch. He allowed a small, conspiratorial smile as he swung the door open.

"Would you like to wait out here?" he asked.

"Aren't you afraid I'll run off?" she replied with an arch of her brow. He shook his head.

"Violet the prisoner has far too much sense to run off from Archie Neville again."

She sighed. "Yes, unfortunately, she does."

John offered a sympathetic look as he stepped inside and left her to watch the people bustling past. For a while, she was content to sit on the steps outside the shop and let the world pass her by, happy to have more than four white walls to look at.

Eventually, a spark of inspiration struck her, and she reached into her pocket to withdraw her sketchbook and a pencil, opening to a blank page, and raising her gaze to the little butcher shop across the street. She liked their sign – a fattened pig carved into wood, surmounted by the name of the shop in letters painted in bold red: Smith & Sons Butchers. She began to sketch out the front of the shop, with its big, diamond-paned front window and awning of green and white stripes. Two men in aprons were outside the shop chatting, and Violet stared at them for a moment, contemplating whether to add them to the drawing before shaking her head and sketching the door instead. She was just finishing up the little figure of the pig when a bell rang behind her and John stepped out of the shop and came to stand beside her. She glanced up at him and he nodded down at her drawing.

"That's lovely," he remarked, and she allowed the smallest of smiles, always aware that Archie's men were all over this neighbourhood and it would not do for it to look as though she were becoming chummy with her jailer. "Ready to go?"

She frowned as she stood, tucking the book back into her pocket. "What about the supplies?"

"Shipment hasn't arrived yet."

Violet's stomach twisted as he held out a hand to help her up, and she took it, swallowing. "I didn't think we'd have to go back so soon."

His mouth quirked as he contemplated her for a moment before he flashed a quick smile.

"Come on," he said, before taking her hand once more and pulling her back into the alley which ran parallel to the shop. He drew her along to the end, stopping when they reached the mews which cut behind the row of shops. Across the way were the backs of the tenements, and the mews was filled with the shouts of women at work hanging their clean laundry along clotheslines that crisscrossed between the buildings, and the shrieks and laughter of the children who ran about them. John glanced down at her with a smile.

"Head down," he said with a nod, and she gave a quick grin, turning to face him while he shoved his bowler hat over his deep golden hair before inclining his head across the way to another alley which cut through the houses.

"Just a moment," he murmured, glancing around the corner to the gathering of women and children to be sure no one was watching before he whispered, "Now!" and tightened his grip on her hand. They darted across the mews and reached the safety of the alley without any notice. Violet was laughing now, holding her gloved hand over her mouth to stifle the sound while John grinned down at her. He looked up one last time as though checking to see if they were being watched, then nodded, seeming satisfied they were alone.

"This way," he finally said, leading her through the alley and out onto Shaftesbury Avenue. He didn't pause, pulling her out onto the street, instead, to blend in with the crowds bustling along the pavement. They quickly made their way across Charing Cross Road, darting between hansom cabs and drays loaded down with kegs, before making a sharp turn up Greek Street. Finally, John stopped before a shop with a bright blue awning, and he turned to smile at her.

"Thought you might like a taste of home," he said, nodding towards the letters painted on the windowpane – *Maison Bertaux, Patisserie*. Violet's heart soared as she stepped closer to peer inside at the astonishing selection of pastries – éclairs and tarts, croissants and palmiers. She was grinning, giddy, as she turned back to John, who had already opened the door and was gesturing for her to go inside. "Whatever you want."

"Oh, John, this is wonderful," she exclaimed as she stepped inside, greeted by the warm, buttery scent of puff pastry. He came to stand beside her as she bent to examine the selection in the massive glass cases.

"I'm told the owner fled here after the fall of the Paris Commune," he said as her gaze roamed over glossy glazed fruits and tarts piled high with whipped cream.

"One of my friends used to paint the communards during their reign. Beautiful work – I bought one of her sketches." Violet faltered for a moment, thinking of Archie's cruel words. *Your things are gone. You know that.*

She gritted her teeth against the flush of anger as John touched a sympathetic hand to her arm before shaking her head. She would not think of Archie this morning, and she stood and nodded towards the girl who was standing behind the counter, setting out golden croissants from a baking tray. It was a beautiful little shop; a taste of Paris dropped right in the middle of Soho, with pale marble counters and crystal chandeliers and silvered mirror on the wall behind the counter, inscribed with the words *Liberté, Egalité, Fraternité.* The plain red flag of the Paris Commune had been strung up over the door to the kitchen, and Violet grinned before greeting the shopgirl in French.

"Good morning, mademoiselle. May we have two *pains au chocolat?* And two of the Dijon squares?"

"And two cups of tea, please," John added, meeting Violet's gaze. "We can eat here. There's no hurry."

Violet breathed a small sigh of gratitude – she would do anything to avoid going back to the box and its bare walls. More than that, though... she had found herself anticipating every minute she could spend with John. At first, it had been out of relief. He was not Archie, or Tommy, and that was enough to be grateful for his presence. But now, after that rainy afternoon in Bess's room, she couldn't stop thinking of him. Occasionally, that little voice would slip into her consciousness, to whisper that he was the same as the others... he had fucked her, and what need had he for her now? After all, he still maintained his demeanor of polite amiability. He was never short, nor distant, nor cold. *But he's never said he cares for you; he's never asked you to stay. He will never love you.*

That voice had kept her up for far more nights than she cared to admit. But just when the voice began to grow louder, John would always do something to prove it wrong. He got her books. He always brought her good food: sneaking her meat pies from the club, or little biscuits, or fresh fruit, or the occasional sandwich. And, most importantly, she was sure her being let out of the box was partly his doing; a hint or suggestion made to Archie which had convinced her would-be fiancé that he might persuade her if he gave her just a bit more freedom.

And so, she had managed to quieten that little voice, telling herself that he was simply being professional, keeping them safe from Archie's wrath should they ever be discovered. She had even considered, in a moment of carefree joy, when he had opened the door to the club to indicate that she was to go with him, asking him to join her in Paris. Not to visit. To stay. Even the thought had made her chest grow warm, envisioning him living with her in her little flat in Montmartre, waking up with the sun dappling the peach-coloured walls of her bedroom, sliding her hands over his chest, feeling the hard ridges of his muscles, and lower, making love with him before heading to her little studio. John could surely find work with the police or gendarmerie... if he wanted.

Violet blinked away the doubts as she took the seat he pulled out for her at one of the small, marble-topped tables, smiling as he set down a plate with the pastries. The girl behind the counter arrived shortly thereafter with cups and saucers, and a small pot of tea.

John was careful to take the seat which looked out onto the street, and smiled as he lifted the pot to fill her cup.

"We're very close now, Violet. Archie and Tommy have already shaken down a whole section of businesses in Wapping, and they're moving into Limehouse next. I'm already collecting evidence – names, dates, everything." He glanced around the shop with a smile. "Soon, you'll be back to the real thing."

Violet grinned as she bit into one of the Dijon squares, a cheesy, mustardy little tart, and closed her eyes as she savoured the treat.

"Mmm, this is as close to the real thing as I could've hoped for." She opened her eyes once more to find him watching her, the corner of his mouth hitched up. "Thank you, John. Truly. You've made this whole horrible ordeal bearable."

His smile faded as he set down his cup. "I've tried... I felt so badly that you had to be involved at all, I wanted to make sure that you were comfortable at the very least."

Violet shrugged and met his gaze, holding it for a moment before she replied, direct and unblinking, "It hasn't been all bad."

John's lips parted and his eyes grew dark as he stared at her across the little table, the steam from the tea curling up between them. "No," he finally said in a low, husky voice, his mouth turning up. "It hasn't."

Violet bit her lip and her skin tingled as though in anticipation of his touch. Her fingers inched towards his hand, stopping only when a bell rang and the door to the patisserie opened. A woman in navy plaid along with two little girls stepped into the shop amid a gust of biting autumn wind, and Violet pulled her hand back, swallowing the rising heat. John gave a quick smile and cleared his throat as he lifted his cup once more and took a quick sip.

"I've one more stop to make before we head back to the Devil's Den, if you don't mind."

Violet shook her head as she sat up straighter in her chair. "No, not at all. Anythin' to avoid goin' back to that bloody room."

He grinned as he popped the last bite of the *pain au chocolat* into his mouth, swallowed it back with the dregs of his tea, and rose from his seat to offer his hand. Violet quickly emptied her own cup and took it, brushing the crumbs from her lap. She drew on her gloves as he moved ahead to open the door to the tinkling of the bell. Once outside, he gave her a quick, knowing smile before settling his expression into that of unduly burdened minder, and she into resentful captive as they made their way back into the twist of streets that formed Covent Garden.

Passing through the tenements, they found themselves on a narrow street, walking by a greengrocer with stalls of fresh fruits and vegetables on display outside. John paused and turned to her.

"Do you want to pick out a few things?" he asked, gesturing to a table covered in shiny yellow apples.

"Oh, yes," she replied, snatching up one of the apples before wandering further along to have a look at the oranges. John nodded and moved further up the street to a boy standing next to a stack of newspapers. He offered the boy a coin and was handed a paper as Violet turned away to pluck up one of the oranges, examining it for a moment before moving on to have a look at a display of pears. She picked out two, saving one for John, and when she turned to show him, saw that he was chatting with the newspaper boy, a lad of ten or eleven. The boy was smiling as he pulled a little book from his pocket and held it up to show John, who nodded in approval. Violet watched them for a moment, her eyes narrowed, before she shoved the fruit into her pockets and snatched out her sketchbook once more. She drew quickly, capturing the boy's bright smile and threadbare little coat, and was just adding in the lamppost he stood beside when John laid a friendly hand on the boy's head, ruffling his hair before waving goodbye. When he turned and came towards her, John was smiling, and she tucked away her sketchbook and held out one of the pears as he approached.

"Who was that?" she asked as he took the fruit, stepping

away to hand a few coins over to the shopkeeper who was sweeping off the front steps. John bit into it as he joined her once more and started walking with her towards Covent Garden.

"Oh, that's William. I got used to seeing him every morning on the way to sparring practice and asked if he was going to school. He said his mum had him out selling papers since his father died last winter. He's learning his letters and wanted to show me the primer he's reading."

"Oh... the poor lad," Violet said as she tucked the pear and the orange into her pockets before taking a bite of her apple. John nodded.

"I hated seeing someone so young having to work just to keep a roof over his family's head, like I did." He glanced at her. "Like so many of us did."

Violet said nothing as she took another bite of her apple.

"So, I spoke with his mum, told her if he was able to go to school during the day and only sell papers on Sundays, I'd make sure he got whatever he made for selling them during the week." He sighed and bit into the pear, chewing before he continued. "I can't do it for all of them, of course. But he's a good lad, got a good head on his shoulders. Once I'm promoted, I'll be able to do so much more."

He nodded as they crossed the street, and Violet thought back to the boy's wide smile and how proudly he had shown off his book. The image she had had of John with her in her little flat in Paris suddenly seemed like an impossibility, for how could she possibly ask him to abandon the people he seemed so eager to help? How could she ask him to give that up? It was with that question in her mind that the day suddenly became a little less bright.

NINETEEN

They didn't have far to go before John was stopping at the door to a nondescript warehouse. He didn't knock; he simply opened the door and gestured for her to go ahead of him. It was cool and dark inside, now that the sun had slipped below the roofs of the surrounding buildings, and only a bare glimmer of light shone through the windows tucked up below the ceiling high above. A boxing ring, surrounded by a handful of mismatched chairs and a scattering of wooden crates, had been set up to the left of the door, and Violet turned to John with a frown as they made their way past the ring to the door on the far side of the room.

"Is this Archie's warehouse?" she asked as he opened that door as well, revealing a darkened office. He nodded as he turned up one of the gas lamps which sat upon a row of metal filing cabinets.

"Yes... it's where we do most of our training and sparring."

Violet swallowed back the sudden twinge of anxiety turning her stomach.

"Is... is he here?"

John smiled, shaking his head as he took a key from his pocket and opened one of the drawers.

"No, he's off in Limehouse with Tommy today. Took Alexander and the Devil with them, too, so there's no sparring practice, either."

Violet glanced back out at the warehouse as she drew in a shaking breath. "You sure?"

John was grinning as he turned to her with a ledger book in his hands before setting it down on the desk.

"We wouldn't be here if I wasn't," he said as he gestured to the chair nearby before taking a seat behind the desk. She slowly pulled it out and sat, watching as he withdrew a small notepad and pen from his coat pocket and set them on the desk. He opened the ledger book and began writing something in the notepad. She glanced down at his scribbled handwriting, then back up to see his brow furrowed in concentration.

"Part of your investigation?" she ventured to guess, and he nodded as he underlined something, the pen scratching upon the paper.

"Yes." He looked up at her with a crooked grin. "I wasn't allowed in here alone until I brought you in, so... I suppose I must thank you."

She let out a small exhalation of laughter as she pulled her chair close to peer down at the ledger. Neatly drawn columns had been filled in with rows of numbers, and she frowned.

"The bookmakers?"

He nodded again. "I can't take the ledgers with me, or they'll become suspicious, but I can gather all the numbers and the names of who's placing bets." He glanced up at her. "I won't be long, if you want to look around."

"Yes, I suppose I will." She stood and wandered back into the warehouse, gradually making her way over to the boxing ring. Violet closed her eyes as she reached out to trail her fingers along the rope, recalling her first encounter with John Barrow in that cellar at the Fox and Friar. She supposed she had wanted him from that very moment, when she had watched him fighting from the shadows, his muscles shuddering with each impact, his skin slick with sweat, but never had she imagined she would have him. More than that, she had never imagined she would want... more. She opened her eyes suddenly and then, on a whim, stepped between the ropes. Into his territory. It was thrilling, almost, to stand where he fought, to remember the sensation of those same muscles beneath her fingers, the skin damp with sweat, not from fighting, but from pleasuring her. It made her short of breath, and she swallowed.

The sound of the door to the office opening made her turn as he emerged into the shadows. He was smiling as he came towards the ring.

"Looking to spar?" he asked as he stopped before the ropes, his tone teasing, and she laughed.

"Oh, I never learned any proper moves."

He raised a brow as he crossed his arms over his chest and settled his weight onto one leg.

"Would you like to?"

Oh god. Something in his tone made every muscle in her body clench and she drew in a shaking breath.

"I suppose... it couldn't hurt."

John's smile was wicked as he slipped between the ropes before slowly removing his overcoat.

"Well... it might. A little."

Violet bit her lip as she reached up to shrug out of her dolman, her gaze never leaving his as he began unbuttoning his waistcoat, then rolling up his sleeves to reveal forearms corded with muscle. Her heart was racing as he reached out with a grin and took the garment from her to lay over the ropes before he loosened his tie and turned to her now in just his shirtsleeves. It took everything in her to banish the image of him kneeling at her feet, her leg propped up on his shoulder, gazing down at him as he licked and suckled her until she came apart.

She coughed to dispel the memory as he set his hands upon

her shoulders to turn her to face him, then trailed his fingers down the length of her arms to grasp her wrists. Slowly, he pulled her left arm out, away from her body, and cupped her hand in his. He smiled as he curled her fingers into her palm, then folded her thumb across her fist.

"Clench your fist, not too tight," he said, then gently rotated her wrist. "Keep your arm relaxed... you'll be too slow if you tense it up."

Once he had her left arm positioned to his liking, he took the other one and tucked it closer to her body, across her chest, making those fingers into another fist. Her heart was hammering against her ribs as he withdrew, contemplating her for a moment before putting a finger to his chin as his gaze traveled down her body.

"I'm not sure how this will work with those," he finally said, gesturing to the skirts of the pale green sprigged gown which had previously been declared too modest for the meeting between Archie and Edward Brill, but was quite suitable for a day of running errands. She glanced down.

"Can I not box in skirts?" she asked, glancing up at him with a raised brow. He shrugged.

"I can't see your footwork, but I suppose we'll manage."

And that was when Violet said something that shocked even her.

"I could take my gown off."

His lips parted in surprise, but the shock did not last long. The corner of his mouth curled up as his eyes flickered down before meeting hers again.

"Yes, that would be very helpful."

Violet's chest was ablaze now as she slowly unbuttoned the prim little bodice before casting it to the edge of the ring. Her skirts and petticoats followed, and she stood before him in only her undergarments. His gaze, turbulent with lust, held hers as he took her arms and carefully placed her back in the guard position before nudging her left leg forward.

"Put your weight on your toes," he said in a low voice, as he backed away to stand opposite her, raising his own arms to mirror her stance. He grinned at her determined expression before reaching out again to take her left hand in his and pointing to her knuckles.

"Keep your wrist straight – all your force should move in a straight line, so you take less of the impact. Hit with these," he said, touching where her fingers bent nearest her thumb, "not these," he finished, pointing to her first row of knuckles. "Unless you want to break your hand," he added with a smile.

"We'll start with the simplest move, a straight strike. You're going to keep your fist vertical," he said, reaching out to make a small adjustment to the hand she held aloft, "and lean into it, putting weight on your lead foot. Now, pull back, and imagine a straight line from shoulder to elbow to wrist to hand" – he demonstrated the strike in slow motion – "and try to hit me in the nose." Violet held back a smile as she did as he instructed, drawing her arm back, mindful of keeping her fist clenched and her wrist straight, before throwing it forward again. He caught her fist easily in his hand, smiling as he released her.

"Again. Keep your arm up – you're shorter than me, you need to account for that."

She nodded and repeated the punch, stopped once more by his parry.

"Again."

And on she went, drawing back and throwing her fist at him as he made small adjustments to her stance. Just as the muscles in her arm and back began to burn, he pointed to the arm she had been holding against her chest.

"Time to switch."

"What?" she gasped, dropping her left arm and panting.

"You should be able to lead with either hand; you need to

practise on both sides. Here," he said, stepping closer to rearrange her stance, drawing her other arm out, touching her boot with his to adjust the foot she led with. She caught his gaze as he nudged her shoulder back, and it took only that brief instance for an inferno to erupt inside her, burning and searing, as he slowly stepped away to resume his stance opposite her.

"Hit me," he said in a low voice. She couldn't think now, so distracted she was by the pull of desire between her thighs as she drew her arm back and struck out once more. He parried easily, but he was not smiling anymore. He was, instead, looking upon her as though he might devour her, as though she were an oasis in a desert and he was dying of thirst.

"Again," he said, and she struck him. He caught her fist and pushed it back. "Again."

In short order, her other arm was burning with fatigue and a bead of sweat trailed down her spine. She was panting as she drew back before connecting with the flat of his palm. He smiled as she leaned back to set herself up again.

"That was good – if it had been my nose, there'd be some damage."

Violet's chest swelled with pride, and she jabbed at him again, catching the edge of his hand this time. It unbalanced her, and she couldn't pull back, stumbling into him instead as the momentum of the punch threw her forward.

She didn't know how it happened – his arms came around her to catch her, and then he was kissing her, his fingers sliding into her hair as her palms skated up the length of his chest. Her corset came off at some point, she didn't know when, and his hands were cupping her breasts through her chemise, thumbs sliding over her nipples. She couldn't think again; she was drowning, pulling him into her, tasting him, breathing in his scent, as he pushed her back, up against the padded post at the corner of the ring.

"Violet," was his fierce whisper, spoken against her temple

as his hips pressed into hers, letting her feel the full effect of his arousal. "Do you want me to stop?"

Stop? Was he mad?

"Don't you dare," she breathed against his roving mouth, sighing and tilting her head back as he trailed hot kisses over the line of her collarbone, until he was flicking his tongue over her nipple through the fabric of her chemise. She moaned as her fingers curled into his shoulders, and suddenly, his hands were on her thighs, dragging up the hem of her chemise, and he lifted one of her legs up around him before fumbling with the buttons of his trousers. He freed his cock, pulling her hips against his and entering her in one, smooth thrust.

A long, shuddering sigh of relief rasped out of Violet's mouth as he held her to him, finding a rhythm that had them both gasping as he caught her lips in a frantic kiss. She clung to his shoulder with one arm, and the post behind her with the other, delirious with sensation as he tilted her hips to access some well of pleasure deep inside her, his fingers digging into her flesh until she combusted, her shout of release swallowed by his mouth closing over hers. Her legs shook with the force of her climax as he lifted her other leg up around his hips so he was holding her, pinning her against the post, thrusting into her as her muscles continued to pulse around him. He released her with a groan to spill his seed upon her bunched-up chemise, his breath rasping against the curve of her neck.

They were gasping as Violet stood between his arms, outstretched to find support on the ropes, her legs quaking as she closed her eyes, trying to find her equilibrium once more. His hand was on her cheek, turning her face up to his so he could touch his mouth to hers. Violet sighed against his lips as he pulled back and met her gaze.

"Violet," he said again, then smiled softly. "We must be mad."

Violet rose to kiss him again – God, she loved the taste of

him. "We'd only be mad to stop. Don't you want more?" she asked, dropping her voice to a seductive whisper as she touched her mouth to his ear. "Don't you want me?"

The words were said partly to hear them from his own mouth – *yes, Violet, I want you, I care for you. I want to be with you* – and partly because it brought her such pleasure to feel his muscles tense and his breath grow short. He released the hem of her chemise to fall back down to her knees before he took her arms in his hands.

"Want you? Violet... you never leave my thoughts. I cannot sleep most nights for want of you." His voice was a low, raw rasp as he bent to press his mouth to her jaw. "Every morning when I walk into that room with you, it takes everything in me not to bend you over and—" He swallowed back the rest of the words with a strangled moan, kissing her again instead as heat flooded her belly. She sighed as he drew back, shaking his head, his brow furrowed. Violet's shoulders fell as she looked up at him and met a gaze full of regret.

"But I am responsible for you while we're in this... and it is my duty to keep you safe." He tried an encouraging smile as he lifted a hand to brush back the stray tendril which had fallen over her cheek. "I promised I would get you back to Paris."

The sting of disappointment made Violet's throat ache as he gave her one last, lingering kiss before turning away to gather his clothes. She stared at him as he rolled down his sleeves, fighting back the urge to say, "And what then?" What then, indeed? She would go back to her life, the one she had spent three years building, the one that was everything she had ever wanted. He would go back to Whitehall to continue his crusade of fighting crime in the rookery and bettering life for those who lived there; to ensure that what had happened to his sister would not happen again. A worthy endeavour, and one she could not possibly bring herself to deny him. Not when she knew what drove him to want those things.

Violet watched as he blithely gathered up her prim cotton dress, her chest swelling with some strange, breathless emotion, and she realized, in one sudden, horrifying moment... she had fallen in love with him. She was in love with John Barrow. He smiled as he turned to her with her bodice in hand, and she took it without a word, her stomach suddenly churning. Violet had stopped believing in love a long time ago, after a lifetime in Seven Dials had broken her down into a cynical little jade. She had thought she loved Archie, and that had been a lie. Love *was* a lie... wasn't it? Hadn't she seen what men really wanted with women? That was not love. She had sold them what they really wanted instead, and they had been happy to pay for it.

He handed her the remainder of her clothes with another quick smile before tugging on his overcoat. Slowly, she pulled on her petticoats, only vaguely hearing when he said, "Here, let me," as he turned her around to tie the tapes for her. She nodded in silent acquiescence, but she could hardly breathe as his hands worked at the small of her back. She couldn't be in love; it wasn't possible. *Then why do you care if you are to be parted?* That blasted voice again, whispering at her, making her doubt herself. *Why do you care if he says he feels the same? He can't love you; you are unworthy. You gave him what he wanted; you gave it to him for nothing.*

Violet's chest ached now, and she couldn't bring herself to look at him as he draped the dolman about her shoulders, his fingers lingering upon the nape of her neck before he leaned down to press a kiss to the shell of her ear. She squeezed her eyes shut as her silly little heart fluttered at the gesture.

"We should be going – we need to get back to the club before it opens."

Violet forced the words out. "Lead the way then."

His expression was sympathetic as she followed him back out into the street, greeted by a sunless sky and a biting chill in the air. Freed from the confines of the boxing ring and the vulnerability of having his hands upon her, of him inside her, Violet's heart began to slow, and she frowned at herself. Love? No, she was not falling for that again. She was far more comfortable with lust. Lust was simple, a base animal urge. It had served her well during her time in Cora's brothel, it had clothed her and fed her and kept a roof over her head. She was not in love. She could not be – what would it get her, anyway? Only another broken heart when she inevitably returned to Paris, and he remained here, in this city which brought her only bad memories.

Paris. Yes. That was the problem. She had started envisioning a future with him – her impractical fantasies of waking beside him, strolling down the Champs-Élysées together, dining on *pain au chocolat* and coffee on the banks of the Seine – they were just that. Fantasies. She had begun to lose sight of her one, single goal, the one she had carried from the moment she stepped onto that train to return to London. Get home to Paris. Restore her career, resume her life. John Barrow had never been meant to be a part of that – he was but the solution to her problem with Archie, and that would have to be what he remained.

Heart hardened once more, Violet turned to John with a serene expression as he opened the door to the box. She felt no fear now, just the small thrum of anticipation of finally getting out of this place and taking her first, freeing steps onto the ship which would take her back to her little studio in Montmartre, where she could pick up the pieces she had left behind and begin putting them back together.

"I won't be here tomorrow," John said, as he lit the lamp on the small table for her. Unperturbed, she nodded and perched herself on the edge of the narrow bed as he turned to leave. "I'll be going with Archie and Tommy to the Royal Albert Dock. Archie has his eye on the warehouses there." He allowed a small smile at this. "This should do it, Violet – a brand-new warehouse, with thousands of pounds worth of goods inside? He'll pay for that, no doubt."

Violet nodded again. "That's excellent news."

There must have been something in her tone, in the flat calm of it, because he raised a brow at her and seemed to want to say something, but then apparently thought better of it and slowly dipped his head.

"Then I shall say goodnight. Sleep well, Violet."

"Oh, I shall. Goodnight, John."

He frowned again and paused with his hand upon the latch before shrugging and closing the door behind him. The scrape of the bolt being slid back into place no longer set Violet's teeth on edge, and she slept well that night.

TWENTY

Archie was in fine form the next morning; resentful shopkeepers and publicans were already handing over their hard-earned money with the veiled threats of violence, arson, or worse, from the Bruisers, and the promise to keep away any other gangs who dared encroach on their territory. He was confident that Violet was close to accepting his proposal, and John was still winning fights for them at night in the cellars of pubs and warehouses, though his body was beginning to feel the toll. But all in all, the Bruisers were well on their way to being in total control of the East End.

Tommy, however, showed little enthusiasm as they strolled along the docks towards the hulking masses of the warehouses in the distance. Seagulls scolded overhead and hydraulic cranes whirred as they lifted massive crates from ship decks to the wharfs below. He scowled at the dockers shouting to one another until Archie clapped him on the back.

"What's with the mug, eh, Tommy?" he asked. "Sun's out, and we're gonna make some money today." He grinned over at John, who had his hands in his pockets, feeling the weight of the notebook and small pencil he had brought along to record the events of today for evidence. "And my Violet's comin' around, ain't she?"

John cast a sly smile over at the Bruisers' leader. "I told you she would."

Tommy shook his head. "I don't trust Brill, Archie. We killed two of his men – you think he's gonna let that go?"

Archie snorted. "Edward Brill ain't even a proper gangster anymore – he's gone soft, thinks he's better than us 'cause he opened a few schools and he's got bloody reformers singin' his praises." He laughed as they came to the office door of the first warehouse, a giant red brick building dotted with small windows along the façade. He didn't pause in his stride, merely pushed the door open and walked inside as though he already owned the place. A clerk seated at a small desk piled high with papers glanced up, startled, his eyes widening behind thin wire-framed spectacles. Archie sauntered right up to the man who rose, uncertain, from his chair. They no doubt made a frightening trio, and John was careful to keep his expression impassive as Archie stopped and jerked his head in the clerk's direction.

"The owner of this place here?"

The young man's gaze skipped from Archie to where Tommy and John stood behind him, then back again and he slowly nodded.

"Mr. Best is in the back supervising the new shipment."

Archie stared at the clerk, as though waiting for him to continue, but he maintained a befuddled silence until Archie raised his eyes heavenward and gestured towards the door at the back of the room.

"Be a good lad and go fetch him for me, wouldya?"

The clerk dipped his head and hastened from the office, surely glad to be away from the three tall, menacing men who had arrived without so much as a knock on the door. Tommy was still scowling as Archie turned back to them and he cut his brother a sharp look of warning.

"Stop being such a bloody pessimist, Tommy. Johnny's not worried, are you, Johnny? He redirected his gaze now to John, who shrugged.

"I ain't worried. Seems like Mr. Brill is smart enough to know when not to mess about. Not if he values his life."

"You see, Tommy? There's nowt to worry about, not if Edward Brill knows what's good for him."

The younger Neville brother looked unconvinced, and he sent a hostile glare towards John who, for his part, remained expressionless.

The door to the warehouse swung open at that moment and a stout, hard-faced man of middling years entered the office. The clerk was nowhere to be seen, and he closed the door behind him as he turned to the Bruisers with a look of resignation on his face.

"You must be Mr. Neville," he said, not bothering to extend a hand as he nodded towards Archie. He sighed and proceeded without waiting for a response. "You're here for your cut, I suppose?"

Archie grinned. "That I am, Mr. Best, that I am. Not to worry, though, eh? I know them Bethnal Boys been givin' you trouble – be assured my lads'll keep 'em out of your way. For a price, of course." Archie's grin was knowing as the warehouse owner's expression hardened.

"I've been keepin' them out of my warehouse just fine by meself, Mr. Neville. Not sure I need you or your" – he paused and sent a withering glare towards Tommy and John before he continued – "men. Brill said you'd come by, but I don't think we'll be needin' your services."

John swallowed as a charged silence filled the little room. A terrible energy fairly crackled off Archie as he drew himself up to his considerable height and fixed Mr. Best with a frightening glare. Impressively, the other man showed no reaction to this, but John's heart had begun to pound against his chest, knowing what was to come.

"I don't think you understand, Mr. Best," Archie spoke slowly, his voice deceptively calm. "This is not an offer. It's a hundred quid, every month, to keep your business safe. Otherwise, who knows what could happen?"

Mr. Best's lips curled. Clearly, he was a hardened docker, unmoved by such threats, and he shrugged.

"We're doin' just fine on our own, Mr. Neville. I know what Brill said, but I ain't got a hundred pounds for ye."

Archie closed his eyes, then, and shook his head. John's heart now beat a rapid tattoo in his chest, and he could practically see the rage rolling off Archie in white hot waves. The next words he spoke were, tragically, utterly predictable.

"Johnny," Archie said, turning his gaze. John looked up, expectant, and knew the command that was coming his way. "Be a good lad and show Mr. Best here what happens when he don't pay us to keep him and his business safe."

John made one last attempt at stopping what he knew would have to happen.

"Didn't Mr. Brill say we weren't to hurt nobody?"

Archie's expression grew dark. "He also said no one would stand in our way, didn't he?"

And at that, John feigned an indifferent shrug and started towards the warehouse owner, who was glaring at them and had clearly been expecting this reaction, for he started to reach towards his belt for the cosh John knew was hanging there. He caught it, mid-stride, as the man swung back to bludgeon him with it, wrenching it away as he lined up with his free hand to deliver a vicious hook, then stepping forward into Mr. Best's retaliatory strike to head-butt him in the jaw, slamming him into the door to the warehouse.

The other man was clearly no stranger to fighting, but John

was a professional, and he struck without mercy, knowing if he tried to pull a single punch, Archie would have his head, and the whole operation would fall apart just as it was coming together. His muscles burned and his head swam as he rained down dispassionate blows, his knuckles becoming raw as Mr. Best's face dissolved into a bloody pulp. Knowing it would come to this didn't ease the horror of beating an innocent man nearly to death, but the operation must succeed. This must not be allowed to happen again, and John's breath was ragged as he finally stepped away from Mr. Best, who was now lying crumpled in a heap in the corner of the room, blood spattered on his shirt, his eyes swollen shut, gasping a curse from bloodied lips.

John stood for a moment, panting, staring down at the man as the Neville brothers looked on before wordlessly taking their leave. He hesitated for a moment, his hands shaking, his chest tight, before he, too, turned and left the warehouse.

Night was falling, and Violet rose to light the lamp beside her bed before she settled herself back down on the narrow mattress and took up her sketchbook once more. There was a newfound sense of purpose as she scratched her pencil over the page, capturing not John, or railyards or docks, or even the cherub which had been her muse during her brief stay at Bradford House, but the people of the rookery. Something about that boy selling the papers had inspired her, and she drew with urgency, as though her hands could not keep up with the images coming to mind. Soon, her book was full of sketches of that boy in his ragged coat and carefully patched trousers, and before long, she had moved on to the two women with the baby who had admired John. When she was done with that, she began drawing the women she had worked with at Cora's, their faces and smiles and pain seared into her memory.

She was careful this time, however, to keep an ear out for

creaks on the stairs coming down to her room, and when she heard the telltale sound, she quickly tucked her pencil back into its case and slipped it under her mattress along with the sketch-book. The bolt squealed and the door opened a moment later, revealing John Barrow holding a covered tray. Her heart, damnable little thing, skipped a beat at the sight of him, but she quickly suppressed that emotion and rose with a polite nod as he came into the room and set the tray down upon the table. It wasn't until he straightened and met her gaze that she saw something strange in his eyes. Something... harrowing. Without thinking, she took a step towards him.

"Are you alright?" she asked, noticing that his knuckles were bandaged and reaching for him. "What happened to your hands?"

He shook his head, looking away from her as he pulled his hand back and rubbed it on his thigh, as though he would rub away her touch. He cleared his throat and shook his head again.

"Had a fight..." His words caught at the end, and he swallowed, refusing to look at her. Worried now, she reached out and took his fingers in hers again, tugging them so he was obliged to look at her. With her free hand, she touched his cheek, and he squeezed his eyes shut as he leaned into her caress.

"What fight?"

The muscles in his jaw tensed before he opened his eyes, squeezing his fingers around hers.

"I had to do it... I knew I'd have to eventually, but I... Archie was there, I couldn't hold back."

Violet's heart was racing as she brushed her thumb over the sharp angle of his cheekbone. She didn't have to ask. She knew what had happened. Someone had said no to Archie. Edward Brill had told them there was a chance not everyone would fall in line, and it had finally happened. She rose up on her toes and, cupping John's face in her hands, she pressed a kiss to his mouth before pulling away just enough to meet his gaze.

"We knew this might happen... You did what you had to do; we can still make this work. Mr. Brill will take care of him."

John's eyes squeezed shut again and his head moved slowly to the side, still bracketed by her fingers.

"I really hurt him, Violet." His voice was a hoarse whisper, and she kissed him again, not knowing what she could say. They had been aware it might come to this, but it didn't make it any less painful. She pressed her lips to his once more, unsure how else to ease the deep furrows in his brow, nor the lines etched into the corners of his mouth. Her fingers slid into his hair, pulling him closer as his fingers trailed over her hips and his breath stuttered out. Again and again, she kissed him, as though she could pull the grief from him, as though she could take away the memory of whatever punishment he had been forced to mete out in pursuit of a bigger goal; one that would hopefully put an end to all such violence. His fingers were pressing into her waist, pulling her into him, and suddenly, all the walls she had built around her heart to keep the pursuit of her goal to return to Paris as her one and only priority, crumbled like so much dust.

What magic had he woven to be able to do this to her? Violet had spent a lifetime building barriers against these feelings, giving away her body without ever giving away herself, and one soft sigh against her cheek from this man was enough to make her question everything she had known about herself. She wasn't made for love... no one could ever feel that way for her, despoiled as she was. But as his fingers slid up, thumbs tracing over the curves of her breasts, she began to wonder, deep in the sheltered recesses of her heart – could he feel that way for her?

No! she cried out to herself, even as his mouth moved over hers. *Don't fall for it again. You're going back to Paris, and he must stay here. This cannot be and you must end it now. He doesn't feel the same; he never will.*

Violet wanted to scream at that voice. Maybe he could; maybe he was simply trying to keep them safe. But it didn't matter at this moment, for he was not in the right state of mind. He was shaking as their hands moved over one another, but it felt so very good, and it would be so very easy to let him have her again, to ease his pain, to bring them pleasure, and she swallowed back a moan as his fingers fisted in her hair and his hips tilted into hers, allowing her to feel the hard ridge of his cock. Desire exploded inside her, but somehow, her rational mind prevailed, and she eased away with a longing sigh.

"John," she whispered as his fingers tightened in her hair, as though he would hold her there before he let out a shuddering breath and released her.

"We're so close now... don't lose hope," she added as she reached up to brush a lock of his dark blond hair back into place. His brow furrowed and his lips pressed together, but he nodded.

"You're right, of course – I won't. I can't stay... I'm working security tonight and I've reports to write before I go to White-hall at the end of the week." He leaned in towards her, closing his eyes as though he would kiss her again before he sighed. "I can taste that promotion, Violet... but it's so hard to believe I'll actually get it. If something goes wrong..."

Violet brushed her fingers across his temple, drawing his gaze to hers before offering an encouraging smile. "Everythin' is in place. You're gatherin' your evidence. We just stay the course, we keep givin' Archie what he wants... and soon, he'll just be a bad memory."

John finally smiled, very faintly, and lifted his hand to capture her fingers, bringing them to his mouth to kiss them.

"We'll meet in Paris after this... you can introduce me to all your artist friends."

Violet wanted to smile at this – wouldn't that be lovely? Wouldn't it be so nice to show him all she had made of herself? But he belonged here. She knew that, and it was too painful to let herself believe that there could be anything more between them after Archie was gone. She would not see him again, not in Paris, not anywhere. And yet... the grief in his eyes was too much to tell him no, and so she kissed him, very softly, and whispered, "Yes. We'll do that."

He nodded, giving her a small smile before he backed out of the room and closed the door, locking it behind him. Violet stared at it for a long time after he was gone, her throat burning as she tried to hold back whatever terrible, uncomfortable emotion was trying to work its way up from deep inside her. Leaving him behind would be difficult, she could not deny that. Even thinking about their being parted made her ache and... maybe she did love him. But Violet would not allow herself to be heartbroken again. Not after falling for someone like Archie, not after the shame of letting herself be taken in by someone who had turned out to be a monster. And not after being told, for years, that her past made her unworthy of such an emotion, anyway. So, she would do what she did best – she would close her heart to any more of these inconvenient feelings. Her life was waiting for her, and she would not let anyone – not even John Barrow – get in the way of her returning to it.

But that did not mean she could not help him. She still wanted him to succeed, and if that meant getting that promotion, then she would do whatever she could to ease the way for him. And she knew, in the upper circles of British society, that meant having a name behind you. Perhaps several. There was only one person Violet knew could help her with this plan, so she reached under her mattress for the little sketchbook and carefully tore a page from it before digging out a pencil and sitting down to write a letter.

Dearest Della...

TWENTY-ONE

Edward Brill was standing in front of Whitehall when John arrived several days later for his scheduled meeting with Superintendent Culpepper. He nodded towards John as he pushed himself up from where he had been leaning against the stone wall and came towards him, hands in his pockets. John almost stopped in his tracks, haunted by the memory of Mr. Best's face, swollen and bruised and bloodied by his own hands, but the hesitation lasted for only a moment as he came upon the leader of the Limehouse Gang. Brill's expression was unreadable as he stopped under the broken shade of a tree, its branches nearly stripped bare with the coming winter.

"Good morning, Mr. Brill. To what do I owe the pleasure of this visit?" John spoke carefully, knowing he had broken the one promise the other man had asked him to keep. Brill shrugged and looked away for a moment, squinting into the sun.

"I received word from one of the warehouses that you and the Neville brothers stopped in for a visit." His gaze revealed nothing when he turned it back to John, who shook his head.

"Archie was right there, Edward. I couldn't refuse; that

would have revealed too much." He swallowed. "How is Mr. Best?"

Edward sniffed and rolled his broad shoulders. "He's fine... or he will be, anyway. I sent him the best doctors I know; they'll patch him right up." His eyes narrowed on John. "You did a bloody number on him, though."

John pursed his lips and nodded slowly. "I know." He gave a grim smile. "It's why I've never lost."

Edward let out a huff of laughter before shaking his head and reaching into his coat pocket.

"I came to talk to you about a letter I got," he said, withdrawing a plain envelope and holding it up. John gestured for him to come inside the building where they might have a bit of privacy. He found a disused interrogation room and closed the door behind them before turning to Edward and motioning for him to take a seat at the small table in the middle of the room and sitting opposite him. Edward set the letter upon the tabletop and tapped it with his index finger.

"It's from that friend of your girl – Della." He grinned. "Lady Bradford, I suppose she's called now. Imagine goin' from bein' a common pickpocket to a bloody countess. I still tell that story to the folks who's new to London, and they never believe me."

John allowed a small smile at that – it was, indeed, a feat for Miss Della Rose to have made the leap from Seven Dials to Belgravia, but he had personally never seen two people so perfectly matched and so very much in love as her and the Earl of Bradford, and could well understand how she and his former employer had come to be married. He had never given it much thought for himself – service to the earl and now detective work with the Metropolitan Police had left him little time for pursuing such a match, though he reckoned he would enjoy wedded bliss if ever he found the time. Unbidden, Violet's image came to mind, and the starry wonder in her eyes when she had looked up at him as they had lain together in Bess's room. He was quick to dismiss the memory as Edward leaned back in his chair and pinned him with a contemplative look.

John frowned as he glanced down at the letter. *It's from that friend of your girl.* Not his girl. He didn't know what Violet was to him – or if she even wanted to be anything to him. He only knew that her plan was to return to her life in Paris, and that he had no business standing in the way of that. And still... that hadn't stopped him dreaming of her, of imagining waking beside her, bathed in bright morning sunlight, or of cold winter nights with her curled up in his arms. It was never very clear in his imaginings where any of these scenes of domestic paradise were to take place, however. Not here in England... she would never agree to that, and he wouldn't expect her to. But... not in Paris, either. He had far too much to make up to Lucy here. And so, as before, he had come to the conclusion that they were simply not meant to be.

John cleared his throat and turned his attention back to Edward. "And what has Lady Bradford written to you?"

Edward settled his hands over his stomach before nodding towards the envelope.

"She and that toff husband of hers want to host a fundraiser for the Charity Organization Society of London. I've never been keen on their politics meself – bit too choosy about who gets their money, but she says they've got dukes and viscounts and the like on their board. They're tryin' to stop people havin' to depend on charity all together, and I suppose I can get behind that. She's hopin' her husband can get some laws or somethin' passed then."

John frowned. "And why is she writing to you?"

The corner of Edward's mouth went up. "The lady said it were Miss Latimer herself who suggested they hold this to-do at my club since I'm apparently the face of reform in the East End." He shrugged and dusted an invisible piece of lint from his sleeve. "If I didn't know any better, I'd say she's doin' this to help you."

John glanced up at this and saw Edward watching him with a gleam in his eyes.

"Help me? With what?"

He chuckled. "As I understand it, you're up for a promotion at Scotland Yard – though why anyone would want to work for those bastards is beyond me." He gave a knowing smile at that, and John raised a brow before he continued. "I know puttin' the Nevilles and the lot of them away will set you apart, but there's nowt those toffs respect more than a fancy title. And if I host a big to-do with all the cream of society, includin' your boss, well..." He paused and gave a crooked grin. "It's all but guaranteed then, innit? And they might actually have a chance to see what life is really like in the rookery. See what we're trying to fix."

John stared at him for a moment. He had, indeed, posted a letter from Violet to Lady Bradford out at Headingly Hall earlier in the week. He hadn't realized it had been to suggest hosting a high society event on his behalf, especially considering Violet's dislike of this city and reluctance to reveal anything of her past to the people who would judge her for it. And a room full of aristocrats and police were certain to do just that.

After a moment, he lifted his shoulders. "Maybe she's doing it for you. Just like she promised she would."

Edward's lips curled up. "Maybe both." He heaved a deep breath and straightened in his chair as he put a finger on the envelope and drew it back towards himself. "In any case, she wants us to decide when to hold this little party so she can do all her plannin' and send out invitations and the like."

John nodded slowly, thinking, before he spoke. "The night of the raid on the Bruisers. Miss Latimer and I both need to be out of there when it happens and there'll be nowhere safer in the city than a private club full of police and toffs."

Edward inclined his head, smiling. "No, indeed. And when is this blessed event finally happenin'?"

John allowed a small chuckle at that. "In a month's time. The twenty-seventh of November."

The other man rose with a nod and John followed suit. "That's sorted – leave it to me." He paused. "Before I go... who was it you lost?"

John frowned. "Lost?"

He watched as Edward tucked the envelope back into his pocket before meeting his gaze once more. "You told me the reason you was doin' all this was 'cause you lost someone. Who was it?"

There it was. The familiar ache, the twist in his gut. He swallowed before he replied, his voice rough, "My sister, Lucy. Mugging gone wrong."

Edward's expression changed then as he pressed his lips together, the grief in his eyes as familiar to John as his own. "Want to know why I'm helpin'?"

John frowned again – he already knew of Edward's charitable work and his fight for reform but shook his head. "No, why?"

Edward cleared his throat now and glanced away, as though he couldn't bear to look at him as he said the words.

"Lost someone meself. Me wife, Lizzie. Typhoid. Told her I'd make life better for our people, and that's what I'm doin'. So don't fuck it up." These words were said with a pointed look, and John felt the weight of that look down to his bones as Edward made to leave.

"Oh, and Mr. Barrow," he added, turning back for a moment, his expression grim as he slowly buttoned his coat. "I hope you're plannin' to retire those when this is over." He directed a meaningful glance towards John's hands, still wrapped in bandages. John followed his gaze, then looked back up again, his mouth flattening into a hard line as he gave his head a little shake.

"Never want to see another boxing ring again."

Edward held his gaze for a long, uncomfortable moment before turning and leaving the small room without another word. John raised one of his bandaged fists to examine it before sighing and leaving for his meeting with Culpepper.

There was no time to waste; if the raid by the police was to take place in a month's time, then there was still much evidence to collect for John's case to be indisputable. If Archie found even a single way to wriggle out of his inevitable imprisonment, then the past few months would have been for naught. And Violet would never be free.

Unfortunately, the pretense had to be maintained a little longer, and John sighed as he stood to the side of the boxing ring in Archie's warehouse, wrapping his hands in preparation for sparring with the Devil, who was already in the ring trading jabs with Alexander. Tommy looked on, notepad in hand, watching them carefully and calling out the occasional critique.

John allowed himself, during that quiet moment, to indulge in the memory of Violet, who even now was locked away in her little prison. It was something he rarely permitted himself now that their operation was nearing its conclusion. His thoughts of late had focused on making note of everything said and agreed to during his outings with Archie and Tommy to the East End, copying ledgers, creating floorplans of the Devil's Den – in general, attacking the mounds of paperwork that were the bane of every police officer's life, in order to make that final raid in a month's time go as smoothly as possible. It had to, for when he did allow his thoughts to wander, however briefly, they always went to Violet and his promise to her. His promise... and of Violet herself. Of the delectable slide of her skin over his and how it had been burnished gold in the flickering candlelight of Bess's room during that stormy afternoon; of the sweetness of her sex and how he fancied he could still taste her, even after all the time that had passed. Of her harsh gasps of pleasure, and of her scent... all the loveliness of a summer's day. He could not recall a single woman who had so thoroughly come to haunt his senses, his dreams, his very existence, as Violet Latimer had.

The temptation to invite her to stay grew stronger every day, but he did not dare ask her to make that sacrifice, knowing why she had left and how much she had made of herself in Paris. She belonged there, and he fully intended to make sure she returned. Even if it meant giving her up and whatever fanciful future he had imagined for them.

A shout from the warehouse door startled John from his thoughts and he turned, absently, to find Tommy waving to him.

"You're up, Barrow."

John drew in a small breath to refocus himself and started towards the ring when, much to his surprise, Tommy began to shuck his coat and waistcoat, nodding towards the Devil as he did so.

"I'll spar with Barrow today," he said, casting a sidelong look towards John as he approached the ropes, causing John to hesitate for just the briefest of moments before he met the Devil's bemused gaze. The other man shrugged and, together with Alexander, they ducked out of the ring and took up their things to leave as John stepped inside, debating if he should ask Tommy why he had volunteered for this duty. Tommy rarely did any boxing himself anymore as he had found far more success in coaching, but his gaze was unreadable as he stepped into the ring with John, rolling his broad shoulders and flexing his neck.

"What's up with you, Tommy?" John finally asked as Tommy raised his fists and narrowed his eyes.

"Want to keep meself on me toes, don't I?"

John said nothing, easily parrying a slow strike, one meant to assess rather than do damage. They traded soft blows for a few minutes as Tommy tested John's defenses before finally speaking.

"Is that little trollop of Archie's gonna ever bloody marry him? I'm sick to death of hearin' about her," he said with a scowl, stepping back to avoid a half-hearted strike. John managed a negligent shrug as he pressed forward with another in quick succession.

"She's been given till the end of the year."

Tommy's expression darkened as he drew back his arm and slammed it forward to deliver a vicious hook, catching John on the shoulder. A real hit, this time. He was no longer being tested.

"So, what'd we bring you in for if not to use those bloody fists? Go knock her about and get it over with."

John fought to keep his expression impassive as he parried another blow before landing a solid strike in Tommy's gut and stepping quickly away from the retaliating fist.

"I'm not doin' damage to Archie's girl when she's ready to agree on her own. I'm not a fool."

Tommy was glowering. "Archie's not gonna say a bloody word to you and you know it. You're his favourite now, or hadn't you noticed? He can't stop bloody talkin' about you and how you've impressed him, bringin' that slut back from whatever back alley you found her in."

John's chest was heaving as he parried another quick succession of strikes before landing a hook. This was going badly – he had to have both Neville brothers on his side for any of this operation to succeed, and so he shook his head and let Tommy's strike catch him in the jaw, sending him stumbling back as pain exploded through his head.

"He don't know me like you, Tommy – I'll never be family,

will I? I only got lucky findin' his girl, that's all," he said, concil-iatory, as he rubbed a hand over his jaw.

"And how'd she know it were Arthur Potts what turned in Archie? He weren't exactly one for keepin' a secret, was he?"

John shrugged and parried again. "He'd be stupid not to keep that secret. And you know how them girls gossip – can't keep their bloody mouths closed, can they?"

Tommy would not be mollified, however, and he swung again.

"Don't you fuckin' hold back – if you're gonna hit me, go on and do it," he said, goading John with a menacing glare. John gritted his teeth, parried a strike, and retaliated with a crushing backfist that caught Tommy in the jaw, sending him staggering backward with a hoarse laugh.

"That's more like it," he rasped, pushing himself up again to strike back. Sweat slicked down John's back now as they sparred, Tommy seeming determined to send him to the floor, but unwilling to have the match thrown in his favour. He wanted John to fight, and fight he did, until his muscles screamed and sweat dripped into his eyes, burning them until he could barely see. Tommy was no better off, for he was no seasoned fighter, and his punches were growing laboured, though he fought like a man possessed, one determined to put an end to his opponent. It was only when he swung and missed that John finally drew in a deep breath and landed a hook that sent Tommy to the ground. He didn't rise for a moment, but when he did, he was panting and shaking his head.

"He's my brother, Barrow," he said, as he pushed himself up off the ground, reaching for a nearby towel to wipe the sweat from his brow. "I know him better than anyone, for good or bad, and I don't trust that Brill bastard. Get that girl to marry him, sooner rather than later, so he gets his mind off this protection racket or he's gonna get himself right back in Newgate. And find out how she knew about Arthur. She won't tell me nothin'; she's hated me from the start. You hear me?"

The air rasped in and out of John's lungs as he slowly nodded.

"I don't wanna get Archie in trouble, Tommy. I just wanna fight." He paused to drag in another deep breath. "I'll talk to her; get her to say yes – one way or another."

Tommy inclined his head and tossed the towel at John. "See that you do. It's the only thing that might get him to give up all that nonsense in the East End."

He didn't wait for a reply but turned and stepped between the ropes before gathering up his clothes and leaving the warehouse. Once alone in the cool, dim quiet, John slowly wiped the sweat from his face, wincing as he touched a hand to his jaw and drawing it back to find blood smeared on his fingers. Sighing, he pressed the towel to his skin and stepped out of the ring. He had just managed to save that interaction, but there were still three weeks to go until the planned raid of Archie's club. The timing had to be just right now – any slip-up and the operation would fall apart. They were so close he could taste it. And yet, as he had felt in his meeting with Culpepper, it all still seemed so far away. Perhaps Violet's plan to throw a fundraiser in his name was not so far-fetched as he had first believed it. That she had even considered putting herself so publicly on display to further his career made his chest grow warm, and he found his worries slipping away as he dressed and left the warehouse to make his way back to the club, eager for brilliant, emerald eyes and that summery scent.

TWENTY-TWO

Violet was asleep when the squeal of the bolt awoke her. She gasped as her eyes flew open and she scrambled to push herself up from the hard mattress and cover herself, fearful that it would be Archie or his loathsome brother come to hound her into marrying again. She was still blinking, shocked that she had slept so late, when the door opened to reveal John Barrow, breakfast tray and clean undergarments in hand. Her shoulders sagged with relief as he glanced at her with a raised brow, closing the door carefully behind him before crossing the small space to set down the tray.

"Still abed, Miss Latimer? That's quite unusual for you," he said with a little smile. She pushed her fists into her eyes, trying to rub away the lingering haze of sleep before accepting the clothes he then handed to her and letting the blanket fall. As she swung her legs over the side of the bed, she caught his hungry gaze as her bare legs were exposed, pressing them together as her body responded with a dull ache between her thighs. There was a flash of a memory, of his hand on her bare leg, hooking it around his hip, and the stroke of his skin against hers. Violet blinked and shook her head.

"I may have been up a bit too late finishin' a sketch," she said after a moment, as he lifted the lid of the tray to pour a cup of tea before handing it to her. She gave a grateful nod and took the cup from him, closing her eyes as the dented tin warmed her hands before lifting it to take a sip. The heat of the drink helped to chase away the last of her exhaustion, and she sighed before glancing up at him as he set down the teapot.

"I don't suppose... you might show me?" he asked with a hopeful look, but she hesitated for a moment – her subjects of late had grown quite personal and she wasn't sure if she was ready to share them. She finally reasoned he had already seen her most intimate work – the drawings she had made of him – and so she nodded.

"Yes, I suppose," she said, and kneeled beside the bed to lift the mattress and withdraw the little sketchbook. When she rose to hand it to him, she found herself looking up into eyes of deepest coffee brown; eyes hooded with desire. After what seemed an eternity, and before she could do something very silly and almost certainly unadvisable, she drew in a breath and took a step back, thrusting the book at him. He blinked, as though he had forgotten his request, and turned away to open it, giving her the opportunity to change into the fresh undergarments he had brought. It seemed almost silly to have him look away while she changed – had they not seen and explored all the most intimate parts of each other? – but she appreciated his discretion all the same. And perhaps he, too, realized that they were but one smouldering glance away from ripping each other's clothes off again and her being in any state of undress would only fan those flames.

He was quiet, slowly flipping from one page to the next as she fastened her corset and stepped into the skirts of that practical green dress.

"Is this William?" he asked over his shoulder as she tied the tapes before plucking up the bodice. She hesitated, slowly pulling on the sleeves before answering.

"Yes. I was… inspired, I suppose. Do you… do you like it?"

He said nothing for a moment as he turned to the next page and her heart seized in her chest as he turned to face her, his gaze fixed on her sketches. Her breath caught when he finally looked up.

"Violet… why do you not paint people? These are extraordinary."

Violet flushed as she clasped her hands to her chest, unable to stop the quick smile which flashed across her mouth.

"Really? I thought for so long that I was too… cynical, to really capture other people as they are. I thought, maybe I'd lost my humanity. Maybe I couldn't see the good in people anymore."

John shook his head, glancing down to turn to another page, this one depicting Bess, caught unawares one afternoon as Violet had been upstairs in the bar cleaning glasses. She had spied the other woman sitting at one of the card tables, ostensibly eating her supper before the club opened, but she had a novel opened on the table before her and was reading as she absently picked at a plate of cold chicken and cheese. Violet had been compelled in that moment to pluck the sketchbook from her pocket and capture Bess, in all her flame-haired glory, transfixed by the words on the page.

"No," John said, raising his gaze to her once more. "I can see it, Violet. You have a remarkable talent."

Violet's cheeks warmed again, and it took everything in her not to pull him down to her mouth to shower him with grateful kisses.

"Well… maybe it was time I expanded my repertoire," she added, a teasing note in her voice, and he gave her an encouraging smile.

"You really should. I've no doubt that railyards and docks

are fascinating subjects, but these" – he held up her book – "these should be more than sketches hidden away in a book."

The corners of her mouth turned up for just a moment and she tilted her head. "I'll think about it."

His soft smile almost made her close that gap between them and abandon herself to his kisses, but instead she accepted the sketchbook when he handed it back to her, and cleared her throat as she took a careful step back to finish buttoning her bodice, well aware of the view he would have of the curves of her breasts showing over the top of her chemise and warming at the thought.

"I met Edward Brill outside Whitehall yesterday," he said suddenly as he bent to gather her discarded clothes. She glanced up at him as he stood.

"Oh?" she asked, seeing the strain in his expression before he looked away.

"Yes... I'm afraid he got word of our visit to the Royal Albert Dock."

Violet said nothing but waited for him to continue. The corners of his mouth tightened.

"I told him I had to do it; I couldn't compromise my cover."

She did reach out this time and laid a comforting hand upon his arm. "He knew that could happen; he warned us himself."

John sighed as he ran his free hand through his hair. "I know, and I think he understood. He sent his best doctors over."

Violet nodded. "I told you he would take care of it."

He breathed out a heavy sigh, as though he could release the burden with it, and inclined his head in agreement. A moment passed before he spoke again. "Mr. Brill also informed me of a letter he received."

"Oh?" she asked again, innocently, as John finally raised his gaze to hers.

"Yes... from Lady Bradford herself."

Violet waited, expectant, for him to continue, still unsure if he would appreciate her suggestion to host a fundraiser in Edward Brill's club, or if he would find it intrusive and unnecessary. After a breathless moment, his expression softened, and he reached out suddenly to brush a finger down the curve of her cheek.

"You would do that for me?"

Violet's breath caught and her whole body grew warm at that one, soft touch as the rest of the world fell away. *Of course I did it for you*, she wanted to say, *I did it because I may be in love with you, but I can't ever have you. This will be my parting gift.* But she couldn't say that – for many reasons, not the least of which was the ever-present fear that he did not return the feeling, unworthy of it as she was. So instead, she forced out a carefree laugh and caught his fingers in hers, drawing his disconcerting touch away from her cheek.

"Of course I did… I want you to get your promotion. You've earned it, and I know what them toffs are like. It's all well and good to be the best for the job, but they always like a title and a bit of influence to back it up. And Della's thrilled to be able to help."

His smile didn't fade, not really, but it seemed frozen on his face as his fingers slowly tightened around hers before he quickly dipped his head and stepped back. Violet had to fight to swallow back the words she really wanted to say.

"Well, I certainly appreciate your… belief in me." He was smiling again, softly, but she was convinced that there was something he, too, was not saying. Still, she dared not pry further, feeling there were a host of messy and, quite frankly, inconvenient emotions waiting to be exposed. So, she said the only thing that could be said from the jumble of them hiding deep in her heart.

"I want you to be able to make sure what happened to Lucy never happens again."

John's gaze flew to hers, his forehead pinched as gratitude, and then grief washed over his features, making a muscle in his jaw tighten. In one stride, he came towards her to pull her into his body before his mouth closed over hers and his fingers were in her loosely bound hair, tugging her against him as she clung to his shoulders. Desire immediately overwhelmed anything else she wanted to say – or ought to have said – and she moaned as his hands began to travel down the length of her body, caressing, gripping, until he reached her buttocks.

"Violet, I..." he murmured against her lips, kissing her again and again, before he finally said, simply, "Thank you."

And with those two words, Violet squeezed her eyes shut and did the only sensible thing she could – she pulled away, breaking the embrace. The little bed was behind them; she could have pulled him onto it and let him make her feel beautiful and wanted and worthy again, but she couldn't risk the final pieces of her heart.

John sighed and nodded slowly, as though in agreement.

"You're right... we shouldn't... that is, I should be going. I must be at the warehouse shortly for sparring practice." He paused. "The twenty-seventh of November. That's when I'm getting you out of here. Mr. Brill will be hosting your party and the police... they'll be raiding this club."

"Oh." Violet wasn't sure what she felt in that moment – relief, certainly. Despite all John had done for her, she was quite sick of staring at these four white walls and had begun going out of her mind with boredom. And, if all went according to plan, Archie would be out of her life for good. Yet... there was a strange twinge in the pit of her stomach, and she had to force a smile onto her face. "That's welcome news. Then we simply stay the course, eh?"

He gave her a gentle smile and nodded. "Yes. We stay the course." He paused, the smile fading as he dragged in a breath. "Though there is the small matter of Tommy."

Violet frowned. "What of him?"

John sighed as he pushed a hand through his hair. "He's getting suspicious – thinks I'm Archie's favourite." John's quick smile was wry. "And he wants this marriage business over with. Says Archie may give up his ambitions if he's married to you. He doesn't trust Mr. Brill, that's for certain. And he wants me to find out how you knew about Arthur. We'll stick with our story there – you knew one of the girls working at the brothel he frequented, and they overheard him talking to the police."

All at once, Violet felt the familiar squeeze in her chest and she had to close her eyes for a moment against the crush of those four white walls. Her voice, when she spoke, was tight.

"The bastard – he's always hated me. Hated that Archie wanted me – and now he can't wait for us to get married 'cause he thinks it'll keep his brother safe. The irony is delicious." She rolled her eyes and let out a frustrated breath. "So, what do we do?"

John's shoulders lifted. "Give him a wedding date. One which falls after the raid."

Violet thought for a moment, then nodded. "What about Christmas? It's just before the end of the year and I can certainly play the flighty female intent on a Christmas weddin'."

John's smile was grim. "Perfect." His lips parted as though he would say something else, but he gave a quick nod instead and went to the door, turning to her before he left. "I'll see you again tomorrow morning."

"Goodbye, John."

TWENTY-THREE

Before long, they were but two days away from the party and the planned police raid. It started as any other; John arrived early with breakfast and a change of clothes. Violet felt as though she were bursting out of her skin as he entered the room with a quick, if subdued smile, before moving past her to set down the tray he held. He then turned to face her and reached into his coat to withdraw a sealed envelope.

"From Della," he said as he handed it to her. She took it with a nod and tore it open to unfold the letter inside, scanning the words quickly as John watched her, expectant.

Dearest Violet,

I hope this letter finds you well, and that your time in Bradford House has not been entirely dull.

Violet looked up at John as she read the first line. "You still haven't told her I left Bradford House?"

He frowned and shook his head. "No, of course not... I promised you I wouldn't. I even swore the staff to secrecy. That being said..." He paused and gave her a meaningful look. "She's going to find out once she and the earl arrive at Bradford House tomorrow. You should send her a letter."

She sighed. "I will," she said and looked back down at the letter.

I am so excited to see you again and let me assure you, the fundraiser is going to be a smashing success. I have become quite the hostess in my time as Countess of Bradford and everyone was clamouring for an invitation. All of Society will be there and Mr. Brill is very eager at the prospect of raising so much money. More importantly, this is our chance to show people what life is really like in the rookeries, and that the people there are worthy of better lives. Mr. Brill has been so very helpful in offering the use of the Brooklyn Club, and we already have plans for future charities so that no one will have to grow up as we did. And of course, if this helps in Detective Inspector Barrow receiving that promotion, then all the better.

Soon, you shall walk out of Bradford House a free woman, and then Clara and I can finally meet you in Paris. Until then, I remain,

Your dearest friend,
Della

Violet finally looked up as a heavy weight settled upon her chest.

"She's gonna be furious," she remarked as she turned and withdrew the sketchbook from beneath her mattress, tearing out another page to pen a response to Della. John gave her a sympathetic smile as she quickly scrawled an explanation for how she came to be in Archie's cellars rather than in the safety of Bradford House as Della would expect. She hesitated for only a moment before she folded up the page and handed it over to John for him to deliver.

"As long as you are safe and unharmed, I'm sure she'll forgive you."

"As long as she doesn't wring my neck first." Violet gave a wry smile. "Is everythin' ready?"

John nodded as he once again turned to face the door so she might change.

"All set. We will be leaving here at four o'clock in the afternoon as I will require your assistance in clearing out one of the storerooms at the warehouse to make way for a new office. Archie and Tommy will be arriving here at the club at five o'clock for the fight between the Devil and some new fella from Shoreditch, as will most of the Bruisers. The police will take position around Covent Garden at five thirty and move in once the fight starts at six. Meanwhile," he added with a hint of humour in his voice, "we shall be drinking and dancing at the Brooklyn Club with all them toffs."

Violet smiled, but her fingers were trembling as she did up the last of the buttons on her bodice. It was so close she could taste it now – she could see the ship which would take her home to Paris – but there was little gladness in her heart when she raised her gaze to John's broad back, clad in sombre grey wool, and knew she would not see him again once she got on that ship. She shook her head. There was no time to think on that now; she must focus on the operation at hand.

John turned when she gave a little cough, and his excited grin made her positively ache with want.

"Then I'll see you again in two days' time."

He nodded and held up the letter she had written. "I'll be sure Lady Bradford gets this today." He gave an encouraging smile. "We're almost there. Just hang on a little longer."

Violet's belly clenched at those words, but she managed a faint smile as he opened the door, gave her one final, encouraging nod, and left. The bolt slid into place, and now all Violet could do was wait.

John tried to keep his mind focused the morning of the raid. He washed and dressed as usual, walked the short distance to Archie's warehouse and had sparring practice with the Devil, losing himself in the back-and-forth of boxing, pushing himself until his skin was slick with sweat and his lungs were heaving with the effort to breathe. Then he washed again, dressed again, and met Archie at a pub in Holborn, where the owner was quietly informed that the Bruisers would be collecting from them going forward in exchange for their protection. There was no protest this time, and John carefully noted the particulars of the visit in his notebook after they left, heading with Archie back to the Devil's Den.

"Come on, Johnny," Archie said as they swept through the doors to a quiet room devoid of its nightly crowds. "I've got a new proposal for my Violet – think she's gonna agree this time."

John answered with a benign smile as they headed down into the shadows of the cellar where Violet waited. Archie burst into the room without so much as a knock to announce his presence, but she had clearly been expecting them and was standing beside her little bed, clad in her gown of crimson wool, her chin raised, her expression cool. John waited in the doorway, stone-faced, as Archie ambled forward, his grin as sly as ever.

"Mornin', Violet, my love. You're lookin' well," he said, circling her as though she were a prize racehorse for sale. Her gaze tracked him as he came to stand before her, but she gave no response apart from a tightening of her lips. Archie carried on, undeterred. "As I understand it, you was talkin' about a Christmas weddin'."

Violet again said nothing but did glance up at him. His expression darkened suddenly, all his casual cheer dissipating as he looked down at her, and John's muscles tensed as the air grew chill between them.

"Now listen good, 'cause I ain't sayin' this again. I'll give you your Christmas weddin'. We'll get married at Westminster bloody Abbey if you want. I'll even let you keep doin' your little paintings. But we are gonna be married. At Christmas. I've given you more than enough time and I ain't waitin' no more. You say yes now, or I will be payin' Della and her little brat a visit."

John swallowed back the cold rage filling his chest as Violet glared up at Archie, her eyes filled with loathing as he leaned down to whisper into her ear.

"You did love me once, Violet. You'll learn to love me again."

John's heart was now slamming against his ribs as Violet lowered her gaze, her lips pursing as though she were holding back a vicious retort, but in the end, she closed her eyes and nodded slowly.

"Yes, Archie. At Christmas. You have my word."

She winced as he raised a hand and took her chin into his grip, compelling her to look up at him before forcing his mouth onto hers, prompting an outraged gasp from her. It took everything – every fibre of his being – for John to stand there and keep the impassive expression on his face as a terrible, sickening rage filled him. Violet's hands were on his massive chest, pushing at him, but he held her fast as John's fingers curled into tight fists and he imagined all the ways he would smash those fists into Archie's face. He had to force himself to look away as Violet finally worked a hand up to dig her nails into his cheek and thrust him away from her, gasping as he laughed and turned to John, who was fairly shaking as fury coursed through him, but could see the finish line. He knew what was at stake and so grinned as Archie faced him.

"There you go, Johnny – you give a little, you get a little."

John gave a huff of laughter as the other man swept by him and out of the room and turned to leave himself but not before catching Violet's tiny, knowing smile as the door closed on her for the final time.

Later that day, at precisely four o'clock, John opened the door to the box and found Violet ready and waiting, practically giddy with excitement as she ran up to him to fling her arms around his neck and press those soft, lush lips to his. The gesture caught him by surprise, but it did not take him long to return her enthusiasm, wrapping his arms around her and lifting her up against him to deepen the kiss. His hands slid up, fingers curling into her shoulders as she sighed against him, withdrawing after a moment to meet his gaze.

"Let's get the hell out of here," she said with a smile, tucking her sketchbook and tin into her pocket before sweeping out of her prison without so much as a backward glance. Her wide smile faded the moment they opened the door at the top of the stairs, replaced by the look of simmering discontent she wore every time she left the club with him. He pushed her down the hall, nodding towards Bess, who stood chatting with one of the other girls at the bar, before they exited onto the street. Already the light of day was fading as they turned to head in the direction of the warehouse before he pulled her into one of the many narrow alleys which ran between the buildings. They followed the length of it in silence until they reached Floral Street, where a plain hansom cab waited. Its driver never looked at them as they stepped up inside, closing the door behind them and plunging the interior into darkness.

The carriage immediately jerked into motion as John fumbled to light the lantern swinging from a hook inside the cab, turning to take in Violet's wide smile and glittering green eyes once it flared to life.

"I feel as though I'm about to burst," she whispered as she snatched up one of his hands and held it to her chest, squeezing it in her excitement. He couldn't help it; his free hand cupped the back of her head, fingers sliding through silky golden curls, and he pulled her forward to seize her mouth in a kiss. The heat of her skin, the sensation of her tongue sweeping across his, was making him hard, but they were only a short ride to their destination at the Brooklyn Club and reason had to prevail, so he pulled away with a gasp to meet that wide, emerald gaze.

"Just think, Violet – by the end of the week, you'll be on a ship back to France, back to your railyards and factories."

She breathed out a sigh at that, but the sparkle in her eyes faded a little at the words, and she gave her head a little shake.

"I think... I think I'll give people a try this time. See what I can find in them. In people like us."

John gave a small smile and dipped his head. "I think that's a fine idea. Just know I'll be the first to claim an acquaintance-ship when you become a world-famous artist."

Violet's cheeks blushed the prettiest of pinks and John was sure his heart broke at that moment, aching with the knowledge of her impending departure, the one that would take her back to where she belonged. And why the ache? John's breath caught as he looked down into those glowing green eyes, the ones which could be as fierce as they were warm with happiness now, and knew he loved her. He loved Violet Latimer. And he was going to do the right thing and let her go.

The ache grew more painful as he observed her in the swinging light of the lantern, his gaze moving over the proud tilt of her chin and the lush curves of her lips, over the sooty fringe of lashes arching over those magnificent emerald eyes, and the crown of her flaxen hair. And she thought she was damaged? Unlovable? No – she was perfection. And he would have told her this – should have told her this – except the carriage was coming to a halt and the door was opening. She turned to him one last time with an eager grin.

"Ready?"

He nodded. "Ready."

The driver handed her down to the pavement below with John following, and she looked up on an indrawn breath. They had come to a stop directly in front of the Brooklyn Club, and it seemed that Edward Brill had spared no expense for this evening's event. Every window on the white stucco face of the Palladian building glowed with gaslight, and enormous wrought iron urns sat on either side of the glossy red entrance door, each filled with a meticulously sculpted topiary. Massive swags of greenery had been tucked into each window box, and a series of brightly coloured paper lanterns lined the flagstone path leading up to the two-story tall portico. A footman in crisp black livery stood at the entrance, and he nodded at them as John led her inside.

As befitting a club designed exclusively for men of the highest orders of society, the foyer was rich with marble columns and floors. Dozens of paintings in gilt frames covered the crimson damask papered walls, and Violet was wide-eyed as she strode up to a small painting of a woman in wide skirts and a bonnet, peering into a busy street as a young crossing sweeper offered his services; the collision of rich and poor, hanging here in hallways owned by a man who had come from nothing, and paid for by those who had everything.

"Do you know who this is?" she asked, glancing back at John, who shook his head as he came to stand behind her, ostensibly to inspect the painting, but longing for a hint of her sunny scent. "This is a Frith – and look here," she added, stepping towards another painting nearby, her voice filled with awe. "A Van Dyke... oh, is that Titian up there?"

"You've a good eye, Miss Latimer," came a voice from the far end of the foyer. John and Violet turned as Edward Brill came down one of two symmetrical curved staircases which swept up to the second floor. He was already dressed for the evening in a fine black tailcoat and trousers, with shirt and waistcoat of impeccably starched white linen. For such a large man, and one who had grown up hauling crates off ships, he cut quite an elegant figure as he came towards them, nodding towards the painting she was admiring.

"*Woman with a Mirror*," he explained before turning to Violet, who was looking up at the dozens of other paintings which filled the space.

"You've quite a collection, Mr. Brill – I didn't know you were an art lover."

He shrugged and gestured for them to follow him, taking them through the foyer to the stairs he had just descended. Through the doorways on either side of the great space were the card rooms and dining room, each bustling with servants who were busy setting the many dining tables, nudging silver-ware perfectly into place, setting out vases filled with fresh flowers – no doubt brought here at great expense – and aligning all the dozens of chairs surrounding the tables. Edward spoke as they crossed beneath a massive chandelier fairly dripping in crystals.

"I'm told it's a good investment," he said, stopping with them at the bottom of the stairs and turning to face Violet with an arched brow. "I understand you're an artist yourself."

One might have expected self-deprecation at this point, or modesty, as befitting a woman working in a highly male profes-sion, but Violet simply inclined her head and met Edward's steady gaze.

"I am – had a few sketches and watercolours exhibited with the Impressionists back in the spring, and a paintin' at the Salon last year."

"Impressive," he said, nodding. "I'm sure you're eager to get back to Paris, then, eh?"

John saw her eyes flicker towards him, just for a moment, before she offered Edward a smile.

"That I am, and to forget that this whole bloody business ever happened. Detective Inspector Barrow here was kind enough, though, to make sure I was still able to do some sketches." She turned that brilliant smile to him, and John had to swallow back the lump forming in his throat as he glanced at Edward.

"They're remarkable. Though I'm no expert."

Edward raised a brow at this and turned his gaze towards Violet.

"I don't suppose you'd let me see some of your work?"

That smile again. Dear god, she was so beautiful.

"Yes, of course, I have them right here," she said, digging into the pocket of her skirts and withdrawing her sketchbook to hand to him with an expectant look. Edward flipped though the pages, nodding at the sketches of young William and his newspapers, of the people on the streets of Seven Dials, of the women who sold their bodies just as she had. There was a small smile on his face as he finally closed the book and returned it to Violet.

"These are rather good, Miss Latimer." He paused then to withdraw a pocket watch and glance at the time before waving a hand towards Violet's outfit. "Your countess friend sent along somethin' for you. And I've a suit for you to use, detective inspector. This is a high society event, after all – have to look the part," he added with a wink as he started up the stairs, motioning for them to follow. John fought the urge to set his hand to the small of Violet's back as they made their way up into the darkness above, whereupon Edward turned up a gas lamp sitting upon a small Chippendale table at the top of the stairs and led them down a corridor paneled in carved oak, stopping between two doors.

"There's a box in there for you, Miss Latimer. And detective inspector," he said, turning to John and gesturing to the second door. "I've had one of my men leave a suit in there for you. Once you're all dressed up, we'll be ready to get this little party goin'. You two take all the time you need," he added with a smile that seemed a little too knowing for John's comfort, nudging him in the ribs with his elbow before chuckling and handing over the lamp to Violet before he turned and made his way back to the stairs. She turned to John with a bemused expression before shrugging.

"Suppose we'd best get ready," she said, opening the door to the room Edward had indicated for her. As they stepped inside, the single lamp she carried revealed an office, no doubt used by Edward when he wasn't at his warehouse at the docks. A row of single casement windows, draped with rich blue velvet, dotted the far side of the room, and the walls were paneled in deep red mahogany. A heavy oak desk sat before a row of bookshelves, stacked with leather-bound volumes and a collection of ships in bottles, no doubt a nod to Edward's nautical beginnings. John spotted a gas sconce on the wall behind them and turned it up, filling the room with wavering golden light before noticing the pale pink box which had been left upon the desk.

"I believe that's for you," he said, nodding towards it. Violet took the lamp and set it down beside the box before carefully lifting the lid and pushing aside the layer of tissue paper inside to reveal a black velvet jewelry box resting upon a gown of rich green silk. John smiled as she pulled the bodice from the box and held it up with a raised brow.

"What d' you think? Fancy enough for all them toffs?'

John chuckled. "I daresay you'll outshine the countess herself."

Violet's cheeks warmed again, and the dull ache returned to John's chest as he watched her carefully lay the bodice across the top of the desk before reaching for the matching skirt and shaking it out. It was a veritable confection of emerald silk edged with black satin, marked by a cascade of ruffles which fell from the waist to the end of the train. She again turned to lay out the garment, but paused, her fingers smoothing over the material, her expression unreadable in the dim light. When she faced him, however, a little smile curved her lips.

"I've never been to a party with this many toffs before. In Paris, we always had artists and singers and actors... no one stood on ceremony. I'm afraid I'll say the wrong thing."

John let out a soft chuckle as he finally allowed himself to step towards her.

"I've observed my fair share of society events – you just stay by me and Lady Bradford tonight and we'll make it through this together."

She nodded slowly, but her hand fluttered to the base of her throat as he dared another step closer, close enough that he could now see the light of the lamp reflected in her eyes. There was uncertainty in them now, and he frowned.

"What's wrong?"

She shook her head as she gazed down at the spread of exquisite silk laying upon the desk.

"All these fine clothes won't change what I was, not to these people. I know what they'll whisper... she's a common trollop. A whore. She don't belong here; she's a pretender. And the only reason they won't say it to my face is because the Earl of Bradford is a patron, and they dare not offend him."

John opened his mouth to reply, but he couldn't tell her that wasn't true; that no one would think that, because it would be a lie. People would certainly think that if they knew what she had been, and few would be willing to see past that to the beautiful, talented, brave, and clever woman she really was. He could certainly see it and he cared naught what her past was – he had his own checkered past that was, at this very moment, potentially holding him back from everything he wanted to achieve. A successful raid and the support of the Earl of Bradford's friends would go a long way to getting him into the office of detective chief inspector, but there were no guarantees when men of better social standing and no criminal past also sought that role.

And so, not wanting to lie to spare her feelings – he was quite certain she would hate that – he tried another tack.

"You don't have to go down there. Mr. Brill and I are quite prepared to host the evening ourselves."

Her shoulders stiffened at this remark, and she whirled to face him, her eyes narrowed.

"I said I know what they'll think of me, not that I cared. I'm doin' this for you and all those souls like your Lucy livin' in the rookery who deserve better, and I want them to know it."

John could only stare at her, at the wild defiance in her eyes and the proud tilt of her chin, his heart pounding with the need for her, as he thought about how much he loved this woman. And then he kissed her.

TWENTY-FOUR

All the pent-up anger within Violet dissipated the moment John Barrow took her face in his large hands and pressed his lips to hers, dragging her against the hard length of his body. Pleasure and pain, the joy of his touch and the sadness of her impending departure spiralled together inside her, and she clung to him, afraid if she let go the moment would end, and if the moment ended... there would never be another. In recognizing that she loved him, and that this was their last night together, she found her fingers inching their way to the buttons of his shirt as he tugged at the hooks and laces of her bodice, casting it unceremoniously to the floor. She moaned as she trailed her fingers over the bare skin of his chest, over rigid muscles, tangling in the whorl of hair over his heart, pausing to feel it racing beneath her touch.

He tugged up her arms, pulling away her chemise and tossing it to the floor, along with his shirt and tie. He was backing her up now, so her buttocks rested upon the edge of the desk. His hands were on her thighs, pushing them apart as he stepped between them, kissing her, always kissing her. He only pulled away for a moment, then, to stare down at her, his dark eyes wild with some emotion she could not name as he cupped her face in his hands.

"I will miss you."

And Violet responded as honestly as she could, without ever revealing the true depths of her feelings. "I'll miss you, too."

He held her gaze for a moment, his thumbs brushing over her cheeks, and she could have cried, then, for she *would* miss him. She would miss him terribly. Her desire was unbearable now, and it only grew sharper as his hand moved down to slide a finger between her slick folds. She arched towards him, her hands working at the buttons of his trousers as he trailed his mouth down the column of her throat, whispering her name. Finally, she freed his cock, hard and hot and ready for her, just as she was ready for him, so ready that as he notched himself at the entrance to her body, she was already on the edge of coming apart. As he took her hips into his hands and held her steady, sliding deeper and deeper until he was buried inside her, she did indeed tip over the edge into release, crying out as his mouth opened over hers.

She was shaking as his hands slid down the length of her thighs to pull them around his hips, and suddenly, the world beyond the light of the single lamp she had set nearby ceased to exist. Violet's entire being was focused on the muscles bunching beneath her fingers, on the rasp of John's breath in her ear, on his scent – soap and citrus and sweat – and on where they joined, her thighs slick with her wetness, his slow, even thrusts. She was at the precipice once more, longing for him to take her with wild abandon, to pin her to that desk and leave her with something to remember when she was back in Paris, alone, because she could not imagine allowing anyone to become as close to her as John; she never wanted the moment to end. But end it did, as John pulled her nipple between his lips, his free hand reaching between them as he kept up the steady thrust of his hips to find that hard nub of flesh and tracing over it until she splintered. Pleasure spiked through her, wave after wave, as he lifted his mouth to hers once more, swallowing her gasps as he pulled out of her to spend himself upon her belly.

They didn't move for a long time with the unspoken knowledge that when they pulled apart, the spell would be broken, and they would soon have to part ways. Violet's throat ached as she pressed her face into his chest, breathing in his scent, her hands splayed across his back, refusing to release him. She didn't want to cry, didn't want to spoil their final evening together, and she squeezed her eyes shut and tightened her grip, wishing she could ask him to come with her but knowing it would be wrong to do so. He had so much to give here, and she had worked too hard for her life in France to give it up for anyone – even John Barrow.

A small clock on the bookshelf chimed the fifth hour, and the spell had to break. The guests would be arriving shortly, and John pressed one last kiss to her mouth before stepping out from between her legs with a reluctant sigh. Violet could barely look at him now as she sat perched upon the edge of the big desk in naught but her stockings, his seed upon her belly. He said nothing as he bent to gather up his coat and dig around in one of the pockets, finally procuring a handkerchief and coming back to her side. He did not immediately begin to clean her, but instead, touched his finger to her chin, tipping her face up so he was looking down into her eyes. His expression was soft, his ordinarily sharp features blunted by the wavering light of the lamp.

"I will not forget you, Violet Latimer."

Oh god, she was going to cry. She couldn't bear to do that in front of him, not now, and so she forced a grin onto her face and said with as much humour as she could muster, "You'd better not."

He gave her a soft smile and leaned down to touch his lips

to hers, letting them linger there as her throat grew tighter and tighter before he drew away and looked down to gently wipe his seed from her skin. When he finally met her gaze again, he seemed hesitant, pausing before he spoke.

"I'll go fetch that suit. Mr. Brill will be waiting for us."

She nodded as she slipped off the edge of the desk and accepted her chemise when he handed it to her. She pulled it on quickly, feeling exposed with no barrier between her nakedness and his appreciative gaze as he buttoned up his trousers once more. He tugged on his shirt to leave the room, giving her time to pull on her drawers and petticoats before stepping into the magnificent concoction of silk and lace that was the dress Della had provided. She was just fastening the bodice, one which cut low across the swell of her breasts, when he came back inside, a neatly pressed suit and shirt draped over one arm. He stopped in the doorway, his eyes travelling down her form, and he smiled as he glanced back up at her.

"Lady Bradford has quite the sense for fashion, I see," he remarked as he carefully laid his clothes over the back of a chair. She grinned at this as she fastened the last hook and smoothed down the front of the bodice, festooned with ruched silk and jet beads.

"Della never had an eye for art, I'm afraid, but she did always fancy a pretty frock." She paused, nervously touching the lace edging the neckline of her gown. "Is she here yet?"

He glanced over at the small clock as he donned the fine white piqué shirt Edward had left for him.

"She and the earl should be here shortly, before the other guests are due to arrive at six."

Violet nodded as she drifted over to the mirror hanging above a low sideboard to inspect herself. The gown was exquisite, perfectly matching the colour of her eyes, but she could find little delight in it as she carefully plucked out a hairpin which had come loose, curling the lock of hair it had held about her finger before pinning it back into place. Her cheeks were flushed from their lovemaking, and she quickly fanned herself to cool her skin before drawing on the fine white silk gloves which had accompanied the dress, along with the exquisite emerald and diamond necklace and matching earrings from the jewelry box. Thus dressed, she turned to face John, and her breath caught in her throat. He was always beautiful, whether it be in his everyday grey flannel or brown tweed, in the boxing ring with sweat-slicked skin and bruises, or naked in a whore's bedroom on a rainy afternoon. But he was especially handsome this night, the suit of black and white tailored perfectly to his lean frame. She smiled.

"They'll never guess you grew up fencin' on Queen Street."

Violet's beauty would put to shame the haughtiest, most blue-blooded of duchesses this evening, of that John Barrow was certain. She was resplendent in emerald silk and black lace, her golden hair a halo, and he couldn't help smiling at her as he took her gloved hand in his to lead her back down those wide, sweeping stairs to the foyer below. It was a bustling hive of activity now, with footmen and maids running to and fro across the shining marble floors, making final preparations for the guests who were due to begin arriving shortly. His fingers tightened on hers as they reached the bottom step, but her expression remained anxious as she stepped down beside him. He wanted to tell her how breathtaking she was: that he would be proud to have her on his arm, to say out loud that she was his. But he was quite sure that would only make her more nervous, and so he nodded towards the card room, seemingly quieter than the dining room as it would not be in use until later this evening.

"Shall we go and find our host?"

She said nothing, but nodded and accepted his hand once

more as John guided them through the card room, its mahogany floors gleaming, its silk-patterned walls luxurious, to the service door at the back of the space. Beyond was a wide corridor which would take them to the kitchens, and it was there they found Edward Brill. A scullery maid pointed him out standing in the alley beyond the delivery door, leaning against the brick wall, pipe in hand. He nodded when he spotted them, knocking the pipe against the wall to empty it before gesturing for them to follow him back inside.

"The manager just told me your lady friend's here," he said, stepping past them to lead them back through the kitchens. Violet's whole face lit up, and they followed Edward to the grand foyer just as a footman was pulling open the door. Della burst into the room, her pale eyes blazing, followed by her husband, the Earl of Bradford, wearing a patient smile as his wife's gaze went directly to Violet. She immediately scowled and stormed over to where Violet stood at the bottom of the grand stairs, the train of her pale silver gown swishing along behind her before she threw her arms around her friend and pulled her into a tight hug. Edward chuckled and John smiled as Della pulled back just enough to meet Violet's tearful gaze.

"I could cheerfully wring your neck, Violet Latimer," Della said with a scowl before hugging her again. She finally pushed Violet back, holding her by the shoulders to give her a thorough appraisal.

"Though the dress did turn out just as I planned, didn't it, Cole?" She spoke over her shoulder to her husband, who was nodding as he handed his top hat and cane over to the waiting footman.

"It did, indeed, my love," the earl replied, with a nod towards Violet. "You look very well, if I may say, Miss Latimer. Della has been quite worried about you since she received your letter yesterday."

"Worried?" she cried. "I've been nearly out of my mind

with fear! Violet, what could you have thought, turnin' yourself over to Archie like that?" A hint of Seven Dials was beginning to creep back into Della's carefully acquired accent as she took Violet by the elbow and steered her away from the group. The Earl of Bradford now turned a benign smile upon John and Edward.

"Detective Inspector Barrow," he said, ignoring the hiss of his wife's voice from the far corner of the room, "good to see you again. You appear no worse for the wear." He extended his hand to take John's as he looked him up and down before turning his attention to Edward. "Mr. Brill, a pleasure to finally meet you in person. My wife has been singing your praises since you offered the use of your club for this event."

"Glad to be able to help, m'lord, seein' as this is a cause near and dear to me own heart," Edward answered as the two men shook hands before the earl leaned in towards John to speak in a low voice.

"I understand there is to be a raid this evening?"

It was only as he was reminded of the work which was to be done tonight that John was finally able to banish the memory of Violet, perched upon the edge of Edward's desk, her pert little breasts begging for his mouth, holding onto him as though she would never let him go as he had slid himself between her thighs, into her slick, welcoming warmth. He cleared his throat and dipped his head.

"Aye. By the end of this evening, Archie and Tommy Neville will be in the custody of the Metropolitan Police, and the Bruisers will be no more."

Lord Bradford nodded slowly as he withdrew the watch from his pocket and consulted it before giving John a quick smile.

"I shall be certain to put in a good word for you with the superintendent when he arrives."

"Thank you, my lord."

The earl now glanced over to where Violet was speaking with his wife, who no longer looked ready to strangle her friend, before returning his gaze to John, his expression concerned.

"How has Miss Latimer been bearing up?"

John's own gaze slid towards Violet, her beauty making him ache, and he swallowed before answering. "Very well, all things considered. Truthfully, she wanted no part of this, and therefore I believe I'm eternally in her debt."

Lord Bradford gave a knowing smile at this. "It's not a bad place to be, I assure you," he said with a loving glance towards his wife, who was even now leading Violet back towards them, both women now smiling.

"Please do excuse my lack of manners, gentlemen, for not staying for the introductions. It is a pleasure to finally meet you, Mr. Brill."

Edward took the hand she offered and bent in a quick bow before turning on his most charming smile.

"The pleasure is all mine, my lady. And please let me say what an honour it is to have the Earl and Countess of Bradford at my little club. Who'd have thought a gangster from Limehouse would be hostin' every bloody toff from here to Mayfair, raisin' money for the same people we all know they'd sooner forget," he said with a wink, pointedly ignoring the raised brow the earl offered before he chuckled. "Lots to see to before everyone arrives. Enjoy the evenin'," he added with a sly grin as he caught up with one of the footmen walking by and accompanied him from the room.

Della was smiling as she turned to her husband, who looked far less amused as his gaze followed Edward Brill.

"Are you certain about him hosting, darling?"

She laughed and pressed a kiss to his mouth before taking his hand.

"Come along, Cole – I want to see the dining room."

The earl shot John a patiently exasperated look before

following his wife from the hall, and then he was alone with Violet once more.

"Would it be too bold of me to tell you that you are stunning?" he said in a quiet voice, and she flushed, setting off the jewels which sparkled at her ears.

"Not if I can tell you that you've never looked finer."

John smiled at that and held out an arm for her, which she took with a wide grin as he led her into the dining room just as the guests began to arrive. They joined with the earl and countess, who were admiring more of Edward Brill's seemingly endless art collection. A string quartet, positioned in the far corner of the room upon a platform, had struck up a lively melody as Violet tugged at John's sleeve.

"Do you see that little landscape up there, with the white house? That's by Monsieur Pissarro, the man who bought one of my paintin's."

And though John should have followed her delighted gaze to the framed canvas she was pointing at, he couldn't help watching her face, loving the sheer elation in her expression. It made him want to pull her into him and kiss her; to do anything within his power to be the one to make her light up with joy like she was now. He wasn't even aware he was staring at her, struck dumb like some untried youth, until someone said his name.

"Detective Inspector Barrow?" came Lady Bradford's voice, bemused, and he blinked and turned to find her watching him with narrowed eyes, tapping her bejewelled fan upon her hip. Violet had moved on to another painting further down the wall and was leaning in close to inspect the signature, and it took John a moment to realize that the countess had been trying to get his attention before he answered.

"Yes, my lady?"

She pursed her lips, appraising him, before she spoke.

"I had wanted a moment to speak with you... about how

things went with Archie. If I had known... I suppose Violet swore you to secrecy?"

He nodded. "She didn't want you to worry."

Lady Bradford sighed and cast her gaze over to her friend who had bumped into the earl and was pointing out something on the painting she had been inspecting. The tapping stopped.

"Detective Inspector Barrow, I have never been so frightened in my life as when I received her letter – and I have been in more frightening situations in my life than I care to count." She looked back at John now, her pale blue eyes unnerving in their intensity. "I know you can't possibly know what life was like with Archie Neville and I'm certain Violet insisted – but I do wish you had told her no. I can't believe she even suggested that plan to you."

John could only lift his shoulders in defeat. "I tried telling her that we could think of something else, but she wanted no one else hurt on her account... I think you, more than anyone, knows how futile it was to say no."

She heaved another heavy sigh. "Yes, I do, unfortunately." She paused, and a worried look pleated her brow. "Is she... well? He didn't hurt her?"

John was quick to shake his head. "No... no, she was safe."

The countess gave a slow nod, but her hand went to her chest, pressing upon her skin as though to ease a racing heart.

"Good... thank you, then, for watching over her." She paused. "You must have spent a great deal of time together, while she was locked away."

Her tone was carefully casual, but John could see her eyes narrowing on him, assessing. He coughed and lifted his shoulders.

"I made certain that I was trusted enough to be her guard. I wanted to be sure she was safe and be able to communicate with her for the purposes of the operation."

The corner of Lady Bradford's mouth quirked up.

"Well, thank you again for keeping her safe. I know she's eager to return to Paris." She glanced over his shoulder and inclined her head. "I do believe that's your superintendent. Be sure to let him know how valuable Violet was in the success of your operation."

Her look was pointed, and John could see how the two women had managed to survive a childhood together in Seven Dials. He was quite sure that Lady Bradford would gladly murder any who dared lay a hand on Violet, and she the same. He smiled.

"I have every intention of doing just that."

She nodded, satisfied. "Then I believe I shall go find my husband. Enjoy the evening, Detective Inspector Barrow." Her little smile was knowing as she turned and made her way back out into the foyer. John frowned at her receding back, clad in shimmering silk, believing wholeheartedly that Lady Bradford had taken one look at him, seen into the very deepest recesses of his heart and knew, without a shadow of a doubt, that he was deeply and madly in love with her best friend.

TWENTY-FIVE

After Lady Bradford had left the room, leaving John with the unsettling sensation that she knew far more than he was willing to admit, he went to find Violet so he might introduce her to his superintendent. She was standing beneath a massive portrait of a lady clad in garb from centuries past, staring up with an expression of wonder. She didn't look at him as he approached her.

"He's got a bloody Holbein," she said, speaking loudly to be heard over the nearby strains of the quartet and the growing din of voices as more guests entered the room. John recognized many of them as friends and peers of the earl – dukes and viscounts and barons. Even a politician or two. He looked back at Violet who had finally torn her gaze away and was watching him with a smile.

"Ready to go make some money?"

He chuckled and offered his arm once more, spotting his superior entering the room.

"Come along, there's someone I want you to meet," he said, as she laid her hand upon his and followed him through the gathering throngs to the superintendent, who noticed him as they approached and waved him over.

"Ah, detective inspector, there you are! Quite splendid, isn't it?" he remarked, gesturing widely to the room with its lofty ceilings of moulded plaster and walls of watered silk. John nodded.

"It was very kind of Mr. Brill to give us the use of it for the evening."

"Indeed." He grinned. "They'll have to make you detective chief inspector now, won't they?"

John managed a polite smile. "If the board sees fit, then I should be honoured," he said, before gesturing to Violet, whose fingers were digging into his arm. "May I introduce Miss Violet Latimer, without whose assistance we would surely not be here in this room tonight."

"Lovely to meet you, Miss Latimer," Culpepper said, offering Violet the smallest tilt of his head. His reply was utterly benign, and yet there was a coolness in his gaze, a disdainful lift of his chin, as he observed her. Violet smiled dutifully in response, but John could see the tightening of her lips and the narrowing of her eyes as she took in his superior officer's unmistakable contempt.

"And you, as well, superintendent. Detective Inspector Barrow has told me a great deal about you." She made no attempt to elaborate upon this as she turned a winning smile upon John. "I'm terribly parched – I think I'll go find the refreshment room so you two may talk business."

John could hardly call out Culpepper's derision for the woman who had undoubtedly helped him with his decade-long ambition to remove the gangs from the rookery, so he gave her a quick, sympathetic look before nodding.

"Of course, Miss Latimer."

Violet had turned away before he had even finished speaking and it was with an effort that John turned back to his superior with a tight smile. Culpepper was watching as Violet crossed the room before giving the smallest of shrugs.

"A pretty thing, I suppose," he said before turning back to John. "I have had word from our sergeant that the men will be arriving outside Covent Garden shortly. All we need do is sit back and celebrate with some champagne." He smiled, but John struggled to return the expression, knowing that Violet was off somewhere, fuming and embarrassed at Culpepper's treatment. He should have been thrilled at that moment – the months of dedication were finally going to pay off – but all he could do was nod.

"Marvelous," he said, wishing it were so. Culpepper gave him a curious look.

"Is something amiss, Barrow? We have finally succeeded – you will surely be detective chief inspector once this operation concludes."

John sighed and let his gaze drift out over the other guests. "Yes, and I am most grateful for the opportunity."

Culpepper tilted his head and narrowed his eyes as John looked back at him. "I expected you might be a little more enthusiastic. You've been undercover for months now – time to return to real life and set about rising up the ranks, eh?" He tried for an encouraging smile, but all John could think of was Violet and the angry flush in her cheeks, and how all night that heavy weight had been sitting upon his chest – he had wanted to confess he loved her when they had been upstairs, to ask her to stay, but he hadn't because he didn't dare stand in the way of her dreams.

"Yes, of course," he murmured absently, his gaze once more drawn to the ballroom, seeking out that gown of emerald silk. When Culpepper loudly cleared his throat, he finally forced his attention back to his superior and found him frowning.

"Detective inspector, I do hope that you maintained a...

professional relationship with Miss Latimer, during your time with her."

John blinked; had he been so transparent? He was quick to shake his head.

"Certainly. We do have a past acquaintance through the Countess of Bradford, and so she is familiar to me, of course."

Culpepper looked relieved. "Quite so. I know women with her... experience... can cause some men to make questionable decisions."

John's eyes narrowed. The weight lifted, replaced by a terrible, cold fury. A muscle in his jaw twitched and he had to swallow back the words he wanted to say, none of which were appropriate for a high-society event, and instead reply, "I assure you, superintendent, that Miss Latimer's experience has no bearing on how I view her. Please do excuse me." He turned without another word to go find Violet.

He spotted her in the shadows of a small alcove, gripping a glass of champagne and he sighed as he came up to her.

"I'm terribly sorry about that, Violet – he treated me no better when we first met. He has always been supportive in my becoming a detective, but I know my past has always troubled him. Anyone raised in the rookery, whatever they make of themselves, must be, at heart, always a criminal."

"Or a whore," Violet said, her voice raw with anger. John's chest grew tight, hating that anyone would dare make her feel so low, this wonderful woman who possessed more beauty and talent and bravery than Lloyd Culpepper could ever dream of. He touched a finger to her chin, and she looked up at him, her eyes blazing.

"You are an artist, Violet Latimer. And you always have been."

Her expression softened, just a little, when they were interrupted by someone coughing loudly. They turned to find Edward Brill watching them with a raised brow.

"If I'm throwin' this whole party just to get you some promotion, then you'd best get out there and start hobnobbin' with these toffs. Miss Latimer," he added, turning his gaze to Violet. "Since you're the expert on these things, I've a new paintin' my solicitor insisted I purchase as an investment, but I think he was tryin' to fob it off on me. Perhaps you'd have a look, tell me if it's worth what I paid?"

Violet glanced at John, then back to Edward and nodded.

"Of course, Mr. Brill. Lead the way."

She left without another word, and John sighed. It was, indeed, time to start hobnobbing. After all, if Violet could withstand the pointed looks and disdainful sniffs of his superintendent, then he could certainly handle mingling with a viscount or two.

Violet was finally beginning to enjoy the evening. The music was lively, the art was impressive, the champagne was flowing, and there were no more scathing looks sent in her direction. Della had finally calmed down after the surprise of the letter and the fear that Archie must have taken out a terrible revenge upon her, and they laughed and chatted just as they had in the old days, marveling at how far they had come from living in a brothel in Seven Dials. They were already planning their visit to Paris when Della spotted John Barrow across the room, speaking with her husband. She let out a small huff of laughter.

"I'm sure they're discussin' the particulars of Archie's case." Her expression grew serious as she met Violet's gaze. "Cole really is very sorry he wasn't able to help you, Vi. You mustn't blame him... I made him promise he would stay out of the business of spyin'."

Violet shrugged as she snatched up a glass of champagne from a passing footman. "It all worked out in the end."

Della's gaze was assessing as she took a sip from her own

glass. "Yes, Detective Inspector Barrow has informed me that you were paramount in his success." She paused. "I know you didn't choose to go to Archie because you wanted to help. What on earth made you go back to that place? Why would you take that risk?" Della asked, placing a beseeching hand upon Violet's arm, and her heart twisted painfully, seeing the concern in her friend's eyes. She managed a brave smile and placed her hand over Della's.

"He was never gonna stop, Della – you know that. He was killin' people tryin' to find me. He murdered a fella I knew from Cora's... and that was the last straw."

Della's jaw dropped in shock, but after a moment, she nodded, though her eyes shone with unshed tears. An awful guilt crept through Violet, knowing how worried her friend had been for her.

"I do know, Vi... but if he ever found out..."

Violet gave her head a vehement shake. "Don't even think it, Della. It won't matter after tonight. I'll be back in Paris before the end of the week and Archie will be rottin' away in a prison cell where he belongs."

Della put on a haughty expression. "Good riddance. We shan't give him another thought. But I expect a grand tour when Clara and I arrive. A celebration of your return," she added with a smile, tugging on Violet's arm so they might stroll around the perimeter of the room, outsiders to the last, even with the benefit of Della's title. No one looked askance at them, but neither did anyone approach them and Violet grinned.

"We'll drink champagne until we burst and stuff ourselves with croissants. D'you know there's a lovely little French patisserie right around the corner from here? Detective Inspector Barrow took me there a few weeks ago and it was just like being back in Montmartre."

Della's brow went up. "Did he?"

Violet narrowed her eyes at her friend. "What?"

Della lifted one shoulder and sipped her champagne. "Seems you two have become rather close. I believe I caught him starin' at you earlier."

Violet managed a scoff but couldn't find the will to meet Della's inquisitive gaze. "We helped each other out of a tight spot. He'll get what he wants, and I'll get my life back."

Della was silent for a moment, her gaze moving over the crowded ballroom. When she looked back at Violet, she was smiling.

"He's a fine man, and there is no one more deserving of that promotion." She took another sip of her champagne before giving her a nonchalant glance. "I don't suppose there is some handsome Frenchman waiting for you back in Paris?"

Violet chuckled. "There are a lot of handsome Frenchmen, but none waitin' for me."

"Pity. I've heard they make excellent lovers," Della said with a wicked glint in her eye, and Violet let out an amused sniff before she looked away with a sigh.

"If you must know the truth, Del, there was no man in France. Not once in two years."

Della turned to her now with a sympathetic look. "I suspected as much. Not once in any letter did you mention someone... it can be so hard to let go of our pasts."

Violet drew in a breath. There was no fear in telling Della the truth; they had shared the highest highs and the lowest lows together and had never felt the need to conceal uncomfortable truths from one another.

"I didn't come home intendin' to change anythin' about that. I was very happy on my own. But then I was spendin' all that time with Detective Inspector Barrow – John – and somethin's grown between us." She let out a small laugh. "We were... together... upstairs before this very party."

Della grinned, her brows rising. "So, he is a very fine man, indeed." The smile faded as she contemplated her friend. "But he's not coming with you to Paris, is he?"

Violet slowly shook her head. "I wouldn't even ask. And I'm not stayin' here for him."

"Well, that is a bit of a problem. Unless... this was a mere liaison?"

Violet took a moment to glance towards the ballroom, not wanting to be overheard before meeting her friend's curious gaze once more.

"I don't know. Della, I think... I think I may love him. Isn't that silly?"

"Why would it be silly for you to love him?"

Violet scoffed. "I was a whore, Della. I fucked men for money. And never once did I see the use in lovin' any of them."

To this, Della only gave a sad smile. "And at one time, neither did I." She glanced over Violet's shoulder, then back to her, touching a hand to her arm. "I'm gonna go find my husband. You should go find Detective Inspector Barrow."

And without another word, Della stepped past her and disappeared into the crowds. Violet watched her go as a heavy weight settled upon her chest. She was not even certain if it was love she felt for John – so how could she tell him she loved him? And even if she did... they were on two different paths, in two different countries, with an expanse of sea between them. All she would end up doing was breaking her heart again, and she had no intention of letting that happen. Sighing, she swallowed back the last of her champagne, deciding that if she had to be stuck at this party with a bunch of haughty aristocrats, she might as well get good and scammered. She was scanning the crowd for another footman when Edward Brill materialized, nodding when he recognized her. He came to stand beside her, saying nothing as they both looked out over a sea of silk and jewels and feathers. After a moment, he spoke, leaning in close so she could hear him over the din.

"You hidin' from all these toffs, as well?"

Violet gave a wry smile. "Maybe. But this evenin' isn't for me. It's for Detective Inspector Barrow. I'm just meant to be hidin' out while the police do their work at Archie's club."

He nodded. "Very good of you to do this for him, considerin' what they think of us."

Violet shrugged and looked up at Edward. "It's what he really wants. And he helped me when I needed it, so this is how I'm helpin' him."

Edward nodded again. The string quartet had struck up another lilting tune and the din of the crowd rose and fell before he spoke again. "I suppose you're headin' straight back to Paris after tonight?"

Violet was staring out at the ballroom, all the people blending into a kaleidoscope of colour as tears pricked at her eyes. She couldn't see John, though if she had, she might have begun weeping at the thought of never seeing him again. She swallowed back the rising ache in her throat and inclined her head.

"Yes. I'll stay at Bradford House tonight and travel to the train station tomorrow afternoon."

"Then I'll give this to you now, in case we don't see each other again tonight," he said, and Violet turned to see him holding out a sealed envelope. She gave him a quizzical look.

"What is it?"

Edward smiled as she took it. "A proposal."

She frowned down at the envelope, and when she looked back up again, he had already turned and was heading out of the room. Shrugging, she slipped it into her pocket and forced herself to wade into the throngs. Her head was beginning to spin from the effects of too much champagne, and she needed to eat something. The refreshment room was just on the other side of that massive foyer, and so she made her way through the guests. She was just rounding a corner when she bumped into a gentleman who turned immediately to face her.

"Oh, superintendent, I do apologize," she said, an angry flush rising up her chest as she recalled his disdainful appraisal of her. She refused to let it show, reminding herself that she was here to get John his promotion, and so plastered a dazzling smile upon her face.

"Ah, Miss Latimer, I had hoped to see you again. I do believe I was remiss in not thanking you earlier. Your assistance in the capture of the Neville brothers cannot go unremarked upon. Detective Inspector Barrow is most grateful for your help."

The tightness in Violet's chest abated at these words, and her smile softened.

"Why, thank you. It was a difficult time, but I'm glad it worked out."

He gave a slow nod and seemed to be considering her before he spoke again. "I take it you shall be returning to Paris posthaste?"

"Yes," she said slowly. "I'll be catchin' the afternoon train to Dover tomorrow."

Culpepper looked relieved, finally smiling at her. "Very good. I should hate for Barrow to become distracted."

"Distracted?"

He chuckled and took a sip of his champagne. "You're a very pretty girl, Miss Latimer, and I worried you had become close in your time together. He is quite set on this promotion, but no man rises to become detective chief inspector if he's involved with, well... a woman of your... experience..." He trailed off now, giving her an embarrassed smile.

Violet might have smiled in return. She didn't know. She was frozen to the spot, people swirling around her as she stared back at the superintendent, with his greying hair, clipped neatly, and his immaculately tailored suit. She seemed to recall the hollow feeling she had on the train to Headingly Hall after Archie had found her in Paris. She felt the same now, only worse. Much worse. My god, how could she have been so stupid? How could she have let herself fall for another man who was wrong? He was wrong. *Wrong.*

She couldn't breathe, and the room was beginning to spin around her. He could have loved her back or not, but it didn't matter in the end because he was never going to be with a whore. He was never going to go with her. Because she was unlovable, and she should have known it from the start.

Violet mumbled an excuse of some sort and turned on her heel, tears scalding at the backs of her eyes as she pushed through the crowds to the card room. She had to get out. She had to get out of this place. She would get on a train tonight; she couldn't wait. A sob was burning in her throat as she found the door, the one which took her to the kitchens, to the way out. A footman said something as she passed; she didn't hear him. Pots and pans banged, and the cook shouted as she stumbled through the kitchen, but she was insensate at this point; she couldn't hold the sob back any longer, and just as she made it outside, it burst from her. Her chest heaved as she buried her face in her hands, letting the tears fall, letting the cold night air wash over her. She should have been angry; she should have raged and screamed and cursed, but all she could do was weep uncontrollably at the knowledge that all her worst fears had been confirmed. Violet Latimer was a whore, and she always would be. No one would love her, and she was wrong to love anyone in return.

TWENTY-SIX

John was smiling and nodding politely to a man whose name he couldn't remember – he might be a baron but, quite frankly, he didn't care. He had barely heard what the man had said, anyway. He had been determined to let Violet go, to never reveal what he really felt for her, so that there was nothing holding her back when she returned to Paris. Why, then, was he so angry? Why was his stomach twisting in knots as he nodded inanely and muttered monosyllabic replies? Culpepper's words would not stop ringing in his head, telling him that the woman he loved – he knew that now – was unworthy of it. The implication was undeniably meant to let him know that he should not involve himself with Violet. It shouldn't matter, then, if she was leaving anyway. But it did. It did matter that she had been deemed unworthy by his superior, despite the fact that she had, without question, saved this operation for them. That she had helped them remove one of the worst gangs in London from the streets.

His future with the Metropolitan Police suddenly seemed so... pointless. If Violet had no value to them, how would he ever have it? His beginnings were just as low; his background just as spotty. Violet Latimer was unworthy of love, according to Lloyd Culpepper. So, what of John Barrow?

The room suddenly seemed too crowded; too hot, too noisy. Violet had been kind enough to arrange this event just for him, but now he couldn't wait to get out and have a moment of peace to think about what it all meant and if, after two years of hard work, nearly getting himself beaten to death on a weekly basis just to maintain his cover and doing the same to others... it had been worth it.

The baron was asking something about police procedure, but John was already turning, muttering his excuses as he sought a moment to think. The card room would still be empty, and he pushed his way through the guests, only to hear someone calling his name. The voice was familiar, and he turned to see, much to his shock, Bess, of all people, weaving her way between the clusters of partygoers, with a footman trailing in her wake and calling after her.

"Mr. Barrow!" she called again, gasping as she finally reached him. The footman came up behind her and took her by the arm, sending John an apologetic look.

"Very sorry, sir, but she said it was urgent and barged in before I could come and find you."

Bess glared at the young man and snatched her arm back as John waved him off. "It's alright, I know her."

She stared the footman down as he gave her one last, suspicious glance.

"Very good, sir," he said, and turned to leave them in the middle of the busy ballroom.

John tried to steer her towards a quiet corner so he might find out how she had found him and what matter was so urgent that she was gasping for air, as though she had run all the way here from Covent Garden. She immediately tugged her arm back and when he turned to her with a puzzled expression, she clapped a hand down on his shoulder and pulled him towards her.

"He knows," she hissed into his ear, and he drew back to look down at her, confused.

"What are you talking about? Bess, what are you doing here? How did you find—"

"He knows!" she said, louder, and John's heart began to race as the unspoken implication dawned upon him. He stared at her, his chest growing cold as her fingers dug into his shoulder, urgent. Someone bumped into him, but he barely noticed as Bess's face turned white and her eyes grew wide.

"Archie knows it was Miss Latimer who turned him in!"

The noise fell away. He was no longer hot; he shivered as a chill crept through him. He was hardly aware of anyone around them as he stared at Bess, mouth agape. Her eyes were wide with terror, and after a moment where he was only aware of the blood rushing at his temples, he finally blinked, immediately straightening to search the room. He was looking for only one thing: a rich emerald gown and a crown of golden hair. His heart was threatening to burst from his chest and his hands had started shaking. He couldn't see her. He whipped around to face Bess.

"How does he know? Tell me everything." He was speaking as he took her by the arm again and led her through the crowds so they might have somewhere private to speak before he went to find Violet.

"It were Tommy," she was gasping as she followed him out into the foyer. "We was in the club, gettin' ready to open for the fight, and he come in – he was furious, Mr. Barrow, he was shoutin' for Archie, sayin' that bitch turned him in, askin' where she was."

They finally reached a deserted corner in the card room, and John turned once more to Bess, whose face had grown even more ashen as she spoke. She swallowed.

"I knew she'd gone off with you, but he was sayin' you weren't at the warehouse. I know you're not really one o' them," she added in a low voice, looking up at him, and he frowned.

"What do you mean?"

"You're not like the other fellas... you're a good fighter, but I could always see you didn't want to be fightin'. And I ain't stupid like they think I am. We girls see things, we hear things, and I know you and Violet were together."

John leaned back, shaken, but there wasn't time to parse that bit of information.

"Where are they now, Bess? Are they looking for her?"

She nodded. "Aye, like I said, they was lookin' for her at the warehouse, and now they've got men all over the rookeries tryin' to find you both. And I knew I had to find you before they did. I saw the papers; I saw Mr. Brill was hostin' a big party tonight and I know you was workin' with him, so... I came here."

"Shit," he muttered, knowing that if Archie and Tommy had left the club to go looking for Violet, the raid was going to fail. It was all for naught, and even if this party was an enormous success... his promotion was lost. He shook his head; no time to think about that now, because if the Neville brothers found Violet, she was as good as dead.

"Thank you, Bess. You'd best stay here until we know it's safe to go back to Covent Garden – Mr. Brill can find you somewhere to rest. I have to go and find Miss Latimer to warn her."

He was gone before Bess could reply, darting through the crowds, cursing them for their impedance as he frantically searched for that distinctive green gown. He checked the ballroom, the dining room, the corridors back to the kitchen. He even bounded up the stairs to search the office where they had made love. She wasn't here. *She wasn't here.* He was gasping now as fear choked him, and he had to pause at the top of the stairs with his hand on the newel post to try to breathe. *Lady Bradford!* She would know where to find Violet. He tore down the stairs, seeking out a head of raven-black hair and a gown of shimmering silver, his frustration mounting as he failed to find her, as well. He was frantic now, ready to begin roaring at the people around him to find her, to demand if they had seen a woman in a gown of green. He had made a second search of the ballroom when he turned to find himself face to face with Culpepper once more.

"Ah, there you are, detective inspector, I was looking for you. I wanted to—"

"Have you seen Miss Latimer?" John cut him off, taking his superior officer by the shoulders and staring at him with wide, panicked eyes. The older man frowned in confusion.

"Well, she must be here somewhere. I spoke with her not twenty minutes ago."

"Spoke with her?" John shook his head. "What about?"

Culpepper shrugged, confused as John released his grip on the other man's shoulders. "I only wished to thank her for her contribution to our operation and enquire if she was returning to France."

"Returning to France?" John blinked, confused. Why would Culpepper care what she did after tonight? The older man shrugged again.

"Yes. I was rather beginning to worry that she was becoming a distraction to you, Barrow. You two seemed awfully intimate earlier and I simply let it be known to her that any involvement you might have with a former... prostitute" – Culpepper lowered his voice to say the word – "would be looked down upon within the department. I wouldn't want you to lose your promotion over that... woman."

In the midst of his panic, it took a moment for the words to register with John, but when they did, his vision clouded with rage.

"*What?*"

Culpepper at least had the good grace to look embarrassed

before he replied, "She left in quite a hurry after that, no doubt to seek out her friend the countess."

Fuck! John wanted to scream at the man, and his fists were curling at his sides, but he managed to draw in a sharp breath. When he spoke, his voice was taut with anger. "You have to send word to the sergeant; the Neville brothers are not at the club – they must delay the raid. Tell him now!"

He turned without waiting for Culpepper's response. Violet was gone and she was in danger. And it was all his fault.

The tears dried up just as Violet reached Piccadilly, and she was beginning to regret having left the party in such a hurry, for her expensive slippers were now ruined and her feet positively ached. She realized, belatedly, that she must be a sight, wandering without purpose down the street, her cheeks stained with tears, wearing an evening gown with neither coat nor shawl to cover her bare arms from the deepening chill, and so she hailed a passing hansom cab.

Now that she had nothing left to cry, all she could do was sit and stew and hate herself for her foolishness, for thinking that John Barrow would ever want to be with her, for falling for him in the first place. She understood now, all too clearly, why he had never so much as said he cared for her or asked her to stay.

He got what he wanted, though, didn't he? Violet let out a shuddering breath and buried her face in her hands as the voice, the one she thought she had finally silenced, began to whisper at her again. *He was never going to be with you because you are a liability. He was never going to choose you over his career. He got his bit of fun.* Violet pressed her palms into her eyes with a strangled cry, trying to erase the image of his face from her mind; of John smiling down at her, of falling into his arms during their boxing lesson, of the feeling of his hips wedged between her thighs, bringing her pleasure she had not thought herself worthy of feeling again. Not until he came along and made neither judgement nor comment on her past.

The tears sprang forth once more at that thought, her heart wrenching inside her chest, a sensation so painful that she let out a low, keening moan. He had made her feel valuable; he had made her feel loved, even though he had never said the words. And it was all a lie – he would get his precious promotion on the back of her imprisonment, and what had she? Just another broken heart and the renewed determination that she would never love again.

That bitter resolve brought her all the way into Belgravia and the high brick wall surrounding Bradford House. At least she could hide away in her room, let the darkness consume her, and steal away at dawn to return to the one place where her past wasn't known, and thus did not matter.

Once the driver handed her out and drove on, she looked up at the high limestone walls of the house. All the windows were dark, and she sighed, relieved that at least she would not have to face the concerned looks or questions of the staff. She would rid herself of this gown, along with the memory of John Barrow and his touch, so gentle for a man accustomed to such violence, and his smile and his stupid beautiful eyes. Jaw set with angry determination, she slipped through the gate and strode through moonlit paths and the shadowed outlines of trees and shrubs, to reach the back door.

Violet was just rounding the corner, her steps quick and quiet, when she heard whispered voices, followed by a small, mewling cry. She paused, mid-stride, frowning, but not before she came around the corner to find two dark shapes leaving the house. They stepped into the light of the lantern hanging from the wall outside, and she froze. Tommy and the Devil. And in Tommy's arms – little baby Clara. Violet's heart lurched into her throat as she was torn between the instinct to run and getting Della's daughter away from these men. In the end, the decision was never made as the Devil looked up and spotted her peering around the corner before taking a few quick strides towards her and closing his hand around her wrist. He then hauled her into the light of the lantern and pushed her towards Tommy, who was now grinning as he looked her up and down.

"Oh, Violet... why do you keep gettin' caught?"

She gasped as the Devil threw her to the ground at Tommy's feet before raising a pleading gaze to him.

"Put her back, Tommy – I know you only came here for bait. Well, I'm here now. You can take me to Archie. You don't need the baby anymore."

Tommy chuckled, low and dark, and prodded her to rise with the toe of his boot. He was shaking his head as she stood on trembling legs.

"Baby? I wouldn't be worried about some fuckin' brat when you got much worse comin' your way." He took a step closer and leaned down, so his face was just inches from hers. Violet's breath caught. "You turned in my brother, didn'tcha?"

Violet's stomach plummeted and she could only stare back at Tommy, her mouth agape as the terrible realization sunk in. He sneered and looked over at the Devil.

"Come on, Archie'll want to know she's found."

Run, the voice whispered at her, but she followed without protest, numb with shock, as the Devil took her by the arm. How could she run when they had Della's daughter? Who knew what they would do to her if she ran?

A carriage waited for them a block away, and Violet was unceremoniously shoved inside. The Devil took the driver's seat and Tommy followed her inside, carrying the baby, miraculously still sleeping. Violet pushed herself as far into the corner as she could, keeping her gaze fixed on Della's daughter.

"Why don't you let me hold her, Tommy?"

His smile was dark in the sallow light of the cab's lanterns. "No."

She let out a small, shuddering breath and turned her gaze out the window to watch them make the familiar journey back to Covent Garden. In the midst of the shock of finding Tommy and the Devil absconding with Della's daughter, Violet had quite forgotten the events of the night, for she now knew only a deep, dreadful fear. It was rising up through her, chilling her insides, and though she did her best not to let it take hold, her hands were shaking as they crossed into Covent Garden. She was careful to peer down the alleys and side streets, hoping to see the police wagons which should be here for the raid, but the streets remained empty as they drew closer to the club. After a stretch of unbearable silence, Tommy finally spoke.

"Suppose you thought we'd never find out, eh?"

Violet said nothing. What could she say? He sniffed.

"It was Arthur's woman – the one he nearly beat to death. Found her in a brothel in Shoreditch. Went lookin' for her meself 'cause I never believed a word you said." Tommy's lip curled as he glared over at her, and her stomach clenched. "I never trusted you. And I never trusted that Barrow bastard." He paused. "Where is he, anyway?"

Violet swallowed and tried to make her voice strong when she spoke, but feared it came out as more of a choked rasp when she replied.

"I gave him the slip at the warehouse. I don't know where he went, and I don't care."

Tommy eyed her suspiciously before he spoke again. "I asked Arthur's girl what happened when he was arrested, and she said he never ratted on nobody." He paused again, his eyes practically gleaming with vicious delight. "She did say she saw you with a copper a few days later; thought he was just hasslin' you for solicitation. It didn't take much effort to add up that you was the one what turned in my brother, Violet."

The air grew chill in the cab and Clara murmured in her

sleep. Violet's throat was so tight now she could barely force the words out.

"He wouldn't let me leave, Tommy."

Tommy remained unmoved, his gaze narrowing on her. "You said you loved him. And he loved you – don't fuckin' understand it meself, but he woulda given you anythin'."

Violet shook her head as a shaft of light from a streetlamp slid over the interior of the cab. "I stopped lovin' him. I stopped when I saw what he really was."

"And what was that?"

A moment of silence. "A monster." Violet's voice was the barest whisper, but Tommy made no reply, his gaze sliding away from her to face forward. Little baby Clara still slept in his massive arms.

Violet let out a shaking breath. She was going to die tonight. None of the rest seemed to matter... John or Paris or her art. What did it matter when she knew Archie would kill her tonight? He knew now that she was responsible for his eight-year incarceration, and he was going to kill her for it. Tears were stinging at her eyes once more, but she blinked them away, determined that she would not allow her fear to show. If she was going to die tonight, it would be with dignity and defiance, not mewling and begging for mercy. She straightened her shoulders as the carriage slowed and they drew upon the Devil's Den. There was no one outside – undoubtedly everyone was in the cellars for the fight if it had proceeded as planned. She swallowed as Tommy opened the door and stepped out of the carriage without so much as looking at her and disappeared into the club with the baby. Violet pushed herself off the seat and leapt out of the cab, determined not to let Clara out of her sight for as long as she could, but the Devil was there, snatching her wrist before she could take even one step towards the club.

Fighting the urge to resist him, knowing it would gain her nothing and fearful of his retaliation, she gritted her teeth and allowed him to drag her inside. When she realized they were heading back down that corridor and into the dreaded box, she couldn't help digging her heels in and trying to pull her arm back. Unfortunately, it was very much like trying to beat back the tide, and his merciless grip remained steady as he pulled her down the hall and to the stairs. Her heart was beating so hard now her chest ached and the shadows at the bottom of the stairs seemed so much more ominous than before. That same fear she had going down them for the first time – that if she went into those shadows and let the door close behind her, she would never come out – had returned, but this time she knew it was true.

The Devil did not light the lantern for her as John had, though she wouldn't have expected him to. He pushed her inside and closed the door behind him, and it was the squeal of the bolt sliding home that finally tipped Violet into the despair she had been battling so hard to resist. The darkness closed around her as she pressed her palms flat upon the door and leaned her forehead against the cool wood. And though she was sure she had nothing left to cry, she wept. Great, shuddering sobs wracked her body as she finally saw the end, wishing, despite everything she had learned tonight, that John was here with her now.

TWENTY-SEVEN

John could think of only two places where Violet could have possibly gone. The first didn't bear thinking of – that she had gone directly to the train station to get out of England as fast as possible. More likely, he hoped, she had gone to Bradford House to collect her few belongings and change into something more practical for travel, and so, it was there he went, hailing the first hansom cab he found and asking the driver to make haste.

He was fairly vibrating with apprehension as he settled uneasily upon the faded leather squab, desperate to reach Violet before she left, to tell her what he should have told her from the moment he knew – that he loved her. If he had, Culpepper's words would have meant nothing to her. But he knew how she would have interpreted them, instead – that he had used her and had never had any intention of being more to her than a lover; that he thought her a detriment to his career. John cursed as the cab rattled over cobblestones, clenching his hands into fists to stop them from shaking. He could only imagine Violet's devastation, how his good intentions had only served to make her feel worthless, and he swore, in that moment, that he would make sure that she knew she was loved, whether she returned the feeling or not.

If only the blasted cab would go faster! It seemed as though an eternity passed before they were finally drawing up to the brick wall surrounding Bradford House, and John leapt from the cab and thrust a handful of coins at the driver before throwing open the gate and racing towards the house. He paused, though, as he reached the back door, for a light was on in the kitchen, though ordinarily the servants would have long since retired for the night. His heart began to race as he let himself into the hall and turned, hesitant, towards the kitchen, from which there came a murmur of anxious voices. Swallowing hard, he made his way towards them and found himself in the doorway. Harris, the butler, was standing before the large table with a robe hastily thrown over his night-clothes. He was holding Mrs. Cooper's hand as she wept. Another woman, younger, stood beside the housekeeper, and she, too, was in tears as she looked up and spotted John. Her small gasp drew Mrs. Cooper's attention, and the older woman glanced up. She looked baffled for a moment before relief filled her expression, and she drew away from Harris to come towards him.

"Mr. Barrow, what on earth are you doing here?"

John could only stare at the unusual scene before him, blinking in confusion as he finally met her tear-filled gaze.

"I... I thought Miss Latimer had returned for the evening. Mrs. Cooper, what's wrong?"

She opened her mouth to reply when there came a knock at the door through which he had just arrived, and they both turned at the sound. When John looked back at her, her expression was stricken.

"It's the police... someone took our little Clara."

John watched in horror as she stepped aside for Harris to open the door, admitting a sergeant and a constable John recognized in passing. They looked surprised to see him as Harris directed them into the kitchen.

"Detective Inspector Barrow?" Sergeant Shelby said in a quizzical tone as they shook hands. John's mind was racing as he gave a quick, absent nod towards the constable. "What are you doing here?"

"I..." he began, then turned swiftly back to Mrs. Cooper. "Someone took the baby?"

The housekeeper gave a shaky nod and waved towards the young woman who was with them in the kitchen. "Miss Yelland here is the nursemaid, and she went in to check on the babe before retiring for the evening, as she always does if the lord and lady of the house are out. And she saw..." Mrs. Cooper paused as her voice caught, and Harris took up her hand once more to give it a comforting pat. "The cradle was empty. We called for the police immediately and have sent one of the footmen to fetch home the earl and countess."

The sergeant was replying, speaking in a comforting tone, but John barely heard the words. They didn't matter, in any case, for he knew precisely who had come to this house and taken Clara, remembering with chilling clarity the words Archie had whispered to Violet when she had dared to refuse him: *I hear our Della's had herself a wee babe.* He burned with rage at the thought of it and turned just as the constable was withdrawing a small notebook and pencil from his pocket.

"You must get word to Superintendent Culpepper at the Brooklyn Club. Tell him to keep the men on standby but do not enter Covent Garden until I get word to him. I know where the baby is and I can get her, but the police cannot be seen in the area. Tell him I shall find him in Whitehall when I get the girl."

The sergeant was nodding as John turned to Mrs. Cooper, who looked on with wide, fearful eyes.

"I will get Clara back, Mrs. Cooper. Do not fear. The men who have her are only using her – they have no intention of hurting her." And even though he said those words in a confident tone, he could not be sure of their truth. A flicker of fear raced through him, but he pushed it down as he stepped past the two policemen and made for the hall. There was no time now to consider where Violet had gone; he must get that child back unharmed. He only hoped that he wasn't too late.

A change of clothes, borrowed from one of the footmen, was quickly procured so John might discard his eveningwear before he raced out into the street to hail the nearest hansom cab. He threw himself inside as he shouted for the driver to make for Covent Garden, clutching the seat the whole ride over and tapping his foot as though he could somehow urge the horse to go faster, then finally shouted for the driver to stop a few blocks over from the Devil's Den. When he reached the club, he found the streets around it were empty and he frowned. The fight should be at full pitch right now, though perhaps with Archie and Tommy out looking for Violet, it had been delayed. He ran a hand through his hair to tousle it before drawing in a deep breath and making his way up the stairs and into the club.

He entered a room devoid of people save for Tommy Neville, who sat at the bar with a glass of whisky in one hand. Cautious, John made his way towards the other man, who turned to look at him with narrowed eyes. Settling his face into as furious an expression as he could manage, he came to stand beside Tommy, who tilted his head.

"Where's the girl, Barrow?"

John shook his head and slammed a hand down on the bar. "She fuckin' took off." He kept his answer deliberately ambiguous, for there was a strange look in Tommy's eyes; something suggesting he was testing John. Tommy paused before he spoke again.

"Found out a little somethin' about Miss Latimer while you two was out."

"Oh?" John answered vaguely, reaching for the bottle of whisky Tommy had left out and filling an empty glass. Another pause.

"It weren't Arthur Potts who turned in Archie. It was her."

At that moment, John was convinced that in another life he could have been an actor. His gaze hardened and his shoulders stiffened as he took a slow, deliberate sip of his whisky. He was shaking his head as he set down the glass and wiped the back of his hand across his mouth.

"That deceitful little—" John couldn't bring himself to attach any unsavoury titles to Violet, and so he shook his head again, as though in disbelief. Tommy was watching him carefully as John glanced up with a dark look, one he drew from the simmering fear and rage that came from that babe being stolen away in the night by this man. "I'll find her, Tommy. I'll find her for your brother, and she'll wish she'd never been born."

The suspicion in Tommy's eyes finally dissipated and he gave a sniff of laughter. "No need for that, Barrow," he said, draining his glass and slipping from his stool. John raised a brow as Tommy took up the coat he had draped over a nearby chair. "She came right to us, she did. Got her down in the box, and we even got Della's brat. Archie's goin' down soon, and I assure you, when he does, she will most certainly be wishin' she was never born."

John's breath stilled in his throat. Violet was here. He wanted to be thankful that he knew where she was, but Archie had made very clear what he intended for the one who had got him sent to Newgate, and knowing she was in his grasp once more made his belly clench with dread. She must have come right upon them as they were stealing away the baby, and a shiver of fear raced up his back, knowing what Archie would have planned for her. He hid it well enough, though, giving a dark little grin and nodding in approval. "The Bradford baby, too? She'll fetch a decent ransom," John said in a carefully casual tone, and Tommy shrugged.

"Maybe, but I told Archie he was better off tossin' the brat in the Thames – too much bother otherwise. Ain't no one knows we're the ones what took her, and it's best if it stays that way."

John paused to empty his glass. "I dunno, I heard the earl paid Della ten thousand pounds for her little bit of thievery. Imagine what he'd pay to have his daughter back, eh?"

Tommy seemed to ponder the question for a moment before he shrugged again. "Might be worth keepin' her alive a little longer, then. I'll see what Archie thinks. Meantime, I do know that he wants us out of here – cleared the crowd out after the fight and everythin' so he can confront Violet proper, like."

John hid a sigh of relief. This was good... Clara was alive and would remain unharmed for the time being, and Violet was down in the box. She, too, was unharmed, but her time was very quickly running out. He had to get Tommy out of here so the police gathered on the outer edges of Covent Garden could reassemble. They could take Archie tonight; John would bring them Tommy, and the rest would fall with their leaders gone.

"Well, then," John said with a sigh as he set down his empty glass, "I say we head on over to the Fox and Friar, get ourselves a drink and a meat pie, and leave Miss Latimer to what's comin'." He was grinning as he took up his own coat and followed Tommy to the doors.

"I knew not to fuckin' trust that girl," Tommy was saying as he dragged on his coat. "Never appreciated what Archie did for her, gettin' her and Della outta that bloody orphanage, givin' them a roof over their heads and food to eat. Thought they was too good for us once they saw how we ran things." He scoffed as they stepped out onto the street, where a light flurry of snow had begun to fall, dusting the cobbles white. "A bloody Seven

Dials whore and a common pickpocket thinkin' they was above a few beatin's – how do they think we got to where we're at?"

John let out a disdainful sniff as they crossed the street to make their way towards Seven Dials. A man, dressed in patched trousers and coarse wool, stood outside one of the brothels with a flask in hand, muttering inanely to himself. Tommy walked by him without so much as a glance, but John met the man's gaze, just for the briefest of moments, and gave an almost imperceptible nod before they rounded a bend, and the stranger was gone.

Violet waited in the silent darkness for a long time. Or perhaps it had only been a few minutes. She could not tell as she felt her way to the narrow bed that had been the source of many sleepless nights for her and gingerly sat upon it. Despair and fear battled inside her, threatening to overwhelm, but she stubbornly refused, focusing instead on her anger, letting it wash over her in waves. She would not die here tonight, she decided; no – she was getting out and she was getting Clara back. It seemed an insurmountable task, she thought, as she looked around the tiny room, letting her eyes adjust to the dark. The barest glimmer of light streamed in through the tiny window, but it was just enough to create shadows in the corner of the room, to highlight the edge of the bedframe. Archie had been seeking the one who had turned him in for eight long years, determined that that person would die for their transgression. She was trapped in this tiny room with no way out save for one door, and there was no way that Archie was letting her out of here alive.

Violet shivered and bit back another rising sob. She mustn't despair; there was no gain to be had from it and it wouldn't get her out of this room. Seeking to distract herself until Archie arrived to deliver his punishment, she turned her thoughts to the one person who had occupied them since she had first seen him fighting in a cellar in Seven Dials. John Barrow. And though thinking of him distracted her from reflecting on her imminent demise, she now felt the full force of the heartbreak in knowing that he, too, thought her undeserving of love. That the reason he had never asked her to stay was because it would have made him a laughingstock at Scotland Yard.

Violet seethed as she dashed away unbidden tears. She was right, then, to leave this place and never come back. She was right to be alone, to care for herself and no one else. With that resolution, a cold, hollow sensation settled itself in the pit of her stomach, but she welcomed it because... at least it didn't hurt.

The squeal of the bolt sliding open made Violet's heart lurch and she jumped up from the bed with a gasp to watch as the sliver of light between the door and the frame grew wider, the door opening to reveal Archie, with little baby Clara cradled in one, massive arm. Her heart thundered as he stood in the opening, watching her with an unreadable expression. They stared at one another in silence. Violet was sure he would be able to hear the deafening thud of her heart as it beat against her ribs, and she drew in a long, shaking breath to slow it down as he took one step into the room, then another. She felt faint now; she had expected shouting and swearing and violence, not this cold, calculated calm. It unnerved her. Her breath was growing short as he took another step closer, and she swallowed as he finally spoke.

"Eight years, Violet," he said, his voice low and gravelly. "Eight years I spent in that place." He was shaking his head, but Violet's gaze was fixed on the baby held in the crook of his arm. Clara was beginning to stir, thrusting her little arms out and murmuring as she woke. She looked up only when Archie spoke again. "You were the only one what ever showed me a bit o' kindness, and I risked everythin' to get you out of that orphanage. I did it for you. I killed a man to do it. And what did I get in return?" He grew quiet, never answering his own question before he spoke again in a low voice. "Did you really hate me so much?"

His gaze narrowed on her, and though his words seemed to indicate he had been hurt by her betrayal, the rage glittering in his eyes suggested otherwise, and she chose her words carefully.

"I didn't hate you, Archie," she whispered, fighting to keep the tremble of fear from her voice. "I didn't hate you," she repeated, softer. It was a lie – she loathed him down to her very marrow, but if this was how she got out of this room, she would spin the tallest tales ever told. "But I didn't want to marry you. I was... I was scared of you. You'd changed. And I knew you wouldn't let me go."

He didn't move, but his mouth did flatten into a hard line. Clara was awake now, her tiny fists curling as she let out a plaintive cry, but Archie barely blinked.

"And what did you do, instead?" he hissed. "Became a whore – you'd have rather sold yourself than be married to me."

Violet swallowed again, pressing her hands to her sides to stop them shaking. "I'm not a whore. I'm an artist—"

"You're a fuckin' snitch," he snarled, lunging forward suddenly to reach for her. Startled, she tried to move back but he caught her wrist in his free hand and tugged her against him to push his face into hers. "I promised I'd kill whoever it was put me away, and don't think for one fuckin' moment you're the exception." He paused and tilted his head to observe her as she struggled against his iron grip. Clara was wailing now at the commotion, flailing her little arms, and kicking against Archie's chest as a flicker of annoyance crossed his broad face. He blinked, the emotion passed, and he was glaring at her again, his face growing redder as his grip tightened, making her gasp.

"Archie, please... you're hurtin' me—" She gasped again as he twisted her arm, forcing her to bend over lest he break it. His voice was growing louder now, and the unnerving calm was abandoning him as his anger grew.

"You loved me, though, didn'cha Violet? I was gonna give you the world and you got me sent to that fuckin' hellhole for eight years."

Violet cried out as he finally released her and she fell to the ground at his feet, panting as she looked back up at him. Clara was screaming now, and this only seemed to further incense Archie, who scowled down at the baby. A dark, dangerous rage clouded his gaze, and Violet knew if he got angry enough, that she would not be the only one to suffer his wrath this evening. She had to get Clara out of here, and she knew of only one way to break through Archie's red haze of fury, so she pushed herself up off the ground and faced him on quivering legs.

"I'm sorry, Archie... I'm so sorry. Let me hold her – I can get her quiet for you."

Archie sneered, ignoring her offer. "Sorry? You're not fuckin' sorry. You were happy to see me go, thought I'd forget about you. Thought I'd let whoever snitched get away with it."

Violet shook her head to focus her thoughts, trying to keep her voice calm even as her mind raced, envisioning all the worst possible outcomes of this evening.

"Archie, come on now, give me the baby. You do harm to the daughter of an earl, and you won't just go away again – they'll hang you," she said without acknowledging his words.

He was pacing now across the width of the small room, his furious gaze fixed on Violet as Clara gasped and cried.

"I shoulda known it was you – the second I go to Newgate you take off with that bitch Della. I shoulda known," he said again in a low growl, shaking his head at himself. Violet was frantic now as the baby writhed in his arms. He swore under his breath before he looked up, fixing her with his darkening gaze. "Tommy said I oughta take you down to the docks and tie a fuckin' stone to your ankles – and send the whelp in after you."

Violet took a step forward, shaking now, her hands clasped

in front of her. "Archie, just give me the baby, I can quiet her for you."

"Who would even know? Who even knows you're here?" he continued, as though he hadn't heard her. Violet winced as Clara's cries rose to a frantic scream.

"Archie, the baby... let me have her."

"But that's too quick an end for you, isn't it? Of all the people who could've ratted on me, you doin' it makes it worse... so much worse."

Violet swallowed back the scream rising in her chest, knowing she must stay calm. He wasn't thinking now, just raging, and so she said the only thing she could think of to break through the haze.

"I'll marry you, Archie. Just give me the baby. I'll marry you. I'll do whatever you want, just let me get her home."

Archie finally looked up at this, his gaze clearing as he finally seemed to realize the state Clara was in and glanced down at her with a disgusted sneer.

"Here," he said, thrusting the screaming child at her. "Shut her up, will ya?"

Violet accepted the baby with a sob of relief, immediately hugging her to her chest and caressing the silken hair on the back of her head. Clara finally began to quiet, and Violet closed her eyes.

"I'll marry you, Archie. I'll do it. If you'll still have me," she said in a strained whisper as she gently rocked the baby. Archie only laughed.

"Marry you? *Marry you?*" His voice rose to an alarming volume as he took a step towards her, his massive chest heaving. The door was open behind him. "So you can run off again? So you can break another promise?" His grin was wild now, his eyes glittering with fury. "Tossin' you and that brat in the Thames would be too good for you."

Violet swallowed hard as she shifted Clara, now murmuring quietly against her chest, to one arm.

"I'll marry you, Archie," she repeated stubbornly. "I'll give you everythin' you ever wanted. I did love you… I can love you again." She clenched her free hand into a fist at her side, aligning her wrist just as John had taught her. Her shoulder tensed as Archie let out a snarl of disgust, stepping closer and forcing her back towards the wall.

"You're not gonna get the chance, Violet. I'm not fallin' for it again, but I am gonna make sure you suffer as I did." His mouth twisted into a cruel grin as he finally backed her up against the wall. "Maybe eight years'll do it. Eight years in this room like I done it in Newgate. And at the end…" He let the sentence trail off, giving her a knowing look. Violet gave him a half-hearted push with her free arm, and he laughed as he stepped away, nodding as though he were very pleased with this decision. "Yeah, that'll do it. Eight years for you, Violet, and a swim in the Thames at the end. But the brat has to go," he added in a dark tone. As he reached for Clara once more, Violet drew in a deep breath. She would only get one chance. Her fist tightened, she drew her arm back, and struck as hard as she could.

Violet took only a moment to recognize the sound of crunching bone as she connected with Archie's nose. His roar of rage echoed in that tiny room, but as she had in Paris, she did not stop to contemplate the results of her attack. She clutched Clara to her chest and darted around Archie who snatched blindly for her, before racing for the door. Up the stairs, into the hall, her heart beating mercilessly in her chest as she reached the door to the club and thrust it open.

What greeted Violet in the street made her come to a skidding halt, and her eyes widen in shock.

The street outside the Devil's Den was full of dozens of police and wagons. Violet blinked in surprise, then turned when she heard someone screaming her name.

"Get outta my way!" a familiar voice shouted, and she squinted in the dim light of the streetlamps to see Della pushing her way through the crowd, followed by her husband and a handful of officers. She raced across the street, still wearing her fine silver evening gown with the earl's topcoat thrown hastily over her bare shoulders. Violet slowly made her way down the stairs to the street, still in a haze as the fear began to subside, leaving her shaking.

"Clara!" Della cried as she reached Violet, who immediately held out the baby for her mother to sweep into her arms. Her husband reached them a moment later as the group of policemen filed up the stairs behind Violet and into the club.

"He's in the cellar," she murmured as they stormed past her, truncheons in hand. One of the men nodded at her in acknowledgement before shouting an order as the earl closed his arms around his wife and daughter. Della was sobbing in relief, and after a long moment, she finally turned and gave Violet a tearful smile.

"What would I do without you, Vi?" she whispered, and Violet finally managed a grin.

"Anythin' for you, Del."

It was only now as she came to her senses that Violet realized her hand was aching from hitting Archie and she winced as she flexed her fingers. How on earth did John manage to do that night after night? Realizing where her thoughts had wandered, she instinctively glanced up to try to find him in the crowd of officers who milled about on the street, but there was no head of dark golden hair to be seen. A shout came from inside the club, and moments later a group of men led Archie Neville out into the street. He had been shackled and his face was smeared with blood, and he swore viciously as he was led to a waiting wagon. A sergeant stopped beside Violet, his thumbs thrust into his belt loops.

"You Violet Latimer?"

"Yes."

"That broken nose your doin'?" he asked, motioning towards the wagon into which Archie was being unceremoniously shoved and the door slammed behind him. She looked down at her swollen hand.

"It is," she replied, and the sergeant gave an approving nod.

"If you don't mind, we'll have a few questions for you when you're ready."

She inclined her head. "I'll be here."

He nodded and left to join the other officers, leaving Violet standing alone on the street, still wearing her lush emerald gown. Della caught her eye after a moment and, carefully handing her daughter over to her husband, came to stand beside her friend.

"Are you alright?" she asked, and Violet let out a shuddering breath as she looked out over the street where officers still milled about. The wagon with Archie had already left.

"Yes, I think so. I will be."

Della gave her a small smile. "Did you give Archie that bloody nose?"

The corner of Violet's mouth lifted as she met Della's gaze. "I broke it, apparently."

Her friend let out a little laugh. "Well done. That was a lucky hit."

Violet shook her head. "Not lucky. John taught me." She swallowed and looked away. "Where is he, anyhow?"

There was a moment of silence. "As I understand, he's at the Fox and Friar, placing Tommy under arrest. The Devil was there, as well, and they've taken him in, too." She paused. "I suppose it's all over now. You can go back to Paris."

Violet let out a long sigh. "Yes," was all she said, and Della's expression softened.

"Were you able to speak with him at the party?"

Violet looked away from her friend again, out over the police who were slowly dispersing, as tears pricked at her eyes.

"No... no, I didn't talk to him. But I did have a chat with Superintendent Culpepper."

"Oh?"

Violet's throat was burning now as she desperately held back the wave of tears threatening to burst from her. She swallowed but couldn't raise her voice above the barest whisper when she spoke.

"I really thought he liked me, Del. I thought he could look past what I was... I almost asked him to come with me to Paris." She let out a choked laugh as tears began to blur her vision. "I was wrong about Archie... and I was wrong about John Barrow."

Della touched a hand to her shoulder, and Violet turned to face her.

"What do you mean?"

A quaking breath escaped Violet. "Superintendent Culpepper made it very clear that John couldn't hope to win that promotion if he were involved with me. What was I to him, then, Della? Why did I fool myself into thinkin' he... he liked me?"

Della's laugh was soft as she folded Violet into her arms. "But he does like you, Vi! Have you gone blind during your time away? Have you forgotten what a man in love looks like?"

Violet frowned as she withdrew from her friend's embrace. "I know what a man in lust looks like. And maybe that's all I ever saw. Maybe I'm right... love isn't for me."

Della's expression darkened suddenly, and she leaned in close to speak, her voice a low hiss.

"You listen to me, Violet Latimer, and you listen good." It seemed that three years being Countess of Bradford had not diluted the Seven Dials pickpocket Della had always been, and she let the full force of that background come out now as she pointed an accusing finger at Violet. "I will not hear you talk about yourself as though you're worthless. I would surely be dead now if not for you, and I would surely not be Countess of Bradford if *you* hadn't told *me* that I was worthy of it. And so, I'm tellin' you now, you are the best and most talented person I know. And if you say once more that whatever you were means you can't be loved, then I shall do worse to you than a broken nose! Because *I* love you – you are my very best friend in this world, Violet, and you deserve love as much as anyone."

Violet dashed away the tears which had fallen down her cheeks as Della straightened and gave her a stern look, though there was a humorous glint in her pale blue eyes.

"I don't know what Detective Inspector Barrow thinks of you," she continued as she pulled off her husband's topcoat to drape over Violet's shoulders. "Though he doesn't strike me as the sort who would hold your past against you. But it doesn't matter. If it's Paris you really want, don't let me or Detective Inspector Barrow or anyone stop you."

Della looked over at her husband now, who was gently cradling their daughter against his chest and sighed. "We should be going home – I'm sure the police will be wanting to speak with you. And thank you, Vi... as always, I would be lost without you."

Violet gave a small smile. "I'll be along shortly."

Della touched her arm before she crossed the street to her family and Violet turned to the waiting sergeant. Perhaps Della was right. Perhaps John had done her a kindness in never sharing what he might or might not feel for her. It didn't matter, in the end. Violet had already made her decision.

The small hours of the morning approached as John finally filled out the last piece of paperwork which would complete the stack that sat upon the desk beside him. He sighed as he straightened in his chair, rubbing a hand over his face. He was weary down to his very bones, and he knew he could have waited until the morning to finish up the seemingly endless number of forms needing to be filled out, but he had wanted to be done with it. He should have been elated – it was over. Two years to become a detective, months of undercover work with dozens of scars and bruises to show for it, and now Archie and Tommy Neville were safely behind bars. The rest of the gang were being rounded up even as he rose from his chair to stretch his back. The streets would be safer for it, and the hard work of clearing out the slums to make way for sanitation, for schools, and for better homes could begin.

He *should* have been elated. But as he tucked the completed stack of paperwork into a folder, he only felt... hollow. He might not find out if he would become detective chief inspector for several more weeks, once all the higher-ups and Culpepper had met and discussed the merits of each candidate. And now... he couldn't really bring himself to care. He had wanted that position more than anything; he thought it would be his redemption, his way to make up for the loss of Lucy, to ensure that the senseless crime which had taken her would not happen again. But now... he was not so sure.

John knew he should go to Violet, to tell her that whatever Culpepper had said to her, he was wrong. John would marry her a thousand times over, promotion or no, and never regret a moment of it. But it was too late... or too early perhaps, and he had no wish to disturb her sleep, for she was surely exhausted from the events of the night.

He couldn't help a little smile as he pulled his borrowed overcoat from a hook on the wall and opened the door to his office only to be greeted by silent corridors. The sergeant who had brought in a bloody-nosed Archie Neville to be locked away in a holding cell had told him the remarkable story of one Violet Latimer, who had emerged from the Devil's Den just as the police were assembling outside, kidnapped baby in hand. They had found their quarry in one of the cellars, cursing mightily and nursing a broken nose, one for which the lady had claimed responsibility. She had departed the scene with Lord and Lady Bradford to return to their home in Belgravia.

John hated that she had been put in such a position to begin with, but could not help admire how she had managed to escape with herself and little Clara unharmed. Unfortunately, in wishing he could have been witness to her landing what must have been one hell of a facer on Archie, he started to remember the day he had taught her those very skills, alone in the warehouse together, and how desperate they had become for one another, so much so that he had taken her up against one of the posts surrounding the boxing ring. How eager she had been; her legs wrapped about his waist, her fingers digging into his back, her cries of pleasure driving him mad with desire. He should have told her then and there. *I love you, Violet Latimer.* She deserved to know that, even if it did mean nothing in the end. Even if he never saw her again.

Yes. He would tell her. As soon as was reasonable, he would go to Bradford House and tell her that he loved her but that she must return to Paris, to her life, to her art. She would go knowing she was loved. Warmed by this decision, John breathed a sigh as he stepped out into the early dawn, the rising sun still hours away. He would rest for a bit back in his rooms before making his way to Belgravia, and he tugged his collar up higher to block the biting chill of the wind as he crossed the courtyard.

"Detective Inspector Barrow," a familiar voice spoke nearby, and John turned as a hulking shape separated itself from the shadows and came towards him.

"Mr. Brill," John replied, nodding in recognition. "What are you doing here at this hour?"

Edward motioned for them to continue walking as he fell into step beside John. "Wanted to see how it all went – only got a few bits and pieces, but I couldn't very well leave my own party."

John glanced over at the other man. "Did it only just end?"

Edward grinned. "I throw very good parties."

John chuckled as they crossed the empty street. His smile faded as they turned to head towards Covent Garden. "It did not go as planned, but the end result was the same. The Neville brothers are in custody, and the rest of the Bruisers are being brought in as we speak."

Edward said nothing for a moment as they drew upon Trafalgar Square, but he did give a slow nod before he finally spoke. "Well, good bloody riddance to the lot of them."

They fell quiet again as they passed by Nelson's great monument when Edward gave a sudden laugh and nudged

John with his elbow. "I hear your woman gave Archie Neville a facer he won't soon forget. Bloody brilliant."

John responded with the barest hint of a smile, his thoughts consumed with the memory of Violet throwing a strike at him, only to tumble into his arms, letting her warm, sunny scent fill his nostrils. He coughed to dispel the thoughts and shook his head.

"Not my woman."

Edward gave a hearty laugh at this. "You two was up there, shaggin' in my office and starin' at each other all moony-eyed the whole night, and you're gonna tell me she ain't your woman?"

John immediately stopped and turned to Edward with a threatening scowl. "Were you spying on us?"

Edward only chuckled in response and turned away to continue walking, forcing John to follow along. "I've no need to spy on the two of you, but I do know what goes on in my club. I'm not blind, man," he said with another little laugh. John frowned over at him as they passed beneath the wavering yellow light of a streetlamp. There was no use prevaricating.

"How long have you known?"

The other man laughed again. "From the day you two walked into my office at Limehouse." He paused, his smile vanishing as they crossed a deserted road. "My Lizzie used to look at me like that."

They finally came to a stop in front of the little brick building where John rented his rooms, and he nodded up at the row of windows above them.

"Fancy a drink? I've got some very fine whisky."

Edward lifted his massive shoulders. "Nah. Got a busy day ahead of me, undoin' all the damage those Neville bastards did. I'm sure you'll be busy, too, bein' detective chief inspector and everythin'," he added with a wink. John gave a noncommittal shrug, looking away as he was once again torn between that desire to do good and how much that position would help him achieve, and Culpepper carelessly reminding him that women like Violet, despite all she had done for their operation, were of no value to men like him. Edward narrowed his eyes.

"You know," he began, his tone carefully indifferent, "I think I've a mind to expand. Your little party tonight has inspired me. All these charities is run by people who've never needed it. Think I'll start me own. Men like us," he said, inclining his head towards John, "we know what it's like to need help. We know these streets better than any of them."

John nodded, though in truth, he was not really listening, contemplating instead how he planned to tell Violet how much he loved her, and that Culpepper was a snobbish prick.

"You know what?" Edward said suddenly, and John glanced over at him. "I think I will have that drink, after all."

TWENTY-NINE

John never did get any rest that night. He and Edward spoke for a long time over a bottle of the very fine whisky, and when the leader of the Limehouse Gang went home with the light of dawn limning the edges of the rooftops, John also left. For the first time in his life, he allowed himself to hope, and he made the journey to Bradford House on foot, as the streets were still empty, with only a few delivery vehicles beginning to make their rounds.

He did not make his way to the back door this time, choosing instead to ring the bell at the front, rubbing his hands together in excitement as he waited for Harris. He had already decided, over his glass of whisky with Edward, that he was going to go with Violet. If she'd have him, he would go to Paris so she would never have to give up her art, and he was bursting with the need to tell her. The door opened a few moments later and the butler looked relieved as he spotted John standing beneath the portico.

"Ah, detective inspector, how good to see you. We are all so very relieved to have Miss Clara home safely. We must thank you, of course, for your quick response and getting those fiendish kidnappers off the streets," the older man said with a fierce scowl as he guided John towards the drawing room.

"I am relieved as well, Harris," he replied as he plucked the derby hat from his head.

"Please, allow me to fetch Lady Bradford – I know she wanted to speak with you."

John nodded as the butler departed, and, too anxious to sit, he made his way around the room, absently tracing the edge of the limestone mantel and glancing out of the tall windows to watch the snow swirling in gentle eddies across the empty street. He gave a little smile at the wintry scene beyond the rippled panes of glass, feeling lighter than he had in ages, longing to run to the bottom of the stairs and shout Violet's name, to pull her into his arms and tell her the wonderful news.

Thus, he turned with a grin as the door opened to reveal Lady Bradford, wearing a simple floral wrapper, her dark hair hastily pinned up on the top of her head. Her pale blue eyes were sunken with exhaustion, but she offered a wan smile as she crossed the room.

"I was going to stop at Scotland Yard this afternoon to speak with you, but I'm glad you're here, detective inspector."

He chuckled. "I am almost certain that it was three years ago now that I asked you to call me John."

Her smile brightened and she nodded. "Of course... John. And you must call me Della. I still do struggle with the titles, you know." She paused and her expression grew solemn as she reached for his hand. "I wanted to thank you for helping get our Clara back safely. Cole hasn't left her side since we brought her home last night. He's still sleeping with her – he's never going to forgive himself for allowing that to happen."

John shook his head. "He couldn't have known – I had thought the whole raid was in hand until Bess warned me. But you're very welcome. Though, most of the credit should really be given to Miss Latimer." He paused and glanced towards the door. "Is she... awake, by any chance? I have a few things I must discuss with her. About the operation," he added quickly. It was only when Della looked up at him with a softly sympathetic expression, that his heart plummeted, and his chest tightened.

"John... she left."

"Left?" For a moment, the words confused him. She was supposed to be here; she was taking the afternoon train. Della gave a somber nod.

"Yes... not an hour ago. She wanted to be on the earliest train."

For a moment, John was speechless, and he stared down at Violet's friend with his mouth agape before he finally shook his head.

"I don't understand... was she not to take the afternoon train? I had wanted to... say goodbye. And to thank her."

Della's lips pressed together, and her shoulders lifted in an apologetic shrug. "I'm sorry. She was rather... shaken... by what happened last night. She came home after speaking with your sergeant and gathered her things. She left for Charing Cross soon after."

John was already turning and jamming his hat back on his head as he made for the front door, and just as he was reaching for the lever, Della's hand stayed him, and he turned to face her.

"The first train leaves in half an hour." Her expression was knowing, and he gave her a quick nod before he tugged the door open and stepped out onto the portico.

By now, John's heart was in his throat as he raced through the gates and out into the street, searching frantically for a hansom cab, cursing when he found naught but drays with morning deliveries and a single rider on a great black gelding. He cursed into the quiet of the snowfall, but there was nothing for it. He ran.

. . .

It was the same train, and the same hollow feeling as when she had arrived here in this very station only a few months' past. But so much had changed in that time – so why did she feel so empty? She should have been sad, or heartbroken, or even angry – but she felt nothing. Violet sighed as she stood upon the platform at Charing Cross, staring as the train which would take her back to Paris pulled into the station with a deafening whistle, its wheels squealing as they slowed, smoke billowing all around her.

She had spoken to Della in the wee hours of the morning to tell her that she must go; that she wanted to be on the first train out of London bound for Dover. She couldn't bear the thought of seeing John again and having to say goodbye. Perhaps Della was right... maybe John wasn't the sort to judge, but Culpepper's words had cut her so deeply that she couldn't bear to know the truth, regardless of what it was. And there was the other truth in what he had said: she *had* been a prostitute. And if John was seen to be having a relationship with her, he *would* suffer for it, perhaps even lose the career he had worked so hard for; the one which would help to ease the guilt of his sister's death. Violet would not be the one to hold him back, no matter how much he had hurt her.

And even as she clung to the idea that John had never felt anything for her, it didn't stop the terrible ache of leaving behind something she had never thought she could have again: love. She closed her eyes to hold back the threat of tears as the train finally came to a screeching halt. The doors opened for the passengers to depart, and Violet stood on the platform, her single suitcase in hand, as they flowed around her, voices blurring together as she thought of John's last words to her: *You are an artist, Violet Latimer. And you always have been.*

She cursed under her breath as a single tear slipped down her cheek. Finally, the porters were calling for the train to be boarded, and Violet dragged in a long, shaking breath, straightened her shoulders, and marched forward. Her only consolation in leaving would be a return to her art, and her new source of inspiration. It would no longer just be railyards and factories. Violet was ready to capture the people just like her; the people who had grown up with nothing and who had no voices to speak for them. She was ready to show the world that, even if men like Culpepper did not think so, people like Violet were worthy – of love, of hope, of something better.

Violet clung to her newfound inspiration as she stepped aboard and found an empty seat. She set her suitcase down beside her and finally leaned her head back and closed her aching eyes with a sigh. She supposed she would rest the whole way to Dover as she had not slept in a frighteningly long time, and she was exhausted down to her very bones. It seemed fitting, then, to be leaving as she had arrived – sleep addled aboard a train, with naught but her suitcase and a broken heart.

She shifted in her seat as the train filled, smoothing down her skirts and trying to make herself comfortable in anticipation of a much-needed nap, when her fingers trailed over a sharp bump in her left pocket. Realizing what it was, she opened her eyes and reached in for the item. It was the envelope Edward Brill had given her at the party. A proposal, as he had called it. She had shoved it into her pocket without much thought earlier that morning as she had changed out of her lush emerald evening gown and had not had a moment to actually read the thing. She slid a fingernail beneath the seal and withdrew a sheet of paper before unfolding it and beginning to read.

John's legs burned and his chest throbbed, but he did not stop, and he did not slow as he raced up The Mall, dodging early shoppers and workers, too terrified that if he stopped to check the time, he would miss her; he would never get the chance to tell her he loved her and that he wanted to be with her. Always.

His arms pumped wildly, and his lungs heaved as he pushed himself faster, faster, heedless of the shouts of disapproval and the glares that followed in his wake. Soon, the great iron roof of the train station came into view over the tops of the other buildings, now dusted with snow, and then the elaborate façade was revealed as he finally reached the building, swerving to avoid a newspaper stand, past the tower dubbed the Eleanor Cross, and up the stairs into the station. His pulse pounded in his ears, and he found himself whispering under his breath, "Please, please, please." A whistle sounded from the platforms beyond the ticket counter and panic was settling its claws into him as he darted around a group of waiting passengers to throw his hands down upon the counter.

"Dover," he gasped to the shocked gentleman behind the bars. "What platform for the train to Dover? Police business," he added, glancing anxiously towards the inside of the station.

"Platform three, sir—" the man started to reply, but John was already off again, sparing only a glance for the signs which directed him down a set of stairs to reach platform three. He was down them in a flash, his chest now throbbing from running flat out for... how long had it been? The train had been due to depart half an hour after he left Bradford House. Wild now, he searched for the sign for platform three, found it, and let his gaze fall... to an empty track.

He stared. "No..." was all he could say, the word ripped from a heaving chest as he gaped, breathless, at the space where the train had been. He turned, looked out of the large opening to the platforms, and there it was, a smudge of black with a puff of smoke rising from the top, nearing the point where the track disappeared into the distance.

"No," he said again, shaking his head in disbelief. He walked, his legs shaking, towards the vanishing train, gasping for air, but soon it was gone. She was gone. He rubbed a hand over his face, closed his eyes, and looked once more. There was not even a trace of smoke to be seen.

Violet was gone, and she had left thinking that her past was an embarrassment to him; that she was not loved. Worse, that she was undeserving of it. His face was burning and the muscles in his legs were quaking, and so he slowly lowered himself onto a nearby bench and dropped his face into his hands, finally taking a moment to catch his breath as a crushing ache settled in his chest; the guilt of not having told her how he had felt. Just as he hadn't told Lucy.

"No," he whispered into his fingers, closing his eyes against a wave of anguish and the cold it left in its wake. He sat on that bench for a long time, cursing himself for a coward and a fool, until the snow began to drift onto the platforms.

"John?" came a sudden, soft voice behind him, and he whirled in his seat.

It was Violet, her suitcase clutched in front of her, looking down at him with a confused expression. John leaped up from his seat, shocked and elated she was still here. Her eyes were red-rimmed – from exhaustion or crying he could not tell, and was hurt to think it was either – so he said what he should have already told her, what he had been terrified to think she might have left without hearing:

"I love you, Violet."

Her whole countenance changed at those words. The pinched, weary look dissipated and her eyes widened as her cheeks warmed. His heart thundered in terrible anticipation, worried that he was too late, that she had already taken Culpepper's words to heart and whatever he said would not matter. After what seemed an eternity, during which he was barely aware of the world around them and the chill in the air, her lips turned up in a hesitant smile and she slowly set down her suitcase before she launched herself into his arms.

John caught her with a noise somewhere between laughter

and a sob, and he held her. Even with his muscles quivering and his chest heaving, he held her, and there were a thousand other things he wanted to tell her, but he couldn't even think, so great was his relief, and so he simply tightened his hold on her. She said nothing, either, just melted into him and buried her face in his chest with a long, shaky sigh.

When the platform began to grow busy once more and the whistle of another train arriving broke through the quiet of the snow-filled morning, they finally drew apart, though John still held her gloved hands.

"I thought you'd left," he whispered, his heart still racing inside his chest as he looked down upon her, at the emerald eyes which he so loved, as the relief still pulsed through him. "I thought I had lost the chance... to tell you..."

Her lips, so lush and pink, curved up just a little as she stared up at him and he couldn't help it. Surrounded by strangers who would most certainly disapprove, he leaned down and pressed his mouth to hers, joy and relief bubbling through him. When he pulled back, just enough to murmur against the soft curve of her cheek, he knew with absolute certainty of the truth when he spoke the words again, "I love you."

Her eyes were shining as she touched her fingers to his face and smiled. "I love you, John. And I'm gonna stay."

John blinked and he frowned, confused. "Stay? No, I came to tell you I would go with you. To Paris."

And now it was Violet who frowned, furrowing her lovely brow. "No, John. You worked so hard for your position—"

"I'm leaving. I'm leaving the police. Culpepper told me what he said to you..."

Violet's mouth flattened into a hard line, her expression hardening as he caught her hands in his and squeezed them.

"I will not continue to work for someone who thinks that I would be diminished by loving you, when that couldn't be further from the truth. I am better for it, and I was devastated to think you had left without knowing that."

Violet swallowed and closed her eyes before she shook her head. "John, I'm stayin' because I have seen the good you're doin' for others." She looked up at him. "I will not take that from you. I can paint anywhere," she added with a smile and this time, it was John who shook his head.

"And I can do good for others anywhere. There are people in need of help in Paris just as there are here. I spoke with Mr. Brill last night—"

He stopped when she withdrew a sheet of paper from her pocket and held it out to him.

"I, too, have spoken with Mr. Brill," she said with a little smile, as he took the paper, bemused, and started to read. After a moment, he looked up, unable to hide his wide grin.

"A commission?"

She nodded eagerly.

"But what of Paris? Violet, all you've wanted was to go back. You almost got yourself killed to go back."

Violet only smiled. "And you did everythin' you could so I could go back, as well, didn't you? You made sure there was nothin' keeping me here. That's why you didn't tell me you loved me before... I see that, now."

John swallowed. "I wanted to tell you a long time ago... I *should* have told you I loved you, from the moment I knew."

"But you didn't want me to have to make that choice."

He only shook his head, and she raised herself up to touch her mouth to his.

"And you don't have to. I'm choosin' this. I'm choosin' my art, the art Mr. Brill will pay me to make, because it can help, too. He wants me to show the world what life is like in the rookeries – all the very worst of it, and the best of it, so people can see for themselves. I'm doin' this for me... and I'm doin' it to help you. Because I want to."

John only held her hands tighter, as though he could implore her to change her mind through that alone. "Violet, you hate it here. Paris was your fresh start... I want you to have that."

Violet only gave the smallest of smiles and reached up to touch his cheek. "I'm stayin', John. Culpepper and the lot of them don't matter – if you love me for all that I am, and all that I was, that's good enough for me." She laughed, the sound as bright as summer among the snow now whipping about them in the wake of the arriving train. "Edward Brill is gonna pay me more than your superintendent makes in a whole bloody year – what do I care what he thinks of me?" She bit her lip and gave him another little smile that made his whole chest throb with want. "Say it again," she whispered.

John breathed out. "I love you, Violet Latimer."

And Violet Latimer, hard-nosed, hard-raised and utterly perfect, giggled at the words.

"And I love you, John Barrow." She raised a brow. "But if you're leavin' the police, what else are you gonna do?"

He gave an exaggerated shrug and finally stepped away, boldly taking her hand in his as they turned to leave the platform. "I believe Mr. Brill has been playing matchmaker with us. We spoke last night, and I shared my reservations about returning to Whitehall. He has been wanting to expand his empire for some time now, and that includes his own foundation... he asked me if I would like to join him, in whatever capacity I deemed appropriate. Wherever I deemed appropriate." He looked over at Violet as they stopped at the bottom of the stairs. "I told him I would be honoured, and that I would be more than happy to accept a position... as long as it was in Paris. So I could be with you."

Violet chuckled and raised herself up to touch her mouth to his.

"He is quite the matchmaker, isn't he? I always suspected he knew more than he was lettin' on."

John's smile faded as he tightened his grip on her hands.

"Just know, Violet... should you ever change your mind, should you ever want to go back to France, I will be with you..." He paused as the idea came to him, so suddenly it almost took his breath, and yet, so very obvious. He smiled. "Marry me, then, Violet. I will go with you to the ends of the earth, wherever it is you want to make your art, as long as we do it together."

She stared up at him, her eyes wide in disbelief as other passengers bustled past them, but he was hardly aware of them as the corners of her mouth hitched up in the faintest of smiles.

"You wanna marry *me*?" She spoke as though she could hardly believe him, and he reached up to touch her cheek, not able to hold back the laughter bubbling up inside him.

"I do. I don't think I've wanted anything more in my life."

Her eyes were still wide. "I never thought that I'd..." She trailed off, swallowing as her eyes began to glisten and he leaned down close to murmur against her ear.

"I would consider myself a very lucky man indeed, if you were my wife. And I fully intend to spend the remainder of my days showing you that you are loved, Violet Latimer."

And finally, she smiled, and she squeezed his hand.

"Then my answer is yes. I'll marry you, John." She laughed again, the sound like bells ringing, and he caught her in his arms to press his mouth to hers, his hopelessness, his uncertainty about his future demolished with those few words. Whatever he did going forward – with the police, or with Edward Brill, or anything else – he would do it with her.

"I love you, Violet," he whispered again, "I love you, and I'm so sorry that you spent even a moment doubting it."

Her smile was bright as she looked up at him. "I'll never doubt it again."

EPILOGUE

One Year Later

"Violet! The carriage is here!" John called up the stairs of the small, colourful rooms he and Violet were renting at Place du Tertre, right back in the heart of Montmartre. It was only their second visit to the city after John had proposed. The first visit had been brief, to allow Violet to collect what remained of her belongings after Archie's destruction of her flat, and to bid farewell to her friends and fellow artists. A year had passed since then, spent in tireless hours to establish Edward Brill's new foundation, dedicated to reform and the eradication of poverty in the slums of London, with John acting as the chairperson. Violet's paintings of the people and places of the East End had stirred much controversy for their grim reality, but they had shone a necessary light and were becoming much sought-after. Finally, after putting off the wedding to dedicate themselves to their new charitable endeavours, Edward had approached Della and they had set about planning the nuptials themselves.

John and Violet had married on a sunny September morning, almost a year to the day after she had found him in a cellar in Seven Dials, and then were forced, with many smiles and well-wishes, upon a train to take a much-deserved honeymoon. Thus, they found themselves back in Paris, and Violet was finally able to give John the grand tour they had discussed so long ago; one that had seemed impossible at the time.

Violet didn't answer John right away, finding that her heart was drumming too loudly, and her throat was too tight. Her fingers shook as she smoothed down the front of her bodice, but she was grinning like a fool as his footsteps sounded on the stairs, and he opened the door to their room, one filled with sun, made warmer by the soft peach plaster walls. She was still in the water closet, with the door closed over, and his soft knock sounded a moment later.

"Violet?" he ventured. "Della's train arrives in an hour... we must leave now if we are to be there on time."

She let out a shaking breath and managed to compose herself before opening the door to find her husband dressed and ready to leave to fetch Della and Clara from the train station for their first grand tour.

"Do you know that she's expectin' again?" Violet said suddenly, and John shook his head.

"I wasn't aware. We shall have to take her to dinner to celebrate."

Violet stepped past him into the bedchamber to gather up the dolman she had draped over the back of a chair and check her reflection one last time in the mirror hanging above the small vanity, tucking in a stray curl as she did so. She caught his gaze in the reflection but did not turn to speak.

"She was always a little sad that since she never had any family to speak of, her children would have no cousins or aunts or uncles to grow up with."

John nodded vaguely as he straightened his cufflink. "Lord

Bradford has brothers and a sister... they have plenty of family to make up for that."

Violet gave a solemn shrug of her shoulders, still watching him from the mirror.

"But they all live so far... Adelaide's all the way in New York. She's got nobody in London, except for me. We're sisters, though... or as close as to sisters as you can get. So, I told her... don't be sad, Della. Our baby will be as much a cousin to your children as any of Cole's family."

John was nodding absently as he withdrew his watch to check the time before he paused, and her heart skipped a beat. His gaze met hers.

"Our baby?"

She nodded, barely able to suppress her smile. He gaped as she slowly turned around, expectant, then let out a sharp breath as he took three quick steps to reach her before tugging her into his arms and squeezing her so hard she thought she might burst. When she gasped his name, her tone tinged with laughter, he pulled back, reaching up to brush his thumbs over her cheeks, now wet with tears, and pressing kisses to her face.

"Our baby, Violet... how long have you known?"

She was laughing and crying and kissing him, having held in the secret for weeks now until she could be sure.

"I've already missed my second course... I wanted to be sure. John, I never thought I could have this, I never thought..." She trailed off, overwhelmed now as she considered when she had first come to Paris, when her art and her friends had sustained her, when she had happily forged her own path, free of the constraints of her past. And she still had her friends, and her art, and she had never dreamed that her work would be so impactful, that her name would be spoken with respect, that people would fight to own her paintings. But now... she had so much more. More than she had ever thought she could have, on those dark, lonely nights in the orphanage. John grinned and kissed her again as he wiped away the tears.

"And I surely never thought that I could be so lucky as to have someone like you... I love you so very much, Violet." He kissed her again, a fierce, breathless kiss before finally releasing her and smiling. "We'd best go deliver our good news, then."

He took her hand to guide her down the narrow stairs to the carriage waiting outside. The tables in the square were full of Parisians taking advantage of the sunny day as the romantic strains of a busker playing his accordion on the far side of the busy space filled the air. There were already several artists at work behind their easels capturing the scene, and Violet nodded towards one of them as John handed her into the carriage.

"I'm comin' out here tomorrow to paint the square. I want to remember this place when we go back to London."

John grinned as he stepped in beside her. "I can think of a few things I'd like to remember," he said with a wicked glint in his eyes as the door closed behind them and he took her into his arms. And Violet needed no painting to remember what came after.

A LETTER FROM THE AUTHOR

I couldn't possibly have given a whole story to Della and failed to acknowledge her dearest friend, Violet, who surely deserved a happy ending of her own, having grown up in an orphanage with Della. Her meeting with John in the first novel was brief, but enough for me to see the potential in their story, and I sincerely hope you have enjoyed reading *A Brush with Scandal* as much as I enjoyed writing it (especially as a former art student, myself).

If you would like to join with other readers in hearing all about my new releases and bonus content, please do consider signing up for my newsletter:

www.stormpublishing.co/allison-grey

Additionally, reviews – even short ones – go a long way in helping other readers discover my books. If you have a few spare moments to leave your thoughts, that would be hugely appreciated!

Follows on Amazon and BookBub are also welcome, and you can find out more about me and my books on my website:

www.allisongreyromance.com

I hope you'll stay in touch – I have many more stories to share!

ACKNOWLEDGEMENTS

I would like to begin by acknowledging, as always, the hard work and dedication of Kate and the whole team at Storm Publishing who never fail to push me to make my writing the best it can be, and to the narrator of this audiobook, Katy Sobey, for truly bringing my characters to life.

I would also like to thank all my readers, for all their support and kind words – they make this business of writing worth every minute.